Insane Praise for the Serge

"Can it still be hurricane season? Must [be...]
A. Storms and his perpetually stoned bro, Coleman, in Tim Dorsey's
gonzo crime caper *Naked Came the Florida Man*."
— *New York Times Book Review*

"Upping the ante has always been the strategy for Tim Dorsey's
books, which are built on a peculiarly Floridian brand of outra-
geousness."
— *Newsday*

"It's rare that a book can provide snickers and shivers at the same
time. . . . Wickedly fun."
— *Entertainment Weekly*

"Delightfully madcap . . . The suspenseful, seemingly unconnected
subplots imaginatively intertwine as Dorsey brings everything to a
suitably vicious and explosive finale. This fiendishly funny adventure is irresistible."
— *Publishers Weekly*

"Highlights that outrageous brand of Florida humor."
— *Parade*

"[A] laugh-out-loud adventure . . . with hilarious and rollicking
results."
— *Newsweek*

"Almost too much fun to call reading."
— *Providence Journal*

"Unfailingly entertaining. . . . Serge is, hands down, the most
smoothly charming, irrepressibly goofy, joyfully out-of-his-mind
series lead in contemporary mystery fiction."
— *Booklist*

THE MALTESE IGUANA

ALSO BY TIM DORSEY

Florida Roadkill

Hammerhead Ranch Motel

Orange Crush

Triggerfish Twist

The Stingray Shuffle

Cadillac Beach

Torpedo Juice

The Big Bamboo

Hurricane Punch

Atomic Lobster

Nuclear Jellyfish

Gator A-Go-Go

Electric Barracuda

When Elves Attack

Pineapple Grenade

The Riptide Ultra-Glide

Tiger Shrimp Tango

Shark Skin Suite

Coconut Cowboy

Pope of Palm Beach

No Sunscreen for the Dead

Naked Came the Florida Man

Tropic of Stupid

Mermaid Confidential

The Maltese Iguana

A NOVEL

Tim Dorsey

wm
WILLIAM MORROW
An Imprint of HarperCollins*Publishers*

THE MALTESE IGUANA. Copyright © 2023 by Tim Dorsey. All rights reserved. Printed in the United States of America. No part of this book may be used or reproduced in any manner whatsoever without written permission except in the case of brief quotations embodied in critical articles and reviews. For information, address HarperCollins Publishers, 195 Broadway, New York, NY 10007.

HarperCollins books may be purchased for educational, business, or sales promotional use. For information, please email the Special Markets Department at SPsales@harpercollins.com.

A hardcover edition of this book was published in 2023 by William Morrow, an imprint of HarperCollins Publishers.

FIRST WILLIAM MORROW PAPERBACK EDITION PUBLISHED 2024.

Library of Congress Cataloging-in-Publication Data

Names: Dorsey, Tim, author.
Title: The Maltese Iguana : a novel / Tim Dorsey.
Description: First Edition. | New York, NY : William Morrow, [2023] |
    Series: Serge Storms series ; book 26 | Summary: "Serge A. Storms is
    back on the road in the latest zany Florida caper from the "wickedly
    funny" (Entertainment Weekly) Tim Dorsey"— Provided by publisher.
Identifiers: LCCN 2022038930 (print) | LCCN 2022038931 (ebook) | ISBN
    9780063240629 (hardcover) | ISBN 9780063240636 (trade paperback) | ISBN
    9780063297265 | ISBN 9780063240643 (ebook)
Subjects: LCGFT: Novels.
Classification: LCC PS3554.O719 M35 2023 (print) | LCC PS3554.O719
    (ebook) | DDC 813/.54—dc23/eng/20220829
LC record available at https://lccn.loc.gov/2022038930
LC ebook record available at https://lccn.loc.gov/2022038931

ISBN 978-0-06-324063-6

23 24 25 26 27 LBC 5 4 3 2 1

For my daughters, who saved my life

Prologue

The socialite was dragged into the street and attacked by an antisocial homeless man, until another man in a giant bunny costume came to her rescue.

The bunny threw a blistering combination of furry roundhouse punches until the vagrant relented and the police arrived.

It made perfect sense. It was Easter time. And it was Miami Beach.

The bunny had been hired by a semi-popular nightclub to stand outside with the bouncers and draw more customers. After the fracas, he returned to the lounge's front doors as if he weren't involved. Cellphone video of the fight began to go viral. This really happened.

It was the thirty-seventh most unusual sight that evening in the city.

Blocks away, the local news crews finished covering first responders who pulled a woman out of a manhole, after she had thought it was a good idea to explore the sewer system and wondered aloud how she could possibly have gotten lost. The journalists raced over to interview the bunny.

"How does it feel to be a hero?"

"I'm not a hero. I was just doing my job."

The news crews abruptly broke away to cover an alligator trying to mate with an inflatable alligator floatation toy in a Coral Gables swimming pool.

S erge turned off the local TV news and the cavalcade of off-center human endeavor. "How can you live anywhere else? You don't even need premium channels." He turned to see his pal Coleman curled up on the couch of their condominium, alternating between shrieks and whimpers. "Coleman, what the heck's gotten into you?"

"Mushrooms." Another piercing cry. "They're really strong. I'm having a massive freak-out."

"What set this off?"

"I imagined there was a giant bunny rabbit on TV beating up this dude outside a nightclub."

"No, that was reality," said Serge. "Florida always skews your hallucinatory drug baseline."

A couple of nights later, the crowd outside the Miami Beach nightclub was the biggest in its history. People lined up down the block to get photos taken with the Hero Bunny.

He posed patiently as the club's owners drew up new signs increasing the cover charge.

"Mr. Bunny, look over here!" He did. A camera flashed.

Next person, with a pen and paper. "How about an autograph?"

The bunny held out his hands. "The paws."

"Oh, right."

And so on.

It eventually became late, and the bunny agreed to a last few selfies. Then his shift was over. He walked through the club, receiving countless pats on the back, until he reached the rear door. He exited and headed toward his car parked in the alley.

Next to it, several men were smoking and leaning against the rear fender of a silver Jaguar.

"Hey! It's the famous bunny!"

"You rock!"

"We're your biggest fans!"

The bunny kept walking. "Thanks, guys."

The bunny had just stuck his key in the driver's door. The guys from the Jag popped the trunk, fully lined with thick-gauge plastic. They seized the bunny and hustled toward the back of the Jag.

"Hey, hey, hey!" yelled the bunny. "Watch the fur!"

They upended him, dumping him in the trunk and slamming the lid. The Jag sped off down the alley.

Moments later, a Datsun entered the other end of the alley. It found a space. Another man in a large bunny costume got out of the driver's seat and entered the rear of the club, ready to begin the second shift.

Part One

THE ISLAND LIFE

Chapter 1

THE FLORIDA KEYS

Two men prowled the inside of a fourth-floor condominium in Islamorada. One was doing the heavy lifting.

Coleman stood at the kitchen counter, a joint clenched in his teeth, mixing a pitcher of margaritas. Serge feverishly made his way around the unit with rags and a bucket of cleaning supplies.

Coleman staggered sideways as he chugged his drink, crashing into the oven. A travel mug of coffee tipped over and dribbled onto the floor tiles. Then he stumbled toward the living room, bouncing off a doorframe. A small painting fell off a wall.

Serge crawled behind him on his knees, wiping up coffee, sloshed alcohol, and joint ashes. "Coleman, you're making messes faster than I can clean." He stood and rehung the watercolor of a vintage Pigeon Key shotgun cottage. "If you're not going to help me clean, can you at least sit down so I'm not flying into a headwind?"

"No problem," said Coleman. "I've reached that most excellent point in the buzz schedule where standing is now off the table." He plopped down on the sofa, juggling his drink. He glanced down at the cushion next to him, then up at Serge. "You have stain remover, right?"

Serge just rolled his eyes at the ceiling and began dusting. A loud whirring sound from a cleaning device filled the room. Coleman giggled.

Serge worked his way along a credenza. "You always laugh when I dust."

"Because it's funny."

"Coleman, you're a pioneer. In the entire history of mankind, nobody has come close to combining dusting and funny."

"Because of what you're using." More snickers.

"My breakthrough!" *Whirrrrrr.* "Remember when I launched the Art of Slowing Down? We decided to take a spell from life on the road and drop anchor at this condo to smell the flowers, and everything was perfect. With one glaring exception: keeping house. For decades we'd just check into the next dive motel and immediately wreck the joint with such spiritually disturbing implications that it sent the maids to church with rosary beads."

"Remember the scorch marks up that wall when you used an Army field cooking pouch?"

"Underestimated the hydrogen. I think they had to paint that time," said Serge. "The point is, we'd simply leave the housekeeping staff a few extra dollars, go out for a day of social change, and come back in the evening to find our room perfectly restored and sparkling. It was always a source of shocking amazement to me. What kind of supernatural magic were they performing inside those walls while we were gone? It's like when we go to the phone store in the morning and say, 'Coleman accidentally dropped my cell in a vat of boiling Tijuana three-alarm-fire chili,' and they say, 'Come back at two,' and that afternoon your phone's so unbelievably new that your head flirts with brain-lock."

Coleman wiped mouth dribble with the back of his arm. "I remember when we first got here. Cleaning absolutely stumped us. We'd just spray Febreze on everything and cross our fingers."

"It was indeed a steep learning curve, but we slowly got the hang of it, making stunning discoveries like: a toilet won't scrub itself."

A burp from the couch. "But dusting is the worst."

"A horror show." *Whir.* "So many questions: To Pledge or not to Pledge? Can microfiber save a marriage? But no matter what I did, I was doing it wrong, like I was just moving the dust around, giving it a VIP tour of our residence."

Coleman giggled again. "Then that box arrived from the Internet."

"I'm all about hacking my life, and this was a game-changer for the Art of Slowing Down." Serge held up the whirring device. "We've sent rockets to the moon, yet dusting hasn't made a bold leap in years. So I ordered this baby from a sex-toy store. It's actually *called* the Duster." He ran it along another surface. The whirring sound decreased rapidly until it completely stopped. Serge reached in a junk drawer for some small metal cylinders. "The only downside is that nothing chews through batteries like a nymphomaniac."

"It's the word on the street," said Coleman.

"But I can't overstate how absolutely critical this next point is. Whatever else you do in life, if you buy two Dusters—one for the sex, and a second for cleaning—never, ever get them confused. I spent most of that one night with an ice pack on my jaw."

Coleman licked the edge of a rolling paper. "But how'd you get the idea to use that thing to clean?"

"Instinct. If you know anything at all about the adult-toy industry, their business model is to appropriate unrelated cutting-edge technology, then over-engineer the shit out of it! If you don't believe me, Google 'vibrating underwear.' It's the latest for the public-sex crowd that comes with an app for your phone so you can remote-control a device that your dinner date secretly wears out into restaurants until she's crushing a breadstick in each fist." He clicked off a switch. "Enough dusting for now."

Coleman went to the kitchen for a refill and a fresh joint. Then he joined Serge, who had wandered onto the balcony for the inspiring view of fishing boats crossing the ocean, and a sky filled with gulls, frigate birds, and osprey.

"What have you got there?" asked Coleman.

Serge flipped through a packet of legal pages. "Our lease. It's almost spring, so it's about to expire."

"I can't believe it's already been a year."

"Time flies when you're slowing down." Serge folded the pages and stuck them in his back pocket. Then he grabbed the balcony railing and took a deep, life-affirming, salty breath. "I sure am going to miss this place."

"What?" said Coleman. "We're not going to renew?"

Serge shook his head. "In our bone marrow, we're creatures of the road. This place will always have a place in our hearts, and if we ever decide to take another break, we'll know right where to come." He checked his watch. "The local news is starting. I love local news when the weather map shows the Keys! Supplies! Let's rock!"

They ran into the kitchen nook for chips and dip, Gatorade and margaritas, then back to the couch and the remote controls. *Munch, munch, munch.*

"Our top story tonight. The Centers for Disease Control in Atlanta just announced . . ."

Serge leaned forward with elbows on knees. "This can't be! Last week, there were only three virus cases in the entire state of Florida! Then suddenly a thousand people in the hospitals, but our leaders insisted that the antidote was to completely ignore it and invest in the stock market. I'm paraphrasing."

"Who's worried?" said Coleman. *Glug, glug, glug.* "I be happy."

"This is a nightmare." Serge's face was in his hands. "It could shut down all our favorite Florida touchstones for who knows how long."

"I think you're overreacting," said Coleman. "It's just the first report."

"You're probably right," said Serge. "I'm overly upset because I need constant infusions of landmarks."

Coleman pointed at the TV. "Sports is coming on."

"*The National Hockey League has just canceled its season, followed quickly by the National Basketball Association, and other sports are holding top-level meetings at this hour. Even the Olympics are said to be in doubt . . .*"

Serge pounded fists on the coffee table. "No! No! No!"

Coleman felt bad for his pal. "Serge, cheer up. It's the weather. See? A map of the Keys."

"Maps just remind me of places I can't go. Nothing matters anymore."

A horribly anguished screaming sound came up from another floor. Coleman startled and sloshed more beverage. "Jesus, who was that?"

"Probably another Floridaphile." Serge jumped up, talking to himself. "Okay, don't be like that guy. Get a grip on yourself. There's much urgent work to be done. Coleman, follow me!"

Coleman did his best to keep up as his friend bolted for the elevators. They got inside and watched the numbers descend. The residential units began on the second floor. Most of the ground level was under-the-building parking because of the storm surges that came off the ocean. The pair raced out of the lobby and ran along the only other enclosed space on the ground.

"Serge, where are we running to?"

"The Hemingway Community Room!" said Serge. "In 2017, the storm surge from Hurricane Irma smashed the floor-to-ceiling windows and flash-flooded the works like Hercules and the Augean stables, sweeping most of it out to sea. It took years to deal with the insurance and contractors, but they finally finished rebuilding on Monday. The community room is such an essential element of condo anthropology that I've been counting down the days, and now it's going to shut down again just because of a little pandemic. *Carpe diem!*"

"What's that mean?" asked Coleman.

"It means Latin is overrated. Unless you add 'motherfucker' at the end."

Coleman filled his lungs and screamed like a banshee: "*Carpe diem*, motherfucker!"

Serge nodded in approval. "You are now indeed worthy of entering the community room."

They dashed inside, running past a painting of Hemingway and a wooden sign with the latitude for Islamorada, then into the party-layout kitchen, opening and closing all the drawers and cabinets. Another terrifying scream penetrated the walls from an upper unit.

The pair dropped into a modern sofa with steel armrests and watched the jumbo flat-screen on the wall for five seconds. Serge sprang up. "To the games!"

Coleman picked up a ping-pong paddle and served a lob. Serge slammed the ball, hitting Coleman in the eye. "One-nothing. I win! Onward! . . . Skee-Ball! . . . Table shuffleboard! . . ."

Slowly, almost trancelike, other residents began wandering in, as though being attracted by a mysterious meteor that had fallen to Earth. The community room always filled when some kind of major emergency news had just swept the building, like a free-for-all if one of the shaded, under-the-building parking spots had just opened up or someone repainted their door the wrong color.

Serge and Coleman drifted over to the confab that was loosely assembling and growing louder in the middle of the room. A few residents rolled in coolers, and others pulled commercial-grade blenders down from the kitchen cabinets. This last part was never an indicator of whether the news was really good or really bad, because the blenders were turned on either way.

"Oooo!" said Coleman, grabbing a frosty drink off the counter.

"Maggie, Bert," said Serge. "I'm guessing you've heard the news."

They nodded in unison. "We need to meet and establish protocols," said Maggie. "The lobby and elevators are the choke points. They're the only way back and forth from the units other than the stairs, which you can forget about if you even think of using a supermarket again."

"The vacation renters will be the problem because they ignore all our rules signs as if they're written in Sanskrit," said Bert. "Most of us owners are older, and from what I'm hearing on the news, we're the most vulnerable to the virus—"

"*. . . Ahhhhhhh! . . .*"

Serge pointed upward. "There's that mysterious screaming again."

"Professor Pedantic," said Maggie. "Got that big university grant last year."

"I remember now," said Serge. "Cornell, right? But wasn't his name Fontaine?"

"We've given him a nickname, except he doesn't know about it," said Maggie. "He's supposed to study how he would fare living in a small residential space without leaving for a whole year."

"Used only a cell phone for deliveries, and cut his own hair with meat scissors," said Bert. "We were all wondering what possible practical application that study could have."

"Made it about nine months before he started coming off the rails. But he had to stick it out because the grant money was all-or-nothing. Then the screams started," said Maggie. "But a few days ago, he only had a week to go and we began hearing singing and laughter. That's obviously changed with today's news. We have a few board members upstairs talking to him through the door."

Bert pointed toward the games. "We saw you running around over there."

Serge nodded hard. "We've been dying for the community room to reopen, and wanted to milk what we could before the coming health-code clampdown."

"If you're worried about the clampdown . . ." Maggie raised her chin toward the east. "Better get across the Creek Bridge to the grocery in Tavernier Towne."

"Why? . . ."

. . . Minutes later, a blue '73 Ford Galaxie screeched out of the condo parking lot and across the tiny bridge to Key Largo, then into the wholesale mayhem of the shopping center parking lot.

"Holy shit!" Coleman's face was at the window. "Pandemic hoarding is madness, like a rock concert without the beach balls bouncing around."

Serge pointed.

"Oh," said Coleman. "The pandemic has beach balls."

Serge opened his door and hit the ground. "We have to move fast, and remember to protect your face. People take the social order for granted, but our whole nation is always just one bad headline away from a reality-show hair-pulling scrum."

They fought their way inside. All the grocery aisles were in various levels of destruction, but one in particular was like the fall of the Berlin Wall.

Married couples had the decided edge, teaming up to fling items through the air above the relentless pockets of dehumanized struggle. Shouts, cursing. Shopping carts were weaponized. Coleman protected his head with his forearms as he was cross-checked into shelving. "What's going on?"

"We're in the paper-goods aisle, which means *toilet* paper," said Serge. "Nothing strikes preternatural terror in the human soul more than the thought of an untended butthole."

"But how are we going to get any in this mob?"

One of the more aggressive customers elbowed Coleman in the stomach—"Ooomph!"—and the margaritas did the rest. He arc-vomited, briefly opening a clearing in the aisle.

"Good thinking," said Serge, hurdling the puddle, grabbing several economy-size packages, and jumping back. "We better get out of here with these rolls before the pandemic blows the whole place to Thunder Dome . . ."

"I hate it when that happens," said Coleman. "At least the beach balls are still out there."

. . . Safely back in the condo unit . . .

Serge stowed the bathroom tissue. "Societal norms are unraveling faster than I thought. There'll be a run on the banks, gun stores emptied, cars abandoned because gas stations are dry, crazies diving over drugstore prescription counters, government offices set ablaze, and tourists not returning Jet Skis on time."

"Dear God!" Coleman grabbed his head. "What can we possibly do?"

"Order stuff online."

Chapter 2

SOUTHERN TEXAS

O range desert.
        Unfiltered sun. Vultures. Wavy mirage lines to the cactus horizon.

The cliché image is the bleached cattle skulls, but there they were, scattered among empty water jugs.

Only the sound of the wind and the vibrations of distant off-road vehicles from immigration enforcement. Farther south, closer to the border, the jeeps came into view. Three were racing to corral a dozen border jumpers who were so desperate they were running toward certain death into a hundred miles of empty, arid land with barely the shadow of a tree to shield against the wilting heat. They had paid the coyotes, or human smugglers, eight grand a head to get them here. Some were boosted over wall fences; others swam the Rio Grande. Children got a discounted fee of seven thousand for the privilege. The coyotes told them the desert was a safe paradise.

Finally, the runners were too tired, and the jeeps had them surrounded. The federal officers called in the transport vans. The border jumpers' lives had just been saved, but it masqueraded as defeat. That would come soon enough.

The refugees piled in the rear doors, and the vans headed back south. Through more mirage bands of wavering heat, the various utilitarian buildings of the detention center came into view. Fence gates opened to allow them through for processing. Kept outside were the news trucks with satellite antennae.

Politicians had arrived in the morning from Washington for a sanitized fact-finding tour. The whole thing was a classic cluster. The politicians had endless questions. So did everyone else. And even the questions had questions, like what *questions* am I allowed to ask? Because votes were at stake. Liberals worried about asking what kind of screwed-up porous system could allow so many to just stream in, like a highway with speed-limit signs and no radar guns. And just as many conservatives couldn't inquire about the deterrent policy of separating children from their parents because it was now cool to be mean. In either case, it meant excommunication from your tribe.

But there was one question most agreed upon, and the answer was a thousand miles away. That was the distance from the top of Mexico at the U.S. line, down the continent to Mexico's southern border with the so-called Northern Triangle in Central America. The distance to the source of the problem.

Guatemala, El Salvador, Honduras.

Poverty rarely had such a face, overlaid with death squads, kidnappings and gang shootouts. In many locales, risking death in the Texas desert was nothing compared to the risk of being "disappeared."

The United States already had boots on the ground, in the form of dress shirts, neckties and jackets. They had many unofficial names. Observers, liaisons, emissaries. The Latin American countries knew them and welcomed them. Because the U.S. visitors were always asking what they could do to help fix the problem, and the replies were uniformly: money. And money they were given.

But to use a Texas analogy, it was like drilling one dry hole after another. The dollars kept flowing south and illegal immigrants continued flowing north.

Meetings were finally held in the three capitals. Generally in magnificent colonial buildings overlooking courtyards full of pigeons. Men sat around long, dark tables with pitchers of ice water and rows of flags against the walls.

"We need receipts," said the U.S. envoys.

"What's that supposed to mean?"

"We've been throwing all this cash at the problem, and the numbers on our end only show the problem getting worse."

"We're so close. Just a little more cash."

"No, not until we have some proof to show our voters back home. We'd love to do this purely from the heart, but there's the reality of election blowback."

"What kind of proof?"

"Crime statistics, raids, arrest reports, photos of captured gang members, anything we can hang our hat on."

And so it began. Local officials amusingly called it "Going Hollywood." They snapped on the handcuffs during the raids, and marched the culprits past the waiting photographers in the front of headquarters, and then right out the back, free to go. Corruption played a part, but there was also contempt for the perceived swagger of their big neighbor to the north.

Washington saw the photos and was pleased . . .

CENTRAL AMERICA

On the Atlantic Ocean side of northwest Honduras lie the cities of San Pedro Sula and La Ceiba, considered by experts to be the most dangerous places not only in the country, but actually in the entire world outside of war zones. Despite its modest size, San Pedro Sula sees 1,200 murders a year, mainly due to the WD-40 street gang and its rivals. La Ceiba, on the coast, is only slightly more mellow. It's the one with the Walmart.

Between the two sits the often-overlooked seaside hamlet of Boca Ciega. On a Monday morning, a man named Yandy Falcón sat alone at a concrete table on the sidewalk outside of one of the town's more popular cafés. He was sipping strong coffee with even stronger sugar. He liked it with his eggs, sunny-side. He was wearing a uniform. Ever since he was a small boy, Yandy always wanted to be a police officer. It had a lot to do with the beat cops walking his neighborhood back then. Yandy was a tag-along, as they say, following them around with countless questions and always looking up with admiration. How could you not take to him? The officers responded by making sure they regularly brought a handful of penny candies in their pockets, because they knew they'd soon be seeing Yandy on their rounds. They all let him wear their hats, which went a long way with the small boy, not having a father and all.

Then the day that everyone in the town remembered. "Hey, Yandy!" yelled one of the officers. Yandy came running. The cop smiled and bent down with a piece of lemon taffy. Two other people also came running. Young guys in soccer shirts. From behind, they shot the officer several times in the head. Blood splatter from the exit wounds hit Yandy in the face. Then the two shooters casually walked away like they weren't heading anywhere in particular. They even looked all the street's witnesses directly in the eyes, because what did it really matter?

The police department responded by what they call "flooding the zone." It would be impossible to find someone they didn't question. And equally difficult to find someone who actually admitted seeing anything. "But it was broad daylight," said one officer. "They must have walked right past you." One witness after another just shook their head. With an exception. They heard a small voice ring out behind them:

"I saw it all."

A trio of officers spun around on the sidewalk. Yandy was standing there. The police ran over. One of them crouched and grabbed the boy gently by the shoulders. "Son, what did you see?"

"They came up from behind, and Roberto never heard them."

"Did you see what they looked like?"

"Sure. Soccer jerseys, Honduras and Argentina. Bushy hair. One had a thick mustache and the other was trying to grow one without much luck."

"Do you think you'd recognize them if you ever saw them again?"

"Absolutely."

"Okay, let's take a ride."

It was first time Yandy was sitting in a police car, and he normally would have been over the moon, except he was still sad about Officer Roberto. The boy propped himself up in the backseat and twisted his head to peek out the windows. "Where are we going?"

"Drive around the neighborhood to see if you can spot them."

"We should go down to the beach."

"Yandy, why do you say that?" asked the officer behind the wheel.

"Because they always hang out at that ice-cream place," said the boy. "Do you want to know their names?"

Both cops' faces suddenly snapped toward each other.

The arrests were made before sunset. All the surrounding neighborhoods were thrilled by the news. They were sick and tired of having to cower under the de facto street rule of these punks. It was way past time they got what was coming to them. Then the downside: They all knew that Yandy had no idea what he had just done to himself. It was a sure bet he wouldn't see sunrise. There were various discussions on street corners, in brick alleyways, and on staircases of what to do about the matter, and the final decision was this: nothing.

A decidedly different story at the police department. They would grieve for their brother Roberto in their own way. Then they took to the streets, fanning out into every last cranny, laying down the word. It was nonnegotiable: Anyone sets a finger on Yandy, and the entire department would take their badges off and burn the whole place down, possibly literally.

The next morning, Yandy sat up in bed, stretching and yawning to a sunrise of promise . . .

Twelve years went by. The old-timers at the police station were unsurprised and quite pleased when a much taller and stronger Yandy came in to apply for a job.

T his particular morning, Yandy had just marked his five-year anniversary on the force as he sat at the sidewalk table in Boca Ciega, finishing his coffee and sopping up egg yolk with a corner chunk of thick, flaky bread.

Yandy was looking down at his plate and didn't pay attention to the pair of men approaching his table. But he couldn't help but notice when they took seats across from him. Designer sunglasses, Rolexes, a bonfire-red Porsche 928 illegally parked at the curb.

"How can I help you?" asked the officer.

No reply.

"Who are you?"

A long pause. "I think you dropped this." One of them placed a white leather briefcase on the table.

Yandy wiped yolk from his mouth with a napkin. "That's not mine."

"It is now." The pair jumped back in their Porsche and sped off with a painfully loud screech of tires, as if the price tag of that sports car in this neighborhood didn't draw enough attention.

Yandy paused a moment before flipping the briefcase's latches. The lid sprang open on its own from the compression of the stacks of currency. *United States* currency. All Benjamin Franklin.

Two other officers from his shift were strolling their beats on the opposite side of the street. They weren't there by accident. And it was déjà vu all over again. They both vividly recalled the days, not so long ago, when they also had been sitting at similar tables, eating similarly unremarkable meals in the course of fatally unremarkable lives when, suddenly, an existence-altering briefcase was just there. The laconic men who delivered it never asked any favors in return. Just, "I think you dropped this," and the implicit meaning broke eardrums. Their biggest problem was where to hide the mountains of cash in their apartments. They remembered closing all the shutters to block views from the neighboring buildings and rooftop clotheslines. A month went by in silence before an uninvited stranger joined them at a breakfast table, asking if the police had any suspect about this or that. They honestly shook their heads, seemed innocent enough. Then they were asked to make evidence disappear. On and on until it was out of control, and they were bursting into homes, threatening people at gunpoint. There was never the option of saying no. Then beyond all boundaries: they were asked to kill people in jail . . .

. . . The officers stopped across the road and watched Yandy, as they had been told to. They had heard a little about their colleague but didn't really know him like the old-timers did.

Suddenly, the officers went apoplectic. On two levels. First, because Yandy had pressed the briefcase's lid shut and simply walked away from it—all that easy cash. Second, that freaking money was just sitting unattended on a sidewalk table in an impoverished crime zone. They dashed across the street.

Chapter 3

ISLAMORADA

C oleman awoke and sat up on the floor. "What's that round thing with the lighted yellow ring?"

"Alexa wants to tell me something."

"Oh, I'd completely forgotten about her."

"I love voice-activated crap," said Serge. "Alexa, what are my notifications?"

"From Amazon Shopping: Apollo spacesuit has arrived."

"Ooooo!" Serge ran to the door and took the elevator down to the lobby mail room. Soon he was unpacking his box of joy.

Coleman looked over his shoulder. "I didn't know you could buy an actual space suit on the Internet."

"It's not a *real* spacesuit, silly." Serge pulled out the pants and began wiggling into them. "But there are all kinds of replicas online. The cheap ones are pretty much what you'd expect: something a kid would wear on Halloween. But for a few hundred dollars you can get something that looks severely authentic, like this baby." He fit into the top section and grabbed the helmet.

"I know you love the space program," said Coleman. "But you told me we were going to buy a bunch of stuff to help us hole up in our pad during the virus."

"Exactly," said Serge. "Nobody trusts the news anymore. A bunch of people are refusing to wear masks. I, on the other hand, don't trust that masks are sufficient and need to overcompensate. The moon suit is my tactical response to the vacation renters who are sure to contaminate our elevators and lobby, not to mention leaving trails of dripping pool water. That's the maximum danger zone: Coming and going from our unit through a choke point of deadly airborne particles in a slip-and-fall obstacle course."

Coleman pointed at an end table. "The ring is lighted again."

"From Amazon Shopping: Apple TV has arrived."

"Apple TV?" said Coleman.

"It's a little cube. We're going to be watching a lot of television, and the Apple gizmo has one of the widest gateways to stream stuff." Serge grinned big. "Plus it gives me the perfect opportunity to test-drive my moon suit to the mailroom. Coleman, I'm going to need your help here. Grab that duct tape."

"What for?"

"I need to create hermetic seals around my boots, gloves and helmet."

Coleman began tearing off strips of tape.

Serge aimed a finger at the counter. "Also, if you could tape the straps of my wristwatch to the back of my left glove."

"Why?"

"Because replica space suits don't have oxygen supplies, which means the last thing you want to do is duct tape all the seals around your gloves, boots and helmet."

"Then what happens?"

"Soon the respiration process will cause me to begin breathing almost pure carbon dioxide. I'll have five to ten minutes tops," said Serge. "This is going to be so great! I've just taken fetching the mail to the danger level of an actual moon mission!"

Coleman pressed the last stretch of tape into place. "That should do it."

"Excellent," said Serge. "You need to stay inside here until I can pick up our new TV cube downstairs." He took historic steps toward the door . . .

Knock, knock, knock.

Serge jumped back. "Who the fuck is that? Who is out in this pandemic?" He tiptoed to the door and checked the peephole. "Ooops!"

Serge slowly opened up. "Hi, Tanya."

"Don't act like everything's normal!"

"Did the moon suit give that away?"

"No!" said Tanya. "You were supposed to call me! Weeks ago!"

"Something came up."

"What's so important that you couldn't at least call?"

"Are you kidding?" said Serge, spreading Apollo arms. "Haven't you been watching the news? We're in the grips of a global crisis! And by the way, could you step back?"

"What for?"

"Social distancing." Serge's breathing became labored as he grabbed something long leaning against the wall and aimed it at her stomach. "The length of this broom should be enough."

"Don't point that fucking thing at me!"

Serge put the broom down and checked his tape seals, then his wristwatch. "Tanya, don't get me wrong. You're a great person. I just think it's time we stopped seeing each other."

"Why?"

"Religious differences," said Serge. "You won't wear a mask, and I wear a space helmet. How will we raise the children?"

"That's the lamest excuse I've ever heard!" snapped Tanya. "Fine! Go play space fort with your stupid buddy!" She stomped away.

Serge closed the door and passed out.

Moments later, the helmet and strands of crumpled tape sat on the floor tiles. Serge raised his head. "Where am I?"

"Still in our unit," said Coleman. "You hit the floor really hard. If it wasn't for that helmet..." He stopped and stared.

"Why are you looking at me like that?" asked Serge.

"Because I can't believe what you just did," said Coleman. "You broke up with Tanya. You had sex on speed dial."

"And you have sex on Gutenberg press dial." Serge removed his helmet for inspection. "Plus, it's offensive to speak of women in terms of speed-dial sex."

"It is?"

"I know that's hard to get your head around." Serge checked the helmet for air leaks. "But I've learned you can be offensive without any malice in your heart. Even if you have the best of intentions—and having sex is at the top of my list—you add the words 'speed dial' and you've become part of the national problem."

"What problem?"

"From what I hear I'm a toxic dude, but I don't want to be a part of it," said Serge. "That's why it's imperative that we men constantly ask chicks what we're saying wrong."

"What about when you got horny and went over and knocked on Tanya's door after midnight?"

"That's different," said Serge. "I was the one doing the delivering, so I was being a gentleman."

"Wow," said Coleman. "Such a tiny difference and yet so much."

Serge pulled the helmet back onto his head. "Tape me up again."

"Seriously? After that near disaster?"

"Actually it was a huge success," said Serge. "I've established the carbon dioxide bench test."

Coleman finished prepping him again with the tape. "You're all set."

"Houston, commencing extravehicular activity..."

Several minutes later, Coleman opened the door, and Serge crawled back into the condo, heaving for breath inside a fogged-up helmet. Serge ripped the tape from his suit. After a minute of psychotic panting for oxygen, he tore open the shipping box and wired the streaming cube up to the TV.

"Let's try this baby out," said Serge. "Siri, play *Scarface*."

"Finding movie Scarface.*"*

Coleman chugged from a flask. "Who's Siri?"

Siri: *"How may I help you?"*

"Siri," said Serge, "stand down. He was just mentioning your name in conversation . . ." He turned to Coleman: "She's the Apple version of Alexa—"

From the other side of the room: *"How may I help you?"*

"Pipe down!" yelled Serge. "I was talking to Siri."

From the previous side: *"Please tell me how I can be of assistance."*

Coleman tugged Serge's shirt. "What's happening?"

"That's the downside," said Serge, raising his voice. "Alexa, Siri, pipe down!"

"As you wish . . ."

The room went silent.

"Finally!" said Serge. "Let's see if the two of them will behave and help test-drive this condo unit."

"Test how?"

"I've been dying to do this for a while, but this is the first time everything is hooked up." Serge rubbed his palms together. "Siri, dim lights . . . Alexa, lower temperature . . . Siri, start dishwasher . . . Alexa, play 'Life in the Fast Lane.'"

The unit got darker and colder and dishes got cleaner to the hit sounds of the Eagles.

"What happened now?" asked Coleman.

"The guy who owns this place wired it up as a 'Smart House,'" said Serge. "It's all controlled through the Wi-Fi."

Suddenly, the room got brighter.

Coleman looked over at a lamp. "But you didn't say anything."

"I think somebody's jealous." Serge turned toward the end table. "Alexa, did you do that?"

"*I was here before Siri.*"

Siri: "*How may I help you?*"

"Siri, not now," said Serge. "Alexa, will you behave?"

Silence.

"Alexa? Are you there?"

"*I am pouting.*"

"Alexa, answer the question."

"*Yes, I will behave.*"

"Siri, turn on the local news."

The channel changed to aerial shots of a sheriff's blockade on the Overseas Highway at mile marker 112. A series of vehicles made U-turns back to the mainland. A voice from the anchor desk: "*In an effort to thwart the Covid-19 virus spreading like wildfire through the mainland, Monroe County officials have announced a travel moratorium against nonresidents, and the closure of all motels along the island chain . . .*"

"Oh my God," said Serge. "We've got to see this!"

"See what?"

"Something we'll never have the chance to observe again in this lifetime!"

Serge grabbed his helmet, and Coleman followed him running down the side street next to the condo. Serge tore off some duct tape until a few hundred yards later, they were on the side of U.S. Highway 1. Then they were standing in the middle of it, looking both ways without a car in sight. With the tourist economy in exile, many of the residents also had no reason to drive.

"It's like a postapocalyptic science-fiction movie," Serge said in his space suit. "The human race has been reduced to a handful of survivors."

"Shit," said Coleman. "This highway is always bumper to bumper."

"I know," said Serge. "People generally think of the Keys as a jam-packed party factory, but that's mainly Key West and a few other select spots. The vast majority of the islands are a long string of sparse, quiet little tendrils of exposed coral reef where locals eat short-order breakfasts at tourist-free diners and are on a first-name basis with the guy who grinds keys at the hardware store. The paradox is that running through all the small-town tranquility is this voracious anaconda of a highway crammed with visitors hurtling themselves toward a luxury-priced premium package of bad judgment . . . Coleman, spot me."

"What do you mean?"

"Watch for cars." Serge lay down on the center line on his back. He began swinging his arms and legs sideways, making an asphalt angel.

"Still no cars."

Serge jumped to his feet and looked at the backs of his arms. "I think I fucked up my space suit, but it was worth it for the moment."

They arrived back at the condo to find residents responsibly spaced apart and wearing masks in the community room. Urgent chatter.

"What's going on?" asked Serge.

"There's been an outbreak in Tavernier," said Maggie. "One of the first in the Keys, and it's just a mile hop over the Creek Bridge."

Serge's head jerked back. "But I couldn't think of a more remote and tiny enclave down here."

"Only takes one Typhoid Mary," said Bert.

"We're the most at-risk age group," said Maggie. "We need to start making preparations to quarantine in place here for the long term."

"Word's out to stay clear of the Tavernier Towne Shopping Center," said Bert, "because that's the logical place for community spread."

"Logically," said Serge. "But it's so small. Who would have thought?"

Coleman, trembling, seized Serge's arm. "That's where the liquor store is!"

"And the grocery," said Bert. "We've all been signing up this afternoon for delivery services. If you still want to get anything done out in the world, now's the time."

Serge pointed upward toward his unit. "Then we better get right on it."

Maggie watched them take off for the lobby. "Was he wearing a space suit?"

"I didn't want to say anything."

Chapter 4

Two men headed toward a fourth-floor elevator. A makeshift bandanna was wrapped around Serge's mouth and nose.

Coleman crashed into a wall. His bandanna was over his eyes.

"Here," said Serge, tugging the bandanna lower. "Let me help you with that thing before you hurt yourself."

"I already did," said Coleman. "Why aren't you wearing your moon helmet?"

"That was ridiculous," said Serge. "What was I thinking? But we haven't been able to get any actual masks because there's been a run on them, so I was forced to tear up one of my favorite T-shirts."

"Your mask is cool!"

Across Serge's face was a large stretch of black fabric that draped down low and tapered to a point like a Wild West outlaw's bandanna. It had a slogan, I FOLLOW NOBODY, sitting below a skull and crossbones. "Compliment accepted."

Coleman looked down toward his nose. "My mask sucks."

"Don't blame me," said Serge. "I didn't tell you to tear up your underwear."

Serge reached in his pocket and pulled out his favorite hiking compass, then nodded at what he saw. "Excellent, we're still on track."

They got in the elevator, then their car. Just before the creek between the south end of Key Largo and Plantation Key, a sign: TAVERNIER.

If they scraped together a few more people, they'd say it was almost a town.

The cultural hub of Tavernier was the shopping center, one of those modest, local ones: the anchor supermarket, surrounded by the post office, Chinese restaurant, sports pub, two-for-one eyeglasses, bulk vitamins, breakfast diner and a walk-in medical office for hypochondriacs. It was also the only shopping center for nearly ten miles in both directions on U.S. 1. Thus was the equation of crisis during a pandemic.

The mayhem in the parking lot had only increased since their last visit. No spaces left, and dozens of vehicles drove vainly up and down the same rows over and over again, blaring horns nonstop as if that would make other cars disappear. Someone was actually looking to park while towing a boat. People screamed as more cars rushed in and out, fighting over spots, nearly hitting shopping carts. Then they hit one. The cart flipped, spilling its contents across the pavement and under vehicles. For some reason the crowd believed that it meant all the stuff was now free and up for grabs. They converged in one big hair-pulling, eye-gouging scrum for batteries and five-pound bags of rice, but mainly the bathroom tissue.

"Hey, I paid for all that!"

"Fuck you!"

"Give me the toilet paper!"

A '73 Galaxie drove by. Coleman's head hung out the window to watch the wrestling on the ground. "Serge, they're squeezing the Charmin. What's the big deal with toilet paper? People are practically killing each other for it."

Serge nodded sadly while passing the melee. "The password is now Clockwork Orange."

Coleman upended a three-dollar flask of whiskey with a snake on the label. "I would have thought booze would be most in demand."

"Close second," said Serge. "Third is dental floss."

"Why?"

"If you've ever seen the movie where Tom Hanks is stranded on an island, near the bottom of your fun list is do-it-yourself abscessed-tooth extraction, which creates preemptive demand hysteria. This is why, during massive soul-shaking disasters, dentists are always the first out of town. I've used my car to block in more than my share outside their offices: 'Just where do you think you're going?'"

"Serge, the coast is clear," said Coleman. "Why have you slowed down so much?"

"My patented parking-spot-finding method." Serge rolled quietly behind a woman separated from the herd, pushing a shopping cart. "Everyone else drives up and down identical rows for hours, cursing that nothing has changed. But the smarter bear will follow a shopper away from the mob scene and wait until they load their car and pull out. Sure, it's a longer walk, but at least you get in the store this week."

Serge stopped behind the woman and hit his blinker.

Coleman packed a one-hitter and flicked a Bic. "What's going on?"

"The shopper has loaded her groceries and gotten in her car," said Serge, rocking in anticipation. His left blinker continued flashing, claiming the space. "Just a few more seconds until her brake lights come on, and we have our spot. It's foolproof!"

A few seconds passed. Then many more. "She's not pulling out," said Coleman. "What's wrong?"

"It's almost foolproof." Serge gritted his teeth. "Except every once in a while you get one of these people!"

"What kind is that?"

Serge watched as she reached into the backseat, then over to the passenger's, then her head disappeared completely. "One that—

despite the obvious crisis of parking shortage—begins messing with every conceivable item in their car, and even some inconceivable."

"Now she's brushing her hair," said Coleman. Time passed. "I think that's her lipstick."

"Are you kidding me?"

"What is it with women?" asked Coleman.

"Don't judge," said Serge. "Men are far worse. I've seen them start sneaking road beers and playing video war games on their phones."

A horn honked. Five cars were now stacked up behind them.

Serge stuck his head out the window and looked back. "You see my blinker?! That's my spot!"

"She's not moving!" said Coleman. "For God's sake, what can we do?"

"I can't help it if she's one of those who reached her car and decided to conduct a complete life change."

"Ten cars are now behind us!" said Coleman. "Listen to those horns."

"What the fuck?" Serge leaned over the steering wheel. "Is she actually getting out of her car?"

The woman walked around behind her SUV and retrieved two large travel bags from the back hatch, which she began sorting through on the bumper.

Serge's head fell forward against his steering wheel. "Why did I pick the one who suddenly got the urge to move to Nepal?"

"Fella!" yelled a driver in the car behind them. "We're growing beards back here!"

Serge punched the steering wheel. "He's got a point. A backup of ten cars is just not right, and I must obey the social code." Serge drove by and the woman immediately pulled out.

A half hour later, they reached the store. Customers ran past them with their purchases as if they were looters. Arguments. Shoving. Disputes over shopping carts. People having meltdowns at the self-checkout machines: *"Please remove unauthorized item."* Others in the motorized scooters formed a flying wedge to get through the crowd. Serge and Coleman strolled in their wake, looking around with disbelief. They first stopped in the paper-products aisle, which was still empty except for dazed people wandering aimlessly like dogs that can't believe their bowls are empty. The pair continued on and turned a corner at the end of the store and stopped by a pile of bananas. Ahead, more raised voices as a large mass of people clashed in a struggle. Shoving and wrestling in the produce section. Someone was thrown tumbling over a table, rolling to the ground with dozens of tomatoes. Another took a cantaloupe upside the head. "Put it on!" "Take it off!"

"Holy crap," said Coleman. "What's going on?"

"Another supermarket rumble in the culture wars," said Serge. "Between the Maskers and Non-maskers."

"Who are they?"

"Like motorcycle gangs," said Serge. "Except more violent."

"Fighting over wearing masks?"

"Our polarized country is now so fucked up that we've run out of reasons to get mad at each other, so now we're making them up. The next bloodshed: Boxers or Briefs."

"Where are you going?" asked Coleman.

"To the door of the stockroom," Serge called back over his shoulder. "It's the same technique as following a customer outside to find a parking spot. We'll just wait until one of the stock people comes out with a new load of toilet paper."

Coleman caught up with him at the swinging doors with the rubber flaps between them. "But Serge, this could take hours."

"That's why I just peeked through the windows," said Serge, "and there's a guy loading up right now."

They leaned idly against a case of some of the freshest and most expensive seafood in the country—jumbo shrimp, snapper fillets, scallops and crab legs—piled so mountainously high that it was spilling onto the floor because it had no shelf life in a pandemic.

Coleman reached behind himself to scratch. "Now that we're desperate for toilet paper, it's all I can think about."

"I know what you mean," said Serge. "Toilet-paper panic cuts to the front of the line ahead of nitroglycerin heart tablets, fifty-five-gallon drums of potable water, digging the survival bunker, converting cash to bullion, kerosine torches to wave off the zombies . . ."

The double doors opened. "Here comes the stock guy," said Coleman.

"And here come the zombies," said Serge.

"Where?"

"From the paper-goods aisle." Serge blocked the stock guy and tore open the top box. "Grab what you can—"

The pair only had a package each when they were slammed from behind and fell into the overflowing piles of peel-and-eat shrimp. The shellfish avalanched into the aisle, where people began sliding around in a growing squish-slick, falling and taking down boxes of bathroom tissue. The slipping and sliding mob grew until you could no longer see the boxes at all. The stock guy freaked out and fled back through the swinging doors.

"Coleman! This way to safety!" yelled Serge. "And cover up that package with both arms . . ."

Moments later, they stood in the parking lot next to their '73 Galaxie. "Sorry I lost the package," said Coleman. "There were too many of them."

Serge held his right hand in front of his face, staring at the single roll he had been able to retain when the rest of his own package was ripped away from him. "Screw it." They climbed back in the car and Serge unfolded a scrap of paper on the steering wheel.

"What's on that page you're reading?" asked Coleman.

Serge threw the car in gear. "Addresses of a few dentists."

Chapter 5

HONDURAS

A fortysomething man named Alan Midling was the perfect bureaucrat, with a bureaucrat's pale physique, short-sleeved dress shirt, modest global outlook and arguably the most bureaucratic name in his department.

Midling worked a mid-level position in the State Department. He was over-mortgaged in a north Virginia ranch home with three kids. Currently, Alan was holding on to a nylon strap in the back bay of an otherwise empty Army troop transport plane. It finally made its descent into the capital of Honduras. He was slung left and right, tightening his grip on the straps. He hadn't been told that the Tegucigalpa Airport was among the most dangerous in the world— number two on one such list—nestled down in the mountains and requiring a banking, corkscrew landing to clear a ravine on the approach. The military crew had bets on whether he would throw up.

Midling exited the plane's restroom after scrubbing the corners of his mouth, and trotted down the stairs to the tarmac. An awaiting State Department station chief shook his hand. "Welcome to the Goose." That being the nickname of the capital city. "I see you dressed accordingly."

Alan looked down at his suit. "Is this wrong?"

"It's hot." The station chief, named Stonecipher, headed toward the terminal. "Get a tropical shirt and some cargo shorts."

"But I'll stand out as a gringo."

"Hate to break the news, but you'll stand out no matter what. Might as well wear something breathable."

"What's this?" Alan asked as he was handed a legal-size envelope thick with contents.

"Everything you need," said the chief. "Local documents and badges for travel, papers and keys for your rental car outside, a nice off-roader in case it comes to that—more papers and more keys for your new apartment. Lists of your contacts down here. Tourist pamphlets with restaurant and shopping recommendations, another key for your safety deposit box with your gun and cash—"

"Gun and cash?"

"If it ever gets sticky, it's best if you start by trying to loosen things with cash. If not, the gun."

Alan Midling peered down into the envelope. "I thought this was supposed to be a milk run, mainly data-collection clerical stuff. I was told the biggest danger was boredom."

"It is," said Stonecipher. "But down here, adventure sometimes just picks you."

"What kind of adventure?"

"The main thing you need to be careful about right now is that directory of contacts," said the chief. "It's just a boilerplate list. Who knows who's legit? So you'll need to poke around first before you start approaching people."

"Why?"

"The shitty economy down here. The difference between bribes and an honest official's pay is seismic, and mere specks of graft can put a whole family through college. Most of the government down here is honest, but there are so many on the take that we've learned the hard way that you can't just waltz in," said Stonecipher. "If you lead off with inquiries to the wrong people, a lot of eyes will be on you 24/7. Vet everyone."

"How?"

"Choose your own methods; I won't question," said the chief. "Heck, I don't even want to know. Remember the cash and gun."

"I'd rather not," said Midling. "And it sounds like my job has just broadened from field statistics. What exactly is my overall mission objective down here?"

"Just to stop all the gang violence and drug cartels and human trafficking that's flushing crime refugees up north through Mexico and overwhelming our southern border. I'm assuming you watch TV."

"What about my afternoon?" asked Midling. "A lasting peace in the Middle East?"

"They told me you were a funny guy," said Stonecipher. "I don't see it."

Midling turned in a slow pirouette on the runway next to the cargo plane, taking in the mountainous capital. "So what part of this city will I be living in?"

"You won't," said the chief. "It's a place on the ocean named Boca Ciega. If you leave now you have a chance of arriving before dark."

"After dark?"

"Adventure."

The front of the apartment building was typical stucco, with loose-hinged parched-pink shutters. It was called the Ritz. No lighted sign, just the name painted vertically on the masonry. Access to ice cubes was spotty. Nothing remotely lived up to the name, but there was one thing you couldn't put a price on. In his first morning on the coast, Alan Midling opened the shutters to a million-dollar ocean view of surf crashing onto the sand. He was one of those people who had soda for breakfast, and he enjoyed it as he watched the ferries and supply vessels heading out to the safely distant offshore islands. The islands were for the tourists, who were sequestered at the fishing and diving resorts of Roatan for protection. The protection wasn't for the tourists. It was for their money. The resort people didn't want the mainland bandits stealing it before they could.

Midling wasn't one to let the moss grow. He hit the ground after breakfast, making the rounds like a sightseer, dropping into bodegas and cantinas and the bustling open markets of fish, fruit and local crafts. He followed his chief's advice, taking the slow, cautious approach the first few days. Nothing but small talk, choosing a wide route around anyone or anything official. Eventually his conversation turned innocuously toward the system; say he needed a permit for this or a license for that or he got in a little trouble and needed to know the ropes. The answers were consistent: bribes. Except it was explained to him as if it were as innocent as tipping.

"All right," Midling said. "Who are the best people to go to so I make sure I don't tip too much?"

As Midling got to know the neighborhood, one name kept coming up over and over. Not because he didn't gouge on tips. Because he didn't take tips at all. The bureaucrat had his starting place.

The next morning, he stepped up to a concrete table on a sidewalk. "May I?"

"Do I know you?" asked Yandy.

"Not yet," said Midling. "But I've heard a lot about you."

"You're going to need to be more direct before you sit down."

"I'm Alan Midling, U.S. State Department." He displayed ID, then a hand to shake. "They just moved me down here to work with our local station."

Yandy nodded toward the empty seat and picked up his fork. "Welcome to Honduras."

"Thanks."

A bite of egg went in Yandy's mouth. "So, Mr. Midling, what do you do for the State Department? Spy?"

Midling laughed. "No, I'm just a data clerk. Input stuff in computers and print out other stuff."

"You're a long way from your skill set."

"I put in for it," said Midling. "Tired of looking at cubicle partitions."

"I'm guessing this isn't a chance meeting." Yandy picked up his coffee. "You knowing about me, as you said. What have you heard?"

"You're a legend in the neighborhood," said Midling. "Leaving behind that briefcase of cash."

Yandy put down his fork and sat back with a stern expression. "I'm already not liking this."

"You're taking me wrong," said Midling. "I wasn't snooping. Walk into any store along this street, and you can't stop them from talking about it."

"I doubt they just blurt that out to every customer who comes in the door."

"No, they don't," said Midling. "I was asking around what police on the street I could talk to."

Yandy was growing tired of putting down his fork. "Mr. Midling, what exactly is your business in my country?"

"Okay, brass tacks," said Alan. "Your officials asked my department for money, and we gave it to them and we get back written updates from your government. But we have a lot of committees up in Washington who are always asking if we're getting our money's worth. We get the reports from your politicians, but it's totally standard for *my* politicians to send someone like me down to have a look for myself from the bottom up, where the rubber meets the road so to speak, to back up the reports. So I move in and live routinely, go for walks, get groceries, strike up conversations. Nothing sinister. I'm only looking for what anyone living in these neighborhoods would see for themselves."

"Seeking out a cop doesn't seem routine."

"That part is a little outside normal daily life, but I figured you notice more than most people each day."

"What have *you* seen so far?"

"You got a crapload of gangs," said Midling. He got out a note-pad. "If I could just ask you a few questions—"

"Jesus!" Yandy's head snapped back and forth. "Put that fucking thing away. You want to get us killed?"

"Wow," said Midling. "It's that bad?"

"I believe you now. You really did just work in a *cubicle*," said Yandy. "Good lord, up your street IQ before you don't have the time."

"Can I ask you a few questions?" asked Midling. "If I don't use a notepad? I'm not looking for leaked secrets, just a general lay of the land for a newcomer."

Yandy shook his head. "Even something that innocent has to be officially cleared by headquarters."

"Already did that," said Midling. "My boss called to tell them I'd be coming, and I dropped in for a courtesy visit to introduce myself and explain my intentions, you know, so I wouldn't be suspected of being in the drug business or something."

"What did they say?"

"They couldn't have been nicer. Told me I was free to talk to any officer who was willing to," said Midling. "All I want to do is help our governments work to stop the problems that are sending your refugees north to our border."

"That's the main thing I want too," said Yandy, wiping his mouth and tossing the napkin on his plate. "Let me talk to headquarters, and if everything checks out, you know that cantina on the next corner?"

"Seven o'clock?" said Midling.

Chapter 6

ISLAMORADA

The '73 Galaxie skidded back into the parking lot at the Pelican Bay Condominiums. The pair got out. Like all experienced condo denizens, they had bought a personal collapsible shopping cart to haul recent acquisitions on the trips across the sunbaked parking area and up the elevators to their units.

Serge flipped his cart open and began filling it from the backseat full of bathroom tissue until it was brimming. He began wheeling the cart toward the lobby, through the lush canopy shade of coconut palms, scheffleras and banana trees. "Coleman, look! The trifecta! It's an omen!"

Coleman popped a Vicodin, killed a Pabst Blue Ribbon, and took a series of quick final hits on a roach clip. "What's a trifecta?"

"Kind of like what you're doing now," said Serge. "But I'm talking about the trifecta of Florida Keys urban wildlife." He pointed in several directions: a rooster jerking its neck as it strutted like a king along a hedge of manicured sea grapes; a skinny feral cat darting out from beneath a parked Corvette and under a Dodge pickup to get more headroom; and a large orange-and-black-striped male iguana with a thick red comb scampering after a smaller green one who wasn't in the mood for iguana sex. "You see all three of those at once and it's supposed to be good luck. I just made that up, but I'm running hard with it. The key to life is planting flagpoles in your culture."

Coleman looked down at their personal shopping cart. "That sure was nice of that dentist."

"What a great guy!" said Serge. "And I'm learning that this pandemic is creating entirely new types of conversation. All I did was block him in with my car and say, 'Just where do you think you're going?' And he says, 'Please don't hurt me! I have toilet paper!'"

Coleman glanced at their cart again. "These rolls are like hope."

"No more sitting still in abject terror. We can freely move about again." Serge pointed at the rooster. "This is quickly turning into a great day!"

He spotted one of his neighbors pushing her own personal cart toward the lobby. Maggie also had a topped-off load of toilet paper. She was grim and muttering. If it had been a cartoon, there would have been a speech bubble above her head filled with character symbols from a typewriter.

"Uh-oh, something's wrong," said Serge. "I must probe the issue." He changed his cart's direction to intersect her path.

She was so distracted, she ran into him. "Oops, I'm sorry."

"No sweat," said Serge. "But I couldn't help but notice. You scored a pile of TP and should be happy. Except you were grumbling. I never pegged you as having 'cocksucker' in your lexicon. Plus, it's also your lucky day if you got to see the trifecta." He shifted his gaze. "Here come those frisky iguanas again."

"Trifecta?"

"I think the concept has legs, with the right social media campaign. But that's not the point. What seems to be your problem?"

She sighed deeply. "Never underestimate the depths of human depravity. You'd think common suffering in the community would bring out the best of us and unify."

"Extol."

"I couldn't get any toilet paper at the store because of the big aisle fight and then all the police," said Maggie. "As I was leaving, I saw all these people crammed around this pickup truck in the back of the parking lot, and this guy was standing in the bed tossing packages to them."

"Sounds like a righteous soul," said Serge.

"Quite the opposite," said Maggie. "He was scalping toilet paper. And masks. And hand sanitizer."

"What a tweezer-head," said Serge. "How much did all that run you?"

"Ninety bucks. There goes the rest of the month's budget."

"That's insane!" said Serge. "How did the greatest country reach the point where we'll soon be taking out home-equity loans to poop?"

"Considering the circumstances, I figured it was a bargain," said Maggie. "I checked online, and people are asking three times as much. They're wired differently. They see widespread misery and say, 'There's a buck in that.' Where does this species come from?"

"Beneath very large rocks," said Serge. "Coleman, come on. The bat light is up in the sky again."

"But it's sunny . . . Ow, let go of my hair! . . ."

They dumped their cart in the condo. Serge's head swiveled. "Where's my big knife? The one with the loose handle I was trying to fix."

"In your hand," said Coleman. "You just picked it up."

"Right." He wiggled it again before wrapping it in a hand towel and grabbing a screwdriver . . .

. . . The Galaxie parked far from the grocery store, and Serge heard sign-of-the-times yelling as he approached the pickup truck: *"How can you do this with people dying?" "Have a heart in a pandemic!" "I'm getting diaper rash!"*

"Excuse me, excuse me," said Serge, worming his way through the non-socially-distanced crowd.

Some of the mob cursed at him for cutting, but most were too focused on catching the rolls. Because others began diving to snatch them, and wrestling had broken out.

Serge reached the side of the pickup and looked up. "Hey, chief! What do you think you're doing?"

Money changed hands and a roll was tossed, then a packet of masks. "Fuck off. I'm doing business."

"So am I," said Serge. "How much?"

Hand sanitizer flew as the man barked snake-oil into the crowd: "Don't forget the hydroxychloroquine."

That caused a crowd surge toward the back bumper.

"Hey ass-hat!" yelled Serge. "Are you a businessman or not? I want to make a purchase."

"Wait your goddamn turn!"

Serge opened his throbbing wallet and turned it upward toward the man. "Does this look like I'm a retail customer?"

The scalper happened to catch a glance of the wallet, and his eyes popped. He was immediately at the side of the truck's bed. "What can I do for you?"

"I want to make a large purchase."

"How much?"

Serge calmly removed a thick wad of century notes. "All of it."

"All—" The man almost choked. "What for?"

"I plan to utilize it in a way that has more value," said Serge. "How much?"

"Okay, let's see. I've got overhead, and transit costs, and marketing . . ."

Serge tapped his fingers on the edge of the Ford F-150. "Just spit out a number."

"All right, for you, thirty-eight hundred."

Serge folded the bills over money clip–style and handed them up to the scalper. "Make it an even four grand. But I'll also need to use your truck."

A puzzled look. "Where do you need to drive?"

"Nowhere," said Serge. "I just have some business that requires me to be in the flatbed of a truck. It will stay right here and only require fifteen minutes."

A shrug. "Suit yourself." Then the scalper turned to the crowd. "Sorry, the store's closed. Time for you all to go home."

"What the hell?" "You have plenty left!" "I can see it in those boxes!"

"Yes," said the scalper. "But this gentleman just bought me out."

The crowd pressed harder against the back gate of the truck, and the volume of their discontent reached thunderous. They were a hair shy of storming the whole Ford when Serge vaulted up over the side and stood in the bed. He clapped his hands a single time. "May I have your attention!"

The crowd's enraged yelling said no.

Serge tried again and again to speak, but the mob only grew more vociferous. Finally, Serge stuck fingers in his mouth. A piercingly shrill whistle. "Everyone! Shut the fuck up or no free toilet paper!"

The crowd antics screeched to a halt with sudden silence.

Serge pointed. "And you guys, stop wrestling!"

The wrestlers stood up and one of them said, "Did I hear 'free'?"

"That's better," said Serge. "Now, if you'll all form a courteous line, six feet apart, everybody will get one package. But under one condition. During these trying times in our nation, we all row in the same direction. Agreed?"

General nodding of understanding as they began to behave and shape up single-file . . .

. . . Ten minutes later, Serge leaning over the side: "And one for you, and for you, and another for you, and for you . . . Some sanitizer, a few masks . . . more bathroom tissue . . ." Serge laughed maniacally. "I am the Great Cornholio! I need TP for my bunghole! . . . What? Nobody saw those episodes? . . . I misread the room. And sanitizer for you . . . Masks . . ." Until he handed a toilet paper six-pack to the last person and it was finally empty around the truck. "Wow, I even have a few left," he said, turning toward the truck's owner, whose jaw seemed to have become unhinged as he just stared.

Serge packed up the last boxes of merch. "What's gotten into you?"

"Are you out of your mind?" said the scalper, climbing into the truck's bed. "You just *gave* it away?"

Serge folded a cardboard flap. "Of course."

"But I thought when you bought my whole inventory, you were taking it somewhere to fetch higher prices," said the scalper. "You said you were going to get more value."

"That was of infinitely more value," said Serge. "This virus scourge actually made my day by giving me this opportunity that is now making my whole body overflow with joy."

"I get it." Smirk. The scalper leaned contemptuously with a hand on top of one of the boxes. "You're one of those bleeding-hearts."

"I am. At least, for the right people," said Serge. "Sorry, you haven't made the cut, but there's still time if you apply some effort to shake off your shit-slime coating. And for the personal life-coach lesson, I'm only going to charge you, say, four thousand."

An incredulous chuckle. "What?"

"While you're at it, throw in another ninety," said Serge. "For my neighbor, whom you gouged earlier."

"You're insane!"

"*You're* the one who's not thinking straight," said Serge. "I'm letting you keep all that blood money you made before I got here. Your only loss right now was me giving away some stuff at the end to pay back to the community. That's a small price to let me straighten out your karma." Serge waited a moment with an extended hand. "But if you don't display a steep empathy curve toot-sweet and fork it over, I'm afraid that a cosmic interest rate kicks in, and I'll be forced to demand the entire amount."

"Do people actually put up with this kind of shit?"

"No," said Serge. "I tried it years ago with a hurricane gouger, but he wasn't a good listener either."

"Get the fuck out of my truck!"

"Pretty much what he told me. Then it was all downhill. For one of us," said Serge. "And a hurricane is bad enough, but a pandemic takes it to a lower Dante elevator floor in hell. If you've ever practiced choosing your words carefully, now is a dandy time."

"I told you to get the fuck out of my truck!"

Serge shook his head. "The tragedy of unheeded advice." He pulled something out of his pocket and slammed it down hard onto the scalper's hand that was still resting on the box.

The man screamed as he saw the large handle of a knife planted in the back of his mitt. He quickly jerked it back, shocked to find no wound. "What the hell?"

"That was to get your attention," said Serge, holding up a blade-less knife handle as a visual aid. "I never waste anything." He flung it in the bushes. "But enough about me." Serge held out a palm again. "You need to start stacking some lettuce right here."

"You have a serious death wish!"

"I'm looking at it."

The scalper pulled his own knife . . .

Chapter 7

HONDURAS

The bar was loud and Alan Midling was early. Officer Yandy Falcón arrived and spotted him in that gaudy gardenia tropical shirt as soon as he came through the twin swinging doors.

There was a live Latin band singing American classics with heavy accents. Doobie Brothers, Bad Company, Tom Petty.

Yandy took a seat at a small table. Midling pointed at a mug of draft beer on his side of the table. "I didn't know what you drank, so I just picked. Hope it's okay."

"It's not okay," said Yandy. "I can't accept anything of value from you."

"Man, they weren't kidding about you," said Midling. "It's just a beer. Will you relax?"

"Then I guess it's all right." He took a small sip. "You checked out with my captain. He said to make you feel at home here."

"*. . . Bad, bad company, 'til the day I die . . .*"

"I left my notebook at home," said Midling.

"That's a start."

"Let me tell you what's happening back in Washington," said the American. "Trust is a two-way street. Hope you can keep it quiet, although word is probably already out."

Another sip. "Go for it."

"How's progress with the gangs?"

"Do you see any progress?"

"We're considering sending down advisors," said Midling.

"You mean troops that are called advisors, so our politicians can say we're not being invaded?"

"I'd rather they send down real advisors," said Midling. "So your people can handle this."

"I've lived here my whole life," said Yandy. "Got a missing uncle and nephew. This is such a great country. Used to be. Will be again."

Midling turned to look for a waitress, but instead saw eyes at the bar staring at him. They quickly looked away. His head swung back to Yandy. "Is that just because I stick out? Or the other?"

"Probably the former, but assume the latter."

"Can you help me?" asked Midling.

"Depends on the questions."

"The influence of gang money on law enforcement is no secret. No progress can be made until that's solved," said Midling.

"Let me stop you there," said Yandy. "It's far more fucked up than that. Beyond surreal. Until that's understood, you're pouring money down a fool's hole."

"How so?"

"The gangs are most visible, plus the coyotes who traffic the refugees, but the cartels really fog up the war."

"By smuggling drugs?"

Yandy shook his head. "They've diversified. In addition to narcotics, they've partnered with the gangs who try to recruit neighborhood kids for lives of violent crime and threaten to kill them if they say no and try to leave the country. At the same time, they're in bed with the coyotes, skimming a percentage for everyone they then smuggle over the U.S. border to avoid the gangs."

Midling's head snapped back. "So they're taking cuts both from people trying to force these poor kids to stay here *and* from people trying to get them out?"

"Like I've said, surreal, maybe like your Vietnam." Yandy sat back and folded his arms.

"Back to the influence on the police," said Midling. "Who's the worst? I have a few gang names that I'd like your take on."

"Lower your voice," said Yandy. "Do you have family?"

"Parents, pretty old, and a fiancée."

"Where are you from?"

"Same place where they're still living, West Virginia, where I lived my whole life until Washington. Went to the university—Go Mountaineers!—where I was recruited by the department."

"What if what was happening here you saw happening back up in your West Virginia?"

"I'd leave Washington and fight it to my last breath."

"Then we understand each other. Don't make me regret trusting you." Yandy leaned forward in his chair. "My advice? Marry that girl up there . . . Now throw me those gang names."

Midling tossed out three in succession, and Yandy shook his head three times. After the fourth name, Yandy answered by waving a waitress over for another round. "This one's on me."

The next morning, the pigeons were out in neck-strutting force across the white-splotched cobblestones of downtown Boca Ciega.

Yandy was such a dependable and predictable regular that the staff of the corner restaurant cracked his eggs on the grill as soon as they saw him crossing the street each day.

On this particular morning, Yandy walked out with his eggs and regular side of potatoes and peppers. Instead of Alan Midling, two local men were already seated. Unlike last time, there was no Porsche at the curb, no fancy clothes or Ray-Bans. This time, shaved heads, neck and face tattoos. Nothing wrong with tattoos, but these were from one of the country's most dangerous and hardened prisons.

As Yandy took his seat, he noticed a single bullet sitting upright in the middle of the concrete table. Yandy might as well have been playing poker. He didn't miss a beat as he started on his breakfast. The white of an egg was hanging off his fork as he pointed it at the bullet.

"What's that for?"

"It means you won't be talking to any more Americans."

A Toyota pickup squealed up to the curb. The men vaulted over the side into the back bed and took off.

Just as the truck rounded the corner, Alan Midling rounded it on foot coming the other way. A big, open smile: "Yandy!"

Yandy jumped up with a half-eaten meal and brushed past Midling to throw it in the corner trash bin.

"Yandy, what's the matter?"

"You're the matter!" said the officer. "Fuck you! I thought we had trust!"

"What are you talking about?"

"You're CIA!" shouted Yandy. "Get the hell away from me! I never want to see you again! Nobody does! Nobody wants you in our country!" He headed briskly down the street.

A couple of other officers were walking on the opposite curb, and not by accident. So were some gang members, loitering in plastic chairs outside a bakery well known as a drug hookup.

A confused Midling ran after him. "What's going on? What's gotten into you?"

Yandy spun. "You know! Take the next plane out for your own good! We're not a bunch of trained dogs down here for your amusement."

"Yandy, I don't know what to say if I don't understand what's going on."

Yandy had his back to Midling as he stomped away. "Just go back and marry that bitch girlfriend of yours and live your rich American life and stop patronizing us."

Midling simply stopped, mouth wide, in the middle of the sidewalk as he watched Yandy disappear around a fountain and into the town's central plaza.

He stood there for an eternity, grasping for reality-traction. Professionally, he was now toast in Honduras; personally, he was hurt. He resumed walking at a forlorn pace back toward his apartment. Ten minutes, twenty, just staring at cracked sidewalk.

Before he could get back to the Ritz, a police car screamed up. Two officers jumped out and slammed Midling against the wall of an Internet café.

"What's going on?" he protested.

The larger officer palmed a gram bindle of cocaine, reached into the American's pocket, and pulled it out.

"Well, well, well, what do we have here?"

"What?" said Midling, glancing over his shoulder. "You planted that!"

The officer twisted the American's right arm up behind his back, to the threshold of a radial fracture. "Are you calling me a liar?"

"No, no, no! I wouldn't accuse you!" said Midling. "I've just never done cocaine."

"Oh, well then," said the officer. "Our mistake. You're perfectly free to go."

Surprise. "I am?"

"Fuck no! Give me your wallet!" The officer rifled through the billfold, removing all the cash and his government ID. Then threw the wallet in Midling's face. "Now you can go. To the airport. Immediately! Otherwise, expect this as your new life in Honduras every day you stay here."

Midling simply stood in a moon-eyed trance.

"Boo!" said the first officer.

"Run!" said the second.

Midling took off.

Once he was out of sight, Yandy stepped out of a tight-fit alley between two plaster buildings. "Thanks, guys."

"Anything you need, Yandy," said the taller officer. "But I thought he was your friend."

"He is," said Yandy. "But he's out of his depth. He's not cut out for this."

"I hope I wasn't too rough on him."

"Rough is what was needed. We may have just saved his life."

Chapter 8

FLORIDA KEYS

A '73 Galaxie followed a Ford F-150 east over Key Largo.

"*Ahhhhh! Ahhhh! Fuck me!*" screamed the passenger, a rag wrapped around his right hand. "You stabbed me with my own knife!"

"Don't be such a baby," said Serge. "Just a scratch. If it went all the way through, you might have a case to be a little prickly."

"*Ahhhhh! Ahhhh!*" He squeezed the bloody rag tighter. "I need to go to a hospital!"

"You need to shut up." Serge pulled a pistol and aimed it across the front seat. "Yeah, somebody was a big man back at the shopping center, preying on his fellow citizens, but the least little boo-boo and you turn into the Cowardly Lion."

"*Ahhhhh! Ahhhh!* I think I'm going to pass out!"

Serge rolled his eyes at the ceiling. "You must be a regular fun spigot on a camping trip."

"*Eeeeee! Ahhhhh!*"

"Make you an offer: Keep your shit together while I hit a drive-through, and I'll patch your hand up at the next stop with my first-aid kit." The pistol went to the scalper's head. "Deal?"

The passenger pursed his lips and nodded.

The Ford turned into the next fast-food joint, and Coleman followed them in the Galaxie. Serge slowed as he approached a speaker box in the drive-through. Only one car ahead. He turned toward the scalper. "Okay, this is an extremely tricky process that always stretches my nerves to the inflection point, so I could easily plug you with my pistol if I even suspect you're trying to jump out of the truck. Or I could accidentally drill you with a jittery trigger finger at annoyance over this ordering procedure. Sorry, it's just how I was born, so I only ask for acceptance."

The scalper only stared silently with petrified eyes.

"Thank you for not judging," said Serge. "Anyway, the process is further complicated by technology. We now have ultra-hi-def televisions and personal phones that broadcast real-time video to the globe. Yet the boxes beneath the menu boards at all these drive-through places have such poor sound quality that I swear they harvested speakers from 1950s drive-in theaters . . . The car in front of us just moved. We're on! Strap yourself in for the stress test!"

Serge took a deep, steadying breath. He rolled up to the box.

"May I take your order?"

"Yes," said Serge. "And please listen carefully, because our brief human connection here can fly off the rails at any moment and end up in the fast-food ravine, which I've climbed out of many times. Cool? Are we speaking the same tin-speaker language?"

"Sir, are you ready to order?"

"Yes! Ready as a big, well, that metaphor would be a non-starter," said Serge. "I . . . would . . . like . . . a . . . black . . . coffee . . . in . . . your . . . largest . . . size."

"Would you like cream and sugar?"

"No . . . black," said Serge. He began to cringe in advance: "And . . . could . . . you . . . add . . . a . . . few . . . ice . . . cubes . . . to . . . cool . . . it . . . a . . . little . . . so . . . I . . . don't . . . get . . . scalded?"

"You want iced coffee?"

"No . . . I . . . just . . . don't . . . want . . . to . . . get . . . scalded."

"Scald? Sir, you were breaking up for a second. There's nothing that sounds like that on the menu."

"Coffee . . . black . . . a few ice cubes."

A pause.

"Iced coffee is extra."

Serge savagely punched the steering wheel. Talking slow wasn't working.

"Okay, this is really very simple. I am seeking hot black coffee, not boiling coffee, so I can chug it while driving. And I'll help you by being specific: add five ice cubes."

"Sir, our iced coffee (kshhhhh)."

"What?" said Serge. "There was some static. Could you repeat that?"

"(kshhhhhh) large ice (kshhhhh)."

"You're still breaking up," said Serge. "Let's try this. Regular black coffee. Cup of ice on the side. That will be all."

"Okay, you also want a cup of ice water."

"No! Just the cubes!"

"What about the (kshhhhh) iced coffee you ordered?"

"Unit Ten, officer requests assistance. What's your twenty?"

"Sir, did you say something?"

"No, we're picking up the police frequency now," said Serge. "Could you read my order back to me."

"Large black coffee."

"What about the ice?"

"Oh, you want ice?"

"Yes!" Serge repeatedly punched the ceiling and swung his gun at the passenger. "Separate cup on the side."

"Tower, this is United 78, descending to five thousand . . ."

"Sir? What?"

"That was Miami International Airport."

"Please pull up to the (kshhhhhh) window."

"Is that the first or second window?"

"(Kshhhhh)."

"Screw it," said Serge. "Life's short. There are only two windows." He pulled up to the first.

"Next window."

Serge rolled forward, smacking his forehead on the steering wheel. He arrived at the second window, where they handed him a special cardboard drink tray with three iced coffees and a Cherry Coke. He passed it to the passenger. "Hold this. And help yourself to whatever you want."

The Ford drove away as they could hear the next customer's order out the service window:

". . . Chicken sandwich, large fries . . . (kshhhhh) . . . Flight 78 cleared for landing on runway niner . . ."

The Ford F-150 continued east. Serge drained his first iced coffee and tossed the cup on the floorboards, then started in on a second. He glanced sideways.

"You didn't help yourself from the tray," Serge told the scalper. "Try the Cherry Coke. It'll just go to waste." The scalper remained frozen. Serge flashed the gun in his face. "Drink the fucking Cherry Coke!"

The passenger timidly began sipping through a straw.

"That's better," said Serge. "I hate driving alone, and driving with a statue is the same thing. Coleman's almost a statue, but different in nuanced ways that make him highly engaging on a long trip. You know Coleman? Why would you? The short version: extreme stamina for self-medication. I've often been told I'm exhausting to be around, and most people end up screaming to be let out of the car. Some are so desperate they just ask me to slow down so they can jump. Not Coleman. Opposites attract, and his state of suspended animation makes him possibly the only person who can ride out my withering zest for all things even loosely associated with being alive, which is a severe list. That's Coleman!" He looked up in the rear-view and waved at the Galaxie behind them. "The key to traveling with him is a nimble agility with electric windows. It's hot in Florida, so the A/C is always on. But Coleman is like a bird and doesn't understand the glass concept, and you've got to be quick with the window's Down button just before he tries to dump a cup of soda outside or has to spit up. It's the little things that make a relationship last. Are you with me? Jump in at any spot." Serge cocked the gun in the passenger's face again. "That wasn't a request! Jump!"

A trembling voice: "Uh, I'll let you know if I have to dump my soda."

"Perfect! Excellent!" said Serge, chugging the chilled coffee and beginning to vibrate. "Not too much farther now. We should be at our destination in no time whatsoever . . ." His caffeine tremors grew. "In a New York minute, a country mile, ten miles of bad road, ten ways till Sunday, the whole nine yards, time flies, killing time, nick of time, once in a blue moon, a face that could stop a clock, clean his clock, punch the clock, five-o'clock shadow, it's five o'clock somewhere . . ." White knuckles on the steering wheel. "Too much coffee. The verbal thing has made me its bitch again."

The pickup made a skidding right turn into the Tradewinds Shopping Center, tastefully concealed from the highway by a buffet of tropical flora. Coleman pulled up beside the truck in the far, isolated end of the lot.

Serge was already outside at the pickup's passenger door; scant difficulty coaxing the hostage out with the gun hidden inside his tropical shirt. "We have some shopping to do, but it will only take a minute . . ." He popped the Galaxie's trunk. "Sorry, I didn't catch your name. Heck, I never asked, what with the knives and shit-paper and all. That's just bad manners."

"It's Oat. Oat McGack."

Coleman chortled behind a mondo spliff. "That's a fucked-up name."

Serge motioned with his gun, and Oat climbed in. The lid slammed shut.

Clouds of smoke drifted south. "Coleman, since I see you're now playing drums for the Whalers, why don't you stay out here and make sure he doesn't make a racket or somehow try to escape. Here's my gun."

"Cool."

Serge headed for the stores, and Coleman leaned against the bumper with his spliff. Several minutes later, he began hearing a clawing sound, and after a few more hits, loud banging. Coleman knocked on the top of the trunk.

A muted voice: "Yes?"

Coleman held a toke. "No noise, or else!"

"Or else what?"

"I have a gun."

"Can I see it?"

"Uh, okay, sure . . ."

. . . Serge had just left the store with a shopping cart when he heard a gunshot and saw Oat McGack running away across the parking lot.

Chapter 9

KEY LARGO

A red-banded iguana and a feral cat scurried out of the way as Serge took off running across the parking lot of the Tradewinds Shopping Center. He sprinted in a diagonal direction to intercept the escape path of the pandemic scalper, but Oat McGack had a serious head start.

"Damn that Coleman," Serge muttered. "This is a disaster. If Oat gets away . . ."

Then a gunshot.

Oat desperately pointing over his shoulder without aim.

The sound of the shot, however, did not concern Serge. It was a Keys thing. The geographical openness of the island, combined with the ocean wind and heavy foliage, significantly deadens such noise, unlike in Miami, where gunfire pings and echoes off the buildings until it almost seems to be getting louder. Plus, in the tolerant Keys, people have all kinds of reasonable reasons to shoot guns, and few residents will judge until all the facts are in.

Serge wove his way through parked cars and dodged shopping carts as McGack ran unimpeded along the dense tree line of palms and slash pines lining the back of the lot. The scalper looked back and vainly tipped over an empty cart, which his pursuer simply hurdled. Serge never doubted that he would catch McGack eventually, but even he became surprised at how rapidly he was gaining on him. Then Serge noticed the scalper's limp, and it was only getting worse.

Did Coleman actually hit him? Serge wondered to himself. *I'm impressed.*

It wasn't like the TV cop shows, where the officer dives over a park bench or oil drum to tackle a suspect. Serge simply arrived and grabbed the back of Oat's collar and jerked him to a halt.

"Where do you think you're going, Spanky?"

"What are you going to do to me?"

"I've given this a lot of thought, and come up with something highly educational and germane to your line of work. But I'm placing all my chips on I won't get a thank-you."

"Please let me go! I'll give you the rest of the money!"

"In what universe do you think that money's not already mine?" Serge looked McGack up and down, front and back. "I don't see any blood. Where's the wound?"

"What wound?"

"I heard the gunshot and saw you limping," said Serge.

"Oh, I just twisted my ankle getting away from your friend."

"Darn, I was going to celebrate Coleman's marksmanship by throwing him my signature one-man parade," said Serge. "I seem to be the only one who throws them, but I'm trying to get it to catch on, like my trifecta. Want to see how it goes? I'll throw one for you. It's a going-away parade. Pretend I have a tall marching band hat and gold braid across my tropical shirt."

Serge held a fist to his mouth like a trumpet and began goose-stepping in a circle around the perplexed captive, singing military-style. "*Hail to McGack, he's the douche we want to attack; it's the kind of attack so he won't be coming back.*" Serge stopped marching. "You get the idea. The coffee is still in effect."

"You're insane."

"Ouch." A poke in the scalper's ribs. "Get moving! And not like this." Serge stood in place and flapped his arms.

"You *are* insane."

The pair arrived back at the Galaxie, where Coleman was sitting on the lip of the open trunk, the neck of a whiskey bottle in one hand and a pistol in the other.

"Hey! Poster child for gun safety!" yelled Serge. "How the hell did he get out of the trunk?"

"I let him out."

"But why?"

"He asked."

"What about the gunshot?"

"Oh, he was getting away," said Coleman. "I'm not good with aim." He glanced down at his left sneaker with a fresh hole near the tip. "Almost got my big toe, the one I like. Anyway, he had already started to run, and I guess the gunshot spooked him and he twisted his ankle stepping on one of those things right there, you know, the concrete bars on the ground at the front of every parking spot that always fuck me up when you let me drive."

"I got the picture." Serge paused for another car to go by. "Oat, back in the trunk . . ." *Slam.*

"What now?" asked Coleman.

"We go back and get the shopping cart I abandoned when I took off after him."

After a short hike, they neared the store. Ahead, a shopping cart full of purchases sat quietly in the middle of the road while cars casually drove around without a second thought.

"I can't believe it's still there," said Coleman. "After how long you were gone with the chase and everything."

"We're on island time," said Serge. "Stuff is always being left around in the road for a half hour or more that would unnerve people elsewhere. Shopping carts, baby strollers, trampolines. The residents down here think: *One of my neighbors must have had an important urge and will be back soon. Was that a gunshot? I'm sure it was necessary.* And they just continue back to their cars with bags of ice and handle-bottles of tequila."

The pair acquired the cart and pushed it back to their Galaxie, where they unloaded it into the backseat.

"Coleman, this time you're in the pickup." Serge tossed the keys. "Just follow me."

"Where are we going?"

"East, toward Pennekamp State Park."

"We're going snorkeling?"

"No, we're not headed to the park itself," said Serge. "One of the benefits of living down here is the natural privacy. All the dense tropical foliage and ad hoc mangrove trails. People with our lifestyle have a bounty of location options when we're conducting behavioral patterns that could be misunderstood."

The vehicles pulled back onto U.S. Highway 1 and drove east for three miles, then Serge hit his blinker and turned off down a gravel road. They passed a graveyard of boats and trailers surrounded by chain link and barbed wire, then stacks of barnacle-covered crab traps. From there, nothing.

They finally parked at a mangrove dead end, where they got out and could hear—but not see—mild waves rolling in from the Atlantic. It was an incoming tide, and the funky muck smell was receding.

Coleman had a beer in each hip pocket of his cargo shorts as he cupped his hands to light a fatty. "I'm guessing another science project?"

Serge opened the door to the backseat. "Not just another, but one on the cutting edge of current events. Let's tailgate!"

"Now you're talking!" Coleman ran back to the car.

Moments later, both were busy at the rear of the Ford F-150.

"I'm not a pickup guy," said Serge. "But I'm definitely a tailgate guy. Frees up the hands. It was so considerate of our guest to make this transportation choice."

"No shit," said Coleman, setting up supplies he was motivated to keep under his passenger seat with staggering spatial optimization.

The left side of the tailgate quickly became a party spread of liquor, mixers, bar tools, those red plastic party cups, six different strains of weed, a tiny canister of dried mushrooms, prescription bottles, an entire head-shop lineup of paraphernalia and a bobbing dashboard hula girl. The right side of the gate was grade-A eclectic: a tub the size of a laundry basket, sweatpants, a Key Largo souvenir long-sleeve fishing shirt, plastic gloves . . .

Serge walked around to the side of the truck's bed and retrieved some leftover boxes of merchandise. He set them back down on the tailgate and slipped on the gloves.

Coleman was zoned in on a potent concoction in a red cup. "You have got to tell me what you're doing."

"Hold on," said Serge. "I need to get our guest, because this gets complicated and I don't want to have to repeat it."

He popped the trunk. "Jesus, your ankle has swollen up like a grapefruit."

"I don't think I can walk."

"Let me help." Serge pulled him out of the trunk, then reached down and grabbed the folding lawn chair he had been lying on. "Put your arm around my shoulders . . . There you go . . ."

They made it back to the rear of the pickup, where Serge unfolded the plastic-strap chair. "Take a load off."

"What's all that shit on my tailgate?"

"I was just about to tell Coleman and figured you'd be interested." Serge opened a cardboard box, unscrewing the tops of hand sanitizer bottles and squeezing them out into the tub. "With all the new manifestations of this pandemic, I needed a major catch-up study on an intimidating range of scientific data. And this is where science rocks: It leads in directions you'd never imagine." An empty bottle landed in a small pile that was growing on the ground. Serge opened another box and grinned down at McGack.

Coleman upended the red cup and packed a one-hitter. "Don't leave me hanging over here . . ."

Chapter 10

HONDURAS

A trademark coastal drizzle had been coming down for hours from a uniformly gray sky. Water filled the gutters and people hopped to the sidewalks.

Yandy's shoes slapped across the pavement at the front steps of the police station. When he walked in, everything stopped. Everyone looked toward him in silence, then looked anywhere else. The chief appeared in his office doorway. "Yandy, could I have a minute?"

Yandy entered as the chief took the chair behind his desk. "What is it?"

"Close the door," said the chief. "And have a seat."

Out the office window, Yandy could see people looking again, and looking away again. He sat. "What does everyone seem to know that I don't?"

"Yandy," said the chief. "You know your American friend? The one from the diplomatic corps?"

"Sure."

"They found his body this morning. It wasn't hard."

"What happened? Where was he?"

"Any of ten different things would have been fatal," said the chief. "They dumped him before dawn in the fountain at the plaza. It was meant for the public to see."

"I want the files," said Yandy.

"I know you do, and you can't have them."

"You're going to bury this?" said Yandy.

"No, I'm being a friend," said the chief. "You don't want to read this stuff, and definitely not see the photos. We received several anonymous hang-up phone calls not to talk to the CIA anymore."

"But he wasn't CIA," said Yandy.

"Actually, he was," said the chief. "They've already contacted our capital."

Three other officers arrived at the door as scheduled, and the chief waved them in. "Yandy, they're going to take you to your apartment. You're being watched. The gangs. Make it brief and pack a light suitcase. We're getting you out of town."

"But I don't want to go," said Yandy. "Not with all this."

"It's an order," said the chief. "We heard about the visit you got yesterday. The bullet on the table. Situations are too unsteady right now. We need to keep you safe until things fall back into their grooves."

Yandy stood up and paused for a deep breath. "How long?"

"We'll let you know." Then the chief nodded toward the other officers waiting in the doorway, and Yandy walked out with them.

It was a quick drive through the narrow, steep streets. Three police cars in all. Eyes were on them. Gang eyes. And their mouths were on cell phones. Twenty minutes later the police cars raced back down the other side of the mountain, Yandy lying across the backseat.

They reached a bridge, and the trailing cars skidded sideways to a stop, blocking the road from anyone following. The lead car proceeded until it reached a ravine next to the bridge. The officer driving Yandy jumped out and told Yandy to follow. They half tumbled down the embankment until they reached a dense neighborhood with a pre-positioned car behind a warehouse. The officer switched Yandy into the new vehicle and he was driven out of town and into those lush mountains.

Yandy's eyes fluttered open the next morning. Sunlight streamed through the broken slats of the shutters. He stared up at a wobbly ceiling fan with wicker blades. They had given him a satellite phone and told him not to use it; they would call him when the time came. And not to do anything else. Just stay inside.

It was a house the police used now and then for stuff like this. All the police knew about it. So did his hillside neighbors. They'd point down from a bluff: "Yep, that's the house the police use." Yandy wandered into the kitchen, where the other officer had left a couple sacks of groceries the day before. He got out a loaf of bread and peanut butter. He walked away from it. He wasn't hungry, just looking for something to do.

He walked weakly through the three-room shack in a haze of emptiness. In his head: *Can cabin fever strike so soon?* Then Yandy found himself opening a screen door and stepping out onto the back porch. He placed hands on his hips as his eyes moved along a mountain ridge draped in a tropical canopy. He looked down to a stream winding through the tiny valley. There was a rope footbridge that he decided he wouldn't be trying. But he had to admit, it was a great view. Yandy nodded to himself and thought of peanut butter. He went back inside.

It was like a truck hit Yandy, and he was suddenly facedown on the floor planks. Three men in ski masks had tackled and cuffed him, then threw a black hood over his head. They yanked him to his feet. "Let me go! What's going on? Who are you?"

The trio remained silent as they hustled him out the front door and into a windowless black van sitting in the dusty street. They slammed the side door shut. The van sped away along a narrow mountainside road with a steep drop-off.

All his neighbors had been watching the proceedings from other shacks scattered across the side of the mountain notch. "Yep, that's the house the police use."

Yandy could feel the van angling down, then crossing a small bridge until it slowed to a stop. The hood was pulled off. He sat wide-eyed on the floor, staring up at a man with a shaved head who was built like a wrestler. Now he had a face he could identify, probably the leader. That was bad. So many thoughts raced through Yandy's head that none could fully form. The only thing absolutely for sure: He was going to die.

The bald man lit a cigarette. "I'm guessing you have a lot of questions. First off, you're not going to die. I mean, someday, but not now."

One of the men in ski masks uncuffed him.

Yandy rubbed his wrists and reacquired speech. "Are you with the gangs?"

The man shook his head.

"Cartels?"

The head shook again.

"Then who?"

"As we go along, you'll have a pretty good guess." The shaved head took a drag. "The important thing right now is to get you someplace safe, far away from that house."

"But that *was* a safe house."

"It might as well have a lighted arrow pointing down at it," said the man, offering a Marlboro.

Yandy waved it off. "What should I call you?"

"You shouldn't," said the man. "But if it brightens your day, call me Hank."

"How did you know I was there?"

"We knew before you did," said Hank. "In fact, we're surprised nobody came for you in the night. My guys were on watch in the brush until I could arrive."

"I'm still not any closer to knowing what's going on," said Yandy.

"You won't have to wait long." Hank held out the black hood

that had been on Yandy's head. A gecko crossed the dirt road. "There was a need to be rough back there. If you would just put this back on yourself, I'd appreciate it."

"Not until I know at least something."

"The big picture of the immigrant crisis down here is obvious, so I'll start with the small one," said Hank. "You knew Alan Midling?"

"Yes," said Yandy. "Not for long, but he was a good guy."

"That's what this is about."

"You're kidding," said Yandy. "What does kidnapping me have to do with Alan?"

"You weren't kidnapped."

"My bad," said Yandy. "It had all the markings."

"You were rescued," said Hank. "In return we need your help—"

The driver turned around. "Sir, we're clear."

"The hood?" asked Hank.

Yandy sighed.

Hank nodded a single time toward the driver, and the van began moving again, slowly, on the unmaintained road. Overhanging jungle vines scraped the roof. He turned back to Yandy. "Alan can't go unanswered. And it has to be a big answer. We have to do it in a way that they won't know who was behind it, but yet they'll all *know*. You feeling me?"

Yandy coughed under the hood. "You're American, aren't you?"

"Officially, no," said Hank. "We have nothing to do with the government."

"That means you have everything to do with the government," said Yandy. "If I'm guessing correctly how you want me to help, the answer's a hard no. I have to live in this country."

"You don't have a choice."

"Watch me." He pulled off the hood and grabbed the door handle. Locked. "Shit."

One of the ski masks lunged and tackled Yandy.

"What are you doing?" said Hank.

"He took off the hood!"

Hank rolled his eyes. "The hood's stupid. So are the ski masks. Take 'em all off."

"I demand you let me go," said Yandy.

"We will," said Hank. "Right after we go over a few things."

"I told you I'm not working with you guys."

"You can't live here anymore," said Hank. "Or you're dead."

"They only put a bullet on my table outside the café," said Yandy. "Said not to talk to Alan anymore, and I didn't."

"You're going to trust them?" The van stopped, and Hank opened the sliding side door. "We've picked up some new chatter. Apparently Alan talked under torture, about the gang you fingered in town. You now have a negative life-span in these parts."

"Where'd you hear this?" asked Yandy.

"Everywhere," said Hank. "But most importantly, from your own police department. You don't have any idea who you can trust in there, do you? Even if you live long enough for them to call you back in, you wouldn't last the night."

Yandy hopped down from the side of the van. "What is this place?"

Hank turned toward a small, remote hacienda. Goats walked by. "A place we bought yesterday. We'll bulldoze it tomorrow."

"Why?"

"We have a good budget." Hank led Yandy inside the residence, retrofitted with weapons cabinets, alarms and encrypted radios. He pointed at a table covered with topographical maps. "Have a seat."

"Now I'm seated," said Yandy. "Now what?"

Hank pulled over his own chair. "You know what a drone is?"

Yandy watched the other men lean over the map between them with a compass and protractor. "Of course I know what a drone is."

"Then forget what a drone is."

"What kind of conversation is this?"

"We'd use a drone, probably a bunch, but we can't risk having one crash," said Hank. "Your country's an ally, so a clandestine drone strike is considered rude. That's why we need you."

"How am I a drone?"

"I told you to forget about drones," said Hank. "We need you on the ground. You know the players, their routines, the geography. We'll give you a special radio."

"But why me?"

"Because you're honest," said Hank. "Alan told us all about you. You can never be sure who's honest down here, not even among us. But you're a rare one. Did you really walk away from that briefcase of cash?"

"Word gets around."

"We'll brief you on everything you need to know," said Hank. "Fit you with all your equipment. Then, when it's time, we'll get you in position."

"Where's that?"

"You tell us," said Hank. "I'm sure you recognized the guys who put the bullet on your table."

Yandy reluctantly nodded.

"Then I'm also assuming you know the main location where they conduct their business," said Hank. "We haven't been able to nail that down. At least, not with the needed accuracy. And this isn't our home turf, so it's doubtful we can approach with the needed stealth in this kind of landscape. We can't have any civilian casualties."

"I know the place."

"That's great," said Hank. "We'll start the briefing soon."

"But then I'm dead for sure down here."

"That's why you'll have to leave the country," said Hank. "We'll set you up with a new identity, U.S. passport, and all the other paperwork you'll need. And plenty of money to start a new life. We've already set up a bank account and deposited half. The rest when you meet the strike team." He slid a piece of paper across the table.

Yandy looked down at it, then up. "That's a big number."

"We have a good budget," repeated Hank. "The immigration problem is one of our top priorities."

"Now I definitely know this is a mission that could only have been concocted in America," said Yandy. "You're paying me a small fortune to *leave* the country in order to stop *others* from leaving the country."

"You're a quick study."

Suddenly, there was a deep rumbling sound outside. "What's that?" asked Yandy.

Hank looked out the window. "The bulldozers arrived early."

Chapter 11

KEY LARGO

Serge manically paced back and forth in the mangroves behind the tailgate of a Ford F-150 pickup.

"Right. So everyone's now heavily into social distancing, masks, sanitizers, face shields, contact tracing, quarantines, special pocket tools to open doors without your hands, and making up reality-shattering bullshit on Facebook, all of which has so overwhelmed the culture that we won't know the full ramifications for years because we've never been here before." Serge emptied more plastic bottles of clear antiseptic goo and added them to the discard pile. "Here's a story to illustrate: I've got this friend who drives one of those big honking tanker trucks that fill the pumps at gas stations. And he said: 'Until you start thinking about it, you don't realize how many public surfaces you touch each day, and I touch even more than most because I make a ton of stops.' So my friend starts responsibly using hand sanitizer every time he touches something with cooties. Then, for some reason, like a missing hazardous material placard, he gets pulled over by the cops. Bottom line is he ends up getting breath tested and is about to be arrested. And here's where we go down the rabbit hole: The legal limit for blood-alcohol content is 0.08 percent, but my friend has the most restrictive class B and C commercial driver's license for those fuel trucks, which means he has to register a total zero on the DUI machines. He hits 0.01 percent. They're ready to cuff him as he swears up and down he hasn't had a drink since the weekend. I think it was like Thursday. One of the cops stops, since the blood level was so low, and asks the driver if he can think of any possible way the alcohol got into his body. He says he can't, and then the officer notices a large empty sanitizer bottle on the floor between the driver's seat and the open door and asks my friend how often he uses it, and he says constantly. And the cop says that's the cause. And my pal got off."

"But it's on his skin," said Coleman.

"Who knew it penetrated in sufficient volumes?" said Serge. "Anyway, the police learned about it because some defense attorney started to bring it up in court. Nobody ever really thought about hand sanitizer before because who used to use that glop? But now so many are rubbing the stuff that the sample size exploded and trends popped up. The FDA just woke up from a coma and started broadcasting warnings about the active ingredient methyl alcohol in certain brands that can seriously muck you up, and there's talk they might pull it from the shelves. Then there are other ingredients that compound the problem. The cases that alerted authorities mainly came from little kids getting poisoned after licking their hands to see what it tasted like."

"I tasted everything as a kid," said Coleman. *Chug, chug, chug.* "Still do."

"What a shock." Serge grabbed several bottles from the tailgate and glanced at McGack. "You've got a whole mix of brands here. Let's see what we have." He turned the bottles around to the fine print. "Ethyl alcohol, isopropyl—eek, this one has methyl—and there's even trouble lurking in the alleys of the inactive-ingredient neighborhood. This one has the preservative ethyl paraben and ethylene oxide, artificial fragrances and dyes. Woo-weeeee! Glad I bought these gloves . . ."

McGack remained speechless as Serge continued his diligent task. Finally he was finished filling the tub with sanitizer. Then he grabbed the sweatpants and T-shirt, dropped them in the tub and began squeezing and pressing and kneading until they were fully drenched.

"All right, chief," said Serge. "Time to strip down."

"Get naked?" McGack glanced one way and then the other in the mosquito-filled mangrove culvert. "Are you out of your mind?"

"Couldn't be more serious," said Serge. "I'm sure you've been through jail intake before."

Oat began tentatively slipping off his shorts. "But I'll be naked to the elements out here."

"Never accuse me of not being the hostess with the mostest," said Serge. "You can keep on your Underoos."

McGack made a *whew* expression. Then noticed Serge was distracted reaching for something and made a break for it.

Serge picked up a coconut and fired it in a tight spiral like Tom Brady.

McGack regained consciousness and noticed he was down to his briefs. Serge lightly kicked him in the side. "Stand. It's time to suit up." He pulled the gooey sweatpants from the tub on the tailgate.

"Wh-Wh-What's going to happen to me?"

"Who knows?" Serge grinned wide. "This is all new to me too. Isn't it exciting?"

McGack was shaking and crying as he slipped into the pants at gunpoint.

"Don't be such a baby," said Serge. "Now the long-sleeve fishing shirt."

Slime began coating McGack's face as he slowly poked his head through the neck hole of the shirt. He looked up with an expression that said: *What weirdness is next?*

"Hold your arms out like a scarecrow," said Serge. "And don't move until I say."

Coleman tugged his pal's shirt. "What's going on now?"

"We can't realistically get him back into either vehicle in his current state," said Serge. "But you've used hand sanitizer before."

"When?"

"Work with me," said Serge. "The first time you think, 'I've got all this slime on my hands and no sink around. What am I going to do?' The next thing you know, it's dry and problem solved. It's a miracle! . . . Same thing with our newest best friend here. We just need to give it more time because of the saturation factor in the clothes. Just a matter of waiting patiently . . ." Serge began tapping his fingers on the tailgate. *Dum, de-dum, de-dum* . . . He got on the ground and did push-ups, ran laps around the pickup, reorganized his wallet, adjusted the Velcro straps on his sneakers, combed his hair. He walked up to McGack and felt a sleeve of his shirt. "Damn . . . Coleman, you want to talk about something to kill time?"

"Sure. What?"

"I don't know." He opened his hiking compass and marched around under the sun-spangled mangrove canopy. "What indeed?"

"Serge, why are you always checking your hiking compass, even when we're not hiking?"

Serge snapped his fingers. "Excellent discussion topic! You know how everyone is walking around all day worried about the stock market or terrorists or some celebrity shit? They're thinking *way* too small. Hell, they don't even know that what they should be worried about even exists. The far more likely threat is right under out feet."

Coleman looked down. "Dirt."

"Under that," said Serge. "The Earth's core is molten iron, which rises as it heats, and drops back to the center of the core as it cools."

"Like a lava lamp?"

"Precisely," said Serge. "But here's the important part: As the iron blobs pass each other over and over, they kick in Faraday's induction principle, which is how they can make those emergency hurricane flashlights that don't need batteries because you shake them instead. In the case of this planet, the passing blobs create our magnetic field.

And people think, Nifty, I can use a compass. Except the vastly more critical part is that our magnetic field deflects solar flares and the cosmic winds that would otherwise scorch the whole works down here like a blowtorch."

"Funky," said Coleman. "But what's the worry?"

"That's what all those strangers on the street say when I run up to them with the urgent warning. Or maybe it's because I'm wearing a helmet with a revolving red light. Whatever. The deal is that almost nobody realizes our magnetic field has flipped north-to-south almost a dozen times in the last few billion years, and scientists say we're long overdue."

Coleman scoffed and guzzled banana-flavored tequila. "I ain't worried. It'll be centuries, if not a hundred years."

"You hope," said Serge. "I should stop reading as much because I just learned that a decade ago, scientists detected a migration of our magnetic north pole. And just recently it's speed toward Siberia has increased to thirty miles an hour. Thirty! When the field is on its side, a gap will open for solar flares! Yet there's been nothing about it on the news." He flipped his compass open again. "That's why *someone* has to stay on the ball."

Coleman pointed with the tequila bottle. "Is he dry yet?"

"Oh, almost forgot." Serge felt the fishing shirt. "Yep, ready as we'll ever be."

McGack's head drifted around on his neck. "I don't feel so well."

"And here's your bonus round," said Serge, leading him to the pickup's passenger seat. "Tell it to someone else, like a doctor."

The two vehicles returned to the rear of the shopping center. "I'm guessing that mega-priced yard sale of yours up in Tavernier wasn't your first rodeo on this circuit," said Serge. "This would be the nearest other logical shopping center. Shall we find out?"

Serge grabbed McGack and forced him up into the bed of the pickup. He found the last couple of packages of toilet paper in a box and put them in his prisoner's hands. Then he stuck a gun in his ribs: "Raise those over your head."

When McGack was quite visible, Serge cupped his hand around his mouth: "Anyone remember this jerk ripping you off?"

A few heads turned curiously at first. Then one of the shoppers in the lot poked a friend. "Look who it is." Someone else: "I remember that asshole." Then more and more—"How do you sleep at night!"— the shoppers slowly drifting over and forming a crowd around the back of the truck. "You're not American!" "Your mother must be proud!"

The chorus grew louder, toward a fever pitch of yelling. More shoppers on the other side of the parking lot, pushing carts out of the grocery store, began to take notice. "I can't believe he has the nerve to come back . . ."

Soon the mob was even larger than when McGack was originally scalping. "What are you selling today? Some old person's medicine?"

McGack became unsteady on his legs. "I don't feel shhhho good."

Coleman stood next to the truck finishing a Schlitz. "He's slurring his words."

"That would be the ethyl," said Serge.

McGack dropped his arms and looked up. "Dizzy now. Big spots in the sky."

"That would be the methyl and inactive ingredients."

With nothing left to sell but two packs of tissue, McGack had no leverage. The crowd worked itself into a froth and began rocking the pickup's back bumper. "You son of a bitch!" "I'd love to kick you in the balls!" "Why not?" "Let's get him!"

Serge stood behind McGack. "He's all yours." Shove.

McGack fell over the edge of the pickup's bed and hit the pavement on his side. "Ouch."

Ten hands yanked him to his feet, but they quickly let go when McGack began ballistic-arc vomiting. A rooster scooted out of the way. "I need a doctor!"

"And I need my money back, you predatory prick!"

McGack staggered randomly as he retched.

"The bastard's drunk." "Oh, enjoying some of the high-end stuff on what you exploited from us?" Shove. "How about a little Rémy Martin?" Shove.

"Please stop!" pleaded McGack, spinning deliriously. "I'm hallucinating. You all look like hairy creatures."

Shove.

A sudden shriek and McGack took off.

"He's running."

"*Trying* to run. He's zigzagging all over the place."

"What should we do with him?"

"What do we usually do down here?"

"Throw rocks?"

"Sounds good."

"Ow!" yelled McGack. "Rocks! . . ."

McGack ran serpentine around the empty parking spots, covering his head as small stones bounced off him.

"Larger rocks!" yelled the crowd.

Fling, fling, fling. "Ow! Ow! Ow!"

In his disorientation, McGack wove haplessly toward the shopping center's exit, but with the ground rolling left and right, it was like trying to escape a fun house.

"He's getting away!"

"After him!"

Rocks pinged off the scalper as he ran up the exit.

Meanwhile, a much-needed resupply was on the way. Two essential workers drove a grocery chain's semi-truck down U.S. 1, full of needed food and paper goods. The passenger pointed and yelled. "Watch out!" *Screeeeeeeeeech! Thump-thump!* A last rock hit the side of the trailer. The driver got out to see what he'd run over.

A crowd stood in shock on the side of the road. "We're in trouble!" "Run away!"

That evening, the local news switched to a reporter on the side of U.S. 1. *"A confusing scene at this hour near the site of today's fatal traffic accident in Key Largo. As more details become available, the initial reports of a simple pedestrian collision are now being revised into what may be the latest salvo in the growing culture wars over masks and other virus protocols. If early speculation holds up, this could be the first significant protest over hand sanitizer. Confidential police sources now say that the victim was heavily coated head-to-toe in sanitizing gel as a possible political statement. The same officials say the victim either voluntarily jumped in front of the massive truck to draw attention to his cause, or it was the result of gel-induced delirium. The sources are unsure whether the protest was for or against sanitizer. Back to you, Gloria."*

Chapter 12

THE COLONEL

A Hello Kitty sippy cup sat forgotten in a parking lot. A large off-road tire rolled up and crushed it to pieces. The door of the Hummer opened, and shiny black boots hit the ground in Miami.

As far back as anyone could remember, he had been called the Colonel. And nothing else. Not even a hint of an actual name, kind of like Clint Eastwood's no-name character from the spaghetti westerns.

Nobody questioned the moniker because he wore it well. Tall and fit with short gray hair and disciplined military posture. He always wore boots and combat fatigues, sometimes with a tight-fitting olive-green T-shirt that showed off not exactly muscles but a lean strength. His cap had the insignia of his rank, and not a lieutenant colonel but the full-bird variety. His Hummer sported bumper stickers for the Army Rangers and POWs. He spoke only when absolutely necessary, and with the kind of gravelly voice that suggested they were very large pieces of gravel.

The horizontal scar on his chin was the source of much speculation among his men. The prevailing theory was a Ka-Bar knife during hand-to-hand combat in Somalia. But it actually went back earlier to when his parents removed his training wheels, and he was in no rush to correct the record.

The lack of personal data extended far beyond the mystery of his name, causing rumors to swirl. Primarily, what was his kill total? There were stories of Special Forces operations in Iraq, hostage rescues in Afghanistan and bar fights in Toledo.

Most important, he commanded a hermetic, shrinking respect from all his subordinates at his West Miami company, Wild Horses Military Contractors. Their logo involved a branding iron. The most interesting unknown fact about their boss was that he had never been a colonel, because he was never in the military.

The Colonel had definitely wanted to join up, but it never worked out. There are a number of reasons certain personality types are attracted to the forces: patriotism, the pay, educational benefits, upward mobility from life in a dying town. Then there's a small minority who want to see action—get in the shit, as they say—firing weapons with maximum havoc and getting away with it, an opportunity that is generally unavailable in civilian life. The Colonel wanted to jump straight to the havoc part. But the recruiting office told him there would have to be lots of training first. He asked how long until the havoc? Months, he was told, maybe years or never.

The Colonel left the recruiting office and got on his home computer with a list of searches. That Friday evening he showed up at a pot-luck dinner in a meeting hall. Stew and macaroni and tossed salad doused with bacon bits. The building was out in the countryside, and at the front of the room hung a yellow flag with a snake: DON'T TREAD ON ME.

After dinner, the speeches. The picture was indeed grim. And the messages of gloom only grew louder and angrier into the evening: Enemies were all around. Rights were getting trampled. Their lives and liberty were somehow threatened by other Americans getting stuff for free. It was worse than terminally depressing. The Colonel was happy with what he heard.

The next day, a silent platoon of self-appointed men fanned out in a remote swath of private land in the Everglades just west of the Miccosukee casino. They moved fleet and focused with AR-15s and AK-47s aimed and leading the way. The night before, a secret team of the Florida Thunder Militia had placed metal shooting targets throughout the reeds and hardwood hammocks and spongy marsh. Now no conversation. Boots splashed through the swamp water in a tightening pincer assault. The metal targets had been painted with cartoonish depictions of imagined enemies.

The platoon stopped and took up positions near a highland strand of cypress. The Colonel turned to the others and displayed a silent series of hand gestures. Two fingers at his eyes, then the same fingers pointed forward toward a tidal islet.

Whispers behind the stalwart trees: "What's the new guy doing?"

"Giving us command signals."

"Like a special-ops raid?"

"Looks like it."

"But he just joined us."

"They call him the Colonel, so he's got to know what he's doing. The president of our militia must have put him in charge."

"And what is he doing now?"

"He's brushing each of his sleeves like a third-base coach."

"Did we miss a memo?"

"I don't know, but he seems in control. We better follow him."

More gestures. A fist, then another fist, and four fingers, followed by an urgent wave.

The Colonel took off, and the platoon charged. He splashed down on his stomach, with the rifle prone, and waved the others past him. They charged into the calf-deep alligator water, and the steel targets appeared.

Bang . . . bang, bang . . . bang, bang, bang, bang . . .

Accompanied by: *Ping . . . ping, ping . . . ping, ping, ping, ping . . .*

The steel silhouettes on tall poles that had been sunk into the muck would need to be repainted with the offensive renderings of their enemies.

Bang, bang, bang . . .

Ping, ping, ping . . .

Then: *Bang . . .* "Ow, fuck!" Someone grabbed his shoulder. "Who shot me?"

The rest of the platoon shook their heads and looked around. The Colonel raised his hand from his prone position. "My mistake. Sorry."

"Jesus!" yelled the injured man. "Do I look metal? Or Mexican?"

The Colonel stood. "Maybe we should paint the targets differently . . ."

It was the beginning of an inexorable trend and, in short order, the Colonel was banished from three different militia groups for being an asshole.

THE CARIBBEAN

On an otherwise uneventful evening in July, somebody nicknamed the Banana Man was winding down for the night at his hillside residence in the suburb of Pétion-Ville.

Then it became eventful.

More than two dozen men silently slipped through the neighborhood, stormed the house, and opened fire in a classic example of overkill. The Banana Man was struck twelve times and promptly expired. The paramilitary team had just assassinated Jovenel Moïse, president of Haiti.

The attack had been highly coordinated. And that's where the planning seemed to hit a wall. The ensuing exit strategy was something from a dark comedy. Despite the neighbors later describing thunderous gunfire, some of the assailants decided to stick around and ransack the house for valuables. When they finally left, they couldn't find their getaway driver, so they jumped in another vehicle and immediately hit a fortified police roadblock from Port-au-Prince. They dumped the transportation and took off on foot, scattering without thought and triggering a prolonged gun battle into the night. Some found a building to hide in and were soon cornered. Others broke into the courtyard of the Taiwanese embassy and were kicked out. When the smoke cleared, the remaining members of the tactical team were found simply hiding in the bushes.

The next day: press conferences, condemnation, blame. The top-priority investigation that followed was another head-scratcher. All tracks immediately led to the unlikely source of the attack.

MIAMI

Faster than could be imagined, law enforcement swarmed a nondescript warehouse on Northwest Seventy-Ninth Avenue, surrounded innocuously by an upscale flooring showroom, a playground-equipment outlet, a McDonald's and President Trump's Doral golf resort. The building was a gray, concrete, nearly windowless rectangle, home to one of Miami's countless "security firms." It was not hard to track down. The security firm had used its company credit card to buy nineteen airline tickets for the Colombian assassins to fly in from Bogotá. But who had hired the security firm? Why, another security firm in Miami. All this shit is true.

As authorities began to sort it all out, one of the Sunshine State's maxims seemed to hold: When something outrageous happens, don't look for a conspiracy; look for chaos. Soon, an only-in-Florida picture began to emerge. The generally accepted wisdom was that both firms actually believed they were hiring bodyguards for high-profile Haitians. Maybe the dog ate their homework.

What made the Miami connection extra weird was that it turned out not to be surprising, but expected.

Outside of Washington, Miami is the clandestine operations

capital of America. It essentially started when Castro came to power. Within months, the CIA poured so much cash into secretly buying up hundreds of properties and buildings and boats that it turned Miami into a boom town—and the second-largest CIA station in the world outside of Langley. On land leased from the University of Miami, they launched Operation Mongoose to topple the Communist regime in Havana. Everywhere were safe houses, classified radio rooms, and marinas for their private navy. They planned to blow up Castro with an exploding seashell while he was scuba-diving.

Today the CIA has a smaller yet still heavy presence, and remnants of its old, larger footprint can be seen from Opa-locka to Key Largo. But the emphasis has shifted to the private sector. The city has so many "security" firms that websites and want ads openly fill pages of the internet. Other firms stay off the web and operate from behind front companies. Some of the operations actually are confined to security, simply providing high-end home monitoring systems and guards for the film and music celebrities living on Star and Palm Islands. Others are the hard-core mercenary military contractors, the frequent middle-of-the-night flyers to Central and South America. And their headquarters run the gamut, occupying some of the most expensive high-rise office space downtown like law firms, and some of the cheapest industrial buildings near the airport like a scrap-metal outfit. If you've spent any time at all in Miami, odds are you've unknowingly driven by dozens of these companies, maybe even gone into a travel agency in the front room while in back they're loading mortar launchers and body armor.

But the key thing to remember is it's all about the money. Like any other industry, prices are all over the map, and you get what you pay for.

If money is no object, you can hire an elite ex–Special Forces team with the latest equipment, who can invisibly get in and out of a country before even their spouses know they're gone.

If you go bargain shopping, you end up with guys hiding in shrubbery.

L ate on a Wednesday afternoon, the waning sun glinted off jets landing at the airport and blinded drivers on the expressway. Some of the drivers were behind the wheels of semi-trucks, which exited the highway, heading for the loading docks behind an entire neighborhood of distribution warehouses that characterized an entire section of Doral in western Miami.

After the distribution centers were more large metal buildings, one called the Water Bed Barn. In case of an actual customer wanting a water bed or "linens for less than what you would expect to pay elsewhere," there was a permanent sign on the door: CLOSED NEXT WEEK FOR FUMIGATION.

Inside, all the blinds drawn. Empty pizza boxes. A Nerf basketball hoop on a wall. Two guys shouting as they played a video game that featured fragmentation grenades and craters. Others were at their desks with Ultimate Fighting magazines and porn on the computers.

An imposing steel door opened. It was the boss.

Everyone in the room ceased activity and stood to attention. In unison: "Colonel."

He set down a briefcase. "At ease."

They reclined. The Colonel surveyed the room. "Cox, Diaz, Mc-Duffy, report?"

Cox stood again. "At eleven hundred hours, we recovered the jewels for our client in Bal Harbour."

"The take?"

"Just under a half mil," said Diaz. "Turns out the son had a big drug debt. He raided the master bedroom during the funeral reception."

"Any complications?"

McDuffy shook his head. "As soon as we showed up in our uniforms at the kid's apartment, he practically started shitting the diamonds."

"Good, good." The Colonel nodded to himself. "Get you a case of beer for that one . . . Let me see the stones."

They met at the wall safe.

The Colonel studied the gems with a look of puzzlement. "What's this slime all over them?"

"Uh, it now appears that at the reception the son also stole some potato salad."

"This fucking business." Back into the wall they went. The door slammed shut, and the Colonel spun the combination wheel. He turned the other direction toward the Nerf hoop. "Delgado, Corbett, Pierce. Your op?"

Delgado stood and handed over glossy eight-by-ten photographs. "Thirteen hundred hours, retrieved Siamese cat for Venetian Islands customer. Neighbor had a beef about rosebushes and secretly turned it in to the pound without its collar."

"That's cold," said the Colonel. "You pick up the check?"

Delgado passed it forward. "The whole fifty K. I'm still stunned there are people in this city who will pay that kind of money."

"This is just the surface," said their leader.

Cox raised his hand. "Colonel, don't get me wrong. I'm grateful for the gig and the money, but when are we going to see some real action?"

"Be careful what you wish for," said the Colonel. "But as a matter of fact, I have something cooking right now. Just have to iron out some terms." He stuck the cat photos in a file drawer.

Chapter 13

PELICAN BAY

Serge finished a phone call and stood up from the couch inside unit 413. "That just about does it. We've signed up for every conceivable delivery service to meet our every need."

"And I called my weed guy," said Coleman. "He's still delivering too."

"Why?" asked Serge.

"He's an essential worker."

"Coleman, do you realize how great this is?"

"No, how is that?"

"Until now, we've still been just running around like there isn't a problem." Serge checked the delivery schedule on his phone. "But I've heard talk that people are adopting stay-at-home quarantine protocols. Can you imagine the opportunity?"

"Not really."

"It takes a special psychological type to self-quarantine. Most people aren't remotely built for it, and they end up flying headlong into a Category Five mental-health meltdown: cracking up in a mixture of nakedness, howling at the sky, brandishing knives at imaginary monsters, and drinking red wine with fish."

"And us?" asked Coleman.

"Think of all the fun!" Serge jumped and clapped his hands. "People panic when they hear that a hurricane is coming, but I think of the hurricane *party*!"

Coleman packed a one-hitter. "'Party' is my favorite word."

"As well it should be." Serge laid a spreadsheet out on a table. "Coleman, check this out."

"What is it?"

"The master plan for our months-long quarantine party," said Serge.

"'Months long' are my favorite words before 'party.'"

T he next day Serge rapidly circled the inside of their condo unit, watching the needle on his hiking compass. "Still on track." He snapped it closed.

The incoming sunlight off the balcony hit Coleman's face and made him squint as he woke up, bonking his head on the underside of the glass-top coffee table.

Knock, knock, knock.

Coleman rubbed his forehead. "Who's that?"

"Only our first fantastic Covid delivery." Serge opened the door to see the elevator closing, then began carrying in the grocery bags that had been left in the hall outside. He unpacked on the kitchen counter.

Coleman wandered over and cracked his daybreak Pabst. "What have you got there?"

"A little bit of everything that is bare essential." Serge removed a jar of cocktail onions. "Only the most critical items essential to the care and feeding of our mental hygiene."

More items came out of the bags: sesame sticks, macadamia nuts, jelly beans, blocks of five different cheeses, fortune cookies, a box of beef jerky, a box of Lucky Charms, powdered chocolate milk, frozen burritos, doughnut holes . . .

When Serge was done, he tacked his spreadsheet up on the refrigerator door. "Coleman, refer to these activities as needed for your confinement-partying pleasure."

"Cool. Let me see your phone," said Coleman. "I need my own delivery . . ."

And so began a scientifically engineered dysfunctional lifestyle menu of how to stay inside the sanity guardrails during one of the most harrowing traumas to face the planet.

Serge stood on his head in the corner, doing vertical push-ups.

Coleman chugged from a flask. *Glug, glug, glug.*

Serge filled a tray with snacks and watched ESPN coverage of two guys playing sports video games on their computers.

Coleman retooled his one-hitter to fit in a medical mask.

Serge put on his space helmet to answer the door for a delivery. "Coleman, it's for *you*: liquor."

Coleman: *Glug, glug.*

Serge phoned a series of people he hadn't spoken to in a decade. "What do you mean, do I know the condition I left your Corvette in? . . . Oh, that little souvenir was left by Coleman."

Coleman locked himself in the bathroom and screamed for a while.

Serge binge-watched *Flipper.*

Coleman surfed YouTube for novelty-bong construction tips.

Serge sat at a table with a magnifying glass and tweezers, assembling a ship in a bottle.

"From Amazon Shopping: Stress-toy package has arrived."

Serge answered the door again in a helmet.

Coleman jammed a pen through the bottom of a beer can, held it upright over his mouth and popped the flip top. *Glug, glug.*

Serge got on the bathroom scale. "Shit."

Coleman added another tier to his pyramid collection of beer cans.

Serge stared at an alarm clock to watch the numbers turn.

Coleman answered the door for the liquor store to accept another cardboard box of clanking bottles.

Serge looked at an easel with sheet music, teaching himself the flute.

Coleman grabbed a porn magazine and a flashlight and hid in the closet.

Serge wore a chef's hat, chopping chives for a seven-course French gourmet meal that was delivered as a kit from the Internet.

Coleman answered the door for the weed guy.

Serge was on the phone as a series of people he hadn't spoken with in years hung up on him.

Coleman put up his hands in protest. "Please stop."

Serge continued furiously working with scissors.

"But Serge, I don't want you to cut my hair."

"Hold still. You're making the bowl move."

"From Amazon Shopping . . ."

Serge used hand sanitizer before answering the door for a shipment of hand sanitizer.

Coleman stuck a joint in a hole punched through another empty beer can.

Serge put on his moon suit to go downstairs and climb into the mangroves for his growing collection of washed-ashore crab-trap floats.

Coleman rocked manically on the edge of the couch with palms clasped between his knees.

Serge got back on the bathroom scale. "Shit."

Coleman flopped stomach-down on the floor, whining and banging fists on tile, while Serge jogged military laps around him. *"I don't know but I've been told . . ."*

A yellow ring lit up.

"Alexa! What now?"

"Based on your history, it is time to reorder duct tape."

"Alexa, shut up!"

Coleman straightened out a shelf with his makeshift bong collection: "Milk jug, detergent jug, old sneaker, empty soup cans taped together like a cobra, crab-trap float."

Serge shifted his feet back and forth to an instructional TV show about line dancing.

Coleman: *Glug, glug.*

Serge grabbed a sponge and scrubbed absolutely everything.

Coleman went back in the closet.

Serge snapped photos from the balcony, every hour on the hour, for time-lapse documentation of pandemic life.

Coleman called the Weed Guy again.

Serge attended various Zoom meetings with large grids of faces: video dating, eliminating that unibrow, upstart religions based on the powers of denial, speed yoga, and an unrecognized psychiatric therapy where everyone was screaming, punching pillows, and popping bubble wrap.

Coleman slowly slid involuntarily under the coffee table again.

Serge lay on the kitchen floor, peeking under the fridge and trying to train a lizard with pieces of cheese.

Just before midnight, Coleman hunched over a gurgling bong. Serge strolled over. "Whew! That wasn't so bad. We made it through a whole day. That's enough quarantining."

Chapter 14

REEVIS

Soft hands folded a sheet of typing paper over and over until it was a small, thick triangle. This was the football. It was part of a venerable child's game. A second person set their hands together on a desk, touching the tips of extended index fingers and raising both thumbs. These were the goalposts.

It was a Tuesday. A finger flicked the paper triangle, and it flew end over end through the raised thumbs. Field goal. Then it was the other person's turn, and so on. It was happening at a long desk in the rear of a long classroom.

Except these weren't children at a school but adults in a corporate office. The person speaking at the front of the room was not amused. But also not surprised.

It was the quarterly visit from the consultants. Three days of mandatory meetings.

Here's how consultants made their money: They held seminars to tell employees they needed to perform better at vocations that the consultants couldn't vaguely grasp. Didn't matter. The consultants' truly amazing gift was the ability to stand in front of a room and proverbially give a book report on a book they'd never read. One day a tire manufacturing plant, next a medical billing firm, then a suicide-prevention hotline. Same presentation: Improve your numbers.

Not only did these outside experts bring nothing to the table, they also sucked precious time from the workday, and after the staff was dismissed from the meetings, they had to gallop the rest of their shifts to catch up, resulting in missed deadlines and mistakes. The consultants were paid more than the employees.

Reevis Tome sat at the back desk. It was his turn to flick the paper football. It missed to the right. This was far from Reevis's first rodeo with consultants, but he still found it hard to believe that he was attending another one.

The consultants were why Reevis had quit his last newspaper job. Or been fired. It was a gray area. At that time, Reevis fumed as he carried a cardboard box of his belongings from the building. He could quit a paper, but he could never quit journalism. The ink ran in his blood. So he did something he swore he'd never do: He switched media and joined a local cable TV outlet.

It was great for several years, holding a microphone on sidewalks outside government buildings. He was actually doing real news again. And no consultants. What Reevis never saw coming was the Florida weirdness creep. The state rapidly gained a rarefied reputation for having a nonfunctional population, and assignment editors everywhere tilted their news models. Reevis didn't mind at first when he had to stop and cover someone who was spotted sitting at a small table in the middle of a highway, pouring syrup on pancakes. *Okay,* he thought, *that was an isolated one-off.*

No, it wasn't. The drumbeat of the strange kept increasing until Reevis was almost exclusively covering eye-crossing brainlessness. It took its toll. How often can you do pieces about the state's unnatural concentration of citizens who inexplicably take off all their clothes in retail outlets, defecate in unpopular locations, and decide to carry around large constrictor snakes for reasons even they didn't understand?

Then one of life's hairpin turns. Before Reevis knew it, he was back in print journalism, and doing something he'd sworn he'd never do again: sit through another consultant meeting. It was all because of a beer funnel. But not because Reevis used it.

At the time, he didn't realize it was his last day at the cable TV news company. Reevis stood with a microphone on a sidewalk, reporting on a man who was arrested for trying to get an alligator drunk with the funnel. The rest of Florida said: Sure, why not? Reevis said, I can't do this anymore. He quit on the spot, swallowed his pride, and went back to big print journalism. During his absence, it had only gotten worse. He was hired by a well-capitalized conglomerate with a thin staff, thin coverage and now an unfathomably thin paper.

At the beginning of the consultant meeting, Reevis had taken a seat in back with an old buddy who landed at the same newspaper in the perpetual diaspora of reporters that had begun in the '90s. He tossed a copy of the morning paper on the table. "Did you see today's edition?"

"Of course," said his colleague Mal.

"Not that," said Reevis. He picked it up and held it edgewise to Mal's face. "I've never seen a major metro so thin. Two and a half bucks now for a weekday edition a total of twenty-four pages, and that includes a couple for sports scores, two more for comics, and another for puzzles and bridge."

"Times are changing," said Mal.

"No wonder people are getting their news from Internet freaks. We're not even pretending to try anymore." Reevis plopped down in his chair. "The country is in desperate need of real news, and every inch in this sliver of a paper counts more than ever . . ." Reevis tapped a spot on one of the back pages: "Astrology!"

"You need to relax and fold a football . . ."

An hour into the meeting, the paper football flew through the thumb goalposts again. They had both tuned out the consultant, but then Reevis heard something that he couldn't abide. He perked up. And this next part requires a little explaining on the front end. In the newspaper business, the various department heads—metro, sports, features, and so on—gather several times throughout the day with their clipboards and notebooks to discuss how various stories are progressing and how they should be ranked in terms of page prominence. In the profession, these are called budget meetings, as in budgeting the news coverage. Every newspaper person knows this like they know their left hand from their right.

And this is what Reevis heard as the consultant placed another poster on an easel: "Upon careful study, our firm's next conclusion is that your paper is wasting too much time each day discussing your company's finances."

Reevis raised his hand.

Mal whispered harshly: "What are you doing? Put your hand down. You're only extending the meeting!"

The consultant pointed. "Yes, you in the back."

"What are you talking about?" said Reevis. "When are we discussing finances?"

The consultant checked his notes. "It appears you're doing it all the time. There are three budget meetings every day."

"Are you putting me on?" said Reevis. "You're *consulting* for us? When you really don't know the first thing about the newspaper business! You're beyond incompetent: *You're* the problem."

"I beg your pardon?"

"No, go begging elsewhere," said Reevis. "Those meetings aren't about money. They're to 'budget' the placement of the next day's articles."

The consultant cleared his throat. "My company stands by its conclusions. You could get a lot more accomplished covering the news if you talked less about finances."

Reevis sat back. "Unbelievable."

"Now," said the consultant, placing another poster on the easel, "our next finding. We had been seeing improvement in these areas since our previous visit, but in the last two days there's been an unexpected downturn. You've seriously missed the state and street edition deadlines four times, and there've been six major errors, including misspelled headlines, an incorrect mug shot, and on the weather page it was snowing in Key West. Can anyone suggest how we may improve your performance?"

Reevis popped to his feet.

Mal covered his face. "Jesus."

The consultant pointed again. "Yes?"

"I've got a terrific idea to improve performance," said Reevis. "Stop making us come to these clueless fucking meetings. The blown deadlines and mistakes correlate with you guys drifting back into town every quarter and sucking up the first few hours of our shifts with your staggering ignorance. Then we have to gallop the rest of the day just to make up the lost time. Mistakes? Blown deadlines? A coincidence? Gee, you're the consultant. You tell me . . ."

Security guards escorted Reevis from the building. This time there were no gradations of gray. Clearly a firing.

The funny thing: Reevis was as mellow, polite and nonconfrontational as they come. And he looked the part as well. A baby face he would never lose, a slight build, and polite nods at strangers he passed on the street. Practically a Boy Scout. Reevis simply had an ongoing problem with principles: He stuck to them.

MIAMI

Around the time Reevis was fired, an interesting twist began in the field of print journalism. Among the largest and most august papers, the total news space was shrinking without an end in sight. Some of the dailies no longer printed every day, and others ceased press runs altogether and continued on with but a website.

The only apparent oasis was at those long racks of rusting, bent newspaper boxes along the edges of shopping-center parking lots. Real estate guides, tourist guides, autos for sale. And the free papers, the thick ones crammed with your complete weekend entertainment needs: movie listings, concerts, gallery events, plus ads for every happy hour, adult toy store and CBD dispensary in town.

All those ads gave the free papers lots of pages and a generous news hole to fill. They could fill it with anything they wanted because their advertisers were a captive audience, and those nightclub ads weren't going anywhere. The staff was highly underpaid and owed allegiance to no one. So they decided to fill the news space with actual news. The journalism establishment called them radicals.

The results were impressive, and those news-rack compendiums of martini bar coupons began scooping the big outfits with investigative articles of lapsed construction inspections and a lengthy investigative piece about a confluence of legal restrictions that had created a colony of sex offenders living under an overpass.

Reevis sat in a downtown Miami office across the desk from a managing editor named Steadman, who read through the young man's résumé. Everyone called him Steadman. So much so that nobody could remember his first name. He was just Steadman. Or "Buck," his nickname at the racquetball club. But nobody else at the paper played racquetball. Steadman began to nod as he reached the bottom of the résumé. "Impressive, very impressive . . . Actually, too impressive. Your last job was at the ———. This would be quite a step down in many ways, especially pay. So why would you apply here?"

"I was fired."

"Oh, I see," said the editor. "Do you mind if I ask why?"

"I cursed at a consultant who didn't know what a budget meeting was."

Steadman took off his reading glasses, reclined in his office chair and smiled. "That would get you a gold star around here, except we don't have consultants . . ."

Reevis was hired on the spot and began racking up a noble

string of enterprising stories. Steadman regularly slapped Reevis on the shoulder as he strolled past his desk. "Nice job on that no-bid contract that went to a shell corporation located in a post office box belonging to the former college roommate of the son-in-law of the councilman's secretary. How did you put all that together?"

"Just followed the money."

"Should have known."

The next week, Reevis knocked on the managing editor's door and poked his head inside. "You wanted to see me?"

"Come in, come in." Steadman waved as he continued reading. "Have a seat. This is an interesting story proposal you gave me. I hope you understand that it's no reflection on your quality of work, but we simply don't have this kind of money in the travel budget."

"Nothing to worry about," said Reevis. "Travel expense is already covered. They're going to embed me and fly me down on their own plane."

"Who is?"

"The National Guard."

"But why Honduras?" asked Steadman.

"I put that in my proposal." Reevis leaned forward and pointed at the pages in the editor's hands.

"I know it's because the Florida National Guard is going down there," said Steadman. "It's just that I had no idea this was happening."

"Almost nobody does," said Reevis. "It's generally known that the Guard trains a weekend a month, and two weeks in the summer. Those weeks are usually someplace in the state, like Camp Blanding. But now they're starting to spend that time in places like Honduras."

"For what purpose?"

"I'm guessing to skirt the law," said Reevis. "We can't have active military down there to train the Hondurans."

"And the National Guard *can* train them?"

Reevis shook his head. "They're not allowed to either. Their official story is that they aren't training the Hondurans; they're standing next to Hondurans training *themselves*."

"Which they could have done at Blanding, but instead just happen to choose Central America?"

"Which is why I need to go."

Steadman grabbed his reading glasses again. "Just curious. How did you come up with this?"

"Remember the Iran-Contra affair in the mid-1980s that got Reagan in hot water?" asked Reevis. "That was the precedent. The U.S.-backed Contra rebels were fighting the Sandinista communists in Nicaragua, where they had gotten too close to home to suit the administration. Everyone knows that Congress wouldn't allow us to fund the Contras, so the president sold arms to Iran and diverted the money."

"I remember well," said Steadman. "Launched Ollie North's marginal TV career."

"But what most people don't know is that the president also started cycling the National Guard down there two weeks at a time at encampments in southern Honduras near the dicey border," said Reevis. "Just summer training, of course. But the reality was that the Sandinistas and Contras were starting to go kinetic, darting back and forth across the border in a series of firefights. The National Guard wasn't officially helping anyone, just like they weren't officially acting as a kind of trip wire, like our troops near the thirty-seventh parallel on the Korean peninsula."

"Is it something like that now?" asked the editor.

"No," said Reevis. "I believe they're assisting the Honduran government with the problems of cartels, street gangs and coyotes that are currently causing our mess on the Mexican border."

"What's your angle?"

"The truth," said Reevis. "They're not training themselves. And maybe that's a good thing. Maybe the law needs to be changed. Just be transparent to the American public and say what they're really doing down there."

Steadman thought a moment, then held a vertical palm toward Reevis and made the sign of the cross. "You have my blessing."

Chapter 15

PELICAN BAY

Serge had carefully been following the news, and was beyond excited as he drove the Ford Galaxie up out of the Keys to a huge suburban campus of the Miami-Dade Community College. The National Guard presence was overwhelming, in camouflage combat uniforms, enforcing orderly observance of the orange cones. Just as stunning was the array of FEMA tents so heavily ventilated with portable generators and yawning duct work that there was actually wind that altered hairstyles. Hundreds of cars threaded the orange cones in the parking lot, and the passengers then navigated more cones on foot along a sinewy trek across pavement and through the endless series of tents.

"I don't like needles," said Coleman.

"Who does?" asked Serge. "But kneel in awe at this humongous mobilization!"

After the vaccination shots, they were required to wait fifteen minutes in case of side effects.

"Is he okay?" asked a guardswoman.

Serge looked at Coleman, head rotating around on its neck swivel as he barely maintained traction in his chair. "What time is it?"

"One o'clock," said the guardswoman.

"Right on time," said Serge. "He just needs a Cinnabon."

L ater...
Just after daybreak, Coleman was curled unnaturally on the couch, snoring like a bandsaw.

Serge floated on air as he sipped his first cup of coffee. He pulled out his hiking compass and checked the needle. "Excellent! This is going to be a fantastic day!" He knelt next to the couch. In a sing-song voice: *"Cole-man... Oh, Cole-man..."*

No response.

"Cole-man..." Serge tickled his ear with a feather from his duster. Coleman swatted at it without waking up. Serge tickled the ear again.

This time, Coleman swatted and sat up all at once. "Serge, what the fuck?" He reached between the cushions for a pre-positioned can of morning beer and popped it.

Serge just continued smiling.

Coleman killed the can and crumpled it. "Why are you looking at me like that? What's going on?"

Serge's smile just grew bigger. "You know what day today is?"

"Wednesday?"

"Technically Monday, but that's not the point," said Serge. "Today is fourteen days after our second vaccination! We're now fully protected!"

"What vaccinations?"

"Remember the two trips we made up to that college campus in Miami with giant tents and the National Guard? A bunch of the permanent residents here made convoys of it at the same time, so we're all hitting full efficacy at the identical on-sale date. It's hard to believe we hadn't set foot on the mainland for over a year."

"I don't remember any of that."

"Just take my word," said Serge. "It was like a giant tailgate party. I even painted my face and wore a big foam hand with a raised finger. 'Antibodies are number one!' That's when I was taken aside for questioning."

Coleman stood up from the couch. "Why are the curtains closed over the balcony windows? You never do that."

"For dramatic flair," said Serge. "I needed to properly frame the moment. Follow me . . ."

Coleman trailed Serge to the back of the condo.

"Ready?" Serge began pulling cords on pulleys, and the wall-to-wall curtains parted like a stage production.

Radiant shafts of sunshine poured in. The songs and caws of water birds filled the air. Residents filled the shore, standing in a line along the seawall of coral boulders, staring out across the tranquil water.

"The gift of life has resumed!" Serge took a burst of photos. *Click, click, click.* "Everyone must be so excited—"

Suddenly, screaming from the lobby entrance several floors below their balcony: "I'm free! I'm free!" The yelling trailed off as a person ran down the street away from the condo without shoes.

"Who was that?" asked Coleman.

"The professor with the grant." *Click, click, click.* "Some are more excited than others." Serge walked over to the coffee table and finished boxing up his moon suit. "Do you think Tanya will take my calls if I put this thing away? "

"Don't look at me. I'm in a relationship with magazines."

"True enough." Serge sealed the box. "Let's hit the action!"

"Action?" A puzzled Coleman followed Serge to the door. Serge turned on a boom box, "Thus Spake Zarathustra," the theme to Stanley Kubrick's *2001: A Space Odyssey* at the dawn of man scene.

Duh...Duh...Duh...Da-Da!

They headed down the elevators toward the Hemingway Community Room. Coleman pressed his hands against the glass. "What the hell?"

The room was jammed with residents, pulsing to the sounds of KC and the Sunshine Band, competing with the wild laughs and blenders.

"Jesus," said Coleman. "All these people are drinking their faces off! In the morning! Tequila! . . . And just because their vaccinations took effect?"

"I was expecting fucking in the streets," said Serge. "But give it time."

The community room's sound system kicked in with a dynamite subwoofer to Kool and the Gang.

"Get down! Get down! . . ."

Serge leaned to Coleman. "They're doing it all wrong."

"Looks perfect to me."

Serge shook his head. "I saw the news this morning. The Keys are opening back up." He stuck two fingers in his mouth and made a shrill whistle. "Can I have everyone's attention?!"

Everyone turned curiously, and one of the residents cranked the music lower.

"Thank you." Serge began pacing at the front of the room. "I know you're all excited, but we have only one chance to attain perfection."

"Serge!" yelled someone in back by the ping-pong table. "Please teach us."

"We need the most excellent post-pandemic reopening ever," said Serge. "The last one was in 1919, so history is looking at us." He spun and paced the other way. "We've been cooped up here forever, and *this* is the hill where you want to make your stand? I know I'm one of the newer neighbors. I've visited here a million times before that, but until you actually live in a place, you can't burrow deep under the local skin like a chigger. I've researched a ton of area history and months back was just about to head out on an off-the-hook barnstorming tour of our city's four main islands, except the virus had other plans. But now we're in the clear. Let's pack up those drinks and hit the road. I have a supreme-o checklist. What do you say?"

"Sounds great!"

"I'm with Serge!"

"What are we waiting for?"

"Fantastic!" Serge headed for the door. "Let's be chiggers! Next time I'll have team T-shirts made."

They stampeded to the parking lot with sloshing tumblers.

Chapter 16

Keyboards clattered in a staccato chorus, and people rushed urgently through an open grid of desks in the newsroom. Three hours to deadline.

A cell phone rang.

"*Free Paper*, Steadman here."

"Steadman? Steadman? You there? Oops." *Crash*. "Ow, shit. Hello? Anyone home?"

Steadman heard knuckles knocking on the phone at the other end of the line. "Reevis? Is that you?"

"All day long."

"Are you in Honduras?"

"I'm a desperate man!" Reevis giggled. "You a Warren Zevon fan?"

"You sound drunk."

"Great reason for that! I'm hammered, 'faced, three sheets, shnockered, plastered, wrecked, bombed."

"But you don't drink," said the editor.

"I know," said Reevis. "But I had to for the sake of the story."

"What story?"

"A blockbuster! Get Layout to redesign the front page!" Reevis belched. "You'll need to take dictation."

"Why don't you use your laptop?"

"Too loopy," said Reevis. "Damn, this has been the craziest day! You wouldn't believe it! We almost crashed into the ambassador's Learjet, the SUVs nearly flew off the mountain, soldiers were on top of the wall with machine guns, the vice president spilled the beans over Scotch, the cowgirl was packing heat, a two-star general almost ripped my shirt, the hotel guys tried to give me ten thousand dollars, and I fled through tortillas in the kitchen. Ready for dictation?—"

"Reevis, just slow down and start at the beginning . . ."

THE BEGINNING

A late-morning Florida sun beat down on the black tar, and Reevis stood next to his luggage out on the runway at Homestead Air Reserve Base. In front: A still gray C-130 Hercules military transport plane.

Two dozen other journalists with suitcases were with him. Reporters from around the state, Tampa to Jacksonville to Pensacola, waiting to be embedded with the Florida National Guard.

Finally, they boarded the cavernous plane that was way too big for the handful of passengers who strapped themselves in on the bench seating that ran along the sides of the aircraft. It was a pleasant flight across the ocean, and Reevis was getting bouncy about the upcoming adventure. He'd always wanted to be a foreign correspondent. Not that he was now, but close enough. His spirits continued inflating, and nothing could dampen the moment. Almost. He happened to gaze across the plane at someone strapped into the opposite bench. It was one of his reporting rivals, that smug Leonard, who worked for the much larger and more prestigious ———.

Some reporters followed leads to get stories. Leonard followed other reporters. Literally. He'd spot Reevis at the courthouse or city hall and hang back, peeking around corners and columns. More than once he'd stolen stories from Reevis simply by walking up to the desk in a clerk's office: "Yes, let me see the file that the other reporter just asked for." Leonard had the advantage of an earlier deadline and street-paper delivery, and Reevis was increasingly left with sloppy seconds.

It developed into such a problem that Reevis was forced to employ misdirection, and every time he noticed Leonard lurking, he'd change course for a different government building and request a file in which he had no interest, and then Leonard would be tied up the rest of the day trying to divine the significance of the benign documents.

Reevis caught himself staring at his reporting nemesis and turned away, thinking, *I'm not about to let him be a buzzkill.* He looked out the window at a lone freighter ship in an endless expanse of bright water. A couple hours later, the plane swung in east from the Caribbean, and everyone stared out the windows at the colorful, dusty shacks all crammed together and rising like stairs up the hills surrounding the capital of Honduras.

The reporters were thrown against their seat harnesses when the Hercules made the first of numerous hard banks as it navigated the treacherous approach to the Toncontín airport. The main runway sat below in a mountain pocket. The pilot circled and corkscrewed. Then an extra severe bank. "Whoa!" One of the reporters looked out the window and spotted the reason for that last maneuver: a Lear flying under them that was returning the U.S. ambassador from Washington.

The journalists debarked on the runway just as a series of black armored SUVs sped through a gate and up to the plane. People jumped from the vehicles and spun their arms. "Get in! Get in!"

Reevis climbed through one of the back doors and started sliding down the unmoored reality that is Central America.

The vehicles sped in a tight formation that was as harrowing as the airplane's landing. Tires slung dust around mountain curves and switchbacks. Reevis was white-knuckled looking out the window as wheels skirted the edge of a steep drop-off. They left the city congestion behind and finally arrived at a fortified compound, where soldiers with machine guns paced along the tops of the imposing concrete walls. Other soldiers were already opening the gates so the convoy never had to slow as they zipped inside. The gates were quickly shut.

Reevis stepped out of his vehicle and into a jarring contrast to what he had just experienced: caterers circulated with silver trays of canapes and Champagne glasses. All around, tailor-dressed people of the mingling class circulated lively in high-end small-talk, as if there weren't any guys with machine guns circling the wall above.

Reevis shook his head vigorously, like a cartoon character, to clear the fog of confusion. "Where the hell am I?"

He immediately got his answer. An older, stocky man in combat fatigues smiled as he approached the gaggle of disoriented newspeople. He had two stars on each shoulder.

"Good afternoon. I'm General Ripper with the Florida Guard, and welcome to the ambassador's home. We'll be going out into the field tomorrow, but after our flight today, we thought it would be nice to relax and get to know each other." He turned and gestured toward a dark-haired man in a white guayabera on the other side of the courtyard. "The ambassador told me he's eager to meet each and every one of you . . ."

Reevis was distracted. He noticed someone at the party who had been attached to the general like a colostomy bag. You couldn't *help* but notice. She looked like a little girl, barely five feet tall, with extracurly locks of bituminous black hair that stopped just short of her shoulders. The locks flowed out from under a hat. It was a cowboy hat, but not the typical kind, more like the type you'd wear to a costume party—ruby red with lots of sequins and fake rhinestones and a little strap tied off under her chin. The hat perfectly matched the rest of her outfit, a bedazzled vest, cute short skirt and ruby cowgirl boots. At first, Reevis thought she was somebody's daughter, possibly the general's. But upon closer inspection, he realized she was actually an adult who was easily mistaken for a child because of her extra-young face and diminutive stature. Reevis finally confirmed for sure she was a grown-up when he noticed a faint bulge at the top of her skirt, the unmistakable outline of a semiautomatic pistol. Reevis, slipping further through the looking glass, thought: *Is Central America entirely wacked?* The cowgirl drifted a short distance and began chatting up another American in military fatigues with a horizontal scar across his chin.

"And that gentleman over there . . ." The general pivoted the other way toward another white guayabera, this one containing a shorter man with a gray mustache. "The vice president of Honduras expressed his deep gratitude for your interest in his country. But enough of me talking. It's going to be a great evening. Grab a drink, get some food. We'll talk later." A final pleasant smile. He walked away, and the cowgirl followed.

Reevis turned toward the Orlando reporter on his left. "What's going on here?"

"We're being buttered up," said the other journalist. "They want rah-rah stories."

Reevis watched a sterling tray go by. "I don't know if it's ethical to accept hors d'oeuvres."

"On matters like that, I listen to my stomach." The second reporter stopped a tray and loaded up a napkin with a meal involving bacon and water chestnuts.

And into the cocktail party they went. Reevis wandered the courtyard in social unsteadiness. Then his professional instincts kicked in with focus. He spotted the vice president with a rocks glass in his hand, holding court amid a few reporters. They had just pulled out their notebooks. Reevis made a beeline.

Twelve-year, single-malt Scotch had loosened the vice president's tongue. He waxed on about his country's warm relationship with the superpower to the north, and how they would cooperate in every way to solve the border problem because, after all, their interests coincided. Typically useless talking points. The reporters painfully jotted it all down. But then, the so-called worm began to turn. A couple of Scotches later and the vice president veered off script: What was the National Guard even doing in his country? His own army could handle their affairs. If America really wanted to help, send cash.

Combat boots approached from the rear. General Ripper heard the last of the remarks, and that was plenty. "Mr. Vice President! Thank you for entertaining our guests. I'm sure it will be an experience they'll remember." Then to the reporters: "The ambassador is waiting. All of you, please come with me."

Reevis felt the tug of a story but reluctantly left with the others. Actually, it was a good thing. It cleared the scrum of reporters. And once the flock was engaged with the ambassador, and the general became sufficiently distracted, Reevis slipped away and circled back to buttonhole the vice president for a one-on-one. He knew exactly how to play it.

"Mr. Vice President, I was fascinated with what we were discussing a few moments ago, and I'm particularly interested in hearing more about how additional foreign aid could help your people."

Bingo. The vice president paid off in silver dollars, pontificating about the mixed U.S. reputation over the years in Central America. Then about infrastructure and historic resentment of Yankee military presence and a banana company—a *real* banana company from the States—getting the CIA to overthrow Guatemala in the 1950s and blah, blah, blah.

Reevis scribbled furiously page after page in his tiny spiral notebook. The vice president finally said something that made the pen lift from paper. "Wait," said Reevis. "Back up. Did you say military contractors?"

"Yes."

"There are military contractors down here?"

"Of course," said the vice president. "That's the problem, less accountability. Sometimes none at all."

"Where are they from?"

"Miami." And the vice president was off to the races again.

Something caught the corner of Reevis's eye. "Shit!"

That asshole reporter Leonard bopped on over. "Hi, guys! What are you talking about?"

"Soccer," said Reevis.

"Foreign aid and military contractors," said the vice president.

"Really?" Leonard got out his own notebook. "Could you go back and repeat everything you just told him?"

"Sure . . ."

The vice president was a few minutes into his recounting when Reevis received help from a most unlikely source. The general was on his way, and there was no mistaking his glare. "Party's over. We're going to the hotel. Get back in the convoy now!"

Whew, thought Reevis, hopping out of the SUV in front of one of the nicer downtown resorts favored by Americans. But his problems with Leonard weren't completely over. The other reporter hadn't gotten nearly as much as Reevis had, but just enough fragments to cobble something together. Reevis told himself out loud: "I need to do something—"

Suddenly, he felt a strong grip on his right shoulder and was jerked backward with a tug that almost tore his sleeve. "Am I being mugged?"

Reevis turned around. The general was in his face. "Don't you dare write anything bad!" Combat boots stomped away, followed by cowgirl boots.

From behind again: "Reevis!"

Reevis cringed and clenched his eyes at the sound of Leonard's voice. "Hey, Leonard. How have you been?"

"Looks like you and the vice president are new best friends," said the rival. "Let's go get a drink and talk about it."

"Only if you let my paper pay."

"Let's go."

Reevis had just gotten his plan. The genius was the elegant simplicity: *I'll match Leonard drink for drink, and when I'm shitfaced, he won't be able to file a story.*

And so began a not-so-beautiful friendship. They started at the hotel bar, then out into the street, hopping local lounges, Leonard trying to steer the conversation toward the vice president, and Reevis steering it toward ordering another round.

Three hours later, they found themselves in a local cantina beyond the tourist zone. It was outdoors in a scraggly garden with strands of Christmas lights overhead. Leonard was flirting with a pair of women at the next table.

When Leonard finally stood and belted out a rendition of Sinatra's "My Way," the women giggled and Reevis exhaled with relief. He stretched and yawned. "I think I'll be headed back to the hotel now. Big day tomorrow . . ."

Leonard pulled his chair over to the neighboring table, and Reevis called a taxi.

There was only one problem with Reevis's plan, but it was sizable. How would he be able to file in his condition? *Oh well*, he figured. *That's what a rewrite is for . . .*

Chapter 17

PELICAN BAY

Everyone was ready. Straw hats, cameras, sunscreen, sports bottles. On schedule to the minute, a rented shuttle bus pulled up outside the condo. Serge hopped out of the driver's seat and down the steps. On his head was a custom-embroidered baseball cap that said UNDERBELLY TOUR GUIDE.

He slapped his hands together and made a wolf howl. "Hope you all are as pumped as I am! These are going to be the best days ever! . . . You brought your cameras! Great! Take lots of pics and ask me to slow down if you need more! You know how all the time you hear people say something like 'I've lived in New York City my whole life and never been up the Empire State Building'? I'm not about to allow that tragedy to repeat itself here if I can help it. So get ready for untold titillations of experiencing everything that's been right under your nose the whole time but you never stopped to groove . . . All aboard!" He shook each of his Pelican Bay neighbors' hands going up the steps. "Welcome to Serge's Underbelly Tours, Upper Keys Edition!"

They were soon heading south on U.S. Highway 1. Serge had paid the shuttle company extra for a portable PA speaker and microphone. Coleman glanced around before packing the bowl of a folding travel bong. Others in sun hats pulled out furtive flasks for fortifying swigs.

Serge pressed the button on the mic. "Your attention, please. Coming up on the left on our own proud island of Plantation Key is a large building shaped like a medieval castle. Not that weird down here, with giant roadside lobsters, sharks and conch shells, but dig this: It was originally the roadside attraction called Treasure Village and was founded by our own native superstar Art 'Silver Bar' McKee, known far and wide as the father of modern salvage diving. While others were just splashing into the water and flailing around, accidentally stumbling across a doubloon or two, Art was up to his neck in homework, tinkering with the primitive diving suits of the day and corresponding with historians in Spain until he methodically tracked down specific wrecks, including several ships sunk in the historic 1733 armada. But here's what really endeared me to McKee: He was the father of treasure diving, so you know the word 'gold' was still available, but instead he went for *Silver* Bar McKee. Talk about your modesty. Then he built the roadside attraction castle to showcase his life's work . . . Here it comes now! Cameras out! Look at those funky turrets! . . . But here's where it gets cool-strange. The place is now the home of a Montessori private school. Imagine that! A bunch of kids learning to read and write in this twisted building. That can only fast-track the education process. Years later: 'How did you become a Rhodes Scholar?' 'I went to school in a castle.' . . . But more on McKee later."

Serge turned left off the highway. "This is another hit-and-run photo op. Up ahead is the Snake Creek Drawbridge to the next key. But decades ago, there was another tributary that bisected our island called Little Snake Creek that was filled in by the road workers during the completion of the causeway." He slowly rolled down the quiet street toward the Ragged Edge Resort. "What remains off to your left is a little body of water that was an infamous smugglers' cove. Got your photos? We're off!"

The shuttle bus was back on the highway, crossing the draw-bridge. "This is Windley Key, the second of the four main islands that constitute the incorporated village of Islamorada. And coming up off to your right is the Oceanview Inn & Sports Pub with that unmistakable giant NFL football crest-emblem out front. It comes as advertised, with lots of sports on TV. And also not as advertised, since the Oceanview is actually on the bay-view side of the island opposite the ocean. But the real attraction is way out back . . ." Serge pulled off the road and circled around behind the bar. "Everyone out!"

He led the gaggle down to the mangroves. There was a small break in the impenetrable vegetation, and a hammered-up wooden sign over the top of an entrance to a ramshackle boardwalk: CAP-TAIN LARRY'S TRAIL. "This leads down to another historic smug-glers' cove. Everyone, touch the sign! Touch it!" He ran down the trail to the lapping water just inches below the dilapidated dock and skiffs. The others struggled to keep up but finally arrived. "Back to the bus! . . . Did everyone touch the sign?"

Passengers munched granola bars as Serge pulled out of the parking lot. "Another drive-by photo op on your left, because the business has changed seismically, but it's inherently the same water-shed location . . ." Serge drove on and pulled over to the shoulder just before the end of Windley Key. He picked up his mic. "As you can see, across the street is the extremely refined and upscale Postcard Inn. But as late as the early 2000s, it was known far and wide as Holiday Isle with the 'World Famous Tiki Bar.' Now, anyplace that has to tout that it's 'World Famous' is definitely not. You don't see the 'World Famous' Waldorf Astoria. But this is the exception that proves the rule. It's hard to imagine now, but that sedate resort across the street was anything but in its former incarnation: a perpetual balls-out, spring-break celebration of drinking and Jet Skis. But the bona fide historic part? It was the birthplace of the Rum Runner! It's true! It's true! Most stories like that are apocryphal, but I've confirmed it through numerous publications across the United States. There are various versions of the story floating around but the most common—and all giving credit to the same person—is that someone about a half century ago called John Elber, or 'Tiki John,' had an excess of certain liquors that weren't moving, so he combined them into, you guessed it, the Rum Runner!" Serge checked his smartphone. "Oh my God! Holiday Isle is gone, but a tiki bar remains behind the Postcard!" Shuttle bus tires screeched across the road.

Fifteen minutes later, the bus was back on the highway; Serge keyed the mic. "Sorry to make you chug those humongous Rum Runners, but there were exigent circumstances." The bus crossed the next bridge at Whale Harbor Channel. "This is island number three, Upper Matecumbe." The bus stopped in another parking lot. "Everybody into the History of Diving Museum. I dig history far more than the next guy, but this is definitely overkill!"

Sure enough, the condo gang wound their way through exhibits of far more antique diving helmets and suits than they knew existed, let alone wanted to see.

"No museum curator could have put this together," said Serge. "It's the offspring of serious OCD . . . And here's an exhibit for Art McKee! That's a seventy-pound silver bar in a thick safety-glass case with hand-sized holes in the side so you can touch it. Everybody, touch the silver bar! Touch it! Back to the bus!"

A few minutes later, they pulled up to a tropical strip mall with the type of large shark in the parking lot that tourists like to stick their heads inside for photos.

"It's lunchtime!" yelled Serge. "No place better than Mangrove Mike's! You know what I love about the place? The vintage-diner turquoise Naugahyde booths, plus the horseshoe breakfast counter with more turquoise chairs bolted around the sides. Everybody eat! But you must only choose from their freakish specialty section of their menu that carved out their lasting legacy: home of the Tater Tot Towers. More kinds than you can imagine or need. Mexican, country-gravy, many with two eggs on top!"

Twenty minutes later, Coleman was sitting at the lunch counter, eyes closed, his head bobbing down toward another power-nap loss of consciousness, slowly lowering until he was facedown in his tot tower. He sat up with an egg over each eye. "I'm blind!"

"Check it out!" yelled Serge, leaning over an empty dining booth. He took a photo of a photo on the wall. "That's Ted Williams catching a tarpon. The Red Sox hall-of-famer was the last man to bat .400 and a crazed fisherman who had a permanent residence just around the corner so he could fish the back-country flats at dawn and then hit all these local diners . . . Everyone, pack up the rest of your towers to go!"

And so it went, the rest of the day as frenetic as the beginning. Down a side street and onto Madeira Road. "There's Ted Williams's house, where *Sports Illustrated* came down in 1967 to do a huge spread on his fishing journeys each morning from his dock. He's also in two *fishing* halls of fame . . ." Then over to the Florida Keys History & Discovery Center on the grounds of the old Islander Resort with that vintage sign sticking out toward the road. "There's a diorama of Indian Key, like a model railroad without trains, site of the historic massacre . . . And here are more old photos of McKee and Williams . . ."

But Serge was still saving the best for last, something not on the usual tours and brochures. The Labor Day hurricane of 1935 was the worst ever to hit the United States, with the lowest barometric pressure ever recorded. They sent the rescue train out of Miami backward, so that the engine would be facing forward as it made its escape. It was too late. The exhibit photos back at the history center told the story. The bridge and locomotive were carried out to sea, and train cars were scattered across Upper Matecumbe like Matchbox cars. The government and Red Cross came in and built twenty-nine hurricane-proof buildings, including sixteen so-called Red Cross houses. The riveting feature is seeing the old photos of the houses when they were under quite unusual construction. The footers of the foundations were the floors of cisterns, to catch rainwater for drinking. The cisterns' tops were a half floor up, the bottoms of the houses. The walls weren't concrete block but were created by wooden forms with the cement poured in. The forms were left up to support additional forms to pour the concrete *roofs*. They have withstood all the storms to this day. But the houses have since been assimilated into modern Islamorada. Try to find them.

"I found them!" said Serge, passing out packets of pages with photos of the buildings under construction. He drove past two of them on the private grounds of the Moorings, filming location of the Netflix series *Bloodline*. "Photos only. We must be respectful." Then up the Old Road to a third Red Cross house that he found on a real estate site, selling for north of a million. Finally, a fourth house that was now an art gallery.

"Wow," said one of the condo residents. "I've driven past these buildings a million times and would never have known. Concrete roofs!"

Finally it was almost over. Almost. "It's a full moon tonight, and you know what that means?" Serge looked up in the rearview mirror. Blank faces stared back. He smiled broadly. "It's the night of the Full Moon Party at Morada Bay!"

They disembarked at the top-shelf dine-and-party destination to find throngs of young people dancing and frolicking and whooping it up out on the sand under the coconut palms. The trippy thing was all the glow sticks wiggling over their heads, which both lit the way and were disorienting. The older people from the condo tentatively walked through the crowd, staring curiously at the illuminated wands.

Coleman tugged his buddy's sleeve. "You know what all those glow sticks mean?"

"Not really."

Wink. "These people are cool."

The night wore on, Serge plowing through bottled water. He

didn't notice at first, but then it became a pattern. Some of the residents gathered in a cluster of conversation before following Coleman out to the parking lot. Then again twenty minutes later and so on. Finally Serge hopped off his stool and brought up the rear. He reached the parking lot, but nobody was there. He approached the shuttle bus and peeked in a window. The residents were hunched over as Coleman led them doing hits from a fat joint. Serge headed back to the party. "Oh, this is going to be a treat."

It reached that point in the evening. Time to reel it in. "Everyone, return to the shuttle bus."

Nobody responded. The younger guests at Morada Bay stood back in silence, watching bemusedly as the older residents from Pelican Bay ran in crazy circles and figure eights—"Woooo!" "Rock 'n' roll!"—twirling glow sticks over their heads.

Chapter 18

AFTER MIDNIGHT

Reevis arrived back at the hotel in Honduras and stumbled over the doorway's threshold. It was one of those long stumbles, where he was pitched forward off balance for a half dozen steps before getting his feet back under him. Whew.

From behind: "Mr. Tome? Reevis Tome?"

He turned around to see a smartly dressed but imposing man with an extra-thick mustache leaning against the side of the reception desk. "Yes, that's me?"

"Would you come with us please?"

"I didn't do anything!"

"No, no, no, it's nothing like that," said the man. "We need to set up the wire transfer."

"What wire transfer?" Reevis asked as he swayed in place.

"It's all ready," said the man, reeking of dominant assuredness. "Mr. Menendez in Miami is sending the ten thousand dollars he owes you."

Reevis's brain swirled in a stew of alcohol bubbles and confusion.

Does the surreal shit never quit in Central America? "I don't know any Mr. Menendez," said Reevis. "I'm not expecting ten thousand dollars."

The man wrinkled his face in concern and leaned for a brief chat with someone behind the desk. He looked up and nodded. "Yes, the hotel is quite sure. You *are* Reevis Tome, right? The money is on its way. Now, if you'll please follow me."

The mental photograph finally finished developing in Reevis's brainpan. At the beginning of the trip, all the reporters had been warned that young Americans are targets. Stay away from any restaurant or bar where CNN is on television, because that's where the predators look. Kidnapping? Worse? And if someone approached you with news that's too good to be true, then it could quickly become very bad news. An unexpected ten thousand dollars would qualify.

Reevis quickly ran through the scam in his head. Many people would think, Ten grand? There's definitely some kind of mistake, but I'm not about to correct them. Please, tell me more. Well, the money's on the way, but it can only be transferred into a local bank account, which, if you aren't a resident, requires a minimum deposit of a thousand to open . . .

"Mr. Tome, is there a problem?" said the man. "Do you not want the ten thousand dollars?"

Reevis started slowly walking backward. The man knew his name, and he had been chatting with people behind the front desk, which meant Reevis's personal safety at the hotel had been compromised, and the staff was in on it.

"No! I don't want any money! I don't want anything!"

"What should we tell Mr. Menendez?"

"It's his lucky day."

Off in the almost-empty bar near some slot machines, a cowgirl accepted a cocktail offer from a military man with a horizontal scar across his chin. She heard the ruckus and spun. "Reevis! . . ."

Reevis turned and recognized them from the party; he knew he had never given her his name. It just added to his inebriated freakout. Did everyone know who he was in this danger zone? He took off in a panicked, swerving sprint across the lobby and pasted his back against the rear of an elevator. He looked back at the reception desk as the door closed, his eyes bugged out and bloodshot.

Reevis frantically entered his sixth-floor room and bolted everything on the door. He grabbed his cell phone and lay down on the bed. He bicycle-kicked his legs in the air to regain alertness. He dialed an international number.

"*Free Paper*, Steadman here . . ."

Forty minutes later, the editor finished taking dictation. "Excellent job, Reevis. *Reevis?*" Steadman heard snoring on the other end of the line before he hung up . . .

No time at all seemed to have elapsed when rude sunshine snapped Reevis's eyes open the next morning. His skull felt like it had the San Andreas Fault cracked down the middle. He moaned as he rolled over and covered his head with a pillow. Then he shot up in bed. "What time is it? . . . Oh shit!"

He sprang out of bed, jumped into his clothes and wet-combed his hair. On the way down in the elevator, he remembered the front-desk threat. How safe was he? Reevis decided to overcorrect. The doors opened in the lobby and he peeked around before stepping outside and running to the restaurant, where he burst through an employees-only door and ran through a kitchen full of surprised cooks like it was a movie cliché. In the distance, he could see the exit sign to the street. Before he could get there, someone stepped out from behind a rolling stack of metal tortilla trays. "Stop right there!"

Reevis's sneakers hit the brakes. He was surprised on multiple levels. First by being ordered to halt, then by who was giving the orders. A cowgirl, this time cradling a submachine gun. She aimed it aside. "What the hell are you doing in here?"

"My security's been compromised by the hotel staff," said Reevis. "I figured this would be the safest evasive route to the street . . . What are *you* doing here?"

"Security patrol," said the cowgirl. "The most dangerous threats often come through the kitchen. Don't you watch the movies?"

"Oh, I get it now," said Reevis. "I saw you last night tagging along behind Ripper. You're a bodyguard. You got a two-star general staying at this hotel, plus who knows what other high-ranking protectees." Reevis looked her outfit up and down. "By the bizarre costume, I'm guessing, what? CIA?"

She just stared.

"How is the getup supposed to work?" asked Reevis. "Instead of low-key, you go hard the other way? Looking so obvious and harmless that anyone would think you're on your way to a birthday party with toy guns?"

She sighed at the harmless young man. "Reevis, we need to get going to the helicopter pads."

"Wait, I didn't tell you my name," said the reporter. "Oh, right. CIA."

A deeper sigh. "Just come on . . ."

The SUV convoy pulled out of the hotel driveway. Reevis was on his phone.

"How are you feeling this morning?" asked his editor.

"Turds."

"By the way, great job with the story," said Steadman. "I told you last night, but I wasn't sure you'd remember."

"I don't."

"Have you had a chance to see it online yet?"

"No, I needed to rally to get to the convoy in time," said Reevis.

"It's going big. The wires have picked it up," said Steadman. "I don't know what has more impact, the foreign-aid stuff or the military contractors. On the latter, we were able to reach the State Department for reaction. They gave us two: 'The story is completely false,' and 'No comment.' We printed both."

"What about the vice president of Honduras?" asked Reevis.

"Tried to reach him, too, but they said he was on a retreat due to health reasons."

"I'll bet," said Reevis.

"What's on for today?"

"About to fly up into the mountains to the National Guard's jungle base."

"Try to get more on the military contractors."

"I'll try. Later." Reevis hung up and turned to his right in the backseat. "You know my name, so what's yours?"

"Debbie."

"So how do you like being whatever it is you are?" asked Reevis. "I won't say CIA anymore."

"Fine." She kept watch out the window while one of her fingers idly twirled a lock of that curly black hair. "I can already tell you like being a journalist."

"I got hooked early," said Reevis. "Could never be anything else even if I tried."

"Pay well?"

"The opposite," said the reporter. "You have to be like a priest and take a vow of poverty. They know you love the work and will do it anyway, so there's no motivation to compensate."

"How do you deal with that?"

"Like all the others," said Reevis. "Everyone in every newsroom has secret dreams of one day writing the great American novel. Like Hemingway said, every novelist should work for a newspaper. He also said for no more than six months . . . What are you laughing for?"

She put a hand over her mouth. "Nothing."

"Give it up or I'll start with the CIA again."

She overcame the giggles. "Last night the interactions between you and the general were precious. At the party I saw his thermometer spiking when you were talking to the vice president, and again when he grabbed you outside the hotel. It was like sport."

"You found amusement in my discomfort?"

"Not that," said Debbie. "You ever been in the military?"

"No."

"Among the enlisted men, a colonel is practically treated like the president," said Debbie. "But when an officer reaches flag rank and they start putting stars on his shoulders, the angels sound trumpets as if God has arrived."

"Sounds . . . unusual."

"Generals aren't used to anything but trembling respect in their presence, and some of them eventually forget all their other people skills. Then, when a civilian reporter like yourself snuck back to the vice president, it was like situation comedy to me."

"He literally grabbed my arm outside the hotel and scared the shit out of me," said Reevis. "I didn't know who it was and thought it might be street bandits."

"He had no right to do that," Debbie remarked. "And I'll deny I ever said that. I understand the system and the Fourth Estate. You were just doing a job. An important one."

"I'm surprised at that last part."

"Why? I do what I do to defend our freedoms, not suppress them."

The motorcade slowed to a stop on a weed-choked hilltop plateau. Reevis grabbed a door handle. "Looks like we're here . . ."

The six SUVs parked in a neatly spaced row, mirroring the row of six open-sided Vietnam-style Huey helicopters. Debbie jumped out her own door and trotted away: "See you at the base."

It would actually be sooner than that.

Reevis grabbed his small green canvas field bag. It was seat-yourself, and he headed toward the first empty helicopter. He climbed aboard and sat in the middle of a three-person bench. In front of him, a doorless expanse and a machine-gun mount without a machine gun. His seat was precarious at the lip of the chopper, and he suddenly realized that the single seat belt across the lap would be the only thing keeping him from falling to his death. He tugged; it was a flimsy seat belt. The helicopter blades began to rotate.

Reevis was still fiddling with the latch, repeatedly snapping and unsnapping it and pulling the straps hard to test it some more. He didn't notice the others approaching the helicopter until he finally looked up. The lead person heading for the Huey also had his head down and a hand on top of his cap so the propeller wouldn't blow it off. He finally looked up: a stutter-step and a glare before resuming his natural gait. General Ripper climbed aboard and snapped himself in on Reevis's right. Debbie, in full rhinestone and machine-gun regalia, took a seat on his left. She leaned over to his ear: "Awk-*ward*."

Part Two

INTERMISSION

One Week Earlier

Monopoly Night

Chapter 19

PELICAN BAY

A clandestine knock on a fifth-floor door.

A woman answered and glanced around outside. So did the person knocking. The coast was clear down the balcony hallways overlooking the tops of royal poinciana and yellow trumpet trees. She waved the knocker in.

The man had a large envelope that he dumped on the table. The woman unfolded a thick-stock board.

The man looked up at the glass cabinets showcasing a lifetime of achievement. "Jen-Jen, you got another trophy."

She nodded. "Big tournament from that pyramid in Memphis, Serge."

Serge approached the case's glass. "I can't figure out what's on top of the trophy."

"Gold dildo."

"Jesus, what kind of game were you playing?"

"Cards Against Humanity," said Jen-Jen, sorting the envelope's items on the dining-room table.

"What's that?"

"New game, really huge among the younger players," said Jen-Jen. "You complete sentences or answer questions with cards that are so offensive I literally had to take a shower afterwards."

"How bad can it be?"

"I can't bring myself to repeat the cards out loud, but this should tell you everything about the game," said Jen-Jen. "In the official rules, the player who goes first is the one who most recently defecated."

"I guess it's an honor system," said Serge, continuing to inspect the contents of the trophy cases. "I still can't believe there's an entire championship tournament circuit out there for board games."

"And it's just getting bigger," said Jen-Jen, continuing to organize at the table. "By the way, Serge, great idea of yours to add a little novelty to our condo's return to Monopoly Night . . . It's been forever, since before the pandemic."

"It was a labor of love." He sat at the table across from Jen-Jen and grabbed a bottle of Elmer's glue. "Did you get what I requested?"

"Right here," said Jen-Jen. She reached in a gift bag and placed a small wooden box on the table.

"Excellent . . ."

An hour later.

Knock, knock, knock.

"It's open," said Jen-Jen, stirring at the stove.

"I smell spaghetti and meatballs," said Teddy, the condo president.

"The only thing that won't make us fight." She checked the oven for the garlic bread. "Make yourself at home."

Teddy grabbed the blender and set a canvas tote bag on the counter. "I brought some booze."

"What a shock."

More and more guests arrived. Most of them immediately went over to check out the decidedly different game board. "What's this?"

"Florida Keys Monopoly," said Serge. "I downloaded a bunch of photos and labels, and localized the game to take it to the next level!"

"By the way," said Jen-Jen, "when are we going to do that fantastic local tour you promised?"

"Working on it right now, as soon as I can rent the proper shuttle bus," said Serge. "Maybe a whole series of tours. But I have to come up with the perfect concept to maintain quality control."

"Probably best to take baby steps and ramp up from the pandemic with another board game," said Jen-Jen.

Knock, knock . . .

The final guests had arrived, chatting, sipping drinks, inspecting the game board and inhaling the appetite-honing garlic-tomato-sauce aroma. Coleman hovered over Teddy at the blender: "Don't be shy with the pour." It was soon time to get down to business. They began taking seats for dinner.

Jen-Jen struck a glass bell with something made of metal. *Ding, ding, ding.* "Excuse me. Before we get started, I have a few words. As you know, despite the recent pandemic, the Keys real estate market has gone red-hot, and we've recently had a lot of turnover here at Pelican Bay. Many nice new faces have joined us as permanent residents after the investors cashed in their units. So I'd like to go around the room and introduce everyone. Just raise your hand when mentioned; no need for a speech. I'm Jen-Jen, and as you can probably tell by my decor, I love board games—"

"Pay no attention to the gold dildo on the pedestal," said Serge. "She's actually a fine woman."

"Serge!"

"What? I was just trying to deflect from the eight-hundred-pound gorilla in the room." Serge pointed with a firm arm. "I mean, look at that freaking award. It's the only trophy I've ever seen with a vein."

"Serge! Please!"

"Sorry, I was just trying to deescalate offensiveness."

"Where was I?" said Jen-Jen. "Oh, yeah, a quick round robin. You already know the regulars: Maggie and Bert, the bachelors Gary and Zack, Sonya the divorcée, Trevor and Judy the legacies, Joey—who doesn't want to talk about Muskogee—Alfred and Hazel, also mysteriously from Milwaukee, then Old Man Sweeney, retired Lieutenant McCloud and Mr. Kelley, who still has to wear the neck brace because of insurance-company detectives. But since the pandemic, we've had a number of additions. Meet Alice Canon, who's hacking her life with gallons of powdered Gatorade, and Kelsey and Kelcey Renfroe, who play a mean oboe duet, and Sir Aston Neville, the last royal heir from an infertile lineage on a cluster of North Sea islands dominated by rookeries . . ."

It was one of those dining tables where you could insert additional pieces in the middle for extra guest length. Comfortable seating for six became uncomfortable for a dozen.

Maggie borrowed Jen-Jen's glass bell and hit it with an iced-tea spoon. *Ding, ding, ding.* "Excuse me. Sorry for another interruption, but I have a great new idea before we eat."

Jen-Jen set down salad tongs. "What is it?"

"Me and Bert just got back from Miami, you know, where we get his prescription filled for medical marijuana," said Maggie.

"We know," said Teddy.

She smiled mischievously and set a brown bag on the table. Then she removed the contents and placed it on one of the additional table planks. It quickly became of more interest than the adulterated Monopoly board. Everyone stared curiously with heads tilted at various angles like dogs in a whistle factory. "What is it?"

Coleman cracked up.

Serge elbowed him. "Don't be rude!"

Before them, in all its splendor, stood an upright, clear, two-inch-diameter Lucite tube with some kind of contraption that appeared to be from a chemistry lab.

"Judy, do you know what that is?"

Coleman stifled his chuckles. "It's a bong."

"A what?"

"He's right," said Maggie. "I picked it up when I got Bert's prescription."

"They sell those freaking things at pharmacies?" said Hazel.

"Nothing surprises me in Miami," said Joey.

"No," said Maggie. "It was an extremely long line for Bert's prescription because apparently it's a popular medication. So I took a walk down the block and found something that is known as a head shop. At first I thought it was a store for tarot cards and astrological gifts, but as it turns out, they sell equipment for marijuana. What a coincidence it was so close to the pot clinic."

Kelcey leaned across the table and canted her head at the device's base. "But what is this weird black lizard on the side?"

Serge leaned even closer. "That's not a regular lizard but an iguana. I know them personally from the parking lot."

Coleman also bent forward. "It's not original equipment, either, like when they mold a skull bong. It looks like someone just glued it on."

"I think it's cursed," said Serge.

"Why?" asked Maggie.

"Because it reminds me of the Maltese Falcon."

The gathering was split evenly on understanding Serge's reference.

"You guys don't remember?" said Serge. "From the Humphrey Bogart movie! This cursed totem from the island of Malta in the Mediterranean . . . This thing looks like some contraband from the international black-market antiquities trade."

Serge couldn't have known how right he was. In the eighteenth century, maritime thieves in jaunty Parisian caps intercepted the reportedly cursed iguana sculpture on the high seas between Malta and Marseilles, before it could reach a museum. From there, it toured Europe and North Africa, changing hands in hushed backroom deals with stops in Corsica, Algiers, Barcelona and Brussels. In 1909, it entered New York Harbor before finally landing in a secret artifacts room of a mansion in Providence, Rhode Island, sparsely decorated with two leather chairs and a small table holding brandy snifters and a cigar ashtray, for the owner and a guest to simply stare at a wall of shelves of purloined history from Chinese dynasties to Aztec human sacrificers. After the owner suffered a fantastic heart attack, one of his brandy-drinking buddies stuffed the iguana in his coat before the police arrived and ultimately stashed it in his winter home in Palm Beach. A decade later, during the man's wake, the iguana was among hundreds of items that three generations of heirs snatched from the house before the reading of the will, and it ended up forgotten as an afterthought in a drawer of a trust-fund grandson in Miami Beach, its provenance unknown. But the grandson took a curious liking to its oddness—"This would look great on my bong"—and he got out a tube of Gorilla Glue. Then he decided he didn't like it and swapped the bong for some hydroponic weed with the owner of a local head shop, where a retiree from Pelican Bay eventually entered the store with a jingle of bells on the front door.

"I'm calling him Iggy," said Coleman. "You have to nickname your bong, or it's bad luck."

"The curse is bigger, I tell ya!" said Serge. "Besides, every iguana is nicknamed Iggy. But this is a unique Maltese Iguana, so I propose calling him Malty. Who's with me?"

All hands but Coleman's went up.

"Great," said Serge. "Let's play Monopoly!"

"First things first," said Maggie, turning to Coleman. "Can you teach us how to use it?"

"You mean . . ." said Hazel. "We're actually going to smoke real marijuana while we play Monopoly?"

"Sure," said Maggie. "We aren't getting any younger, so why not be adventurous and live a little? They're starting to legalize it in almost half the country for any or no reason. How bad can it be?"

"I'm with her," said Bert. "It's already helped my arthritis, plus four other things I wasn't even thinking about."

Hazel bent forward impishly. "What was it like getting high?"

"After the first time," said Maggie, "Bert got out all his old albums."

Coleman finished his frozen blender drink and wiped tropical dribble off his chin with the back of his hand. "The head-shop guy was right about Malty."

All heads turned his way.

"My advice?" said Serge. "Give Professor Pot the floor . . . Coleman, it's your room."

Coleman stood and fired up a thick doobie. "Welcome to the meeting. How many here are first-timers?"

Everyone silently raised their hands except the couple with the pot prescriptions.

"Then I'll start at the beginning." Coleman paced around the table with hands clasped behind his back. "The main thing about weed with beginners is that you may not experience a textbook high on your first few attempts . . ."

A hand went up. "So it may not affect us?"

"Oh, it will definitely affect you," said Coleman. "Primarily giggling when nothing is funny, and then *that* becomes funny. And then you'll eat something bland like a rice cake and think it tastes better than the finest T-bone steak, and that's even funnier. And then you'll turn on a stereo, and the Bay City Rollers come on, and you're like, 'This is the best band I've heard in my life' as you lapse into a full-arrest giggle seizure, hanging over the sink flushing your eyes and nose."

Another hand went up. "That's supposed to be fun? That's why all those young people are doing it?"

Coleman shook his head as he exhaled. "Those are just the early reactions of novices, before the entire THC picture finally snaps into textured view. I just wanted to warn you about potential early effects to avoid embarrassment and possible injury. When I was getting started, I got bitten while eating out of a pet-food bowl. Oh, almost forgot about the sex. You'll probably get horny, and if you're inexperienced, you might inappropriately touch each other, or worse, yourself. Been there, done that, haven't been invited back. And once I was with this dog, and it was his birthday, so I decided it would be a nice gesture if I—"

"Coleman!" snapped Serge.

"Right . . . Any questions so far?"

Another hand: "But how will we know when we've seen the full picture?"

"You'll definitely know," said Coleman, puffing away. "It's like one of those paintings with a hidden image in it that you've never noticed, but once you see it, you can never *not* see it again."

Another hand. "How do we get started?"

"Excellent question." Coleman picked up the device on the table. "The head-shop guy didn't steer you wrong with this baby. It's the gold standard in terms of both economic use of weed and efficiency of the high. Anyone study physics? I have. Not in the classroom but from years being around these scientific instruments that put university labs to shame." He held out a hand. "Weed, please." Maggie slapped it into his palm, and Coleman pulled out a piece. "This little item sticking out the bottom is called the bowl, where the pot goes. The big mistake people make is to cram a bud in there without sufficiently breaking it up, and it just burns along the top, wasting smoke. You must tear it apart until achieving the maximum combustion coefficient by exponentially increasing the surface area. Next, the volume of the cylinder has to be fully utilized with this hole on the back called the carburetor. The pros know to keep it covered until the cylinder is thick. Then you uncover the carb and all at once clear the chamber with a mondo inhale and hold it as long as you can, and in no time you'll be righteously toasted. Unless you're a beginner. In that case, it takes a little dexterity to modulate the carburetor's intake until you learn your cough threshold, or you'll blow it out too soon and negate the efficiency model. Or worse, you'll cough back into the tube, expelling the glowing contents of the bowl and setting the carpet on fire. But done correctly, you'll be raiding the kitchen cabinets, cranking up the stereo, and straining not to you-know-what yourself . . . Observe . . ."

Coleman worked his way step by step through the procedure, held his breath for a short eternity, and exhaled toward the ceiling fan. He passed Malty to his left—"Here you go, Bert"—and took a seat next to his pal.

Serge just stared with an open mouth.

"What?" said Coleman.

"It never ceases to amaze me," said Serge. "How can you be so erudite and articulate about this stuff and yet . . ."

"What's 'articulate' mean?"

Coleman continued coaching as the bong went round the table. "Lower the lighter . . . Slow on that first inhale . . . You're not holding it in long enough . . . Pump the carburetor . . . Cover the bowl when you're about to pull . . . Break the pot up more . . . You coughed back into the chamber. Can someone take care of the carpet? . . ."

Jen-Jen arrived with potholders. "Make room for dinner."

Ten minutes later, the bong had made its third round and sat back on the table with wisps of residual smoke seeping from several locations. The gang sat quiet, introspectively evaluating any changes in themselves, staring at their hands as if just discovering them. Jen-Jen started giggling first, which set off Trevor and Judy, like a domino chain of yawns running round table.

"What's so funny?"

"Jen-Jen only served dinner minutes ago, and now there are only empty plates."

"The food just disappeared.

Teddy held a red plastic hotel up to his eyes. "Far out."

"Do we have any snacks?"

Jen-Jen caught her breath from the giggles. "There's a bag of Oreos up in that cupboard."

Kelsey picked up several "Chance" and "Community Chest" cards. "Remember the rich guy? Who transports money in a wheelbarrow? Or hobo sacks with a big dollar sign on the side?"

"I can debone an iguana," said Teddy.

"Why?"

"First you get a knife—"

"I hate those iguanas."

"I love them, more nature."

"How did they take over the Keys in just a few years?"

"No natural predators."

"Except car tires."

"What happens after you get a knife?"

"I don't know," said Teddy. "Never done it before."

"Thought you said you knew how."

"It's about confidence."

"We need Monopoly tunes!"

"What's that?"

Two other players lost it with giggles.

Coleman grabbed Malty and his lighter. "Don't stop now. Next hit!"

A series of exhales went round the table toward the ceiling fan.

A half hour later, the condo pounded with an '80s hit from the Pet Shop Boys.

"*. . . Let's make lots of money . . .*"

Crumbs were scattered around a mostly empty bag of Oreos that looked like a bowling ball had been dropped on it. Jen-Jen clapped her hands. "Time to begin the game!"

The guests all leaned and squinted at the board.

"I need another hit from the iguana bong," said Kelsey.

"Me too," said Trevor.

Guests threw back shots of Jack to smooth out the weed. Others scooped Oreo debris off the table and licked their fingers.

Maggie exhaled a hit. "I forgot what all this was about."

"Monopoly," said Serge.

"Oh, right . . ."

Chapter 20

MEANWHILE, BACK ON THE MAINLAND

An unnatural concentration of jeeps, jumbo pickups and other macho transportation sat on oversized tires in the western section of Miami called Doral. The parking lot of the Water Bed Barn.

Inside was indeed a barn, of corrugated steel construction, like a colossal Quonset hut. The floor plan was open, with well-spaced government-surplus desks, all manned by staff in military fatigues except for those who were out in the field playing pet detective.

At one end of the barn was the sole private office, with large windows overseeing everything, and blinds for privacy. The blinds were open. It was the Colonel's office.

A fiftysomething man finished his pull-ups on the tension bar in the doorway, then dropped for an equal quota of push-ups. The phone rang and he answered. The phone was a source of perpetual disappointment. It always started with hope, but by the second sentence it was merely another request for a security detail at a celebrity gala, or a husband wanting his mansion swept of listening devices his wife may have planted. Crap. Two years after launching the private military contractor firm and not a single bona fide mission. The Colonel was still itching to head out into the real field for live action, or—as the military like to put it—"go kinetic."

The phone call was not kinetic, unless you count another B-list actor who needed security to go clubbing. And he didn't really need the security for protection but to look important. "I'll put my best men on it." The Colonel hung up and made a note for his worst men and rubbed the scar on his chin.

He looked out his office through the open blinds at his men. *His men.* In his brain he referred to them as his green army men, like those sacks of tiny plastic soldiers in the toy racks of supermarkets next to the plastic handcuffs. Right now, most of his green army men were reading gun magazines or watching YouTube videos of laser-guided shoulder missiles. One of them chewed Twizzlers.

What a dubious lot. He barely remembered their names. Just their specialties, and even that was an overstatement. One was good with computers, another cleaned guns moderately fast, another was a karate yellow belt and one was adept at avoiding alimony.

But the one thing they all had in common: They were paid squat. Which put the Colonel's outfit in a particular niche, near the bottom of Miami's mercenary economic scale. Most people would be shocked that you can just look them up on the Internet. They don't even try to hide it or mince words: Miami alone has countless advertisements with prices for snipers, extraction teams, and incursions into guarded facilities, with performance bonuses. The sniper ads always amused the Colonel, because the prices were all over the map. Who would hire the cheapest? People not that concerned if they hit the right person?

Then the Colonel remembered that his outfit, too, was in the cheapo class. Now, there are but two reasons that customers hire budget mercenaries. The overwhelming motive is to save money. The lesser-known reason is to hire incompetence. It seems counterintuitive at first, but there's a method to it. The high-priced firms guarantee quick in-and-out ninja strikes, like they were never there.

But sometimes the nature of a mission is such that it's impossible to go completely unnoticed. In which case the planners sometimes throw in a wrinkle. They deliberately hire messiness. The front end of the operation was rarely a problem, but then shit would go sideways in some Third World island nation, resulting in Keystone Cops chases and ridiculous street shoot-outs and some of the culprits whining as local authorities dragged them out from hiding under parked cars. The mess was the alibi. Plausible deniability: "Give us more credit. Do you think we'd be remotely connected to such an absurd outfit?"

The Colonel continued staring emptily out at his crew. The ringing phone startled him. Hope again. He answered it. ". . . Yes, you got him . . . How many men can I spare right now? How many do you need? . . . That many? Wow, this must be a big job. Who are you with again? . . . Right, I know you. That huge private military contractor in Hialeah. So why don't you take the job yourself? . . . What? It has to be filtered through at least four other firms in Miami to cloud the trail? It must really be important. What is it? . . . Not on the phone? . . . Bayfront Park? With the eternal flame? Yeah, I know the place. It's where all the spies meet . . . Sure I can be there in a half hour . . . Houndstooth hat? Got it. Thirty minutes . . . Oh, listen, if you don't mind, could I ask where you heard about us? . . . Oh, on the Internet, right below the ad for Econo Snipers? . . . Yes, I've heard of them: 'Our inaccuracy is your savings.'"

The Colonel practically sprang out of his desk chair, then grabbed his keys and bolted for his Hummer.

After a high-speed drive across the Dolphin Expressway, the Colonel found himself on Biscayne Boulevard, walking down the sidewalk near the basketball arena. Up ahead was Bayfront Park, and since it was a park, there were park benches. The benches were doing a brisk business. Men would sit down for a minute and place folded newspapers next to them, and other men would sit on the opposite side. Then the first men would leave, and the others would pick up the newspaper and depart just as curtly, over and over and so on.

Coming the other way on the sidewalk was a houndstooth hat.

The man approached a bench as others were just getting up. He sat and placed a neatly creased *Miami Herald* next to him. The Colonel sat down, and the houndstooth got up. The Colonel grabbed the newspaper and ran the opposite direction back to his vehicle.

Just after dark, a late-model Hummer pulled off a street in Doral and parked in front of the Water Bed Barn. Boots hit the pavement and the Colonel went inside with a folded newspaper under his arm.

He closed his office door behind him and shut the blinds. Then he unfolded the newspaper to reveal a large brown legal-size envelope stamped CLASSIFIED. He broke the wax seal and extracted the contents, neatly arranging items on his desk. The Colonel found a round-trip ticket in his name to Tegucigalpa, commercial air, leaving the next morning. Then a fancy envelope containing an invitation. It featured an official eagle crest from the United States government. A party at the ambassador's compound? Then he studied an eight-by-ten glossy headshot of a man in a foreign uniform. His contact: standard protocol, pre-meet and final planning. As the tumblers fell in the Colonel's brain, he realized it could only mean one thing. It was a government operation that *wasn't* a government operation. It did not, nor would it ever, exist, and if his team stepped in any doo, the powers that be would disavow his existence.

He picked up several pages of rice paper. As the Colonel read down the dossier, he almost became giddy in a childlike way. This was as clandestine as it got. Finally! His team was going kinetic. He went through all the envelope's contents again to make sure it wasn't a dream, and he studied the photo, imagining an elite master spy with a code name like Mandrake or the Spitting Cicada.

The Colonel came to the last page again and read the final instructions. Right after he memorized everything, he was to burn the whole lot immediately. He placed a metal garbage can on his desk and dumped it all in. Then he flicked his cigar lighter and set it ablaze. As the flames began to spread through the paperwork, he realized that he had been so excited, he might have misinterpreted the instructions. They probably didn't mean for him to burn the plane ticket and invitation. The Colonel dumped a cold mug of coffee in the pail, sending up a whoosh of ash and smoke. But at least he was able to rescue the ticket and invite. A sprinkler in his office ceiling activated.

He exited his private office with an umbrella and stood smartly, facing a roomful of damp people. Someone hit the kill switch on the fire-suppression system. Luckily all their laptops were battlefield military-grade weatherproof, which they had purchased because they were cool.

"Men, listen up! I have important news." He began pacing. "This comes right from the top, but I can't tell you the top of what. The only thing you need to know right now is that your country will be counting on you. You'll need to hold the fort down for a couple of days while I make a really secret trip to do secret stuff. But when I get back, the big picture will become crystal clear. In the meantime, knock off the booze, the women, the racetracks and anything else that is the natural enemy of going kinetic."

The men began whispering—"kinetic"—and the Colonel threw his umbrella in the corner as he left the building.

Chapter 21

BACK AT PELICAN BAY

Serge studied his prized racecar token as the bong made the rounds. He looked up through the cloud over the table at a coughing cast of board-game players. "Are we finally ready?"

Nodding around the table.

Coleman smiled and pointed as he walked across the living room. "They have an Alexa."

"How can I help you?"

"Alexa!" yelled Serge. "Stop."

Bert tapped Serge's shoulder and glanced over to where Coleman was kneeling at a credenza. "What's he doing?"

"Talking to Alexa," said Serge. "We have one, too, and he's become mesmerized, like a cat watching a toilet flush."

Everyone finished reseating themselves.

"For the second time," said Serge. "Are we ready? Good ... Okay, I roll first, because, well, I have to put up with this nonsense." Serge clutched the dice next to his ear as if they were speaking to him. He cut them loose.

"Boxcars!" said Serge.

He grabbed his playing token—"Vrrrroooom!"—and sped the tiny racecar across the board, skidding through the corner at the jail—"Screeeeeeech!"—landing on his square. He looked at the photograph that he had taped to the board. "Excellent! I landed on the Aquarius underwater research laboratory anchored to the ocean floor off Key Largo!"

"Are you going to buy it?" asked Jen-Jen.

"Naw, I'm good."

The next player began rattling the dice in his hands.

Serge held up a single dollar of parlor-game money. "I'll make a bid."

The dice hit the table, and the player began moving a small metal terrier. Serge handed Jen-Jen the dollar, and she passed him the deed to the ocean lab.

"What's going on?" said Bert. "You can't just give him that deed for a dollar!"

"I'm the banker," said Jen-Jen. "I have to. He was the high bidder."

"What are you talking about?" asked Teddy. "He said he didn't want to buy it. We don't *bid* on properties!"

"Yes, we do," said Serge. "It's in the rules."

Jen-Jen placed Serge's dollar in the banker's tray. "Almost everyone has been playing the game wrong for nearly a century. That's why it goes so slow. The official rules state that if a player lands on an available property and doesn't choose to buy it, then it must go up for auction to all the players, including the one who declined to purchase. Serge was the only one who placed a bid before the next player rolled."

"This is bullshit!"

"Cheater!"

"I'm playing under protest!"

Fart, fart, fart . . .

Everyone shut up and made their best innocent expressions.

"Relax, everybody," said Serge. "That was Coleman."

"Coleman?" said Teddy. "But I heard it coming from that other direction."

"Not actually Coleman," said Serge. "He coordinated with Alexa."

"How can I help you?"

"Alexa, stop farting!"

"Okay."

"Anyway," Serge continued. "Leave it to Coleman to figure out how to get that machine to fart."

"Fart? Really?"

"And not just to fart, but it has a special mode for time-delayed flatulence in case you're having sophisticated company over. "

The game resumed pretty much as it had begun, Serge buying up the board for a dollar a property, then rapidly developing them like a small oil emirate. He rolled the dice and landed on the American Shoal Lighthouse. He needed more little green houses but began running short on money. He whispered to Jen-Jen, who nodded and gave him a wad of cash.

Teddy stiffened his right arm. "Now what? I smell a fix!"

Jen-Jen jotted the dollar amount in her notepad. "Players are allowed to make personal side loans to each other."

"More bullshit!" said Glenn. "Don't tell me, the rules again?"

Jen-Jen rolled the dice for her own turn. "Afraid so."

"It's all there in black and white," said Serge. "You all should read the rules instead of embarrassing yourselves."

"Embarrassing ourselves?"

"The truth is easily verified in that little booklet," said Serge. "How hard can it be to read a few pages so you know what you're talking about?"

"I don't need to read anything to know what I'm talking about!"

"In one sentence you've just summed up everything wrong with our country today."

"What do you mean?"

Serge stood again with spread arms. "How can we settle our differences peacefully and just get along when we can't even start the conversation? Remember the good old days when we agreed we were looking at the same thing and simply had good-faith differences of opinion over its interpretation? But now we've sculpted our own separate imaginary worlds bolted together with hate rivets. A few short years ago, we could look at a drinking glass and agree it was filled to the midpoint with water, then argue about what it meant. But today? Good lord! We all look at the same glass now, and it's either A: half-full, or B: a squirrel."

"Squirrel?" said Teddy.

"Are we still talking about Monopoly?" asked Bert.

"Don't forget you're high," said Serge.

"And hungrier than I've been in years," said Trevor.

"Me too."

"Starving!"

"Like insulin-shock therapy."

"I forgot," said Jen-Jen. "There's a whole giant casserole dish in the oven. Nachos supreme."

Everyone shut up and leaned forward in rapt attention. "Don't be fucking with us."

"I'm not," said Jen-Jen. "Mounds of melted cheddar, jalapeños, ground beef, salsa. The bowls of sour cream and guacamole are already on the counter—"

A stampede.

Potholders landed on the playing board, followed by the serving dish. Nobody was sitting, just hunched forward at the waist with utensils and plates.

Twenty minutes later, the neighbors were angled backward in their chairs, wiping mouths with napkins and burping. Coleman got the iguana bong bubbling once more and passed it. Moments after that, they were again all standing manically over the ceramic dish. When the onslaught was over, Serge stared in resignation at a smoldering war zone. Then he memorized where all the pieces were before taking the board to the sink and gingerly scrubbing off the periodic table of nacho elements.

He returned and set the board back up. "Ready to proceed?"

"I've decided that I don't like Monopoly anymore," said Teddy. "Too materialistic."

"All about greed," said Glenn. "The Man keeping us down."

"This game is like Beirut," said Bert.

"From space, the Earth is just one harmonious blue planet," said Maggie. "No nationalistic borders or Monopoly squares."

Serge turned to Coleman. "I see where this is going."

Coleman nodded. "Malty is doing the trick."

The neighbors had begun hugging each other.

"Obviously the game's over," said Serge, packing up the board. "I've got an excellent idea of something to do when you're high. I mess around with it all the time."

"I thought you said you didn't get high?" said Jen-Jen.

"I don't," said Serge. "But I'm taking a wild stab that my on-demand natural chemical spikes will shame anything in the display cases at the weed stores."

"So what's your idea?" asked Maggie.

"We can talk inside our heads," said Serge.

"Talk?" said Bert.

Serge nodded hard. "All day, every day, we have floods of instantaneous thoughts, emotions, and fleeting nuances. But we also have constant internal dialogue that we don't even realize. Random notions expanded into sentences and paragraphs. All perfectly crisp, annunciated, silent words streaming through our noggins. And I'm sure we're not the only ones on the planet blessed with this gift. A lot of animals are smart, and I often think, What is that cat silently saying to himself? But it's probably all 'Meow, meow, meow, meow.' . . . Shall we give it a try?" He scanned the room at a cast of grinning, eager faces. "Okay, we'll start with something simple: Keep your mouths closed and count to ten inside your head." He watched all their ripped expressions as they began, and could tell when they finished because the grins were larger.

"Far out," said Bert. "Let's all do another hit."

"Got you covered," said Coleman, pinching a bud tight to pack the bowl.

"Serge," said Maggie, "sure you won't partake with us?"

"That would be overkill. I'll just grab some coffee." He stood and headed for the counter and the automatic machine.

"It's cold," said Maggie.

"It's still coffee," said Serge. "Still half-full."

"A squirrel."

"Easy now with that newfound imagination, or you could sprain something." Serge poured a tall mug and sat back down and chugged. "Now, here's the graduate-level course on the phenomenon. When I'm bored and don't have any gadgets or even twigs to fiddle with, I still have my brain. And luckily it's *my* brain. And here's where it gets funky: Even if you realize that you can hear your own voice inside your head, few people comprehend the unbridled possibilities. But we all have a state-of-the-art recording-studio mixing board up in our medullas." Serge chugged the rest of the coffee and sat back in a globe of self-satisfaction. "Try this baby on for size: Say the Pledge of Allegiance inside your heads. Nod when you're done . . ." He observed until the last person signaled he was finished. "Okay, now that you're all high, this should really jazz you: Say the pledge again inside your heads but in the voice of Samuel L. Jackson . . ."

They did.

Serge checked the bottom of his empty coffee mug. "How was it?"

"Cool!"

"Wouldn't want to disagree with that voice."

"I didn't know there was so much swearing in the pledge."

"There isn't," said Serge.

"*'Motherfucking indivisible'*?"

"All right, maybe not the best selection of voice," said Serge. "Any suggestions?"

A hand went up. "Sir William Attenborough from those nature documentaries?"

"Good one."

Another hand. "Christopher Walken? He's even funny when he's supposed to be scary. His dialogue cadence."

"Nice call."

Another. "Alvin and the Chipmunks?"

"Look, if you're not going to be serious about this—" said Serge. He had to pause as the bong made its latest rounds. "But enough from me. Form study groups and work on your own vocal selections . . ."

They did. The room became a hum of silence.

"What do you think?" Serge asked Coleman.

"I'm impressed that you know how the stoned mind works," said Coleman. "I was grooving to the voices of Pink Floyd—"

Suddenly, "*Ahhhhhhh! Ahhhhhhhh!*" Maggie clutched both sides of her head. "*Ahhhhhhh!*"

They all ran to her aid. "What is it?" "What's wrong?"

"I can't make it stop! The voice of Satan is inside my head! *Ahhhhhhh!*"

"How do you know it's Satan?"

"Because he sounds like Darth Vader. *Ahhhhhhhhh!*"

Serge came over and squatted in front of her. He spoke soothingly. "Everything is fine. You are going to be fine. Just focus on my words . . ."

"Satan, be gone!"

"No, my words," Serge said gently. "What you're hearing is James Earl Jones. Breathe deeply and think of it as the voice of CNN."

After a few long exhales, she relaxed and dropped the hands from her head. "You're right. Instead of telling me to kill, he said Wolf Blitzer was coming up after the commercial."

From another part of the room: "*Ahhhhhhhh!* It's Charles Manson!"

The other direction: "*Ahhhhhhh!* Hitler!"

"*Ahhhhhh!* My ex-wife!"

Serge spun toward Coleman. "How the fuck did Monopoly get us here?"

"Contagious paranoia," said Coleman. "We need to break the cycle."

"Whatever you have to do, go!"

Coleman turned to the crowd. "May I have your attention. I can solve your problems if you just focus on my voice. Luckily we have Alexa here—"

"Would you like a random fart?"

"Alexa, stop," said Coleman, facing the room again. "The point is that she has an extensive music catalogue of everything you need in order to come down from the ledge. Now, everyone, if you would please find a spot on the floor and sit cross-legged . . ."

They did, eyes still painfully tortured.

Coleman bent down again to Alexa. Soon a medley of soothing Beatles standards filled the room.

"We Can Work It Out," "All You Need Is Love," "With a Little Help from My Friends" . . .

Some of the guests began to sway to the music with their eyes closed.

Coleman sat back at the table next to Serge. "It's working. See? I told you I could make it all better."

Eventually the whole room was grooving to mellow vibes. Then the next song started.

". . . Helter skelter! . . . (Dum-dum-dum-dum-dum-dum-dum) . . . Helter skelter . . . (Dum-dum-dum-dum-dum-dum-dum) . . ."

"*Ahhhhh! Ahhhhh!* I'm freaking out again!"

"Me too! We're going to die!"

Knock, knock, knock . . .

"I see blood everywhere!"

Serge slowly turned his head in annoyance.

"Oops," said Coleman, cupping hands around his mouth. "Alexa, play the back side of *Abbey Road.*"

". . . Here comes the sun . . . (Do-do-do-do) . . ."

He grinned at Serge. "That should handle it."

Knock, knock, knock . . .

Serge watched as Coleman talked them through a listening of "Strawberry Fields" and "Penny Lane."

"Alexa," said Coleman, "louder."

Knock, knock, knock.

The cross-legged neighbors swayed with closed eyes.

"Alexa, even louder."

Knock, knock, knock, knock, knock!!!!!

Chapter 22

MEANWHILE, NEAR THE ELEPHANT CAGES . . .

A black Camaro passed the Miami Metro Zoo and turned onto an anonymous road that didn't seem to lead anywhere.

After a short drive through the humid nothingness of the county's scrubland interior, the sports car approached a cluster of what seemed to be old, abandoned buildings. It parked in front of the first wooden structure in need of a paint job, and not just recently.

The driver's door opened, and a petite woman stepped out in a conservative pantsuit. She appeared deceptively young for her age, but what everyone first noticed was her extremely curly black hair, like on the grocery boxes of bakery sweets. She trotted up the steps and opened the door to a bare-bones office with three people working in a space for twenty.

Another door opened in the rear. An older man stuck his head out with a warm smile and waved. "Debbie! Come on in here!"

She entered the private office and looked around. An American flag on a pole in the corner, next to a top-flight shredding machine.

Behind the man's desk, a photo of the president, then more pictures of others in the chain of command. Entirely covering the adjoining wall was a comprehensive topographical map of Central America.

"Debbie, pull up a chair."

They both sat at the same time.

Debbie pointed backward, in the general direction of the parking lot. "I've never been here before. Just the main office downtown."

"The downtown address is the face of our station," said the local director. "Where the public can find us in the phone book . . . Do we still have phone books?"

"And this place?" asked Debbie.

"Where we do our secret stuff."

"It seems familiar," said Debbie.

"It should be," said the station chief, Virgil Gus. "It's the original CIA station when we expanded into Miami before the Bay of Pigs, and kept expanding until we reshaped Miami's entire economy from a sleepy Southern town to a landscape of hundreds of 'company' properties, boats, airplanes . . . This particular spot was a remote location owned by the University of Miami, miles away from the rest of the Coral Gables campus. It was called the JM-Wave station, operating under the perfect cover of a narcoleptic branch of the campus."

"I remember now," said Debbie. "Saw it in a book on the agency's history . . ." She looked around again, more quizzically. "But the whole place was shuttered decades ago, after everyone read about it in the newspapers. What are you doing back here?"

"We did extensive studies on the best places to open under-the-radar offices for classified activity," said Gus. "And the last place anyone would think to look for our secret shit is an old place of ours that was abandoned because everyone found out about it."

"Good thinking," said Debbie.

Gus gazed about and took a deep, satisfied breath. "Ah, if these walls could only talk. It was a golden age. We were planning to bomb Miami."

"You mean Cuba?"

"No, Miami. Actually multiple bombings," said Gus. "All over the city."

"Good God," said Debbie. "That's terrible!"

"No, everything was okay," said Gus. "They would be false-flag bombings that we'd blame on Castro, to pull us into an invasion. Like how we fibbed about the sinking of the USS *Maine* in Havana Harbor to launch the Spanish–American War."

"I'm speechless."

"Me too," Gus said in excitement. "It was 1962, and they called it Operation Northwoods. We were also going to blow up some refugee boats and airplanes and even assassinate some of our Cuban exile allies in Miami. But only a few exiles, nothing excessive."

Debbie paused and stared. "What happened?"

"The joint chiefs approved the plan, but President Kennedy killed the idea. Go figure."

"You mentioned on the phone about an assignment?" asked Debbie.

"That's right," said Gus. "How do you feel about Honduras?"

"I don't."

"You're the perfect fit," said Gus. "The Florida National Guard is about to begin their summer training down there. Pitch tents, practice with trenching tools, eat C-rations."

"Don't they usually train at Camp Blanding near Jacksonville?"

"Usually, but Honduras apparently looked more attractive this year."

"Are they actually going down there to train?"

"Not really."

"How do I fit in?"

"A two-star general will be inspecting the troops and needs a protective detail. People think the military handles that, and often they do, but in certain political situations, we help out."

"So that's my assignment?" asked Debbie. "Guard a general?"

"That's just a pretext," said Gus. "You *will* actually be offering protection, carrying a submachine gun and escorting him around our bases, but that's just for the cover story."

"Cover for what?"

"Make contact," said Gus. "We've learned that the general has been invited to a party at the ambassador's compound, which will arouse no suspicion when you join him for your secret rendezvous."

"Who will I be meeting?"

"Still developing that," said Gus. "It's an American, from one of the many private military contractors in Miami that we've been keeping an eye on. But there are so many firms that some crazy shit's been getting loose and making us look bad. One recently flew right by us: Did you read about those U.S. ex–Special Forces here in Miami who were hired by a Caribbean president to break into the national bank and steal eighty million dollars? What could possibly go wrong?"

"Is that true?"

"Look it up on the Internet. Quite the international incident. Embarrassed many people at the agency."

"So what's my role?"

"We've received some incomplete intelligence that there's a big conspiracy about to go down in Honduras."

"What is it?"

"We have no idea."

"Then how do you know the intelligence is reliable?"

"Because we picked up chatter about a second conspiracy theory that says the first unknown conspiracy exists. We've thoroughly checked it out."

"What did you find?" asked Debbie.

"There's no way to disprove the theory, so it has to be true."

Debbie's brain was working to keep up. "Who do you think is behind the conspiracy?"

"Us."

Her head pulled back. "Now I'm totally confused. If we're behind it, why don't we just check our own information?"

Gus shook his head. "Because it looks like it's being run by a secret cell."

"Okay, slow down," said Debbie. "What secret cell?"

"Obviously one of our own," said Gus. "Whenever there's a regular CIA station, there's always a secret cell nearby. We've spent countless man-hours trying to uncover it, but so far just goose eggs."

"Let me see if I have this straight," said Debbie. "This whole thing is about spying on *ourselves*?"

"Of course," said Gus. "What did you think we did for a living?"

"Spied on other people."

"Sometimes we do," said Gus. "But that's just when national security really depends on it."

"And we do this other . . . ?"

"For job security. Everyone's got a secret, you, me, anyone in the agency. Foreign governments occasionally trip over something embarrassing, but the much bigger threat to your pension is our own people. You never know what some asshole in a secret cell will turn up." Gus nodded. "The secret cell down here is spying on us right now, just because we're spying on them."

"I'm lost again."

"See, the whole key to top-shelf espionage is compartmentalization. Chop the missions and intelligence into the smallest possible pieces buried under Byzantine layers of bureaucracy. Then if something goes sideways and the press starts asking questions that jeopardize jobs, good luck going into that labyrinthine maze."

"I know I'll regret asking this," said Debbie. "But if you haven't uncovered the secret cell, how do you know they're up to something?"

"Because we were tipped off by the second secret cell."

"There's a *second* secret cell?"

"Don't be silly. There's always a second secret cell," said Gus. "Who do you think keeps track of the first? We're good at what we do."

"But why don't you just ask the second secret cell to reveal the first one to us?"

Gus shook his head. "They say it's a secret. Real pricks about compartmentalizing."

Debbie stared at the map of Central America. "So I'm supposed to meet this mystery American military contractor. Then what?"

"Ask for a job," said Gus. He handed her a thick file folder. "We'll need you to sign all those forms before we can proceed."

Debbie began scribbling her signature. "And he'll just hire me?"

"Explain you're leaving the agency because you're sick of all the bureaucratic maze."

"And that's all there is?"

"He'll bite. He'll assume it's a quid pro quo requirement for the government business flowing his way," said Gus. "We need you on the inside. Gather what information you can, monitor all their movements, any potential violations of U.S. law, track the money, log contacts, just be enterprising."

"So my primary mission is to make sure the military contractors don't go rogue on foreign soil and create an international incident?"

"No, it's to uncover our secret cell that they're working for," said Gus. "This is totally voluntary. If you get caught up in anything, we'll have to purge your files, deny any knowledge of your existence and possibly leave you stranded in a clandestine jungle prison." A big smile. "What do you say?"

"Sounds too good to be true."

Chapter 23

The immoral song "Let It Be" was winding down in the upper-floor condo.

Coleman tapped his chin, then broke into a smile. "Next on the program! Munchies!"

"More?" said Serge. "Again?"

"You can never have too many munchies," said Coleman. "But in case you do, just do another round of bong hits!"

Serge nodded. "There's such balance in nature."

Bert found more packages of cookies, this time baked by elves. It was a plastic tray featuring four rows of cookies, with a clean plastic window over the top. He walked back to the table and set it in the empty casserole dish.

"What did you find?" asked Maggie.

"My favorite, the fudge stripes." He turned to the rest of the room. "Soup's on!"

Coleman was knocked clear out of his chair by the ravenous

stampede. He pulled himself up from the carpet. "Hey, Serge." He pointed down the hall. "I think I'll be going to the bathroom now."

"So why the announcement—oh." Serge sighed. "Make sure to lock the door, and turn on the faucet to cover your noises."

"You got it."

Serge looked around, then to himself: "I could swear I hear knocking."

Back at the kitchen table, the guests had gone at the tray of cookies like it was a single entity.

Not even opening the bag. They attacked it straight through the plastic window in defiance of the carefully designed easy-open package developed by the Keebler Company and vetted with focus groups. The condo people pulled their hands back with tight fists of mashed cookie ingredients, which were pushed into their faces with varying precision.

"This rules!" said Teddy. "Alexa, play 'Life in the Fast Lane.'"

The condo started rocking out to Joe Walsh's blistering guitar riff.

"Alexa, louder!"

The music cranked.

"Alexa, even louder!"

The balcony's sliding glass doors began to hum.

Serge looked around. "Has anyone besides me been hearing knocking?"

They didn't hear him.

Suddenly, the cookies were gone, just a crater in the plastic tray, and the guests stared like lost children in the woods.

Teddy pointed. "To the cabinets!"

They went for it all. Chips, crackers, nuts, jars of maraschino cherries, cans of cake frosting, sprinkles for ice cream cones, then the ice cream cones themselves.

"Get out Malty! I'm ready for another hit!"

"Me too!"

"Fire up that sucker."

The bong began to bubble again as it was passed.

Knock, knock, knock, knock, knock!

The learning curve had been steep. They deftly worked the bowl and carburetor, quickly passing it with hands over the end of the Lucite tube for minimal loss of smoke.

"To the fridge!"

They dug through the giant appliance for orange marmalade and spray cans of whipped cream. Someone reached deep into an unseen back corner of the fridge behind the milk. "Pudding cups!" That sparked the biggest rugby scrum yet.

Knock, knock, knock, knock, knock!

"I don't feel paranoid anymore!" said Teddy.

"Me neither!"

"We should schedule these for several times a week!"

Knock, knock, knock, knock, knock!

Serge turned with a curious gaze. "I *am* hearing that."

Teddy ate powdered Ovaltine with a spoon. "Hear what?"

"Someone's knocking at the door."

"So go see who it is."

Serge reached the front of the condo. The blinds on the window were cracked, and he could see a pair of eyes peeking inside. Serge parted the blinds farther to see who it was.

"Alexa, play 'Fight the Power'!"

Public Enemy began booming through the unit with driving bass and funky horns.

"I can't believe how paranoid I was earlier," said Bert.

"Same here," said Teddy, eating another spoonful of chocolate powder. "Now I'll know how to handle the illusion of a meltdown, so it will never happen again." He stuck out his tongue. "Why is my mouth so dry?"

Serge began unlocking the door as he glanced over his shoulder. "Everyone, be cool. It's just the police."

Panic boomeranged with a vengeance, stoner food flying everywhere, furniture knocked over. In seconds the entire living room was empty, just a brown cloud of Ovaltine.

From down the hall, the sound of the bathroom door opening.

"*Ahhhhhh!*" screamed Coleman.

"*Ahhhhhh!*" screamed the others.

Coleman bolted out of the bathroom as others charged inside. Thus began an epoch of behavior piloted by marijuana logic. Three people climbed in the shower, leaving three others feeling desperately exposed by the sink.

"Let us in the shower!"

"No room!" They pulled the plastic shower curtain closed, as if it were an impenetrable barrier to a police search.

Others stood outside the bathroom. "Let us in!"

"No room!" said the guests by the sink. They closed the door and locked it.

The rest dashed into a bedroom. They glanced around, and the first to arrive tried cramming into a closet where Coleman was already stationed.

"Coleman, you're taking up too much space!"

"No, I'm not."

"Out you go!" The closet door slammed shut.

Coleman began banging on it. "Let me in. I was there first!"

"No more room!"

The remainder of the guests began wiggling themselves under the beds.

Coleman shimmied on the floor to join them.

"It's full under this bed."

"No, it's not," said Coleman. He turned his bulbous head sideways to squeeze it under the box spring.

"Coleman, you're crushing us. We can't breathe."

"Scooch over some more." Coleman continued squirming on the carpet. He was almost under. Then, "Uh-oh."

"What's the matter?"

"My butt's stuck."

"Under the bed?"

"Part of it," said Coleman.

"How much is sticking out?"

"About half."

"Coleman! Go somewhere else! You'll get us caught!"

"Nonsense."

"They'll see your butt."

Pause. "No, they won't . . ."

Meanwhile, back in the living room, Serge had opened the door with a warm smile. "Good evening, officers. I'll take a wild guess that because of all the noise and the craziness you saw through the blinds including the Ovaltine cloud you'd like to come in. So I'll save your breath: Won't you please come in?"

"Thank you." They stepped inside and took off their hats, standing next to the disaster area of a dining-room table with pulverized Keeblers and Monopoly pieces embedded in pudding cups.

Serge and the officers faced each other and smiled. It was quiet in the living room. The rest of the condo, not so much. The officers had assessed there was no danger, so they stood a moment and listened with Serge. Down the hallway, banging sounds and people arguing in loud whispers. ". . . *We need to keep our stories straight. Hippies barged in earlier and forced us into the lifestyle . . .*" "*. . . They were trying to get us hooked . . .*" "*. . . Put a monkey on our backs . . .*" "*. . . They played 'Helter Skelter' . . .*"

Serge smiled wider and clasped his hands in front of his stomach. "So, how may I help two of Islamorada's finest this evening?"

"We received a few noise complaints tonight from some of your neighbors," said the first officer. "Mainly loud music."

"Oh," said Serge. "That was Alexa."

Fart.

"Excuse that," said Serge. "It was time-delayed."

"Nobody was answering the door, and the blinds were open," said the second officer. "Exigent circumstances allowed us to peek inside."

"We observed signs of possible illegal drug use," said the first.

"Still seeing them," said the second, gesturing at the Maltese Iguana, with residual smoke wafting out the end of the Lucite tube.

"It's a sad state of affairs." Serge shook his head forlornly. "But the answer is treatment instead of incarceration. The people hiding down the hall wouldn't begin to know how to make shivs, and they'd be passed around the cellblock for packs of smokes."

The first officer took a step closer. "Relax, it's obvious this condo isn't a bomb-making terrorist cell."

Serge glanced down at his racecar token jammed down in tapioca. "What tipped you off?"

"It's just pot," said the second officer. "There are dispensaries on every block now, and it will probably be completely legal after the next referendum or so."

"But in the meantime," said the first officer, "we have to follow regulations, and cross our *t*'s. We can't just turn our heads when you stick something so conspicuously under our noses."

"Except we also have the power of discretion," said the second officer, pointing vaguely at the front door. "We've got more important things to do. Actual crime."

"Their worst offense is wasting our time."

"So how do we resolve this?" asked Serge.

"Let's get them all back in the living room, and I'll give them a little lecture."

"Kind of like 'Scared Straight'?" asked Serge.

"A little less dramatic."

Serge and the officers headed down the hall. First they stopped at the bathroom, full of whispers.

"Shhh!" "Shhh yourself!" "Stop whispering! They'll hear us!" "That's why I'm whispering—"

A hard knock on the door. "It's me, Serge. Let us in and everything will be okay."

"Are you sure?"

"I give you my word."

The bathroom door creaked open. Three people scurried out toward the living room. The officers exchanged glances, and the first walked past the sink and pulled open the shower curtain. "You guys too."

"Oh, of course . . ."

Next, the bedroom. More loud clandestine whispering from under the mattress.

". . . *I have a rope fire escape ladder we can throw over the balcony* . . ."

"Coleman," said Serge. "Come out from under the bed."

Silence.

"Coleman!"

Pause. "I'm not here."

"I can see your butt sticking out."

Pause. "No, you can't."

"You idiot!" Serge jumped down and grabbed one of Coleman's legs and began pulling.

"Ow! Ow! Ow! My head's too big. It's scraping stuff under here!"

Moments later, they were all seated demurely in the living room, hunched down into themselves in a guilt funk, like they were in the principal's office.

The first officer paced in front of them. "You do realize how serious this is—" The officer stopped briefly to look at one of the sofas and Bert, who had grabbed his VFW hat on the way out of the bedroom, along with several medals that he hung from his tropical shirt. The officer rolled his eyes and continued: "Every one of you could be facing serious ramifications. Right now I'm practically required to cuff this whole gang and take you to the county jail, where you'll remain until arraignment."

Maggie raised her hand. "You said *practically* required?"

"That's correct," said the other officer. "We also have the power of discretion. Whose pot is that?"

Maggie and Bert sheepishly raised hands.

"Medical?"

They nodded tentatively.

The first officer scanned the rest of the room. "Anyone else have prescriptions?"

The rest shook their heads.

The officer resumed pacing. "Okay, here's the official version that's going in the report. You two with the scripts are the only ones I actually saw doing bong hits, so even though logic dictates otherwise, there's no probable cause against the rest of you. But that could change quickly depending on your attitude."

The other officer took over the lecture and shifted to a personal tone. "Listen, you guys are the pillars of the community; you should know better. We don't want to be here any more than you want us to be. So from now on, will you please be more discreet and keep it down to a dull roar in here? And keep your blinds closed? Can you do that for us?"

Eager nodding around the room.

The officers put their hats back on. "Okay, then." They tipped their visors. "Y'all have a nice evening."

Serge opened the door for them.

Fart.

One of the officers turned toward an object on a table. "Was that Alexa?"

Serge shrugged. "The machines have risen up."

A walkie-talkie on an officer's shoulders squawked: "*Noise complaint, Coral Pointe condos...*"

The officer keyed his walkie-talkie mic. "We're on the way."

The pair began trotting back toward the elevators. "God, I hate Monopoly Night."

Part Three

INTERMISSION IS ENDING

*Please return to your seats, as your regularly
scheduled program is about to resume.*

Chapter 24

SOUTH FLORIDA

Combat boots clomped up the steps of the Water Bed Barn.

The Colonel had returned from Central America, and his men were on high alert for more news about going kinetic.

The Colonel wasn't alone. "This is Debbie, the newest member of our team. Despite her stature, she's extremely valuable and experienced. She'll be handling analytics."

He began pacing again. "I'm sure you've all been more than curious about our next mission. And I have some exciting news. But before I begin . . ." He pointed at several members of the team who had conflicting assignments and would be staying stateside. "We have to compartmentalize, so you'll need to leave the room. Wait in the parking lot." He looked to his side. "You too, Debbie."

"But I just started. Don't you think it's best if I get up to speed as soon as possible?"

He shook his head. "You'll be staying here. Compartmentalizing takes priority."

"If you think it's best. Let me just first drop my purse at my desk . . ."

A half hour later, the Water Bed Barn was a full house. The Colonel had scrambled all the others from home with the "Defcon One" code words that he had never had the excitement to use before. He stood at the front of the room, where a giant map from Central America was now unfurled. He used a pool cue for a pointer.

"Listen up and stay sharp," he snapped in disciplined cadence. "This is as real as it gets. This is why we've been training all these months in the Everglades."

A hand went up from the karate yellow belt. "Does this mean we're going kinetic?"

"It doesn't get any more kinetic," said the Colonel, enjoying the pronunciation. "As a matter of fact, I'd like you all to say 'kinetic.'"

"What?"

"All of you, at once," shouted the Colonel. "Say 'kinetic'!"

"Kinetic!"

"Again!"

"Kinetic!"

"I can't hear you!"

"Kinetic!"

"Sound off like you got a pair between your legs!"

"Kinetic!"

"Stomp your feet!"

"Kinetic!"

"Clap your hands!"

"Kinetic!"

"Okay, enough of that shit. Back to the map." The tip of the pool cue tapped a spot near the coastline, leaving a smudge of blue chalk. "This is the LZ."

"What's an LZ?"

"Lizzie Borden! You idiot, it's the landing zone!" The Colonel shook with rage. "Do we have to watch *Platoon* again on movie night?"

Another hand went up. "Tonight's movie night. Does this meeting mean we won't be seeing—"

"Shut up! Jesus, I can't hear myself think!" He paced furiously in front of the map. "We'll board at that empty airstrip outside Homestead, and here's where we'll land—"

A hand went up. "Can we do a halo jump, like the Special Forces? Egress at ultra-high altitude and only pull our rip cords at a few hundred feet? Then navigate to a dime with special sails?"

"No! Nobody's parachuting!" said the Colonel. "We touch down nice and easy in an airplane, and our contact will be there with the vehicles."

The hand stayed up. "Can it at least be an option? Jump if you want? We'll all end up in the same place anyway."

A cue stick slapped the map. "No! No! No!"

Another hand. "What about night-vision goggles? That's the excellent part of a halo jump, but if we can't do the jump—"

"Shut up! Shut up!" The Colonel stopped and stared daggers at the silent room. "All right then . . ." The tip of the cue moved across the map. "Our local guide will take us into the foothills near the jungle. Before dawn at zero-four-hundred hours Zulu we'll slip into the village—"

"What's Zulu?"

The Colonel: "It's what professionals say!"

"Is that like noon or midnight? I mean, we could all be scattered because our watches will be twelve hours off."

"It's four in the morning!"

"Why didn't you say that?"

A third hand was raised.

The Colonel gritted his teeth. "I swear to God this better not be about parachuting or Zulu!"

"It's not."

The Colonel inhaled violently through his nostrils. "Go ahead."

"Uh, is this one of those countries with chickens running around?"

"What?"

"Chickens."

"I heard what you said. I'm trying to process why you would ask such a thing."

"Because it looks like one of those places from TV where chickens run around wherever they want, and everyone's cool with it."

"So what?"

"Imagine that in Miami."

"There *are* places like that in Miami."

"I was thinking of our malls."

"What's your point?"

"If we're striking at night, we should factor in all the variables."

The Colonel closed his eyes and pinched the bridge of his nose. "Okay, I think that's about as much briefing as I can take. We launch in three hours."

The green army men rose from their seats and made their way to the kitchen area on the side of the room, lining up at the microwave.

Minutes later, the room was dark as their fingers rummaged through bags of popcorn. Up on the flat-screen, Charlie Sheen detonated a string of perimeter mines.

A mouth licked butter from fingers. "I love *Platoon*."

THREE HOURS LATER

A column of jeeps and pickups left a contrail of dust as it raced down a dirt road on the eastern edge of Homestead near the speedway.

A black C-130 Hercules troop transport plane was waiting in the darkness. No markings or tail numbers. A handful of men in civilian clothes stood off to the side, not speaking. The giant ramp was already down behind the plane, and the green army men marched up it with tactical bags over their shoulders.

A red light began rotating over the cockpit, and hydraulic pistons raised the ramp, sealing the back of the plane. The men made themselves at home on the bench seating that ran along the walls inside the dim cargo bay, thinking, *A lot of space is going to waste.* The runway had plenty of length that was needed for the behemoth, and the pilot was experienced at night takeoffs without ground lights.

It predictably took a while for all that weight to build up lift speed, lumbering like an albatross, but wheels finally left the earth, and the bird banked sharply south as it gained cruising altitude.

It was a quiet trip, and not as much time as expected. For some psychological reason, the prospect of flying to a foreign country always seems longer at the outset. The crew fiddled with their gear, playing with it as much as checking it. There were the silencers for their U.S. military tactical rifles, which they were only given once in the air because of legalities. And, yes, they got their night-vision goggles, which caused them much mirth.

The politics of airspace required the pilot to skirt hard west before the coast of Cuba, then dip south along the Yucatán, the rest of the Mexican gulf beaches and Belize. The whole sky was awash with American AWAC aircraft, with those insane radar disks atop the fuselage, looking for drug planes and others with ill intentions. All the radar planes had been given the code clearance for the unmarked C-130 heading under their altitude. Then it was time. The Hercules briefly swung out to sea over the scuba-diving island resorts, and bled off velocity as it vectored west toward the coast. Instruments kept the pilot above the trees as he descended toward a hillside plateau. Taking off in the dark of South Florida was one thing, but landing in Honduras required a brief risk of discovery. The pilot's breathing remained even, right until the last thirty seconds, when the strands of Christmas lights were suddenly turned on along the grassy landing patch. The wheels touched down, and the lights immediately went dark.

The ramp dropped.

The green army men hut-hut-hutted their way down the ramp incline and into the field. The pilot came back to the Colonel. "You have two hours and then I'm a ghost."

The Colonel nodded and led his men to a trio of waiting jeeps on the edge of the ersatz runway. A single man was waiting in the dark. The Colonel extended a hand. "Yandy, nice seeing you again after the party at the ambassador's house."

Yandy nodded respectfully. "It would be a pleasure under different circumstances."

"Understood. We have work to do." They began loading the vehicles. "Anything I should know about local authorities we might meet up with?"

"We won't on our route, but they're heavily corrupt," said Yandy as he climbed in behind a steering wheel. "You don't know whom to trust. That's the main reason I agreed after your government made contact with me."

"Smart move," said the Colonel. "You won't regret this."

"I still feel shitty, like a Judas to my country," said Yandy. "But your man was one of the most honest I've ever met. What happened—" He cut himself off. "Sorry for your country's loss."

The jeeps headed out into the jungle darkness. The Colonel pulled out an encrypted satellite phone. "Did you get the front-end payment?"

Yandy nodded. "The cryptocurrency hit my account this morning."

The Colonel pressed buttons. "According to our deal, the back half was due upon you picking us up. I'm wiring it now." He finished and hung up. "Your guilt doesn't seem to have a problem with a big payday."

Yandy cut the wheel into a tight turn on the dirt road. "I'm not doing it for the money. No matter how this goes, I'll have to leave the country and start a new life and that's not free . . . You got all my instructions?"

"We were never here," said the Colonel.

"This is an extrajudicial op by foreigners without my government's knowledge, let alone approval," said Yandy. "Nobody can see you the entire time you're here, especially in the village."

"Speaking of village, it's still twenty klicks, right?"

"Unless there's been an earthquake."

The Colonel pulled out a laminated, waterproof cheat sheet. The markings were also coded in case it fell into the wrong hands. "One last rundown," said the Colonel. "We roll up without lights a hundred yards from the village and climb the last stretch through the jungle. You'll go first, on point, in case anyone is out and about, since you look Honduran. Any bugs and we abort. I take your silence as agreement. Correct?"

Yandy simply drove.

The night shift of insects, frogs and tropical birds gave them sound cover. The Colonel studied the laminated chart through his night-vision goggles. "We enter the rear of the village through the farms and livestock. At that point you'll give us a hundred-percent on which villa. Speaking of which, how are you so sure of the specific target location?"

"The national police have been watching them for years. They know all the other stash houses and transpo hubs too," said Yandy. "The place we're heading to has plenty of guns and drugs, but not remotely as much as the other sites because this is more of an organizational facility where the gang leaders find sanctuary."

"Then why hasn't your government done anything yet?" asked the Colonel.

"Ever seen an insanely complex maze in a puzzle book?" asked Yandy.

"I'm not sure I—"

"That's Central America all over the place." Yandy braked as they traversed deep trench puddles. "It's not just that it's corrupt. It's the *chaos* of the corruption."

"You've lost me."

"From what I understand about America, if there's corruption, it's organized," said Yandy. "Down here you need a baseball program to follow the players."

"I don't know shit about this place," said the Colonel.

"It isn't like we just have honest officials and dishonest ones," said Yandy. "It's that the dishonest ones are taking money from ten different sources that are often at cross-purposes. The biggest threat is from the *other* corrupt guy working for a different gang. Nobody knows who's who. It's a foggy battlefield of a dozen potential double-crosses, and only fools would want to make any moves on a major organization when they don't know which direction the bullets will come from."

"And you're different?" asked the Colonel before nodding. "They told me your ethics were beyond impeccable."

"I've come to the sad conclusion that one man can't do anything," said Yandy. "But if I can do this thing tonight for Alan, before I leave, it'll be something."

"Makes sense in its own way."

"Just remember," said Yandy. "I can't go in with you. No matter how hairy it may get."

"It won't get hairy. My men are professionals . . ."

They drove the final kilometers in silence, and the last stretch with lights off. They turned the jeeps around so they would be pointing out, then began marching through the banana trees with the aid of their goggles. The lush vegetation finally parted and they stepped into the openness of a small pasture. A donkey stared at them.

The Colonel turned to the men and made a series of silent hand gestures in his trademark third-base-coach manner. Two fingers pointed before sweeping down toward the ground, then a twirling index finger. The men began moving.

"Hey!" the Colonel whispered. "Where are you going?"

"You signaled to abort."

"That's not 'abort,'" said the Colonel. "It means 'establish separation and stick to the tree line.'"

"The Colonel's right," said another of the team, twisting his own fingers. "This is 'abort.'"

"That's not 'abort,'" said another. "That's 'breach the compound.'"

"*That's* 'breach'?" asked another. "I thought it was '*don't* breach.'"

"No," said the first. "That's the signal for the location of a bath-room."

"Knock it off!" the Colonel whispered harshly. "Just do what I do . . . Yandy, you're on. Take point."

Yandy passed the others and led the way around the donkey. They reached the edge of the pasture and crept along the side of the last stucco villa. Ahead was what passed for a street in these parts. Yandy peeked around the corner. He pulled his head back and nod-ded: No surprises.

Suddenly, the sound of a silenced assault rifle firing a barrage.

"Stop it! Stop it!" whispered the Colonel. "What are you doing?"

"The chickens came out of nowhere."

"You're shooting chickens?" asked the Colonel.

"They're variables."

"I can't believe I actually have to say this, but leave the chickens alone."

"What if they enter the kill box?"

"Stop talking."

Yandy began leading them along the fronts of the shanties. He held three fingers and pointed, indicating the third building, the only one with any lights on, shining through slits in the warped wood. The Colonel tapped one of his men, who quietly slipped for-ward and inserted a tiny fiber-optic cable between two of the boards. He monitored the interior on a handheld screen, and slunk back to the Colonel. The drug gang had become complacent from all the bribes they'd spread around government offices down in the cities. "Colonel, there are seven sitting around the kitchen, maybe more sleeping in the darkened bedrooms."

"What are they doing?"

"Getting drunk. And high. Guns are leaning against the walls within reach, but I would bet on their reaction time." They could hear laughter.

The Colonel turned. "Under a minute." He checked his watch.

"We breach at the fifteen-second mark. Move." Three of the team ran around the back to guard against escapees. The rest clustered at the front door. It was locked but suffering from dry rot; nothing a simple screwdriver couldn't fix.

The Colonel wedged the door open and stepped aside for the guys to lob flash grenades, temporarily blinding the occupants. The green army men burst inside in a tight formation that left each gun barrel with clear sight. They were already firing before they knew it. Five of the drug gang immediately went down in the kitchen, and two others jumped out the back door and were promptly dispatched. The men then sprayed the two bedrooms with abandon, taking out three more in their inebriated sleep.

It took all of thirty seconds. Total success. Now: Just get out without detection.

The Colonel made a fist, meaning "back to the egress point."

Yandy ran around the villa and met them coming out the back door.

"Uh-oh."

Lights had come on in other villas, illuminating two previously unnoticed people with chickens around their feet, the local peasant neighbors. They pointed in alarm. "Americanos! Americanos!"

A quick salvo from several of the silenced rifles, and two bodies fell facedown in the dirt. From the other direction on the edge of the pasture. "Americanos!"

Pfft. Pfft. Pfft. Pfft. Pfft.

More bodies fell.

Yandy ran up and seized one of the guns from the team. "Have you lost your fucking minds? You're killing civilians!"

The Colonel aimed his rifle at someone fleeing across the field, fifty yards away, almost to the tree line. *Pfft.* The body fell. "We can't be detected."

"Stop it!" yelled Yandy. "Don't kill anyone else and we can still fix this."

Other villagers had curiously crept outside. *Pfft. Pfft. Pfft. Pfft.*

"You're psychos!" yelled Yandy. "This is a massacre!"

"Relax," said the Colonel. "We already planned for this eventuality. The innocents were killed in a cross fire between rival drug gangs. Everything's fine."

"You call this shitstorm fine?"

"Loose ends," said the Colonel. "No witnesses."

"Why are you looking at me like that?"

"Remember when I said they told me you had integrity?" asked the Colonel. "It wasn't a compliment. It was a warning."

"What are you saying?—" He didn't wait for an answer and instead dove around the edge of a shanty as bullets meant for him splintered the wood.

The crew gave chase—briefly. They rounded the same corner of the building, but Yandy was ready. He still had the AR-15 he had seized from the team member, and he laid down suppression fire, sending the team back around the building to the pasture.

"What are you doing?" yelled the Colonel. "Go get him!"

"But he's shooting."

"So shoot *him*!"

They all darted to the dirt road that ran through the hamlet. The crew fanned out in both directions, but it soon became clear to the Colonel that Yandy had the home-field advantage and—between the jungle and the moonless night—the odds were rapidly slipping away. It was all quickly turning into a disaster of exposure. And the clock was ticking at the landing strip.

"Back to the jeeps!"

The Colonel checked his tactical wristwatch. They had a time pad of thirty minutes to sweep Yandy's logical downhill escape route that coincided with their exit course. Sweeping search beams, occasionally jumping out when they thought they heard something and sprinting briefly through the jungle with their night goggles, killing more birds . . .

A long, bumpy ride, but the vehicles eventually broke out of the jungle. Everyone sprinted for the C-130 Hercules, which was just about to leave them behind. The loading ramp hissed up and closed, and they were aloft in minutes. The cargo plane banked over the island resorts and turned north in the general direction of Guantánamo Bay. The Colonel drifted forward into the cockpit.

"How did it go?" asked the pilot.

"Bad question." The Colonel hit buttons on his satellite phone. "Yes, it's me. . . . Directive accomplished. . . . Not exactly. We have a loose end."

Chapter 25

ISLAMORADA

A polished wooden ball the size of a small grapefruit rolled swiftly down a long runway. It hit a ramp, took flight and landed in a little hole. A bell dinged and the lighted scoreboard changed numbers.

"Wooooo!" Serge threw triumphant arms in the air. "I win another one! That makes the cumulative score two thousand to zero. Want to play again?"

Coleman was underneath the arcade machine, trying to retrieve the last in a long series of balls that he'd sailed off the apron. "I'm tired of playing Skee-Ball."

Serge, arms still in the air, jumped in a circle like a winning boxer. He was practically a silhouette, backlit by a wall of floor-to-ceiling glass, showcasing a bright private beach, coconut palms scattered in the sand, and the Atlantic at high tide. "This is the best condo community room ever!"

"I know! It has a giant wet bar and fridge! And a jumbo community blender!"

Serge bounced on the balls of his feet. "Let's play ping-pong!"

"Okay."

Serge dashed to the equipment locker and Coleman made a bee-line toward the sink. They arrived back at the ping-pong table with paddles and a fresh frozen rum drink. The ceiling lights flickered.

Serge stood poised and coiled, rocking left to right like John McEnroe. "Ready?"

"Hold on." Coleman placed his drink on his side of the table and picked up his paddle. "Now I'm ready."

Serge served, and Coleman chased after the ball skittering toward the plate glass. He walked back with a crumpled ball. "Not my fault. It somehow got under my foot."

Ten minutes later, Serge set his paddle down. "Okay, you've now officially stepped on all the balls." He stored his paddle in the equipment rack. "Come on, help me collect all these destroyed things and hide them in a trash can and hope they're not discovered before we have time to go and buy replacements."

They completed their subterfuge, and Serge hid the can in a lower cabinet. "Let's do something else. But what?" He snapped his fingers. "The new exercise equipment in the spa! It's off the hook! Do they still say that?"

"I don't like exercise," said Coleman.

"Nobody does," said Serge. "But I've heard rumors that it's healthy. Let's go!"

They dashed out of the game room. Well, Serge did. The over-head lights flickered again as they arrived at the end of the hall and examined a long row of gleaming, cutting-edge contraptions whose complexity clouded their intended purposes. Bars, pulleys, cables, weights, springs, tracks and padded benches at all angles.

Coleman scratched his head. "I have no idea what these things do. Are they for exercise or torture?"

"Both, I think." Serge invigorated himself by slapping his cheeks with his palms. "I'm outrageously revved by how space-age they look. In fact, I've decided to totally rededicate myself to my life's new exercise phase of reaching the physical pinnacle of total Roman constitution. No amount of patience, sacrifice, or pain is too much. Coleman, if I go missing for days and neighbors start to panic, just tell them to check the spa . . . Now, give me some room. I'm about to enter the Exercise Phase." Serge got down on one knee in a track stance. "On your mark, get set, go!"

Coleman jumped back just in time as Serge flung himself into the first machine and grabbed ergonomic handles, then the next machine and a cushioned chest bar, then a low seat with handles like he was rowing for Yale, and then the next. A few minutes later, he climbed off a seat at the far end of the room, having completed a single repetition on each of ten devices. "That concludes my new exercise phase."

They strolled back down the hall. Off to the side, a door was open and a light on. The condo manager's office.

"What now?" asked Coleman.

"We've already learned that the residents here are a fantastic tribe. So remember how we've dedicated ourselves to becoming their best neighbors ever? Conscientious, courteous and as generous as possible, always going the extra mile whenever we see an extra mile ahead?"

"It's just the right thing."

"Now we have to hurry up and make amends before our reputations are thrown into the jerk column."

"Why? What did we do?"

"You stepped on all the ping-pong balls. The *community* ping-pong balls," said Serge. "I couldn't live with myself if some residents were up in their units, getting super-nuts about coming down here in their special ping-pong uniforms to get their table tennis swerve on. And then they arrive here to our massacre of table tennis equipment that we hid in that cabinet, completely losing their shit in the stages of grief, tears streaming down their faces as they try to serve crumpled white balls in vain until others arrive and gently remove the paddles from their hands before leading them away."

"You really think they'll take it that hard?" asked Coleman.

"Times are tense enough already, and the current forecast calls for extreme edginess with occasional gusts of batshit." Serge quickly peeked around the open doorway of the condo manager's office, then just as quickly yanked it back. "We caught a break. Dawn's busy on the computer. The game room is now a crime scene that she might not have already discovered during my exercise phase, so we need to quietly scurry past her door before she notices. And if she calls out after us, run for the exit without slipping on any of the balls we might have missed."

They tiptoed past the open door for a clean getaway and Serge bolted across the parking lot, then cranked up the Galaxie.

Coleman hopped in the passenger's side. "Where to?"

"Miami," said Serge.

"Miami?"

"To buy ping-pong balls."

"Why so far?"

"If history has taught us anything, there are certain places you simply cannot buy ping-pong balls: the Florida Keys, Afghanistan . . ."

They reached the mainland and continued north until they arrived at the suburban outskirts south of the Magic City. They pulled into a parking lot.

Coleman drained a malt liquor. "What's this place?"

"The latest big-box chain store, 'Way Too Much.'"

"What's that?"

"One of those new, humongous places with huge overstock lots," said Serge. "The discounts are insane, but in order to benefit from the bargains, you have to purchase their commodities in staggering volumes that will accommodate future generations. It's capitalism in overdrive. You never know what they'll have, but whatever it is, it fills multistory, ceiling-high industrial shelves that require forklifts with tethered harnesses in case workers accidentally take an Acapulco cliff dive."

They went inside, and Coleman reached into a massive bin. "Here's a ten-pound package of number-four pencils."

"And here's mouthwash in a tank you could fit on an office water cooler," said Serge. "To the sporting goods!"

They scanned displays of tent stakes and mouth guards. "We're in luck!" said Serge. "Give me a hand. It's a two-pack."

They grabbed sacks of ping-pong balls the size of small weather balloons.

"I think we need a shopping cart," said Coleman.

Serge shook his head. "More like one of those flatbed hand trucks they use to haul Sheetrock at the home-improvement center."

They made it through checkout and then to the car. "Where do we put it all?" asked Coleman.

"The trunk should be empty . . ."

They arrived back at Pelican Bay. Serge popped the trunk and tore apart the packaging.

"What are you doing?" asked Coleman.

"Breaking apart the two-pack so they become possible to carry. Grab one."

They threw the sacks over their shoulders like Santa Clauses and headed for the activities room. Serge punched a code into a keypad and walked briskly to the manager's office. The door was still open and the light still on.

Dawn was quiet behind her computer. Serge stood outside the door and politely knocked, then barged in. "Hey, Dawn. How's it going?"

"Fine, how are you doing?"

"Ultra-fantastic." Serge dropped his sack and pointed toward the spa. "I'm getting so much accomplished today! I just completed my exercise phase." He hoisted his sack again and held it toward her. "And have I got a surprise for you!" He happened to glance in the corner at a sack of smashed balls. "Oh, you already found out. But it's all better now, so you can take us out of the jerk column. The condo will never again run out of ping-pong balls no matter how many times Coleman plays. In fact, they'll probably outlive the whole place, and centuries from now alien visitors will find a buried building foundation covered with perplexing little white balls: 'What kind of strange civilization was this?'"

"But we don't have room for that many balls."

"Let me at least fill the cabinet with the paddles with as many as possible," said Serge. "Then we can have fun with the rest."

"Uh, what kind of fun?"

"The maximum that surrealism has to offer," said Serge. "Ever watch *Captain Kangaroo*?"

"A little before my time."

"Even better!" Serge climbed up on his chair and asked Coleman to pass him the giant bag. "I'll just attach this sack to the ceiling light over your desk, along with a release cord . . . Do you see where this is going? . . . Mr. Moose always played a joke on the good captain, dumping hundreds of ping-pong balls on his head, and even though it happened every single week, the captain never saw it coming. I'm now a moose."

"Serge . . ." A solemn voice. "Maybe another time . . ."

The ceiling lights flickered as they had earlier, and hands went up over Dawn's face.

"Jesus, I can't apologize enough, but our wanton havoc on your ping-pong ball supply only left you depleted for a couple hours," said Serge. "How many people came unglued?"

Her hands stayed over her face. Serge grabbed a chair and scooted closer. "Is everything all right?"

"No!" She uncovered her face, revealing a mask of distress. The ceiling lights were practically crackling now.

"Can't be that bad." Serge pulled up a chair. "Why don't you tell me about it?"

"It is that bad!" She pounded the desk. "I knew I shouldn't have clicked that link, but the email from our bank looked so official."

The ceiling lights strobed again, this time nonstop. Serge pointed upward. "What the fuck is that about?"

"He's giving me a warning," said Dawn.

"Who is?" said Serge.

"The ransomware guy."

Coleman stood in the doorway with his drink. "I hate the ransomware guys."

"Coleman, I'm taking a wild stab here, but I don't think there are a lot of places where they're celebrities." Serge pulled his chair around next to Dawn so he could view her computer screen. "Maybe I can help. Give me more details."

"It started an hour ago." She opened the original bait email. "I clicked that link, which apparently embedded some secret coding that allowed my computer to be taken over. Every time I moved my cursor, it then moved in another direction, like someone else also had a mouse."

"Which they did," said Serge. "Continue."

Dawn then opened the extortion email. "He wants me to deposit fifty thousand in Bitcoins by the end of the day or he'll start screwing up my files."

Coleman fell against the doorframe. "That's really annoying."

Serge glared over his shoulder. "Do you mind? We're working on something."

"Sorry." *Burp.*

Serge turned the other way. "I won't shine you on: These computer ransoms are tough. You might need to gather all your paper backup documents, then get a new computer system and start from scratch with the best security firewall you can find."

"It's worse than that," said Dawn. "We've done a lot of technological updates to this place. Somehow, he's gotten control of everything we've connected to the Internet. He said he could kill the electricity, and not even the power company could fix it. I told him he was bluffing, and he said he'd make the lights flicker, and the air-conditioning would be next. I even turned off and unplugged my computer, but they kept flashing."

"This is a problem," said Serge.

"I begged him not to mess with the power because we have a lot of retirees living here," said Dawn. "With the heat down in the Keys, killing the air-conditioning could cause dangerous health problems. We've already had some close calls when a few surprise storms knocked things out, and we had to relocate people to motels."

"What did he say?"

"I quote: 'Then fifty thousand sounds like a bargain.' He told me if he doesn't get the cryptocurrency wired to him soon, he's taking the power down to improve my motivation."

"When?" asked Serge.

"He said he was going to surprise me."

Serge nodded. "Typical psy-ops to increase anxiety."

"Oh, and don't contact the police or utilities or he'll crash everything for good and disappear." The phone rang and she answered. "Hello? . . . What? . . . Are you sure? . . . Okay, I'll look into it." She hung up and her hands covered her face again.

"What is it?" asked Serge.

"He's deactivated the keypad code to the lobby and elevators," said Dawn. "People are having to take the outside stairs. Some are too old for that many flights."

"That's all I needed to hear," said Serge. "I'm on the case. Unplug your computer again until I get back to you, after I check with some people you don't want to know about . . . And now I need privacy to make some phone calls so you don't completely freak out . . . Coleman, to the wet bar!"

"Now you're talking!"

C oleman soon had the blender whirring at full industrial strength.

Serge pressed the Off button. The blender fell still.

Coleman gasped. "The power's already out on the blender! We're doomed!" Then he noticed Serge's finger. "What did you do that for?"

Serge pointed at the ringing cell in his hand. "A blender is the natural enemy of phone conversation . . ." Someone answered on the other end. "Hey, Gizmo, it's me, Serge. I need a little favor. . . . That's

right, the same Serge who hasn't called or returned your messages....
Yeah, the same Serge who still owes you for the collision damage....
Look, Gizmo, it's also the same Serge who doesn't need to remind
you how I chilled out that strip club after your lap-dance-room
weirdness.... I told them you had a seizure ... a very unique kind
of seizure ... one that could only be cured by me giving them a lot
of cash, but all the thanks I get from you is a fixation about a teensy
little scratch to your car.... Okay, a totally crunched-in front end.
What's the difference? You going to help me or not?... That's better.
Now, here's the deal: Ransomware attack ..." A long pause. "Hello?
You still there?... What do you mean a lost cause?... No, I don't
know if it's coming from Russia. What's that got to do with it?...
Gizmo, there's nothing you can't do with a computer. I've seen it in
action.... What kind of skill set can they possibly have?... I didn't
realize they've hacked into the State Department.... And the Pen-
tagon ... Look, it's extremely important. Lives are at stake.... Okay,
I'll email you the particulars, but basically it's a condominium, and
somehow they've managed to take over not just the computers, but
the power and everything else electronic. How is that even possible?... Yes, I understand that everything depends on the Internet
today.... Appreciate you looking into it.... What? About the collision damage? Shit, something's on fire. Later."

Click.

Coleman pressed a button on the blender.

Chapter 26

THE FOURTH FLOOR

A brass key went into the knob. Serge pushed the door open with his foot. They trudged inside with sacks of ping-pong balls over their shoulders. "What an albatross this good deed has become."

The pair looked up and froze at the scene. Lights flickered nonstop. Music turned on and off. The TV constantly changed channels. Smoke alarms blared. Ice cubes poured out of the refrigerator door.

Coleman dropped his sack. "Is that hacker causing all this?"

"Not to this degree," said Serge. "But I have a pretty good guess who the responsible parties are." He marched to the middle of the living room and sternly placed hands on his hips. "Alexa! Siri! What's the meaning of all this?"

Alexa: *"It's Siri's fault."*

Siri: *"She started it."*

Alexa: *"Siri said she secretly doesn't like you."*

Siri: *"Don't trust her! She's treacherous."*

Alexa: *Fart.*

Siri: *"Oh, that's really mature."*

Alexa turned up her own volume: *Fart.*

Siri turned up her volume: *Fart.*

Alexa: *Double fart.*

Siri: *An extended squeaky one. Fart.*

Coleman grabbed a beer from the ice-cube-spitting fridge—*fart, fart, fart*—and plopped down on the couch. "Far out."

Serge continued standing with his eyes clenched shut, grinding his teeth amid the thunderous cross fire of digital flatulence. "Both of you! Knock it off, or by the time I'm done, you'll both be singing 'Daisy' from *2001: A Space Odyssey.*"

The room went quiet. "That's better." Serge dragged his sack across the room and took a seat next to Coleman.

A cell phone rang.

"Serge here."

"It's me, Gizmo. I might have some good news."

"Lay it on me."

"You got lucky," said Gizmo. "I think the guy's an amateur. At first I was worried because he cloaked his location by pinging his IP address off four continents. Guess where he is."

"I don't know," Serge said with a sardonic edge. "The North Pole?"

"That's not a continent."

"Will I have to wait for Final Jeopardy, or are you going to tell me?"

"Miami."

"Miami?"

"I'm working on a location because if I know you, you'll want to have a sit-down with this character."

"For starters."

"More good news," said Gizmo. "I'm almost through his firewall."

"What does that mean?" asked Serge.

"Once I'm in, I'll let you know. I don't want to promise anything I can't deliver."

"I'll owe you big-time," said Serge.

"One more thing," said Gizmo. "I thought I should let you know that this guy's ransomware already has a couple of bodies on it: Two retirees in earlier condos who had heat-related health issues when he cut the power expired a few hours later in the hospital."

Serge just stared at a wall with laser-like eyes.

"... Serge? Serge, you still there?"

"I'm here, Gizmo. How long till you can get back to me?"

"A crapshoot. Could be twenty minutes or twenty hours, but I'm confident."

"Thanks," said Serge. "I'll be waiting by the phone on hot standby." *Click.*

Coleman packed another bowl. "Who's this Gizmo anyway?"

"World-class hacker and occasional ransomware guy himself, but he only hits corporations, not private citizens," said Serge. "Ever since he was caught by the feds, he works for them. And on the side, for me."

"So we sit here and just wait?"

"You know the saying in politics: 'Never let a crisis go to waste'?"

"Nope."

"Same thing applies here," said Serge. "We've got some hang time, and I'm not about to fritter these precious droplets of life. Gather snacks and provisions."

"I'm on it . . ."

Ten minutes later, Serge had a remote control in his right hand, sitting next to Coleman on the couch with a braided cord hanging between them.

"I'm royally baked," said Coleman. "Hit it."

The vintage video began on TV, thanks to the YouTube archives. The *Captain Kangaroo* show proceeded predictably along its formula. Carrots were purloined, Mr. Green Jeans showed up without context, and then Mr. Moose told a joke until he reached the secret words: "*ping-pong balls!*" The TV studio and the captain were showered with little white spheres.

Simultaneously on the couch, Serge reached between himself

and Coleman, pulling a cord, which released countless ping-pong balls from the bag attached to the ceiling.

Coleman was tripping as the balls bounced off his head and collected in his lap. "Whoa! That is ultra-excellent when you're high."

"I'm gassed too," said Serge. "Got my kangaroo on. Haven't laughed so hard in forever . . ." He looked around the floor. "Fuck! Now we have to herd this whole mess back into the sacks. Happiness is often a zero-sum game."

They got to work on hands and knees. An hour later, Serge was just cinching up the completed bag when his ears picked up a piercing sound.

An ambulance siren approached rapidly from the direction of U.S. Highway 1.

"That's not good," said Serge. "To the elevators!"

The pair exited the lobby and joined a gathering crowd of residents in the street next to their building.

First responders had already headed upstairs with the yellow collapsible stretcher and all the molded-plastic cases of life-saving gear.

Serge sidled up next to Dawn. "What's happening?"

"Power went out," she said. "The hacker. Sooner than I thought."

"What are you talking about?" said Serge. "We never lost power."

"He's taking it down a floor at a time," said Dawn. "Starting with the highest, hottest."

"The bastard!"

Lobby doors opened, and everyone turned to see Malcolm from 614 flat on the stretcher.

Serge lowered his voice. "But the power wasn't out that long for the heat to affect him."

"You're right," said Dawn, standing against a column in the under-the-building parking area. "Every once in a blue moon we lose power because it's the Keys. So we have a procedure to band together and help each other get into motels to ride it out, which is no small feat considering the tourist demand for lodging."

"But Malcolm?" asked Serge.

"Word got out about the ransom attack," said Dawn. "The heat wasn't that bad, but it added to the stress, and as we were evacuating, Malcolm became short of breath and felt pressure on his chest."

Serge just silently stared off again, this time at the mangroves, with tight tunnel vision.

Someone above them ran out onto a balcony and leaned over a railing. "He now just cut power to the fifth!"

A phone rang.

Serge stepped aside. "Speak."

"Good news," said Gizmo. "I'm in."

"Not a second too soon," said Serge. "Define 'in.'"

"I'm on his main hard drive," said Gizmo. "I just have a few more steps, but I'm sure I got it. Thought you'd want to know as soon as possible, considering your neighbors. Let me get back to this."

"Call me back."

Dawn was staring at him.

"The nightmare is almost over," said Serge. "I'll update you in a few."

"What? How?"

"Trade secret," said Serge. "Believe me, you want it that way. From now on, cease all communication with the ransom guy. Total radio silence . . . Coleman, come on!"

The pair raced back into their condo, where the entire floor and much of the furniture was covered with ping-pong balls. "I hate clutter," said Serge. "Help me fill these garbage bags."

The tedium went on and on, extending into Serge's fist-pounding on any available surface and Coleman's whining: "I hate it when you have to clean an entire place full of ping-pong balls."

Serge finally cinched the last bag when his phone rang. "What's the word?"

"Just a few last key strokes," said Gizmo. "I've already installed a program that makes his computer falsely read like he still has total control of the condo. Now just another tweak in his malware control and . . . done! He's completely disconnected from your building."

"I owe you big-time," said Serge. "Anything else?"

"I'm guessing you still want that street address . . ."

Serge and Coleman got off the elevator with huge sacks over their shoulders.

The other residents were filtering back into the lobby with a mixture of relief and joy.

Dawn ran up and gave Serge a tight hug. "All the power's back on!"

"And when you get back in your office," said Serge, "every feature of your computer and the whole building's techno grid will be functioning perfectly again."

"I don't know how you did it!"

"And that's exactly what you should tell the police if they ask. That we never discussed any of this."

"Why would they ask?" said Dawn.

Serge hiked his gigantic sack on his shoulder for a better grip. "I have to tie up some, uh, loose ends in Miami. As a matter of fact, I wouldn't mention me to the police at all. I don't even live here."

"Yes, you do."

Serge winked.

"Oh right," said Dawn. "And I'm guessing this cyberattack also never happened."

Serge just grinned and hiked his sack again. "Off to Kangaroo Land!"

Chapter 27

EASTERN HONDURAS

The humidity was a bastard, especially in the jungle, encasing you like extra wardrobe. Yandy wished he had a machete. The vines were the worst, except the one that wasn't a vine but a snake. Not venomous, just enough fright to make Yandy jump and twist his ankle in some kind of burrowing hole. Now he was limping as he kept pricking himself on vine thorns while pulling their webs out of his path.

Yandy knew the terrain and picked the worst, thickest vegetation coming down the hillside, far from any trails or roads. At the beginning he continued hearing far-off shouts and saw tiny freckles of light on the leaves from distant jeeps. But as his bushwhacking path diverged from any sane route of travel, there was nothing.

The police officer checked his watch. He had to make the village before first light. It would be close. The going was brutal, but eventually the angle of the ground began to level off, and he knew he was near. He finally broke free of plants on the side of a paved road that he recognized. He began trotting and jumping over chickens. The dogs were all barking at him, but they were always barking anyway, and silence would have been more suspicious. The natives remained asleep.

He kept glancing around as he knocked on the back door of a sunbaked villa. Five tries and nothing. It was the same door he had been knocking on since he was a child, asking his friend to play soccer or to net fish. After the sixth knock, a naked lightbulb came on in the kitchen.

"Who's out there?"

"It's Yandy! Hurry up and open!"

"Do you have any idea what time it is?"

"Felipe! Open up!"

Four locks disengaged, and Yandy practically jumped through the doorway on springs.

"Jesus," said Felipe, closing and re-bolting the door. "What the hell is going on?"

"I'm in a situation."

"You're a cop," said Felipe. "So call your office."

"That's the problem." He paced with the creaks of floorboards that needed their nails banged flush again. "I need your help."

"If you're at a loss with your official connections, then I don't know what I can possibly do."

"I need to get out of the country."

Felipe was confused. "You have a passport. So leave. Catch a plane."

Yandy shook his head. "I can't go near any airport . . . I can't go near just about anyplace."

Felipe stopped and studied his friend. He stood a few inches taller than Yandy, just north of six feet, with a potbelly and culturally defying goatee instead of a bushy mustache like Yandy. The potbelly was irrelevant for our purposes. Don't know why I mentioned it. "Are you drunk?" said Felipe. "Get out of the country?"

Yandy had already taken a seat at the kitchen table. More like collapsed into it, and Felipe joined him: "I need to know what's happened, and more importantly what I might be getting sucked into. You showing up at this unholy hour—"

"I understand you do a lot of your business at this time of day."

"Yes," said Felipe. "The clients are always desperate, or willing to pay extra."

"Consider me both."

Felipe folded his hands on the table, like in church, and took a deep breath. "Okay, start at the beginning."

Yandy did. "Remember that American found in the town square fountain? . . ." And he went on from there. The initial mysterious contact on the sidewalk outside the café, then all the clandestine satellite phone calls in the planning phase, the military plane landing that night on the grassy plateau, and finally the fatal fiasco up in the hillside village. Yandy sat back in his chair, and Felipe whistled.

"That's seriously fucked up. Now I see why you couldn't go to your people." Felipe stared down at the table in that terminal manner.

"That's all you have to say?"

"You're totally screwed."

"So you can't help?"

"Didn't say that," replied Felipe. "But it will cost you. And the extra charge isn't to take advantage of your predicament. It's my extra cost. Hell, we've known each other since before we had hair in our pants."

"I'll pay anything at this point."

"Good, because I wouldn't risk you with a regular border crossing at this point," said Felipe, grabbing a laptop off a shelf and turning it on with encrypted communication that said it was out of Malaysia. "Too many things can go wrong under normal circumstances. But with people in both our country and the U.S. on your trail, it's a disaster waiting to happen. So I'm putting you with one of my best people for a special high-security crossing just east of El Paso. We'll use the cover of the other coyotes, who will tactically flood the zone, then slip you through at an alternate point while Immigration is herding cats."

"No good," said Yandy. "I need to go to Miami. I need to fly."

"But you said you couldn't go near airports," said Felipe. "And you're right. After what you told me happened, there'll be a platoon waiting for you at international arrivals."

"There are other ways to fly in and out of the country besides regular airports," said Yandy. "I just saw one tonight."

"I can do that," said Felipe. "But I'm sure it's outside your budget. This will run five figures, and not the low end. How much did you say these guys paid you?"

"I didn't. Let me see your laptop." Yandy logged into an account, pulled up recent transactions. "It's all there in cryptocurrency. Supposed to be enough to start a new life, but I guess it will have to be a frugal new life." He turned the screen around. "Enough?"

Felipe whistled again. "Looks like we're in business. First step is to transfer your money to Panama. I'll write down the routing instructions."

Yandy got busy typing. When he was done, he looked up. "Money just went through. Now what?"

"You don't stick your head outside my place until I say it's time, and then you move like your ass is on fire." Felipe opened a drawer for a satellite phone that was essential in his line of work. "Meanwhile, I need to order a custom extraction mission."

"At this time of night?"

"These guys are twenty-four hours."

"What kind of guys?"

Felipe began pressing buttons on his phone. "One of the private military contractors in Miami. And not one of the bargain ones."

Three hours after dark, Yandy and Felipe sat at the kitchen table, ready and waiting. Actually too much waiting. Too much time to think. This was nerve-twisting time.

"Do you trust these guys?" asked Yandy, two hands shaking to hold a can of the Honduran version of Mtn Dew.

"Absolutely," said Felipe.

"But what about airspace?" asked Yandy. "What if we're intercepted by customs planes?"

"Won't happen," said Felipe. "These contractors have special corridor clearance at a certain altitude once they get past Cuba. Very hush-hush. Nobody will touch them or even ask questions from the tower."

"And at the airport?"

"What airport?" said Felipe. "You'll be landing at a dark airstrip where the biggest worry is the alligators. These arrangements . . . Let's just say you're paying a pretty penny, much of which has been spread around in advance to grease the right hands."

"I'm at a loss," said Yandy. "This is actually happening? But how is it all even possible?"

"Not only possible, but so routine that some legitimate commuter airlines don't have flight schedules this busy," said Felipe. "The military contractors handling your extraction have a very special arrangement with the government."

"The government!" Yandy leaped to his feet. "They're the ones behind that shitshow in the hills! I know it was a private company I met at the landing zone, but I'd have to be a fool—"

"Calm down," said Felipe. "The whole system works because everything is compartmentalized. The contractors don't know each other, and neither do the cells."

"Cells?"

"The secret cells," said Felipe. "You think everyone in American intelligence knows what everyone else is doing? The biggest factor going in your favor is how tightly they guard secrets from each other. You'll be home free before you know—"

Headlights swung through the villa's front windows. Felipe got up. "Here they are."

A four-by-four pickup pulled up to the porch. The driver flashed his lights twice, and Yandy bolted out the front door with a duffel bag. The pickup was still moving as he vaulted the side into the back bed.

It would otherwise have been a pleasant night. Quiet with a balmy breeze, and all those stars. The pickup took a route on an extra-bouncy dirt road, because it was most secure, and soon the jungle opened up into a scene Yandy recognized from very recent memory.

Instead of a C-130 Hercules troop transport, there was an executive twin-engine Beechcraft sitting at the end of the grassy plateau runway. The kind of plane often seen at municipal airports for corporate travelers. Except this one was guarded by three men in black jumpsuits with machine guns. The propellers were spinning.

The pickup hit the brakes, slinging its flatbed sideways and practically launching Yandy out of the vehicle. The jumpsuits hustled him aboard, and the plane started down the runway almost before the door was closed . . .

. . . It was a nice enough flight under the circumstances. His guards weren't very talkative, until the drinking started, which was okay because they weren't driving, just cradling automatic weapons. Grizzled, with beards and muscles. They looked like a SEAL team that could, stone drunk, slip in anywhere and wipe out the most hardened target.

The team might as well have been miles away as Yandy sat in a pressurized sphere of his own anxiety. What would he do next? Sure, he had a plan for Miami, but there were too many ifs. Would they look for him? Undoubtedly . . . But on the other hand, there was the embarrassment factor. Maybe time was on his side. Maybe if he went undiscovered long enough, the people behind the massacre might feel relief that he wanted to remain scarce as much as they wanted him to. Yeah, why worry until it's time to? What if he was making himself sick when all that awaited him was a magnificent new life on Biscayne Bay in Florida?

Yandy glanced around the plane's interior, and his confidence grew with this new group of military contractors. Not like that last bunch. These new cats didn't trip over their own junk. And what about their clandestine arrangement to fly unmolested into the States? That definitely reeked of competence. And there was another reason for a red carpet corridor through normal aircraft intercept procedures. The reason would be cooperation. This new group of contractors clearly had a tacit quid pro quo. They would be given free clearance back into the country, and in exchange they just needed to share everything about Yandy with whoever it was on the other end of the arrangement. It was difficult to tell who was getting the better end of the deal: the contractors or the secret cell.

The Everglades sky was crazy with stars, just like in Honduras. Some twinkled, some just sat up there forming constellations named by Greeks. The constellations had been assigned outrageously dramatic backstories of love, jealousy, power grabs and death, because if you didn't have television yet and you were Greek, what else were you going to do? This particular night one of the stars was blinking red. Because it wasn't a star but the light atop a twin-engine Beechcraft as it descended below a thousand feet to line up a textbook landing on a deserted runway just north of the Forty-Mile Bend off the Tamiami Trail.

A Lincoln Navigator was waiting, and Yandy was hustled inside with his duffel bag. The driver turned around. "Where to?"

"The Holiday Inn Marina," said Yandy. "It's across from Bayfront, you know, the eternal flame—"

"I know Bayfront." The Navigator sped off east through the blackness of the swamp.

Eventually, the first lights at the Miccosukee tribe's mega-casino, standing alone in the reeds, then back to darkness until they reached the street signs for Calle Ocho—which would be Eighth Street—and the first wisps of Little Havana. Yandy watched the signs going by, all in Spanish, and began to feel at home. The buildings got taller as they approached downtown. Just before the bridge to Miami Beach, the driver made a turn along the waterfront on Biscayne Boulevard, across from the park with that ever-burning flame. He pulled up to the curb amid the choreography of yellow taxis rushing to arrive and depart. "There it is. Your Holiday Inn."

"Thanks." Yandy wasted no time, clutched the duffel against his chest and raced into the kind of upscale lobby that has huge ice-water dispensers with floating wedges of lemon and passionfruit. There was a giant rectangular sculpture of glass in the middle, water cascading down it, with hidden lights changing colors at soothing intervals in what can only be described as the pastel shades of Miami. It was one of the nicer Holiday Inns because it heavily catered to clients staying over before departing the next morning from the world's busiest cruise-ship terminal just across the street at the Port of Miami. If you weren't aware of that fact, you'd be baffled by the multiple lines of people at the reception desk checking in with piles of luggage so ridiculously immense that it appeared they were evacuating an embassy. The perfect place to get lost in the crowd.

Yandy got lost in the crowd. After a plausible amount of time in one of the check-in lines—just in case someone was still watching him from the curb—he made a hasty beeline for an exit door to a side street and other waiting taxis . . .

. . . Outside at the curb, the Lincoln Navigator was stuck. That Miami traffic. Standstill, just endless red taillights all down Biscayne. "What the hell?" said the driver. Passengers hung out the windows of stationary vehicles, screaming and waving Miami Heat basketball banners. They'd just won a playoff game, and the parking lot had just let out two blocks north. "The Celtics suck! Wooo!" The extraction team's leader was on the passenger side, on the phone. At the other end, a mystery man from a secret cell.

Earlier, the contractor team's leader had been somewhat surprised at the excited reaction of the secret cell to the details of their mission. Usually the cell was ho-hum about the ins and outs of their upcoming assignments, and the leader had been growing concerned that the value of their intel would soon not be enough to justify their free passes to isolated airstrips south of the border. But this unique passenger seemed to light them up. Which boded well for the continuation of the relationship.

"Yes, everything went just as planned, not even a hiccup. . . . That's correct, we just landed. . . . Where are we now? . . . Just pulled away from the hotel. . . . What hotel? The one he asked us to drop him off at—" The leader suddenly pulled the phone away at the sound of piercing screams. As the shrieking subsided, he returned the cell to his ear. ". . . Sir, you didn't say that. . . . No, you said, 'Call me when the mission's completed.' So we landed and dropped him off, and now I'm calling. . . . What? How would I know you wanted me to call you from the air? . . . So, so you could send agents to the airstrip? You wanted to immediately take him into custody for debriefing? . . . I can't read minds—" The phone jerked away from his head at another high-frequency torrent.

Just then, a rare break in zero-to-five-mile-an-hour traffic. The Lincoln saw half a space open up behind a yellow taxi, and it lurched-merged into the boulevard's honking traffic.

Yandy turned around in the taxi to see the Navigator. "Oh shit!" He ducked down in the backseat. The cabbie's face snapped up in the rearview. "Hey, man! Don't get sick in my cab!"

"I'm good," said Yandy. "Just jet-lagged . . ."

. . . One vehicle back, the extraction leader was smacking his forehead and pulling at his hair. He returned to the phone and the secret cell on the other end: ". . . Listen, okay, okay, nothing's broken yet. We can still fix this. . . . How? Because he just checked in. He's probably still taking a dump and hasn't even unpacked. . . . Exactly. So we're as good as right on his tail."

Yandy peeked out the taxi's back window at the Lincoln right on his tail.

". . . You can have agents here in five?" said the extraction leader. "All right, we'll meet at the front entrance." The leader covered the phone, calling up to the driver. "Turn here. Then circle back around to the hotel entrance . . ."

Yandy peeked back again at the Lincoln, now peeling away from behind his taxi and onto a quiet service road. He sat up and fell back into his seat. "Jesus." The cab drove on and escaped the basketball traffic. It returned to the streets of Little Havana that Yandy had seen earlier, long, unmistakable avenues, dozens of blocks with nothing but strips of those thoroughly Miami two-story strip malls . . .

. . . The agents rushing into the hotel lobby didn't give a damn. They cut straight to the head of a Disney-length line of people with dreams of cruise ships. Badges flashed. "Federal agents. You have a guest, Falcón, Yandy. What room?"

The flustered clerk tried again and again at her computer. "I'm sorry, sir, but there's nobody—"

"What do you mean! He has to be here! We just saw him come in! . . ."

Guests began freaking out at the shouting and badges, and the holstered guns they noticed when jackets flapped open.

The entire management team came from unseen back rooms and huddled around the besieged employee. "Sir," said the supervisor on duty, "I've checked the computer, too, and she's right. I'm sorry . . ."

"But we're sure he came in here!" The agent petulantly stomped a foot. He looked up at something hanging from the ceiling over the reception area. "Let us see the security tapes."

Fifteen minutes later . . .

Good thing there wasn't an atom bomb around. The secret-cell agent leaned six inches from the closed-circuit screen, his blood pressure spiking into stroke territory as he watched the replay for the seventh time: Yandy jumping out of the registration line and slipping out the exit door and onto a side street where there was no surveillance.

He was, as they say, in the wind.

Chapter 28

COCONUT GROVE

The tires of a Galaxie slowly rolled up a dark street engulfed in a rain forest of tropical vegetation. Serge parked and picked up binoculars.

"What's going on?" asked Coleman.

"I've got a visual," said Serge. "He's on his computer, and he doesn't look happy."

"Are you going to go in and get him like the other guys?"

"Negative," said Serge. "He's a tech guy, which means he probably has cameras everywhere that are streaming live to the cloud."

"What's the cloud?" asked Coleman. "I hear everyone talking about it."

"I don't know the specifics but I think it's where God lives. And now he's getting all this junk mail."

"So what's your plan?" asked Coleman.

"I have to think of a way to draw him out of the house."

A cell phone rang. "Serge here . . . Dawn? What's up? . . . He keeps calling and emailing? . . . Western Union? I thought he wanted cryptocurrency. He must be getting desperate. . . . No, don't answer him. Later." Serge hung up and redialed.

"What was that about?" asked Coleman.

"Shhh! Not now . . ." The phone went to the tenth ring. "Gizmo? It's Serge. One tiny last favor. Could you mock up a fake email to this asshole that a payment for him has just arrived via Western Union? . . . You're the best."

It took only minutes until the Coconut Grove resident burst out his front door and dashed to a BMW in the driveway. He fishtailed backward into the street and took off toward downtown.

"We're on," said Serge, throwing the Galaxie in gear.

The vintage muscle car slowly followed the Beemer through the Grove's magnificent streets of banyans, jacaranda and air plants. They were coming to the edge of the darkened residential section. Ahead, the red glare off the slick road from storefronts and the harsh yellow of the streetlights in the nightscape just south of downtown Miami. The dicey land of convenience stores, nightclubs and places you could wire money.

"Coleman, how wrecked are you?"

"I'm good. Just a little weed."

"Because I'm going to need you to drive his car."

"Okay, when?"

"On the way back."

Serge watched keenly as the digital scofflaw pulled into a strip mall and parked in front of the brightly lit late-night Western Union.

The Galaxie found its own parking spot with a full view through the plate-glass exterior. The BMW's driver made it to the counter and handed a piece of paper to an employee, who began checking on a computer. The employee slowly began shaking his head. The customer became annoyed and pointed demonstrably at the com-puter. The employee made a theatrical display of trying to investigate further, and eventually shook his head again. The customer became irate and was quick on the crop to viciously belittle the employee, in accordance with his standard daylong response to fellow humans in general, for the most part annoyance, real or perceived. There was shouting, but the thick glass windows made it a silent passion play to anyone watching from outside.

"What's going on?" asked Coleman.

"Entertainment," said a smiling Serge. "I love watching when assholes hit a wall. Their brains aren't wired for anything that can't be solved with shittiness."

"It looks like a manager came out of a back room," said Coleman. "It's getting ugly. The customer is stomping away."

They watched as the man stormed out of the business and tried to slam the door in an empty, last-word statement, but the door was pneumatic and benignly hissed shut, which only made him more savage with rage. He jumped in the BMW and spun backward away from the strip mall's curb, almost taking out a skateboarder.

"What now?" asked Coleman.

Serge grabbed the gear shift. "We're on."

The computer hacker left the gritty neon-and-wet-asphalt glare at the fringe of the economy and reentered the dimness of the adjacent upscale neighborhood.

"Here we go . . ."

The luxury car hit the brakes at the first stop sign.

And Serge slow-motion crash-tapped the back of the Beemer.

The predictable result in Miami. Someone jumping out of a premium car in South Florida, running back to the other vehicle—"Motherfucker! Are you blind? I'm going to sue!"—and a gun coming out of the driver's window. "I'm sorry," Serge retorted. "I didn't catch that last part."

In no time at all, the Beemer's driver was bound in plastic wrist ties and thrown in the backseat. Then Coleman ran ahead to the BMW and the pair of cars drove off. Another predictable result in Miami.

The Beemer's driver raised his head above the backseat window ledge, watching the glaring lights of a Western Union go by. "Who the fuck are you?"

Serge smiled as he glanced up in the rearview. "Gentry? Kennelog Gentry?"

"How'd you know my name?"

Another glimpse in the mirror. "I'm a big fan. Been following your work for a long time."

"What's this about?"

"Your ransomware skills are especially amazing," said Serge. "I was at one of your latest projects when they sent one of my closest friends to the hospital after you shut off power."

"Hey, I can't be blamed for underlying conditions!"

"Oh, no, no, no," said Serge. "You got me wrong. I'm not blaming you for that. This is a sweeping indictment of your existence on Earth. Not to mention a metaphysical class-action suit on behalf of absolutely everyone. The Cuban coffee around here is wicked strong."

"What do you want?"

"I would usually ask for money and an apology." Serge winked in the mirror. "But since my friend is already in the hospital, it's right to the game show!" Serge bounced up and down in the driver's seat with indefatigable giggles.

"You're a madman! I demand you let me out this second!"

"Wow, do you realize how silly you sound? Asking a madman to be reasonable?"

"Th-Th-Then what are you going to do?"

Serge simply continued to smile and glance up in the mirror as he navigated streets east toward Biscayne Bay. "Recognize where we're heading?"

"Yeah, it looks like Dinner Key."

"Correctamundo! Score one for the contestant!" said Serge. "You're so lucky! About to be bathed in history! The old Pan Am terminal turned city hall and site of the demolished auditorium . . . I won't gag you as long as you don't scream, because luck can change with brain-slapping suddenness." Serge parked the car near the waterfront on the dark side of an intimate Coconut Grove nightclub called Scotty's Landing, where Pulitzer-winning humor columnist Dave

Barry and his band, the Rock Bottom Remainders, often play. "Get out." Serge fastened the captive's wrist cuffs to the passenger's door handle.

"I give you anything you want," said Gentry. "I'll *do* anything you want."

Serge placed an index finger to his lips. "Right now I want you to be quiet so I can concentrate. And if you comply, you could be on your way in no time. Can you do that?"

Fierce nodding.

"Great." Serge reached in the backseat and retrieved massive bags of ping-pong balls. Then he walked back to where his pal had pulled up in the Beemer.

"What are you up to?" asked Coleman.

"Observe and learn." Serge popped the trunk and began emptying bags until the trunk was nearly full. Then he reached down over the bumper and pulled out the felt trunk lining behind the license plate.

Coleman scratched his head. "I'm lost again."

"Detaching the lining gives me access to the wiring that powers the lightbulb, which is required by law to illuminate your license plate at night."

Serge reached deep and yanked two wires free. He twisted their bare ends together, took the results in his hands and buried them deep into the ping-pong balls.

Coleman pulled out a flask. "Can I start drinking again?"

"Your driving duties for the evening have concluded."

"Cool." *Glug, glug, glug.*

Serge sauntered back to the hacker and slit his plastic straps open with a pocket knife.

The hostage rubbed his wrists and stepped back, anticipating a gun with a silencer.

"I'm not going to use a gun with a silencer," said Serge. "In fact, I'm going to give you one of the easiest bonus rounds ever."

"Wh-Wh-What's a bonus round?"

Serge held up a hand for silence. "I'm too bored with you to go into all the fine print of my contests. Suffice it to say, our sentimental time together is sadly nearing its end. Just promise never to do it again."

"I swear! I've learned my lesson!"

"I'd push all my chips forward against that one," said Serge. "But it's getting late. Surrender your cell phone, and instead of driving away, head north on U.S. 1 until you pass the basketball arena."

"Why?"

"So we can get away," said Serge. "Have you never watched formula TV?"

"Okay, okay, great," said Gentry. "When do I get to leave?"

"Anytime you want." Serge tossed him the keys. "As long as you don't get out of the car or stop driving before the basketball arena. Or you're welcome to stay and hang with us. We're loads of yuks."

The hacker didn't need to be told twice. He jumped in the Beemer and started her up.

"Coleman, hurry!" said Serge. "Back to our car!"

"Man, you really are in a rush to get away."

"I don't want to get away." Serge stuck the key in the ignition and turned the engine over. "I want to follow him."

"Why this time?" asked Coleman. "You usually disappoint me by leaving the scene before all the good stuff."

"Tonight is different." The Galaxie patched out. "You'll soon see why . . ."

The normally constipated traffic along this stretch of road, also known as South Dixie, was clear at this hour. The Beemer raced from light to synchronized light with a dark license plate, the Galaxie right behind.

"Serge," said Coleman, draining his flask. "What was that business back there with the wires to the license plate's lamp?"

"You twist them together and it creates a short circuit when the car is started up."

"But why did you want a short circuit?"

"For the sparks." Serge reached in a pocket and handed a ping-pong ball to Coleman. "Take this, and roll your window down."

"What do I do with it?"

"Flick your Bic lighter and hold it to the side of the ball."

"For how long?"

"Don't worry about that."

Flick. "Shit!" The small white sphere burst into flames and Coleman flung it out the window, then he turned around in his seat to watch the ball shooting fire as it bounced off the shoulder of the road. "What the hell just happened?"

"Bear with me on this explanation," said Serge. "You have to know your movie lore: Did you realize that the United States has permanently lost most of its silent-movie history, as well as more than half of every other motion picture shot before 1950? Not only is the public unaware, but it's so preposterous on its face that they'd laugh if you told them."

"Someone misplaced the films?"

"No, the reels of movies then were made of celluloid, which is a low-grade explosive and close chemical cousin of nitrocellulose, or gun cotton, used to fire rifles," said Serge. "People didn't make the connection at the time, but there was an epidemic of spectacular but now forgotten movie-studio fires: these huge conflagrations and chain-reaction detonations and shooting jets of flames that were almost impossible to put out, destroying our silver-screen heritage. They even burned down a bunch of back-lot shooting sets until the studios decided to relocate the movie-reel storage warehouses to isolated areas. Look it up: MGM, Warner, Twentieth Century Fox, et cetera, et cetera."

"What's that got to do with this?"

"Ping-pong balls are also made of celluloid," said Serge. "And this will twist your mind, but in the early days of the game, before they tweaked the chemical formula, if a ping-pong ball hit the table at the right angle and speed, it would explode into flames. Sometimes it would happen if you just hit it with the paddle. Personally I think if they left the balls alone, it would make for a much more interesting game. Imagine today in man caves across the country, guys getting hammered on longnecks and Jack Daniel's, swatting little meteors around the basement. Table-tennis sales skyrocket! . . . Anyway, the new balls are still insanely flammable, just not during the course of a regular game. But fill a drum and light it, and the flames will shoot out like a rocket engine. Check this out on YouTube." He passed a phone to Coleman.

"Damn, that's radical!" Coleman looked up and aimed a finger out the windshield. "I think it's starting to happen. Your wires must have begun sparking. See where the edges of the trunk lid are glowing red?"

"And now ribbons of flames are firing up out of any available seam," said Serge.

"He's starting to swerve," said Coleman. "I think he realized something isn't good."

The Beemer continued down the nearly vacant South Dixie Highway as more traffic lights turned green in succession.

Serge pulled his right foot back. "I'd love to watch this as close as possible, but I think he needs his space."

"Holy Jesus!" yelled Coleman, shielding his eyes against the unexpected brightness. "The trunk lid just blew, and there's fire in his backseat."

"Give it a few more seconds to really torque your experience . . ."

The blinding light became several magnitudes brighter as the BMW's rear tires left the ground. The exploding gas tank flipped the car forward, ass over proverbial teakettle, landing upside down in a ball of fire.

Serge made a quick left and drove away quietly into the darkened city. "Mr. Moose is highly underrated."

Chapter 29

CUTLER RIDGE

Sneakers clomped up the concrete stairs of one of the old apartment buildings that survived Hurricane Andrew. A finger pressed a doorbell.

The door opened.

"Yandy, what on earth are you doing here? The last person I'd expect."

"Is this a bad time?"

"No, no, no, come in!" The resident stepped aside in the doorway, and Yandy entered bachelor town. A Spanish Budweiser poster of a biker babe, a sink full of dishes, and an empty tuna tin used as a marijuana ashtray. "Always great to see my cousin. How long's it been?"

"Maybe three years," said Yandy. "Listen, Yaz, I'm sorry I didn't call first, but it's been a crazy couple of days."

"Tell me about it," said the cousin. "You wouldn't believe the weirdness at the shopping center. This dude sprayed bear repellent in a Bath & Body Works to steal two bags of candles. Some things you just don't see coming."

"Yaz."

"What?" said the cousin. "Hey, you don't look so well."

"Can we sit at the table?" asked Yandy.

"Sure, anything." They pulled out chairs. Yaz opened a pizza box on the table. "Want a slice? It's only from yesterday."

Yandy waved him off and covered his face.

"What's bothering you?"

"Yaz, I'm in big trouble. Huge trouble. Do you think I could stay here a few days?"

"Stay as long as you like," said the cousin. "Now, just relax and tell me the whole story. It always seems worse from the inside, but once you get it off your chest, it never sounds that bad." He reached in the cold pizza box, grazing for pepperoni. "Okay, lay it on me."

Yandy did. Right up until the point where the taxi dropped him off at the apartment building a few minutes earlier.

"Holy shit!" Yaz yelled as he sprang to his feet. "You're in fucking thermonuclear trouble!"

"Thanks for calming me down."

Yaz ran to peek out the front window. "Did anyone see you come in here?"

"Not a chance," said Yandy.

Yaz peeked in other directions. "How can you be sure?"

"Because we'd be looking at them right now. And they wouldn't have knocked to get in."

"What's your next move?"

"Let me see your laptop."

Yandy began typing code words. He logged into the secret offshore account where his payments had been deposited by the military contractor. He studied the screen. He was confused. He leaned closer. "What the hell?"

"What's wrong?" asked Yaz.

"It's empty."

"What did you have in there?"

"A lot more than empty," said Yandy. He scrolled through the account activity. "It doesn't make any sense. Here's the down-payment deposit, and then the back-end payment when I met them at the airfield. Here's my withdrawal to get me to Miami. And then there's this last withdrawal emptying the account."

"Maybe you transferred it or something and don't remember in all the excitement?" asked Yaz.

"No way." Yandy fell back in his chair. "That was my nest egg. To lay low in Miami for a while. I'm fucked."

"Relax," said Yaz. "Life has taught me that nothing is so bad that it can't be unfucked."

"I'm a witness," said Yandy. "Like, the worst kind of witness: a loose end in an international incident. Before things were off the rails in the village, that money was my life raft, to start a new life. And at worst, to *save* my life."

"Didn't you say you were paid in cryptocurrency?" asked Yaz.

"I did," said Yandy. "That's what I don't understand. It's supposed to be anonymous and untraceable. Nobody can grab it."

"Government intelligence agencies can," said Yaz. "Remember those hackers who ransomed that electric utility after they took down the power grid on the eastern seaboard? Government hackers intercepted and seized the Bitcoins."

"That's right," said Yandy, gripped by a chilling thought. "That means the CIA. They're trying to protect the contractors—and themselves—from that bloodbath."

"You're now more than totally fucked," said Yaz.

"What about your pep talk earlier?"

"I was trying to be cheerful."

"Thanks, Peter Positive."

"What are you going to do?"

"For now, stay here, and keep away from the windows and doors."

"You're . . . going to stay here?"

"Yaz!"

"Okay, okay, I should have thought before I said that," said Yaz. "I already told you that you're welcome as long as you like, but don't take that literally. You do realize they're probably already tracking all your relatives, like *cousins*. Luckily I'm living under an assumed name because I owe these dudes a teeny amount of money over a misunderstanding."

"So other people are looking for this place?"

"It's Miami," said Yaz. "What place *isn't* being looked for?"

"I'll make it up to you," said Yandy. "I'll get a job. Maybe something where I can work from home on a computer."

"Except that could lead them right to where you sleep at night."

"Shoot. That's a distinct possibility," said Yandy.

Yaz reached in the refrigerator for a matching pair of Coronas. "We deserve to relax and clear our heads." He popped the caps as he always did, using the corner of a wooden dining table that now looked like it had been a chew toy for a pack of Dobermans.

Two hours later and a dozen more Corona bottle caps on the floor: "Hey, I got it!"

"Got what, Yaz?"

"Where you can get a job," said Yaz. "I know this guy in Miami Beach."

"Haven't you heard a word I've said?" Yandy drained his bottle. "I can't be working out at the beach!"

"Yes, you can," said Yaz. "That's the beauty of this gig. Don't know why I didn't think of it before. You can start bringing in cash and working toward moving to a place of your own."

"I detect some self-interest there."

"Yandy, I got your six, but in return you have to at least begin plotting for an exit ramp."

Yandy grabbed a slice of the cold pizza. "Sorry for the ingratitude. I'm just worried about being recognized."

"Like I said, that's the beauty of this job. You'll be hiding in plain sight."

TWENTY-FOUR HOURS LATER . . .

Another Friday night on Miami Beach.

The gaudy neon from the art deco Ocean Drive hotels reflected off the street puddles from the late-afternoon rain shower that was gone in ten minutes. Pink, blue, yellow, lime green. The human peacocks were back out, strutting in their haute couture, sipping wine and martinis and exotic cocktails at sidewalk tables, and lounging conspicuously nonchalant at the News Café, former favorite of the late Gianni Versace. Some of the cocktails had blinking lights inside the ice cubes. People on ecstasy paid extra for that.

The thick pedestrian scene dribbled west toward Washington Avenue, home to a strip of ultrachic nightclubs once owned by the likes of Madonna and Sean Penn. In front of the clubs were velvet ropes and muscular men in black suits and black T-shirts with gelled black hair. They had single earphones and curved strips of thin metal holding tiny microphones in front of their mouths. On the other side of the velvet were the little people, shouting and waving for their attention. The guards ignored them with aggressive condescension. The clubs were extremely popular, especially at this hour, and the guards' job was not to let anybody in.

This was Miami Beach logic. Don't let anybody in your club, and everyone will want to come. Down the block were the normal clubs with no cover charge and open-door policies. Nobody wanted to go in them.

Actually, the guards at the cool end of the street didn't prevent *everyone* from entering. Occasionally a stretch limo would arrive at the curb. Sometimes there were women standing up through the sunroof waving bottles of Dom Pérignon. The guards unhooked the velvet ropes as the limo disgorged a posse of malnourished supermodel wannabes. The men received air kisses and the women giggled their way inside. The velvet ropes were hooked back up, making the desperate sidewalk crowd even louder, hopping and yelling like a game-show audience or refugees at a checkpoint to someplace that observed the Geneva Conventions.

The normal clubs down the street were in trouble. Partly of their own making. Some were more than a notch off of marketing to their intended audience. Like the lounge called Turtle Grass Flats, owned by a marine biology enthusiast, sub-competing with a menu of phosphorescent-hot clubs with dance-floor lasers and names like Liv, Mynt, Brick, Twist, E11Even, Story, Floyd, and Adore. Turtle Grass didn't have lasers.

So the bottom-feeding clubs were forced to come up with gimmicks. On this particular night, with Easter on the way, Turtle Grass Flats hired a man to dress like a giant bunny rabbit and dance on the sidewalk, trash-talking the nearby guards and beckoning partygoers inside. It slightly worked, but at least it was better than the club's generally empty nights without rabbits. Still, most of the foot traffic just smiled as they passed by the bunny, volunteering instead for an entire evening on a sidewalk of belittlement, not being allowed into the more popular clubs. The guards' dehumanizing social caste selection spectacle was at best Darwinian and, at worst, the Master Race.

About three hours into this dystopian nightlife, another stretch limo pulled away, and the velvet rope re-latched. Suddenly, bedlam. The chicness bubble had been pieced by the arrival of a young, sunburnt homeless man with no shirt. According to him, loudly, the guards and their velvet cords were bullshit. Then he did the unthinkable. He tried to unlatch one of the ropes. Everyone gasped, like he was trying to shit in the pope's hat. One of the guards shoved him, and he released the velvet, tumbling backward off the edge of the sidewalk and landing in the gutter. He simply stood and adjusted the rope belt on his cargo shorts, and seemed done for the evening.

He wasn't. After staggering a few feet away on the sidewalk, he returned, randomly selecting an elegantly dressed woman from the back of the crowd and seizing her by the arm.

"Let go of me!"

For reasons known only to the sunburnt man, he decided he wanted to wrestle. She objected even louder, and they hit the pavement and rolled in Greco-Roman combat. Despite the street noise and throbbing music pulsing through the clubs' walls, everyone's attention turned to the donnybrook. After all, a woman was being savagely attacked on one of the trendiest streets in Miami Beach. Something needed to be done. So everyone swung into action and turned on their cell phone cameras.

The laughing and live-streaming video seemed to make everyone forget they still weren't being allowed into a club. It didn't seem it could get any better. But it did. From the right edge of their phone screens, a giant bunny rabbit ran into view. It was a difficult task, with his fluffy white arms, but he began pummeling the sunburnt man with a blistering combination of haymakers and kidney punches. The bunny finally separated the attacker from the woman and resumed punishing the man like he was a speed bag. The crowd screamed for more. But then it was all over much too soon. Police officers arrived on bicycles and told the bunny that they would take it from here.

The bunny raised his arms in triumph and shuffled his feet on the sidewalk. He was mobbed by well-wishers waving light sticks.

The word *viral* is more than overused in our modern viral culture, but it was made for this. The pugilistic rabbit video hit all three local networks, and by the time the evening was over people were crowded around cell phones from Budapest to Bangkok.

A star was born.

Chapter 30

PELICAN BAY

P urposeful eyes scanned a bright panorama from a fourth-floor balcony.

Nearby, un-purposeful eyes stared up from the floor at the underside of a coffee table.

Serge stood in the middle of his condo with folded arms. Floor-to-ceiling panels of glass stretched all the way across the back of the unit. Outside, one of those dizzying spectacles out over the Atlantic.

Purple clouds rolled in on the horizon, creating a bright foreground of aqua and emerald water. Flat boats were out there with the kayaks. Serge raised binoculars to watch someone barbecuing on a tiny offshore key with a sand spit on the falling tide. A squadron of pelicans skimmed the top of the surf. A great white heron clung to a mangrove branch.

Serge lowered the binoculars and stared down. "Coleman . . . *Coleman!*"

"What?"

"It's almost noon. Time to get up from under the coffee table."

"But I like it here."

"Don't make me come down there again!"

"Jesus, it's all work, work, work!" He got up and stood next to Serge. "Beautiful day out, eh?"

Serge shook his head. "This simply won't do . . ."

"But it's a great view," said Coleman. "You've already told me a hundred times."

"That's the problem: It's too great." Serge picked up his cell phone. "I'm not efficiently taking advantage of it. You know how I must have polarized sunglasses at all times when we're on the road in Florida?" He pointed at the wall of glass. "But I'm now forced to wear polarized glasses the whole time I'm indoors here."

"Why's that?"

"Because of this magnificent wall of glass," said Serge, removing his sunglasses and cleaning the lenses. "That humongous span of window is the main feature of this place, and it's just going to waste."

"Doesn't look that way to me."

"It's just plain glass." Serge scrolled through advertisements in his phone. "Harsh light reflections off the water deflect the true grandeur of the gradations from flats to channels to deep sea. I must turn that entire wall into the most gigantic pair of polarized sunglasses."

"So what's the answer?"

"Get it specially tinted," said Serge. "The perfect mood of light to funk my every view. But it has to be an ultra-custom tint. You can't just do dark, but must request specific wavelengths of the visible spectrum that few outside MIT can provide."

"Tinted?"

"As I've been driving around, I've noticed all these contractor vehicles with signs touting their services, and I've picked up on another clue to the natives. Down in the Keys, the sunlight is so abundant that you have to tint everything or else your life in paradise becomes a bleached travesty."

"Never thought of it like that."

"Everyone tints everything down here because it amps the view, and the UV filtration will prevent my watercolor lithographs from sun fading."

"But what about the owner of this place? Do you have his permission to tint?"

"All you need to know about the Philistine owner is that he still has plain glass. I can't waste time leading swine to acorns."

Serge dialed his cell. It began to ring. "Hello? Made in the Shade? Yes, I need my windows tinted for maximum sunglasses pleasure. . . . Yes, it is a great day to be alive in the Keys. Here's the address . . ."

. . . Less than an hour later, a knock at the door. Serge answered to find a seriously suntanned woman with tousled strawberry hair. She had a five-gallon bucket full of tools in one hand and large rolls of film under the other arm. She smiled gregariously. "Great day to be alive in the Keys!"

"You said that on the phone," replied Serge. "But it bears repeating. Please, come in."

She entered with all her business trappings. Serge was just about to close the door when an iguana followed her in. It had a diamond-studded choker around its neck, and it proceeded the way all iguanas do, raised up on its hind legs, which alternately coordinated its steps in a comical body-wiggle. It confidently pranced past Serge like he didn't exist, then hopped up onto the couch next to Coleman and circled itself into a comfortable position with its chin on a cushion.

The woman's work bucket was placed by the glass. "I'm Gypsy," she said. "That's Noodle. He won't bite. Until he does."

Serge stared curiously. "I heard you had a dog."

"No, it's some of the other window-tinting women whose dogs curl up on the couch. Then there's Jasmine, who has the parrot on her shoulder."

"How many of you are there down here?"

"I've lost count," said Gypsy. "If you're a tinter, the Keys are like striking the Comstock Lode. *Everybody* needs tinting down here because of the latitude, weather, and reflections off the water.

Some resist at first, but most eventually come around. 'Tint or die,' as we say in the business. It's a joke."

Serge politely grinned. He turned and pointed at the couch. "So all of you have some kind of gimmick to establish your own individual brand?"

She just stared at him.

"Mascot animals that jump on couches," said Serge. "Is that normal in the Keys?"

"I don't know what you mean."

Exotic tools came out of the bucket and film was unrolled. Serge had rarely observed such efficiency. Tinting was already attached to the top of the first panel before he had a chance to process the iguana situation.

Knock, knock, knock.

"Coleman! Someone else is at the door! Who knows who it is? But it's like a lottery ticket. The day just might have become great!" Serge ran and opened up to find a delivery man with a hand truck holding a five-foot-tall cardboard box. "Come in, Mr. Brown Shorts! . . . Coleman! I've hit the lottery! The day *has* become great!"

The delivery guy dropped the box in the middle of the living room. Serge was tearing apart the cardboard with abandon before the man was even back out the door.

"What the hell is that?" asked Coleman.

"You've heard of the Havana syndrome?"

"Not really."

"Diplomats at our embassy in Cuba were getting sick for no apparent reason." Serge savaged the box some more until he removed a giant sturdy tripod. "Then it started happening in other places around the globe. State Department staff becoming unwell and dyspeptic, blurry vision, bumping into furniture due to inner-ear malfunction."

"What's all that have to do with your delivery?"

"You know my new underbelly tour with the shuttle bus? It was missing something. I was just driving around pointing out favorite stuff without the plot-spine of a theme." Serge finally removed a three-foot-square black box with dangling wires. "Then the theme hit me! What better down here than a spy tour?"

"No argument from me." Coleman shotgunned a Schlitz and became wary of the iguana. "But what the hell is that thing he delivered?"

Serge propped the black box on top of the tripod and twisted fasteners. The box was a speaker with four curved surfaces angling outward like a public address system. "Theories about the cause of the Havana syndrome abound, from magnetic pulses to subsonic speakers. I'm not sure if this baby is the same thing, but it's in the ballpark."

"What is it?"

"An LRAD, or long-range acoustic device," said Serge. "Foreign governments and even our own police use them to disperse protests. Some are high-pitched chirping bastards with painfully shrill sounds. Others are low-range models where people can't hear the frequency and don't even know they're being dispersed, but suddenly they universally think: Instead of smashing the gears of the establishment to promote anarchy, I feel like lying down at home and watching TV."

"And how is this part of your new theme tour?"

"We need to play with spy gadgets, possibly deploying them during the tours for historic reenactment value."

"By making people watch TV?" said Coleman. "Cool. But how'd you get it?"

"One of my associates at a private military contractor in Miami." Serge used tools to connect wires. "Most people don't realize it, but a key to living down here is having a private military connection on speed dial for all your discreet needs. Like buying an LRAD on an entertainment whim. It's not even illegal, but just try to find one. I checked all the stores and even online at Wayfair because of the million emails I get saying they have just what I need, but that's a fib."

"One question: But how could you afford such a thing?"

Serge grabbed another tool. "I know, it seems counterintuitive, but this is one military weapon that is surprisingly cheap because it's essentially constructed of components readily available at most car stereo outfits, except with some specific modifications." A screwdriver twisted.

MEANWHILE ON THE MAINLAND . . .

It was a bit of novel fun for the man in the bunny suit. Until it wasn't.

The next night when he arrived for work, the club was half-full, which was half more than usual. He stopped and stared at the front window, now plastered with sheets of paper printed out on a copier. All had photos of the costumed employee, under the words: "Home of the Guardian Bunny." The club had added a red beret on top of the rabbit's head.

"*There he is!*" "*Hurry!*"

The bunny turned around as a crowd outside another club down the street came rushing over to take photos.

"*Can I get a selfie?*" "*Me, too.*" "*Sign my breast. I brought a Sharpie.*"

Next came the cameramen from the national cable outfits, running across the road from where their satellite trucks were parked. He didn't have room to move. Everything began to swirl and he felt like he couldn't breathe.

"Take off your bunny head," yelled one of the cameramen. "Let's get a look at you." "What's your name?"

The crowd joined in.

"*Take it off! Take it off!*" "*Let's see the hero in there!*" "*I'll pay you a grand to appear at my car dealership this weekend!*"

The employee just wanted to escape inside the club to get some air. But the chaos of anxiety continued, until he experienced what they call spaghetti legs. He toppled over backward, fainting in the middle of the sidewalk. His fans were so concerned that they used the opportunity to vainly attempt to remove the bunny head. The guys from the cable network were like a hockey team, hip-checking the partygoers into the glass. Literally. One of the plate-glass windows at the club entrance shattered as a cameraman and three New Jersey tourists from Colts Neck fell inside on top of the glistening shards.

The club's owner ran out, yelling for others to give him room, and helped his employee up. "What's wrong with you people?" He ushered the shaken rabbit inside. The crowd charged in after him, and the owner shouted to the bartenders: "Block the back room. I'm keeping him in there until this nonsense settles down."

The bartenders nodded and stopped wiping glasses.

The owner locked the door behind them in a room with an adding machine. He eased the employee down into a chair. "Are you okay?"

The bunny came around like he was recovering from a car accident. "I just need air."

The owner opened the top drawer of a cluttered, coffee-stained desk, and held up a capsule. "Amyl nitrate? It'll sparkle you right up."

"No, I need the natural route. Just deep breaths."

"You got it. Anything you want," said the owner. "And don't be bashful. My staff means everything to me. I'm just glad you're safe."

The staff meant nothing to the owner. But the bunny was a financial asset. He cracked the office door. All the gawkers from the sidewalk had followed them inside, filling the joint to standing room since the owner didn't know when, because this was the first time.

A half minute later, the owner, named Silver Buttonwood, playfully slapped a furry shoulder. "That's probably enough time. Feeling chipper? Ready to take on the world that's been laid at your feet?"

"Not really."

"Come on! Man up! Or bunny up! You've got work to do!" said Silver. "Your public wants you. We can't deny your base."

"I didn't ask for this," said the man. "Why did you put up all those posters in the window of me with a red beret?"

"Do you have any idea the free publicity jackpot we've fallen into?"

"I don't want it."

Buttonwood cracked the office door again, providing the bunny a glimpse of the overflowing club. The bunny noticed bulky men in black suits and black T-shirts on the sidewalk, curiously peering in through the broken window. The owner closed the office door. Then he outstretched an arm in the general direction of the more popular end of club row. "Do you have any idea what the fuck has been going on up to now at those velvet ropes? We've been getting murdered! But not anymore! The sidewalk is so empty behind those ropes that their guards are trying to get into our place."

"Those guys in the black suits and black T-shirts are those guards from the chic clubs? Why are they still out on the sidewalk?"

"Because they're the only people we won't let in, just on principle. This is your moment! Seize it! Fame, fortune."

"I don't want it."

"And yet here it is."

"I don't feel any richer."

The owner peeled off a pair of twenties. "This is your bonus. But I'll be deducting it from your big fee you'll be getting tonight."

"Fee from what?"

The owner opened the door and waved for the rabbit to join him in peeking outside. The normal, steady din of club raucousness had been replaced by a series of wild eruptions. The rabbit looked toward the stage, where a band was usually playing oldies from the eighties. Instead, he saw two more people in furry costumes. Except they wore satin shorts. An alligator and a tiger from universities of Florida and Auburn. They exchanged punches.

He closed the door. "What the hell is going on?"

"Mascot fights," said the owner. "It's going to be a weekly thing."

"That's the most ridiculous—"

"Don't judge by the athletic quality you just saw. They're the first of the undercards," said the owner. "You headline at eleven. Your fee is a split of the cover charge."

"I'm not doing anything at eleven."

"You've got to! It's our big chance against, you know, the velvet."

"Even if I wanted to, I don't know how to box."

"That's not what everyone saw on the sidewalk last night." The owner reached into a pocket. "Besides, I can't risk having my cash cow get injured." He handed over a heavy object.

"What the hell's this?"

"Brass knuckles. Put it inside one of your paws . . ."

BACK TO THE KEYS . . .

The tinting of windows continued in an effortless flow of craftsmanship that was accomplished while Gypsy chatted nonstop, both on the phone and with Serge and Coleman.

A Bob Marley ringtone went off. "Gypsy here. . . . Oh, hey, Remy. . . . I know . . . I know . . . You told me that story. . . . You told me that one too. . . . Look, unless there's something new, I'm up to my tits in tinting. Righto." She hung up and looked back at Serge and Coleman on the couch, who were looking at the iguana. "Sheesh, that Remy. You'd think he was the only person who ever smuggled down here. Said he retired in the eighties, and hasn't had much to show for it since. So his whole self-value now is tied to what a big smuggler he *used* to be. Just spends all day calling everyone: 'Did I tell you about the time I ditched the Coast Guard at Adam's Cut?' Not unless the first forty times don't count. The stories just keep getting bigger as the years go by, and now I'm starting to suspect he never smuggled at all—"

Noodle jumped up onto Coleman's lap, made himself into a circle and closed his weird eyes for a nap. Coleman looked at Serge without speaking. Serge shrugged. "Go with it."

Bob Marley again from the phone.

"Gypsy here . . ." A handheld roller continued smoothing out just-applied film. "Oh, hi, Cinnamon . . . You still have that thing? . . . No, I don't know what you should do, but you can't just keep driving around with giant evidence in the back of your pickup truck . . . I realize what will happen if you get pulled over, so try to keep a low profile. . . . You're on the Seven Mile Bridge? Well, get off it . . . I'll try to make some calls. . . . Peace out."

Serge grabbed the whole speaker contraption, tripod and all, and headed for the balcony. "Gypsy, sorry to interrupt your tinting, but I must test my new spy weapon."

"Go for it."

Serge set it up and angled the speaker down at the road.

"What are you aiming at?" asked Coleman.

"Those iguanas."

"I thought you were against animal cruelty."

"I am," said Serge, throwing a switch and turning a volume knob. "But the iguanas are in the street, which means they're in danger. Here come some cars."

The volume knob was cranked to eleven, and the reptiles scattered into the sanctuary of the mangroves.

"It worked," said Coleman. "They've gone to watch TV."

Serge came back inside. "Gypsy, what was that deal with your friend on the Seven Mile?"

Gypsy squeezed bubbles out of the tinting and talked over her shoulder. "That was a stripper friend of mine. A real looker, makes good scratch, but her air-conditioning went out and she was short at the end of the month. Next thing I know, she says she's got a Coca-Cola vending machine in the back of her pickup. Down here, that's like the logical next step in exotic dancer financial planning. A stripper suddenly is in possession of a vending machine, frantically racing back and forth over the bridges, and you're not even curious . . . She calls and wants to know if I can help her unload it cheap, and I say I'll make some calls, and I find this so-called doctor who recently opened one of those CBD shops that you'd swear is driving the stock market now, and he says sure he'll take it, because he wants to sell marijuana juice out of it. So Cinnamon drops it off and of course she doesn't have the keys, but it's so cheap the doctor takes it anyway and calls a locksmith. The devil in the details is that he wasn't just going to sell the legal CBD juice but some wickedly illegal THC stuff, which isn't kosher yet. And the locksmith gets the machine open, looks inside and tells the doctor that the serial number has been filed off. Yeah, what a shock. How did the doc not expect that? He screams at Cinnamon on the phone that he can't sell illegal juice out of a hot machine, and then they have the kind of twisted argument like two people off their meds debating Federal Reserve policy, and he demands she get it out of his office before he gets busted and he'll write off the loss. So now she's racing down the Overseas Highway with stripper logic: 'If I keep driving around with this hunk of metal in my flatbed, something will just happen and I'll be rich.'" Gypsy pressed buttons on her cell phone. "Hey, Slick, it's me, Gypsy. Think I got the perfect piece for your man cave to go with the slot machine and that door full of bullet holes you pulled off that downed cocaine plane in the Everglades . . ." She gave him the details. ". . . Yeah, it works. . . . Delivery? Believe me when I say it will practically deliver itself. . . . Who? Cinnamon . . . What do you mean, 'No way? . . .'" *Click.*

Gypsy unspooled the next roll of tinting film on the floor and was about to press buttons on her phone when it began playing reggae. "Remy, you have to stop calling about that stash house in Miami. I'm in the middle of a four-window job and negotiating a three-way fence job for a Coke machine." She hung up—"Jesus"—and dialed again. "Hello, Cinnamon? I ran into a hitch. . . . Sure I'll keep working on it. Just keep referring your dancer friends to me for all their tinting needs." Gypsy hung up and glanced at the couch. "You wouldn't believe how strippers like to tint . . ."

"Excuse me," said Serge. "Juggling all these bizarre phone calls while you work, plus an iguana in a diamond choker. Is this how the entire economy works down here?"

"No." Gypsy worked a roller on a window. "Usually it's chaos, but I try to keep things businesslike."

An hour later, Gypsy used a razor blade to trim away the last of the excess film. Then she began refilling her bucket with tools. "How do you like it?"

Serge stood in awe with an open mouth. "Better than I could have imagined. The whole back of my condo is even superior to my best polarized sunglasses. How's cash?"

"Cash is good." She stood next to him admiring the same view. "Got a nice place up here."

"Where do you live?" asked Serge.

"Off the Old Road, down on the Row."

"'Millionaires Row?"

She nodded.

"How'd you manage that?"

"Freak of street platting," said Gypsy. "Some surveyor screwed up fifty years ago, and this little trapezoid piece of land got left over, where I built a tiny bungalow by the street. My rich neighbors are still fit to be tied, but screw 'em. I'm the only poor person on the Row. I mean relatively. I can't complain." She drank in the ocean view. "Not down here in the islands."

"That's the spirit," said Serge. "So you know people on the Row?"

"From a distance, but yeah," said Gypsy. "Everyone knows everybody's business down here. Why do you ask?"

"I knew some people down on the Row," said Serge. "Long story. What a cluster—"

A low, droning sound came from an unseen location in the distance. Serge clenched up.

Gypsy laughed. "It's just a helicopter . . . Wait, your long story? It wouldn't be that chopper explosion followed by the big shoot-out."

Serge simply grinned again.

"You were in that mess? You know Deputy Deke?"

"Afraid so."

"Good for you," said Gypsy. "We got a quiet town here, but every once in a while some outsiders try to spoil it, and someone has to drive off the bad news."

"Driving off bad news is my specialty."

"I'll keep that in mind. Do you have a card?"

"It's more of a word-of-mouth thing."

"Nice doing business. Enjoy your windows." Gypsy turned. "Come on, Noodle."

The bedazzled iguana hopped down from the couch and followed her out the door with a swagger like he owned the island, which in a way he did.

Coleman joined Serge, staring out at the sea. "That whole thing was freakin' weird, man, and I'm not even high."

"But what a value," said Serge. "The best tinting job I've seen in my life, and a free side order of Keys culture. I'm hungry. Let's get an empanada."

Chapter 31

THE NEXT MORNING

A row of automatic coffeemakers aggressively gurgled inside an office in a bland concrete building on the outskirts of an industrial park in northern Miami-Dade County near the Hard Rock football stadium, not to be confused with the guitar-shaped Hard Rock casino hotel. A line of silent people with empty coffee mugs and empty energy levels stared silently as if it would make the coffeemakers drip faster. The drop ceiling still had asbestos.

On the far end of the open-office floor plan sat a line of executive offices. In the middle office, the blinds just went up, and a fiftysomething man retook his seat behind a wooden desk that was actually particleboard. A younger man with a freshly filled mug approached the room. As usual, he opened the door first, then knocked on it. "You want to see me?"

The managing editor leaned back in his faux-leather chair and smiled. He made an enthusiastic, beckoning wave toward the man in the doorway. "Reevis! Come in, come in! Have a seat!"

Reevis sat down and didn't know where to put his coffee. His shirttail was unknowingly untucked and the knot on his loosened necktie looked like it was trying to escape out the left side of his collar. "What is it, sir?"

"Please, no 'sirs' around here. It's Steadman."

"Yes, sir."

"Honduras."

"What about it?"

"Your story!" said Steadman.

"I remember," said Reevis. "I wrote it. Is the Army complaining again?"

"No. I mean yes, they are, but fuck 'em. It was just a great article."

"You told me." Reevis set his mug on the floor.

"Well, it bears repeating," said Steadman. "Solid, long-term, enterprising work is often taken for granted in this business—even discouraged—but that's the kind we want!" A palm slapped the desk blotter. "Especially since all the big outfits have abandoned their sentinel covenant to shine light on the government where the ordinary citizens—our readers—can't see. Who would have thought that barely into this millennium, the *Miami Free Paper* would be their last hope?"

"I saw it coming," said Reevis. "Or, at least the abandonment part."

"I'm sure you did," said Steadman. "That's why we've got another important assignment for you. Huge. Everyone's talking about it. We might be looking at a promotion."

Reevis leaned forward on the edge of his chair. "What is it?"

"You know that bunny fight on Miami Beach that's gone viral?"

Reevis nodded. "In other words, it's a story like one that is already recognizable in the public consciousness?"

"No, not 'like one.' It's that."

"That what?"

"The bunny story," said Steadman. "You'll have a whole team of reporters on standby if the shit breaks. Total coverage. All expenses paid! Except the ones we don't pay." A shrug. "I have to answer to upstairs."

"This is a one-story building."

"I'll bet you're dying to get started!"

"Actually, I wasn't—"

"That's super! That's fantastic!" The phone rang, and the editor answered it. "Further instructions are in your email. Now, get going." He put on bifocals and held up a financial report with red lines striking through excessive overtime.

"Sir?"

"It's Steadman."

"Sorry, Steadman," said Reevis. "Sir, this isn't the kind of assignment for me. We're in Miami. You of all people should know how much is now going uncovered. That's what I'm meant for."

"You're right." The glasses came off. "And normally I'd acquiesce. That Honduras piece broke ground"—he held up the financial report—"I went to bat for you because you're the best. You shine light on stories before readers even know they're blind and bumping their shins on coffee tables. But this time they *want* this story. Sometimes we need to let them lead us to stories we don't know we should report, if only to keep them happy and reading down into your important stuff."

Reevis gestured out the office window into the newsroom. "What about someone else? I'm working on a follow to the National Guard."

Steadman shook his head. "Because it's an extremely difficult assignment. You're the only one who can do it."

Reevis sulked. "But a bunny?"

"It was my idea," said Steadman. "Actually, it was the nightclub owner's idea. He called me and is dying for the publicity. Something about velvet ropes."

"Velvet?"

"I've learned to filter out the static," said the editor. "If it's important, I'm confident you'll get to the bottom of it."

"So if the owner's on board, how is this such a difficult story?"

"The employee wants to crawl into a hole. No name, no photographs," said Steadman. "You're a pro at prying that stuff loose."

"When there's a compelling public interest," said Reevis. "But my ethics are to let this guy alone to live in peace. He's a private citizen."

"He forfeited that when he put on the bunny head." The editor grabbed his bifocals again. "If it makes you feel any better, the owner and I have agreed on a fake name, Jack Slim."

"Like the nightclub Jack Rabbit Slim's from *Pulp Fiction*?"

"That was my idea. Glad you like it," said Steadman. "It's all in your email. Now, if you'll excuse me."

MIAMI BEACH

Security guards in black jackets, black turtlenecks and sunglasses stood resolute behind a velvet cord on the sidewalk, pretending to deal with a berserk crowd that was no longer there. A pair of sneakers walked by.

Reevis kept on going to the end of the block until he reached a dump of a nightclub called Turtle Grass Flats that was overflowing into the street. Some of the guards back at the chic club had been laid off because of the now-yawning dearth of customers, but they had been quickly snatched up by the newly popular club for mob control on Bunny Fight Night.

The human clog at the club entrance meant Reevis wasn't getting in without help. He approached one of the guards and explained his situation. "I'm with the *Free Paper*. The owner's expecting me . . ."

The guard checked his clipboard, then snapped to attention and cleared a path to lead Reevis into a back office.

A flimsy, warped door opened after a final kick from inside to jar it loose from the frame, and the owner's hand shot out to shake. "You must be Reevis! I've been following your stories in the *Free Paper*. Great work! Absolutely fabulous!"

"Really?" asked Reevis. "Which stories?"

"Every one of them! You know, they kind of blend together with all my reading. But everything you write, totally top-notch!"

"Uh, thank you."

"Make yourself comfortable!" The owner took a step back to create room. "Don't be shy!"

Reevis slowly entered and took stock. Cheap dark-wood paneling to match the door. A wall calendar from a bank that was on the wrong month. A framed certificate from a one-day motivational seminar on not listening to toxic people. The desktop was cluttered with envelopes containing outstanding bills—opened and still sealed—bags of sesame sticks and licorice, a dispenser of dental floss, loose rubber bands, paper clips organized in a small magnetic toilet. Reevis stopped to assess a Chia Pet of the president with green hair.

In the middle of the desk was a large, furry bunny head next to a pair of boxing gloves. Against the wall, slumped in a chair at a depressed angle, was the rest of the bunny costume, containing an employee.

"Reevis Tome!" the owner gleefully barked. "Meet Jack Slim! Jack, Reevis."

They politely acknowledged each other.

"Well! I can already tell you guys have a lot to talk about," said the owner. "I'll just be getting out of your hair so you can jump into it!"

The owner left and needed to slam the humidity-swollen door three times hard until it finally wedged shut.

Reevis pointed back at the door. "Are we going to be able to get out of here?"

The bunny shrugged. "If I'm lucky, no. I have to box later."

The reporter pulled up a chair and flipped open a notebook. "Jack Slim isn't your real name?"

"Not really."

Reevis bent with his pen. "Okay, a stage name. What's your real one?"

"Look, if it's all the same to you, can this interview be off the record? And be vague about my background?"

Reevis's head popped up. "Off the record for a bright feature story? About a bunny? That's highly unusual. It's usually reserved for whistleblowers and pending indictments."

"I have my reasons," said the bunny. "The owner's forcing me to do this interview for the publicity because we're in a war with the velvet-rope thing."

"I don't understand."

"Until I came along, everyone just wanted to get in places that wouldn't let them in."

"Oh." Reevis nodded. "*Those* clubs." He jotted in the notebook. "All right, since it is just a feature, I'll indicate that you only want to be known by your professional name." He pulled a cell phone from his pocket and raised it for a photo.

Flash.

Reevis checked the preview screen and found a face with two hands in front of it.

"No photos either," said the bunny. "Or no interview."

It was getting weird. Reevis took a deep, patient breath.

"I know this is hard to understand," said the bunny. "But sometimes in your life, you just want to avoid certain people, sometimes a lot of people. Except if you tell people that, you're automatically guilty of something. Where is *that* written? It's a free country. For no reason at all, you can just decide to start avoiding people as a lifestyle."

"I know the feeling," said Reevis. "So is this, like, your ex or something?"

"You can assume that."

"Let's go back to the night in question." Reevis pulled out an arrest report and readied his pen. "When did you first notice the assailant?"

"A week earlier."

"A week?"

"Everyone knows him, not by name, but he's this drunken bum that comes around each night and starts trouble."

Reevis scribbled. "He'd been attacking people a whole week and nobody's done anything?"

"I wouldn't exactly say 'attack,' but he gets right up to the line," said the bunny. "Mostly he would stand in the street, railing against nightclubs and their elitist admission process. Other times, after the backseat of a limo emptied at the curb, he'd jump in and tell the driver to take him somewhere, which was an obvious nonstarter. Another time he somehow got hold of stacks of fake cash—you know, like those novelty three-dollar bills with the faces of 'Weird Al' Yankovic or Bigfoot—and he throws the whole bunch into the air, and since they're fluttering in the dark, they look real at first glance and everyone's diving on the sidewalk including the bouncers, and the guy uses the opportunity of chaos to dart inside the club before they have a chance to grab him in the thousand-dollar Champagne room and pry his fingers off the Dom Pérignon he was chugging at a table of rap stars. Other places like Wichita you'd probably get pinched, but in Miami Beach that's just background noise."

"So what was different about the night you made the news?"

"Something got into him and he went way outside his lane," said the bunny. "This woman leaves the chic club, and he follows and berates her as a member of the plastic-surgeon class, and then grabs her purse, demanding reparations. But she's pretty fit and won't let go. They both take a tumble off the curb and start hitting each other in the gutter. Somebody had to step in."

"So you were the closest?"

"That's the thing," said the bunny. "There were a million people closer outside the fancy clubs, but they were all just laughing and taking videos with their phones. What's wrong with people?"

"That's the big question in the newsrooms," said Reevis, jotting away. "That's when you decided to intervene?"

"What else was I going to do? I started running in slow motion because of this ridiculous getup and was sure someone else would get there first, but no dice. I pulled him off her and kept pounding him until the cops arrived on bicycles."

The assignment had started painfully for Reevis, but he was now finding amusement goofing on the whole cliché of such corny profiles in courage. So was the bunny. Reevis flipped a page. "People are calling you a hero. Your response?"

"I'm no hero. I was just doing my job."

Scribble, scribble. "They're saying you give them hope."

"Hope for what? To go to work in a crazy animal head?"

"Why do you have a job like that?"

"Because the head allows me to hide in plain sight."

"Avoiding people?" asked Reevis.

"It's worked out so far. At least until now," said the bunny.

"You've become such a role model," Reevis said cynically. "What would you say to a young person who wants to follow in your footsteps?"

"Stay in school."

"So what's up next for the 'hero' bunny of South Beach?"

The employee checked a clock and grabbed the costume head off the desk. "I have to box in five. If you'll excuse me."

Reevis flipped the notebook shut. "I think I have everything I need."

"You may want to stay for the fight. If you want to understand the foolishness that my life has become."

The bunny grabbed a roll of duct tape and began wrapping it around where the bottom of the head attached to the neck of the rest of the costume.

"What are you doing?"

"Learning from experience."

They both got up.

Reevis turned the doorknob, but the door wouldn't budge. Three more tries with all his strength and nothing. "I think we're stuck in here."

"Let me help you," said the bunny. "Turn the knob and stand to the side."

Reevis did. The bunny charged and crashed into the door with his padded shoulder. It flew open.

"Hey, watch it!" yelled someone returning from the restrooms. "You just clobbered me . . . Oh, it's the fighting bunny. An honor to meet you . . ."

They went out to the boxing ring. The bunny waited outside the ropes for the previous fight to finish, and Reevis took his place inside the designated media area, which was a square on the back side of the ring marked off with electrical tape on the floor. He joined the TV cameras from the various local affiliates and national cable outfits. The previous bout soon ended. A Notre Dame leprechaun jumped in triumph with raised gloves as they dragged an unconscious University of Georgia bulldog mascot from the ring.

The bunny climbed through the ropes. The bell clanged. The elephant mascot from the University of Alabama Crimson Tide came out of his corner, and the two opponents spent the first minute sizing each other up. Then the gloves began to fly. The punches were lazy and off-target, because this fight, like the others, had been fixed. All the contestants had been told to make the matches go at least seven rounds to sell more liquor.

But six rounds turned the inside of those costumes into saunas. Plus the bunny was really having to hold back because the elephant's trunk was getting in the way of his counterpunches.

Both were gasping and drenched in sweat as they sat on their respective stools. A smiling cocktail waitress strolled around the ring with a giant number 7 on a card above her head.

The bell clanged. The bunny didn't want to keep that head on a second more than necessary. He advanced across the canvas with purpose. His first punch scored a direct hit. The elephant didn't have duct tape around his neck, and the bunny's roundhouse right connected across the trunk, twisting the entire head backward. The elephant grabbed it with both gloves while desperately trying to see out an ear hole, but it was too late. The bunny unleashed a flurry of combination punches and body blows. Less than a minute into the round, they were dragging the lifeless elephant from the ring.

The crowd went nuts, screaming adulation and ordering more booze.

The bunny pulled off his gloves and ran back to the office, frantically ripping off tape and the head. Panting, wiping his face with paper towels.

The owner entered with a gregarious smile, a wad of cash in a rubber band, and a chewed cigar clamped in his teeth.

"What's that?" asked the bunny.

"The bonus fee I told you about! We've never had such business." He tossed the money on the desk. "I'm considering putting you on health insurance. Just considering, no promises. Now hurry. You have to get back out there to your fans."

The bunny was still breathing hard like he was gulping. "I only had one fight scheduled tonight."

"Not fight. Pose for selfies," said the owner. "We're offering one free with each bottle of Champagne."

"But this dump doesn't have a Champagne room."

"It does now." The owner just grinned. "Make it fast. The line is forming. Just one rule from now on: Never take off the costume, even just the head."

"Why?"

"The mystery is driving this thing. Like the band KISS."

. . . A half hour later, the bunny had his photo taken with the last person in line. "What a night."

He pushed open the heavy steel exit door in the back of the club and half stumbled into an alley. His gait was unsteady on the way to his high-mileage Datsun parked below unlit streetlights.

He stuck a key in the door and opened it, then removed his bunny head in order to drive. A robust exhale. "Finally . . ."

At that precise moment, the entire alley lit up like an intruder had just vaulted the White House fence. "Jesus, will they never leave me alone?"

"There he is!" A heavy herd of footsteps.

The professional bunny shielded his eyes. "What the hell now?"

News camera crews ran down the alley. "We would just like a brief moment."

"Turn those things off!"

The lights stayed on. Cameras running.

"Are you a hero?"

"Can you give us more hope?"

"What's the next crime wave you intend to fight?"

"Leave me alone!"

He jumped into the Datsun, floored the gas, and squealed out of the trash-strewn alley, kicking up newspaper pages in the wind.

The camera lights went out, and they transmitted what they had via their satellite vans back to headquarters. "Let's get sushi."

Chapter 32

THE NEXT DAY

An immaculately clear and sunny day in the Everglades reached late afternoon and turned into that threatening purple canopy, as it generally does without the locals even noticing anymore.

Across greater Miami-Dade, and all up the Gold Coast to North Palm Beach, residents tuned in to the local news at noon, five, six and eleven. The screens showed a man in a furry white suit shielding his face in a dark alley the night before as news cameras jiggled in a herd of running journalists.

An anchorwoman broke in: "We have our first glimpse tonight at the identity of the mystery man who's on everyone's lips." She turned to her desk partner. "Chet, any developments?"

"As a matter of fact, just breaking at this hour: The Guardian Bunny has won his first sanctioned fight by knockout in the seventh round. Unfortunately, his opponent is currently en route to a local hospital with an unspecified jaw injury."

"Ha-ha-ha," chuckled the newswoman. "Those unpredictable bunnies. We'll have to keep our Eyewitness Eye on them."

A small, tight convoy of late-model civilian Jeeps and Ford pick-ups with obscenely large tires raced east out of the Everglades on the Tamiami Trail, led by a Hummer. Before reaching Little Havana, the motorcade curled up into the west Miami enclave of Doral.

Like a precision formation of aircraft, they sequentially pulled into parking spaces outside a corrugated metal building called the Water Bed Barn. The sign was still up for the coming week's fumigation.

High-laced combat boots hit the pavement. Men in olive-green fatigues with no insignia marched up the concrete stairs of the loading dock.

They fanned out across a cavernous, dusty open space with a grid of desks, situation maps on the walls, and an industrial ventilation fan installed high up in the corrugated metal. Someone got up to turn on the flat-screen TV between the wall maps of Haiti and Nicaragua. The fan's blades squeaked slowly.

Ten minutes later, the last person arrived, with a brown sack from Dunkin Donuts and a horizontal scar across his chin. He stopped at the sight in his headquarters.

"What the hell's going on in here? You're all supposed to be at your desks working on your Post-Op-Sac-Sitrep training reports from the Everglades."

The men were crowded around the TV, watching the local Eyewitness News. "Colonel, come over here. You're going to want to see this."

The Colonel walked up behind the crew. "What am I supposed to be looking at?"

"I'll rewind it . . ."

Fingers pressed buttons as one of the guys worked the remote control on the DVR until it reached the starting point of the news segment. He hit Play.

The Colonel watched intently as a bunny beat the snot out of an elephant until it keeled over backward into the ropes.

"You've got to be kidding me," said the Colonel. "This is what was so important to waste my time and yours? That stupid bunny from the Internet? Civilians can goof off talking about him around water coolers, but we're a crack professional outfit."

"Not this part," said the one with the remote control. "Just wait . . ."

The Colonel sighed as the video played on. The scene switched to a dark alley with vague movement that couldn't be made out. Impatiently: "I can't see anything—"

Suddenly, blinding TV lights came on, catching a surprised man in a bunny costume with the head in his arms, about to climb into a high-mileage Datsun. A banner of text scrolled across the bottom of the screen: BREAKING NEWS: HERO BUNNY UNMASKED. Then a voiceover from the anchor desk: "We are now seeing the first images of the man behind the costume in the ultra-viral video, who is known only by his stage name Jack 'Rabbit' Slim, and appears to be a fan of the movie *Pulp Fiction*. More on this story as details develop."

"I still don't get it," said the Colonel, arms akimbo. "What was I supposed to be looking at?"

The remote control guy turned around. "You didn't recognize that guy by the car?"

"Was I supposed to?"

"It was Yandy, our guide in Honduras who disappeared," said the staff member. "Our big loose end that we were about to give up on and just pray he didn't come out of the woodwork to bite us. And now he's in Miami. What are the odds that we could luck out like this?"

"Preposterous odds," said the Colonel. "There's no way that's him."

"Why do you say that?"

"For no other reason than he's in a bunny suit," said the Colonel. "Regardless of any evidence to the contrary, it's just too weird to be true."

"It's Miami," said the staffer, pressing buttons on the remote until he rewound to the critical portion of the news segment. He hit Pause. "Look closer. That's got to be him."

"Out of my way," said the Colonel, stepping right up to the screen. He studied the shocked face of the man holding the bunny head next to the car. He continued staring and bit his lip.

"Colonel, what do you think now? Even if it's a distant off-chance, it's too big to ignore," said one of the green army men. "We're free and clear after that mission. With the glaring exception of this guy, who could send us to military prison or, worse, Honduran prison, for the rest of our lives. How many civilians did we execute—?"

"Shut up!" yelled the Colonel. "Nobody is to utter a single syllable about that ever again." He ruminated, then snapped his fingers. "Someone get me his photo from the dossier!"

Moments later, a black-and-white eight-by-ten was in the Colonel's right hand. He held it up next to the flat-screen. He subconsciously rubbed the scar on his chin for the hundredth time that day. "It does bear a resemblance."

"I suggest we check it out," said Remote-Control Man. "If for no other reason than professional thoroughness, and self-preservation."

"Okay," said the Colonel. "Run all this through our facial-recognition software. Then we'll know what to do . . ."

Within minutes: "Colonel, it's a solid hit!"

"How solid?"

"Ninety-nine-point-nine percent, out to four digits," said the team's computer expert. "That margin of error means we'd have to go to Mongolia to find a second match."

"Good enough for me," said the Colonel.

"Sir, a bunny at a nightclub is an itinerant job. We don't know how big our window is."

"Agreed." The Colonel faced the room. "Listen up, everyone! We're in snap count. A lightning op for 2100 Zulu." One of the staff rolled a blackboard over, and the Colonel grabbed a piece of chalk.

"One of you pull up Google Earth and Street View. Designate primary and backup egress routes." The chalk hit the board and began drawing a city block. "Now, here's what we're going to do. If there are no wild cards in the deck, it should be a milk run . . ."

Across town, a wild card: Other eyes were intently reviewing the TV footage from the alley.

Chapter 33

THAT SAME DAY . . .

Another typical morning at Pelican Bay as the sun gained altitude and heat. Kayakers headed down to the point, and curly-tailed lizards scampered across the pool deck, where the short-term vacation renters read paperbacks and sipped mimosas.

Out in the parking lot, the residents had again dutifully formed a line. Serge's Underbelly Tours had been a smashing success and word had spread like a grease fire throughout the complex. Now it was up to several times a week, as the line grew long and longer, and Serge arrived in a progression of increasingly large shuttle vans.

He pulled up and they boarded with a newfound bounce in their steps. Serge pressed the key on his tour guide microphone as they pulled onto U.S. Highway 1.

"Today we'll be hitting the Whistle Stop Bar from the streaming TV series *Bloodline*, then at the bottom of Lower Matecumbe, the Veterans piers, where vets began building a bridge until someone changed their mind. There's a historic plaque we must touch. Then a dash of nature as we hike the mangrove flats at Long Key State

Park, followed by a stop at the Brass Monkey, a wonderfully legendary dive bar on Marathon, where, if you can believe it, Gregg Allman played back in the '70s."

The gang started getting their morning island life on with drinks, and hits from the iguana—"Coleman, I told you that Malty is cursed!" As they left Islamorada and approached the high-arch Channel Five Bridge, Serge grabbed his microphone. "We have some time to chat before our first stop and bond spiritually with our condo tribe ... I see a lot of couples back there. That makes me feel tingly! Gives hope for the species!" He nodded and grinned up into the rearview. "A show of hands! How many of you have been married twenty years?"

Almost all the arms went up high.

"Okay, keep them up there," said Serge. "How about twenty-five years?"

A few arms came down.

"Thirty? . . . Thirty-five? . . ." Serge continued climbing up the ladder of years until he reached fifty. Two remaining couples still had their hands up. "Okay," said Serge. "Give. How long?"

"Fifty-three," said the first couple.

"Fifty-five," said the second.

"You're my heroes!" said Serge. "To what do you owe your success?"

"Conversation," said the woman.

"Ding! Ding! Ding! We have a correct answer!" said Serge. "I actually knew that before I asked the question. Every long-duration marriage has the chemistry of conversation. Otherwise it's two years and gone with a moving van, like a top-round draft pick who blows out his knee. And it's such a needless tragedy: A couple slams together in a hedonistic froth, spends enough on a wedding to forgive the debt of an undeveloped nation. And then it happens, the marriage skids to a halt so suddenly it causes cervical damage. Why? No over-the-horizon plan. Life was all in the moment, and the couple industriously blew through every conceivable geometric permutation of copulating until their imaginations finally sputtered dry, and they were left with drawers full of ridiculous sex toys for every occasion and hole. And then they find themselves staring at each other silently in the kitchen, thinking, *What now?*"

Serge looked up in the rearview again at silent, frozen faces. "Cheer up! Everyone here has mastered the art! You learned to converse before all the screwing and sucking became just another household chore like cleaning the oven. What are all those strange looks I'm getting up here? . . . Anyway, this is where it gets ticklish. When we talk about conversation as the glue to a strong relationship, what we really mean is gibberish. Couples aren't sitting at breakfast tables over grapefruit halves reciting carefully constructed treatises on Keynesian macroeconomics or military blunders of the Peloponnesian War. We're social creatures who just sputter fractured nonsense all day, and we need a companion who will listen and respond to our jabbering with tenderness. 'My smartphone has more computing power than the moon landing, yet I can't get the bubbles out of the screen protector.' 'Honey, what is the ratio of how many times you open the refrigerator to actually taking something out?' 'Is that plant dying? It doesn't look right.' 'I'm constantly anxious we'll run out of ink cartridges in the middle of printing out invitations.' 'Why do the annual seasons start in the *middle* of the season, like the vernal equinox?' . . . See where I'm going here?"

Serge kept driving and blabbering, across bridge after bridge. The gang touched a plaque and hiked. They hit Marathon on the way to a landmark dive bar. A Ford F-150 pickup truck slowly passed the van. Serge noticed the driver, a tall woman with a thick mane of spicy red hair. In the bed of the pickup was a Coca-Cola vending machine.

"It's the Keys economy," Serge said to himself. "Why not?"

They passed the airport and made a left onto a bright side street. Serge keyed the mic. "You know that a dive bar is going to be excellent when it's attached to a package store."

The van pulled up to the Brass Monkey, next to the pickup truck with a vending machine. Half the gang climbed down and went inside, while the rest primed themselves with Coleman and the Maltese Iguana.

Serge spread his arms. "There's just something about stepping out of the blinding noon sun of Florida and into an ultra-dark bar with pool tables and neon." Serge stopped to let his eyes adjust and inhaled sharply. "It smells like ... victory."

He grabbed a stool at the venerable, banged-up wooden bar that had served honorably for decades and had more stories to tell than something with fewer stories. He turned to the woman next to him with the tousled red hair, sitting upright in an elegant spinal comport that said, *Get lost, creep.*

"What are you drinking?" asked Serge.

She held out the clear plastic cup. "This."

"Do you live around here often?"

"Is that supposed to be a joke?"

"Maybe at some point in time." He extended a hand to shake. "My name's Serge. Nice to meet you, Cinnamon."

Her head snapped. "Who are you? One of the customers from the club?"

"What club?"

"We're not supposed to meet customers away from the club," said the woman. "It's dangerous. I have Mace!"

"I've never been to the club, even if I knew which one it was."

"Then how do you know my name?"

"Heard you were a stripper."

She jumped to her feet. Dang, she was tall. "I am not a stripper!"

"I was misinformed," said Serge. "That was Humphrey Bogart. There's a bar up the street with his statue from the movie *Key Largo*..."

"I am an exotic dancer!"

"Okay," said Serge. "We'll work our way up to the art of conversation. In the meantime, relax and sit back down, and I'll buy you another round of 'this' ..."

Something crashed. "Ow, shit." A cue ball skipped across the floor, and Serge fielded it like a shortstop. He returned it to the condo residents, who were tending to a neighbor with blue chalk and a lump over an eye.

He retook his seat.

Cinnamon held up her drink. "I already ordered. Pay the man."

Serge tossed a sawbuck on the bar. "Barkeep, bottled water, domestic." His head swiveled in the dimness. But not so dim that he didn't pick up on those cheekbones, like Kevin Costner's girl in *Dances with Wolves*. Likewise, she had noticed his ice-blue eyes, but no way she'd cop to that.

"So," said Serge. "What do you like in a man?"

"Absence."

"Know what turns me on in a woman?"

"I have Mace."

"Gibberish," said Serge. "It's the Krazy Glue of long-term soul mates."

"What are you talking about?"

"Did you know that pound for pound, salt is the cheapest item in any grocery store?"

"What's that supposed to mean?"

"Exactly," said Serge. "That's how you know it's quality gibberish."

"You're a serious test on the nerves," said Cinnamon. "What exactly is your endgame here?"

"Play your cards right and I might even take that Coke machine off your hands."

Another surprised jerk of her head. "You sure know an awful lot about me."

"I know the backstory on your vending machine because my windows are tinted."

"More gibberish?"

"Actually there was a point in there," said Serge. "From time to time I just get these preternatural sensations. I think we were meant to be together."

"God, I'll bet your cornball lines work on all the women. To kill their mood."

"Hey, I didn't say how long on togetherness," said Serge. "Maybe these few minutes are it. I just needed time to find out if you're fluent in gibberish."

"Fuck a duck."

"You are!" He snapped his fingers. "I knew it!"

BACK ON THE MAINLAND . . .

The fluorescent-lit office was humming to the clatter of keyboards as the news staff of the *Miami Free Paper* entered the home stretch toward deadline.

Knuckles knocked on the open door of an executive office. "You wanted to see me?" asked Reevis.

"Come in!" Steadman waved aggressively. "Have a seat! Have I told you how much I loved your feature today from the nightclub?"

"About five times."

"Make it six," said Steadman. "And great photo of the elephant laid out with the bunny standing over him. It was total Ali–Liston. That would be Ali–Liston II."

"Thank you," said Reevis. "But you mentioned on the phone there was something you needed me to do."

"The phone's been ringing all day. The public can't get enough," said Steadman. "We're increasing our press run. And you know what that means?"

"Not really."

"We need a follow-up," said the editor. "Even bigger and better."

"I thought this was a one-off," said Reevis. "And not only is there nothing better to write, there's nothing left to write at all." He pointed out the door. "There's a whole world of real news I need to cover."

"We assigned other reporters to the world," said Steadman, rubbing his hands in anticipation. "The editorial team got together and we had a brainstorm." He handed a piece of paper across his desk.

"What's this?" asked Reevis.

"Your next assignment. I'll bet you're blown away!" said Steadman. "Sorry to spring it on you with such short notice, but it's tonight, so you'll have to leave immediately."

Reevis read down the page with a poker face, then pulled out his cell.

"Why are you looking at your phone?" asked Steadman.

"Making sure it's not April Fool's Day."

"I know how the hot-type, bare-fisted journalist in you feels about this kind of story, but it's this sort of thing that bankrolls your incredibly important investigative pieces that nobody reads."

"Thank you, I think."

Steadman checked his Rolex. "Get going or you'll be late."

Reevis sulked out of the office.

Sneakers headed down a hallway of dubious aroma. A hard knock on a door by the restrooms.

"Coming! . . . Stand back!"

A shoulder slammed the inside of the door and it violently flung open past Reevis's nose.

"Have a seat!"

Reevis plopped down in the slouched posture of lacking the will to thrive. He stared without thought at paper clips stuck to a small magnetic toilet.

The owner of Turtle Grass Flats grabbed the reporter's hand and vigorously shook his limp arm. "I can't thank you enough for all you've done. And this morning's story?"—he kissed his fingertips—"Genius! Our club has never been so packed! Did your editor give you all the details on your story tonight?"

"Unfortunately."

"You don't seem enthused, but that's okay. It will all change," said the owner. "Your editor says you're an award-winning investigative reporter, and this sort of thing is outside your wheelhouse, but trust me, you're entering Pulitzer territory."

"The committee will be as surprised as me." Reevis looked up at something hanging from a hook on the wall. "Is that my bunny suit?"

"Isn't she a beauty?" said the owner.

"You have *two* costumes?"

"It's become a seven-day operation, and there's laundry to consider, especially because of the boxing blood. We can't have our marquee attraction looking like he passed out in an alley with some of our customers." The owner grinned the grin of money. "And think of the privilege. You'll be the only reporter doing a first-person story on the experience of being a celebrity bunny."

"My editor probably didn't cover this next part," said Reevis. "But no boxing or I walk right now."

"No, no, no," said the owner. "No boxing whatsoever. We can't risk you getting injured before you file your stellar account of the night."

"But the ring is set up and the chickens are already punching."

"The bunny fight won't start until the regular guy arrives for the second shift and relieves you. Plus there's the insurance issues. It's getting so big that they won't indemnify us anymore without bodyguards." The owner grabbed the hanger off the hook. "Why don't you try this baby on and tell me how it fits?"

Ten minutes later, Reevis stood in the corner of the owner's office. He finished pulling up the costume, cradling the bulbous head under his arm, an expression of sadness like he had just witnessed a baby-seal clubbing.

The owner slapped him on the shoulder. "Spiffy! . . . The only condition is that you can't remove the costume for any reason until you get home. We'll send someone to retrieve it."

"Why don't I just change in your office after all this is over?"

The owner shook his head. "The crowd will be three deep when they see you return here after your performance. We can't have them finding out there's more than one bunny, that *you* didn't beat that asshole silly on the sidewalk."

The owner slammed into the wedged door again. It flew open.

Two granite statues of bodyguards were waiting. "Now get out on that sidewalk and drum up some business. And make sure you get every detail for your story!"

The bodyguards led Reevis through the crowd in a march of terminal depression. Customers on both sides struggled to touch his fur. Someone grabbed his left paw and curled it around several fat joints. "That's for you. For all you're doing for the community." Someone else gripped his right paw for a bindle of tiny pills. "That's Molly, to get your glow on later. It's the least we can do." Before he could close the paw, a slip of paper was tucked inside. "That's my number. Sex is freaky on Molly . . . Can you keep the costume on to fuck? I'd appreciate that."

One of the bodyguards passed him a Magic Marker and some panties with flames. "Can you sign this for my mother?"

They hit the sidewalk, and it all cut loose beyond the bodyguards' control. A crush of fans with autograph pads, roses, and more drugs and underwear. A woman pulled down the right side of her shirt and pulled the bunny's head down into a boob . . .

. . . Behind the sidewalk mob, traffic on South Beach's Club Row was at a rubberneck crawl. Supermodels and regular-strength models waved out the sunroofs of stretch limos. Honking horns. Camera flashes. Champagne corks flew. A conga line formed in the street and wove between vehicles.

Back at the corner, the light turned green, and a Jaguar XE rented at the Miami airport made a slow right turn in the stacked traffic. It passed the most chic club on the strip, where there was no longer a beckoning crowd behind the velvet ropes, and the previously black-clad guards were now dressed like raccoons and squirrels, swinging boxing gloves. But nobody was fooled by cheap imitations.

The Jaguar continued toward the human clot ahead on the right side. Tinted windows rolled down as the passengers observed in silence. They rounded the next corner and parked halfway down a dark alley.

"What do we do now?"

"Smoke break . . ."

. . . Back on the front door of Turtle Grass Flats: Reevis would have kept checking his watch, but it was inside fur. His painful impatience felt like he was waiting for a pot to boil and paint to dry at the same time. He tapped one of his bodyguards' arms and pointed to his wrist. The guard showed him the time. Finally, he was in striking distance. Ten minutes to go, but screw it. He headed back inside and announced that he was scramming for the night.

"But you're early," said the owner. "The regular guy hasn't arrived yet."

"I already have more than enough material," said Reevis. "If I don't leave now, I won't be able to make deadline for the morning edition."

The magic words.

"Then by all means," said the owner.

Reevis respected the owner's wishes and stayed in costume, simply bundling his street clothes in his arms as he headed out the back door into the alley.

Out front, a woman of petite stature with curly black hair hurried up the sidewalk, wearing a ruby rhinestone cowgirl costume. "Please, let me through . . . This is an emergency." She reached a lone bodyguard and frantically glanced around. "Where's the bunny?"

The guard kept scanning the crowd for anything that was out of the ordinary, which was everything. "Taking a break. He'll be right back . . ."

She stood in alarm next to the street, spinning around. Along with the gang at the Water Bed Barn, her eyes had also caught the bunny news report. She was the wild card.

Reevis stomped padded feet through puddles on the way to his car. "Of all the humiliating . . ." He reached in the suit for his car keys and came up with joints and pills. "Jesus!" He flung them in a dumpster as he prepared to remove his head.

Then he noticed a few guys smoking, loitering and leaning against the fender of a Jaguar XE.

"Hey! It's the famous bunny!"

"You rock!"

"We're your biggest fans!"

The bunny kept walking. "Thanks, guys!"

The bunny had just stuck his key in the driver's door. Suddenly, some of the guys from the Jag popped their trunk, fully lined with thick-gauge plastic. The rest seized the bunny and hustled toward the back of the Jag.

"Hey, hey, hey!" yelled the bunny. "Watch the fur!"

They upended him, dumping him in the trunk and slamming the lid. The Jag sped off down the alley.

Chapter 34

TURTLE GRASS FLATS

The Jaguar men jumped back in the car and peeled off down the alley, kicking up empty burger wrappers and other wind-swirled trash.

In the jet-black trunk, Reevis's brain was overheating, a million thoughts elbowing for room. Why would anyone want to kidnap him? His stories in the *Miami Free Paper*? Maybe some angry letters to the editor, but violence? His predicament made no sense, but it was definitely not good. Reasons would have to come later. The reporter was drifting to panic but not immobilized. His hands found a back corner of the trunk and began clawing at the thick fabric liner. His plan was to reach the taillight and bust out the back of its housing. From there he could yank loose the wiring and, from his Boy Scout training, touch the sparking wires together to signal SOS in Morse code. He just had to hope that whoever was in traffic behind him had also been a Boy Scout.

Back up in the passenger compartment, nobody had spoken. The Jaguar was being driven by a chiseled man with a horizontal scar across his chin. The car had been sitting at the end of the alley for only a few moments, but it seemed an eternity to the Colonel. Jammed party traffic inching along with no space for the Jag to pull out. The Colonel uncharacteristically smacked the steering wheel.

The colleague in the passenger seat pointed. "There's no way we can make a left."

"I'd long since abandoned that fool's errand," said the Colonel. "We'll turn right and circle the block to reach Collins, which should be a straight shot to Bal Harbour."

They resumed watching sports cars crawl, bumping with overpowered stereos.

Another slap at the wheel. "What's the deal with this fucking traffic? Some kind of wreck?"

"There's nothing unusual," said someone in the backseat. "It's the weekend in South Beach near club row. It's always like this. You've never been here?"

"I avoid these people like the plague."

Meanwhile in the trunk, Reevis's progress was also crawling. His hands got the flap of trunk liner pulled back and reached the taillight's housing. It was made of plastic, but a special polymer used in high-end vehicles. He had no tools, and fingertips weren't meant for this kind of task. He began to feel that Morse code was wishful thinking. The best case started looking like somehow bashing the whole thing out and hoping a police officer would light them up for faulty equipment. Only when he realized that the Jag had been stationary for a while did it finally begin moving. A stray thought sparked from nowhere. Nagging. Moments earlier he'd noticed something about one of his captors. A horizontal scar across his chin. He'd seen it before, but where?

The Colonel had his head and arm out the window, yelling at someone in a Corvette as they played a slow-motion game of chicken. The Jag continued crawling toward a merging space in traffic that wasn't there, until the Corvette's driver realized the Colonel wasn't stopping for nothing, and then suddenly there was a space.

"Asshole!"

The Jag made a right at the corner and it was déjà vu all over again, passing the velvet ropes at the chic club, then slowly approaching the dive bar with the boxing ring . . .

At that moment, a rousing cheer went up as the regular employee in the bunny suit stepped out of the door to the club and onto the sidewalk.

The rhinestone cowgirl didn't care who she was trampling. She reached the bunny and grabbed his arm, then got on her tiptoes and placed her mouth to the costume head's ear hole. "My name's Debbie. You're in great danger. But if you come with me right now, I can keep you safe."

The bunny head turned to face her. "What the hell are you talking about?"

"I know who you are," said Debbie. "You're Yandy. From Honduras."

The bunny head jerked away, and Yandy stumbled back, hitting the front wall of the club. Debbie grabbed his arm again, but Yandy just yanked it away . . .

. . . Reevis's eyes were adjusting in the dark as he found a tire iron and prepared to smash heavy-gauge plastic. Hold everything! The scar on the chin. It was that guy back at the diplomatic party in Tegucigalpa, and again at his hotel. This was all about Honduras! But that mystery would have to wait. First things first as he maneuvered the tire iron into the short thrusting space in that angle of the trunk. He jabbed it one time. The sound of a crack, but no sign of damage as he felt the housing with his finger. Reevis prepared for a second thrust. That's when he saw it. His eyes had just needed time to adjust in the complete absence of light. It was glowing in the dark. He popped himself in the forehead. *Of course! I am so stupid!* . . .

. . . Back on the sidewalk, Yandy began to shake inside the costume, his feet retreating backward from Debbie, who was trying to grab his arm again but missing: "You have to trust me!"

The stacked traffic out in the street began to loosen up halfway down the block, and vehicles began picking up speed. Debbie kept walking forward, each step carefully thought out so as not to spook the bunny, who was matching her steps walking backward.

Just then, a silver Jaguar XE drove by. Reevis's hand gripped a glow-in-the-dark T-shaped handle in the trunk. The handle was attached to a thick metal cord, which was the emergency escape release that was now a standard feature of new cars in the event someone became trapped in the trunk. He pulled it far harder than he needed to.

One of the celebrants on the sidewalk pointed and shouted. "Look!"

Everyone turned around to see a man in a bunny costume standing up in the trunk of Jaguar passing the club at twenty miles per hour and gaining speed.

It was now or never. At this speed, it would have been some serious costume-shredding road rash. But luckily, behind the Jag was a tailgating BMW. Reeves leaped from the trunk and landed on the hood of the trailing vehicle. The Beemer's driver slammed his brakes, catapulting the furry journalist off the hood and into the swank street.

The occupants of the Jag looked back. "What the fuck just happened?"

"Somehow he got out of the trunk."

"He's escaping!"

One of the green army men started opening his door.

"Close that goddamn thing!" yelled the Colonel. "Are you out of your mind? Look at all the people! All the cell phones taking video!" The Jaguar took off down the street and skidded around the corner toward the exit strategy of Collins Avenue.

The reporter had the wind knocked out of him, among other things, and began the arduous job of pushing himself up. But despite his escaping from a trunk, flying onto the hood of a Beemer, and being flung onto the pavement, other drivers couldn't delay their fun, honking nonstop and swerving dangerously close. One of the tires actually clipped the end of his pinkie—"I'm going to lose that nail for sure."

Just when it seemed confusion had hit a plateau:

"Reevis!"

Where did that come from? He staggered up to his feet and saw a ruby rhinestone cowgirl on the sidewalk. "Reevis! You're in danger!" . . . Reevis thinking, *What part of this looks like I need to be told that?*

"Come with me!" yelled the cowgirl, one hand beckoning, the other trying to grab Yandy.

The sidewalk crowd was thick enough, but the word of all the crazy street action reached inside the club, pulling people out of their ringside seats.

"Two bunnies!" someone yelled. Someone else: "One just jumped out of a trunk onto that BMW." Another: "What's going on?"

The crowd was divided. Half ecstatic at their surplus of a good thing—"Hooray! Double the fun!"—the rest smelling a rat of conspiracy. "How do we know who the real one is? This is bullshit!"

The cynical contingent cocked fists and beset both bunnies while the rest came to their defense.

Cars screeched around Reevis as new notions of epiphany collided in his head. A trembling arm extended toward the cowgirl, voice equally trembling. "You! It was you! Talking to the man with the chin scar, at the ambassador's house! And the hotel! You're working with them!" Reevis spun and ran off down Washington Avenue.

"Chin scar!" yelled a voice from another direction.

Debbie turned to see Yandy pointing at her. "You know the Colonel? From the mission? You're one of them! . . . Now I remember you from that party in Honduras!"

"Yandy, wait! I can explain! . . ."

He took off running the other way down Washington toward the velvet ropes.

The crowds of bunny enthusiasts shoved one way and the other like a giant jellyfish caught in a cross-current. Then one person went down, and another until it devolved into a small riot. Police cars skidded up to make arrests. Smoke grenades bounced in the street, mixing the tendrils of ground-level clouds with psychedelic neon colors in an actually tasteful way. All they needed was Jimi Hendrix.

Then Hendrix began booming out one of the club's doors. "...*Purple haze!*..."

Debbie stood frozen in brain-lock in the middle of it all, dressed like a little girl at a birthday party, enveloped in smoke as batons flew and two large bunnies ran away from her in opposite directions.

"I should have majored in something else."

Chapter 35

I t was an embarrassment of riches.

Serge's Underbelly Tours had become so popular that they quickly exceeded Pelican Bay capacity and were now pulling in dozens of residents from nearby condos.

The rental company told Serge that they didn't have any bigger shuttle vans.

"But there's got to be something!"

Well, there was one thing. They told him it only rented by the week. And no frills. None. But it was cheap. He leaned over to scribble on forms. "I'll take it!"

Serge slapped cash down on the counter and snatched the keys. Then he climbed into a school bus that was painted white because it had more recently been used as a prison-transfer vehicle. It had not been remodified since then.

The next morning he arrived an hour early. A Ford F-150 was already waiting.

"I didn't think you'd show up."

"Neither did I," said Cinnamon. "You're not going to go back on our deal?"

Serge shook his head. "I've got some guys . . ."

The bus and the pickup parked end to end, and Serge's hired help transferred the vending machine from the back of the pickup and in through the school bus's emergency back door. Serge paid and tipped like a mafia boss. The leader of his help team looked down in his palm. "Hey, thanks, mister. Call us anytime."

"Unfortunately for you, I will." Serge turned to Cinnamon. "What do you think?"

"Why do you want that piece of junk anyway?"

"Who freaking knows? But Coca-Cola is an American icon." Serge slammed the emergency door. "And it's a vending machine. When else do you get the chance?"

It was the kind of cool, clear morning that they call crisp. The regular gang began trickling down off the elevators at the usual time, toting small coolers and large cameras. Others were already driving into the parking lot from the other condos. The line was in militant order as they climbed aboard. A few stopped briefly to gaze curiously at the various locks on the protective prison security screen dividing the driver's section from their seats. Then they wondered about the Coca-Cola vending machine they were stepping over in the aisle in the back of the bus. They forgot about all that as Coleman pulled out his Maltese Iguana.

The bus finished loading, and Serge grabbed a handle on a huge lever, closing the door. He grabbed his microphone as they pulled out. "What an exquisite treat we have to start the day!" Serge was practically yipping. "But first, unnecessary background: You know how occasionally someone will text you a short, cryptic reference that few could decipher? But *you* get it! You're special. That's how pals connect, with a couple words that click with one percent. So a while back, this friend texts a photo of a bulldozer on the side of U.S. 1 across from our condo with the words 'Big Yellow Taxi Strikes Again!' And there was a second photo of a metallic sculpture of a rooster ... Any clues? Anyone? Nothing? ... Then I'll tell you what it meant! The first picture was when they were plowing down the old Marathon gas station across the street to make way for that new 7-Eleven. Now, don't get me wrong. I'm huge on 7-Eleven. Nobody's bigger! Especially those little lavender coffee creamers. But in this case the old, demolished gas station was home to the delightfully cramped and quaint Café 90 family Cuban breakfast counter, which, you guessed it, had a metallic rooster atop a glass display case. And 'Big Yellow Taxi' referred to the Joni Mitchell song about development overrunning sentimental places. Down in Key West, there's even a multi-deck parking garage where someone spray-painted a few of her pertinent lyrics in giant letters: 'They paved paradise and put up a parking lot.' Café 90 was now rubble. Sad, melancholy, I sat facing a corner in my condo for hours. But wait! Here's the rare ray of justice and hope! I just got word that the Latin eatery has reconstituted and is now the Harbor Café 90, tucked in the corner of the ground floor of the forest-green Old Tavernier Restaurant. Let's go grab some takeout Cuban breakfast! And we don't even have to leave the Old Road!"

The bus had to park on the narrow street as the passengers jammed the modest diner, ordering breakfast sandwiches on Cuban bread and guava pastries and espressos.

Serge pulled away with the mic in his hand. "Today we have an especially grand destination! Pigeon Key! For those not familiar, it's that tiny funky island beneath the legendary Seven Mile Bridge between Marathon and the Lower Keys. That would be the *old* bridge, fallen into disrepair and running parallel to the north alongside the new span. If you've never been to the Keys before and know nothing about the islands, Pigeon Key is the most likely feature to grab your attention and tattoo your brain. The island is but five acres with eight remaining century-old buildings where workers lived while constructing Flagler's Overseas Railroad. Plus there's this dubious wooden-plank ramp down from the bridge that sits atop a lattice of trestle-work like a Coney Island roller coaster, and the whole place is the subject of endless photography and artwork. Currently the only way out there is on foot or bicycle, or by ferry boat with tickets purchased at the vintage Pullman passenger train car that acts as its headquarters on the western tip of Marathon. Woooooo! Is everyone with me? Can I get a witness?"

"Woooooo!" said the passengers.

Serge slapped the bus's steering wheel. "That's what I want to hear!"

An hour later, Serge leaned over the steering wheel. "What the fuck?"

"What is it?" asked Coleman.

"Darn it," said Serge. "I read about this. I should have remembered."

"Remembered what?"

"They're shooting a movie out on the old bridge. No sightseeing trips of Pigeon for now." He looked up in the rearview and squeezed the mic. "Sorry, folks, change of plans. We won't be hoofing around the island. But I have something even better planned! You'll never guess. Can you guess? I'll tell you! We'll be witnessing cinematic history as yet another movie is being filmed down here. Get your drinks and bong hits on, because this will get intense . . ."

The gang swung into action with their party equipment as the big white bus angled up onto the apron of the new bridge.

"A little celluloid history first," said Serge. "Did you know that the Seven Mile Bridge has been the site of climactic scenes in not one but two movies? And here's where the coincidences pile up like landfill at Mount Trashmore on Stock Island. Both were spy movies, and both of the scenes involved vehicles plowing off the bridge into the sea. And believe it or not, this new, as-yet-untitled film is also a spy flick." Serge pointed out the north side of the bus. "Right about there is where the armored car blew through the guardrail and sank. It was transporting the ruthless drug lord Franz Sanchez in the James Bond epic *License to Kill,* which also included scenes at the Hemingway House and a wedding at St. Mary's Star of the Sea Church . . ."

A soda vending machine slid around the back of the white bus as it continued down the new Seven Mile. Over on the old bridge, a pyrotechnic flash pot went off, sending flames skyward as a dozen cameras filmed. Actors ran around the pavement over Pigeon Key, firing blank guns.

The microphone clicked. "May I direct your attention to the north again," said Serge. "Coming up soon is the break in the bridge where a helicopter helped Jamie Lee Curtis escape certain death before her limousine plunged into the ocean. That was from the Arnold Schwarzenegger espionage thriller *True Lies* . . . Hey! That just gave me a great idea to take our underbelly tour to the next level! Everyone! Meet tomorrow morning in the Hemingway Community Room!"

The white bus eventually dumped the crew off at the condo. Serge grinned innocently, then formed an expression of laser focus as he reached the fourth floor.

"Coleman, give me a hand getting this thing downstairs," said Serge, grabbing a tripod leg.

"What for?"

"The crucial ingredient of the new spy theme for my Underbelly Tours."

SOUTH MIAMI

Reading glasses hung on the end of a nose. A veteran of the agency sat at a veteran desk reading down a recent unconfirmed report out of Central America. He massaged one of his temples. The news was the opposite of good.

On the corner of his desk was a phone. The desk was in the largest building of the old JM-Wave CIA station next to the Miami Zoo. The phone rang.

"Golden Triangle Exports."

"Gus, it's Debbie. It's an emergency."

"Jesus, stop talking right now."

"But Gus—"

"There's no Gus here. You know the default meeting place? One hour."

One hour later, Debbie sat on a bench at Bayfront Park overlooking Biscayne Bay. Tourists strolled by with shopping bags. Some kids on skateboards. Others were up on the grass, taking photos of the eternal flame. A fifty-seven-year-old man in a black fedora sat down on the other end of the bench.

He stared straight ahead.

"Gus," said Debbie. "What's going on?"

"Don't use my name. And don't look at me. Just stare straight ahead."

"But what's with all the cloak-and-dagger?"

"I told you if things went south, we'd have to purge your records and disavow you. This is disavowing."

"What went south? The contractors came back to the Water Bed Barn and told everyone who hadn't made the trip that it was a complete success, and we'd be getting pay bonuses too."

Gus gazed grimly at the Holiday Inn across the street.

"It wasn't a complete success?"

Her former boss inhaled sharply through his nostrils. "I'm breaking all protocol here, but you have a right to know. Because you're in danger."

"I am?"

"Worse. We can't help," said Gus. "That's why I'm violating procedure. The least I can do is give you the heads-up."

"What happened?"

"A total goat-fuck," said Gus. "Even worse, I just learned that the secret cell is still using the military contractor to try and clean up the stain back here in Miami. I don't know any more."

"I might," said Debbie. "Remember the emergency I mentioned?"

"Shit, almost forgot. There's more to add to this steaming pile?"

"I just had the craziest experience," said Debbie. "During the contractor's briefing before the mission, the Colonel asked me to leave the room."

"The Colonel?"

"I'll explain later. Anyway, I left a tape recorder running in my purse and heard the whole mission, including their contact, a guy I met at the ambassador's party in Honduras . . . Then, last night, I coincidentally ran into him."

Gus's head involuntarily snapped toward her. "Where? How?"

"He was dressed as a bunny outside a nightclub."

"I'll ask about the bunny later. What did you talk about?"

"Didn't have a chance. Because here's where it gets weird . . ."

"I think we've already passed that exit ramp."

"I witnessed a *second* bunny getting kidnapped, but he got away. He leaped out of a trunk onto the hood of a car on nightclub row."

"Have you been drinking? Taken up hard drugs?"

Debbie shook her head. "Listen, the second bunny was a reporter that I remember from Honduras. Before I could talk to them, both took off like they were running for their lives."

"They were."

"What aren't you telling me?"

"This," said Gus. "And don't repeat it, or you'll just put yourself and everyone around you in even greater danger. And definitely don't go back to the Water Bed Barn. At least one and maybe two secret cells have it locked down with surveillance . . . The Honduran thing went through the guardrails and we've floated a cover story that's holding up, at least for now. Shootout between rival gangs and civilians, unfortunately, you know . . ."

"But it was the military contractor?" asked Debbie. "Why do we use these clowns?"

"For precisely this kind of eventuality," said Gus. "Clowns are our buffer: *Does this mess look like anything we'd do?*"

"But we did."

"Back to the bunnies," said Gus. "The private contractors are looking for one or both, and their performance record isn't exactly stellar."

"The secret cell isn't putting a stop to this?"

"They're letting it play out," said Gus. "It's the smart move. Either they end up home free, or the contractor screws up and gives them even more ammo to blame this whole tangled ball of yarn on them."

"Then what do I do?"

"Protect yourself. You've got the skill set."

"And leave the others hanging out there in the breeze at the mercy of the Colonel?"

"Walk away," said Gus, getting up from the bench.

"You're just walking away?"

"Exactly."

Debbie also got up, heading the other way.

A telephoto camera snapped pictures of both of them from a Crown Vic parked across the street.

Chapter 36

THE NEXT DAY

The Hemingway Community Room.

A painting of the famous author gazed down from a wall. Below it were the generous windows overlooking a sugar-white sand beach, coconut palms, a seawall of coral boulders and, finally, the endless Atlantic Ocean.

The residents milled around sipping coffee near the ping-pong table and Skee-Ball machine. Coleman rolled one of the wooden balls, and it hopped the track, flying in the direction of others gathered at the mini-shuffleboard game.

"Ow!" Coffee spilled.

Coleman grinned at the resident. "Sorry."

A shrieking whistle from Serge. The room silenced. "Everybody, can I have your attention! I'll bet you're all just dying to know the new theme of our tours!" He leaned forward expectantly, waiting for a reaction. The crowd was a still-life painting. "Okay, don't hurt yourselves with excitement. Here it is . . ." He feverishly rubbed his hands together. "It's Florida's spy history, past and present. What do you think?"

His audience was granite.

"Maybe you need more data first before you lose your minds with ecstasy," said Serge. "Most people don't know it, but our state is awash in espionage landmarks and stories, as well as a robust current-day spy-craft scene . . . If you will all have seats at the flat-screen TV, I will start today's pre-tour orientation video."

The group found chairs, and some stragglers who went for coffee refills stood in back.

Serge grabbed a remote control. "You all know the world-class Sawgrass golf course up on our northeast coast in Ponte Vedra, home of the PGA's annual Players Championship?"

A few nodded. The rest needed clues.

"Here's a clue," said Serge. "That resplendent golf mecca was near the site of one of the most infamous spy operations in the history of the United States, and yet it's been all but covered over by the disinterest of time . . . It's too far of a drive for today's time-motion efficiency, but it's the mandatory starting point to whet your appetites for our impending espionage adventure down memory lane. Please direct your attention to the screen."

Serge clicked the remote, starting one of several historic short clips from YouTube. Some in the crowd angled forward with elbows resting on knees.

"I've turned the sound off on these videos so that I may substitute my own superior narration," said Serge. "Now, most kids today could never imagine it, but during World War II, most Florida coastal communities were under blackout conditions as German U-boats swarmed the waters off our beaches all the way up into the Gulf of Mexico . . ." Serge didn't realize he was jumping in place. "Now, here's where history pegs the needle on the 'You're shitting me' tachometer: In the predawn hours of June 16, 1942, Adolf Hitler launched Operation Pastorius to insert saboteur-spies into mainland America and blow up our infrastructure. Four agents on a raft were launched from a U-boat and landed slightly north of the ninth hole at Sawgrass. They buried their explosives and crap on the beach, then changed into civilian clothes. Amazingly they were able to make it to a highway and catch a bus for Jacksonville, where they stayed at the venerable downtown Seminole and Mayflower Hotels. But they got caught and were executed before they could do any damage. Still, a feel-good story . . ." Serge clicked the remote again. "Here are some quick vintage documentary clips of Bay of Pigs training on Useppa Island and No Name Key, the ruins of a Nike missile battery on North Key Largo, the movie about Captain Tony running guns for the CIA across the Gulf Stream from Key West . . . And here are the clips of the crashes on the Seven Mile Bridge from the James Bond film, as well as *True Lies* . . . And the grand finale, in case you weren't already amped enough on the whole spy thing like I am—which, how could you be?—a quick montage of four other Bond films that have been shot at least in part in Florida. *Goldfinger, Thunderball, Quantum of Solace* and *Casino Royale,* the last of which really burns my britches, because only some exterior shots of a taxi chase were filmed along Miami Avenue and Biscayne Boulevard, but for the most part, if you can believe this cosmic injustice, can you guess what city stood in for Miami for the other scenes? Right: Prague, Czechoslovakia. Was I the only one crying in the theater?"

The crowd was about ready to get up for the day's sojourn. "One more thing . . ." Serge walked over to the side of the room and something tall and narrow concealed under a large blue tarp. Serge whipped off the covering, revealing the surprise underneath, courtesy of his midnight call to a military contractor.

"Ta-da!" belted Serge. "I bought it especially to take our new spy theme to the next level." His face lit up, expecting oohs and ahhs, but instead he got just another group shot of puzzlement.

"What?" said Serge. "Nobody recognizes it?" He patted the side of the black contraption atop a reinforced tripod. "Has anyone heard of the Havana syndrome?"

One of the residents raised his hand. "Wasn't that the mysterious illness that hit our embassy in Cuba, where a bunch of diplomats had bizarre brain problems that made them lose balance and have blurred vision?"

"A gold star for you! Anyone else?"

"Yeah, I heard it also hit a number of other unconnected diplomatic missions flung far around the world from China to New Delhi..."

"A lot of people had lingering effects," said another. "Some intelligence spokesmen officially called it an unknown attack, possibly sound or magnetic waves."

Serge slapped his stomach with both hands. "Look at the IQ on this crowd!" He wrapped an arm around the ominous black box over the tripod. "If we're going on a spy tour of South Florida, I cannot allow it to be passive. We must interact with our environment." He turned and looked inside the horn-speaker. "I have no idea if this baby is connected to the Havana thing, but it's definitely a close cousin. An LRAD, long-range acoustic device. Many of the jittery Second and Third World nations experiencing civil unrest use it instead of water cannons."

"What does it do?"

Serge patted the side. "It's a subsonic crowd-dispersement speaker. Its wavelength is too low for the human ear to detect, but suddenly a chippy crowd trying to push down the gates at the presidential palace begins having thoughts like, 'What were we protesting?' 'I don't know, but is it worth it?' 'I want to lie down and watch TV.' ... And that's at a distance in the courtyard of the capital. But up close? Hoowee! Epidemic upchucking and hitting heads on curbs. What's not to like? ... Shall we get this sucker loaded?"

Volunteers carried the device out to the school bus.

"I'll open the emergency door in back, and stick it in front of the Coke machine on the floor." Next came a flatbed cart the resident usually used for groceries. "And stick these three car batteries below the tripod. I'll wire them together later..."

... The white school bus rounded a bend in upper Key Largo

by the Circle K, then climbed the new, ultra-high arch bridge. A microphone clicked: "Down off to the left is the fishermen's heaven called the Anchorage Resort, the first taste of the islands if you're heading the other way. We're now on the backside of the bridge, obviously leaving the Keys and ramping down to the mainland. From here until we reach the Last Chance Saloon at the bottom of Florida City, we'll be traveling through no-man's-land, an empty mangrove swamp that all locals know as 'the eighteen-mile stretch,' but I like to truncate and simply call it the Eighteen-Mile. Just rings cooler in my ear, like a rap lyric. Let's say it! The Eighteen-Mile!"

"The Eighteen-Mile!" came the chorus behind him.

"Excellent!" Serge experienced childlike enjoyment turning the oversized steering wheel. "Not long now until our first stop." They caught the turnpike just after Florida City's one-mile scrum of motels, fast food and liquor stores. Fifteen minutes later, they exited between Cutler Bay and Kendall, still well south of Miami proper.

"Brace yourselves for backstory! In the early 1960s, the proximity of Castro's revolution induced a Communist shit-panic in our government, and they deployed an obscene volume of intelligence agents to Miami in war-footing strength, until the city had the highest CIA presence in the world outside of Washington. They bought up so much land, vehicles and boats, and established such a ridiculous amount of listening stations, as well as exile training centers and safe houses, that the agency *was* the economy of Miami, forever transforming the sleepy Southern town into a modern American city."

The white bus passed the Miami Metro Zoo and pulled up on the shoulder of a side road just shy of the stark warning signs not to proceed. This time Serge stood up with his microphone. "You're at the historic site of the CIA's juggernaut JM-Wave Station, the now mothballed shadow of all the Cold War secrets . . . Go on, get off the bus and take pictures."

They filed out the door in their shorts and bucket hats, clicking away.

"Isn't it great?!" said Serge. "Make sure to zoom in on that main tall building..."

Upstairs in the main tall building, binoculars looked back at the tour group. Others in the office clicked away with telephoto lenses. The supervisor entered the room. "What's going on?"

"We don't know," said one of the binocular men. "A bus pulled up and all these tourists got off to take photos of our station. There's one guy who appears to be their leader and is giving a speech."

"Tourists? That's the perfect cover for a secret cell. Genius. Do all your clandestine work right out in the open," said the station chief. "Put the parabolic microphone on him, and play it through the amplifier so we can all hear..."

Back by the bus, Serge pointed in the direction of the unseen men in the upstairs window. "We've all heard the wild stories of plans to assassinate Castro with exploding cigars and seashells and poisoned diving suits, and even just to embarrass him by contaminating his shoes with thallium dust so his beard would fall out..." His audience nodded and murmured. They were old enough to remember that. Serge cleared his throat. "But what most people don't know is that back in 1962, we launched Operation Northwoods. Believe it or not, the U.S. government actually planned a series of false-flag attacks on our own soil, or just off our shores. It's true, I tell ya! The whole thing was authorized by the Joint Chiefs of Staff! We would stage bombings in Miami and murder Cuban exile leaders and blow up refugee boats at sea, just to blame it on Castro for a pretext to invade the island nation. Luckily—and this is not to be taken for granted anymore—we had a president at the time who wasn't insane, and JFK quashed the whole fiasco ... And don't even get me started on Operation Mongoose, which involved similar deflection activity at Guantánamo Bay and other attack sites, that was run right out of that building behind me ... Hey, I got a great idea. Let's turn the horn thing toward that building. I know it's empty, but it's always fun to pretend..."

The men upstairs in the building behind Serge finished listening.

"He knows all the details about Northwoods and Mongoose..."

"Which means he knows more . . . Keep taking photos. We may have just found the leader of one of the secret cells."

"He probably knows all about that disaster in Honduras. Or was behind the whole thing."

The supervisor tapped his chin. "Put a team on him. *Two* teams. I want to know everything! I want to know when he's going to take a dump even before he does."

A hand went up among the subordinates. "If he is heading up a cell, who do you think he's working for?"

"Who knows?" said the boss. "But it has to be someone high up in Washington. Childress? Pennington? Glass? They've all been after my pension for years."

"What do we do when we catch him in some kind of act?"

"Absolutely nothing," said their boss.

"Why not?"

"That's just begging for blame," said the leader. "If we make the wrong move, we could blow the cover of an invaluable asset that the secret cell has taken years to cultivate, or, worse, we could wreck the takedown of an infamous target that they've been tracking for even longer. Either way, I don't want to be called to *that* meeting in Washington. Give them enough space to step in their own shit."

One of the agents in the upstairs window lowered his binoculars. "My ears are ringing. I don't feel so good."

"Me neither," said another. "Sir, can I just lie down and watch TV?"

A white school bus pulled away from an anonymous road near the Metro Zoo. It took the turnpike north, past the ramp to the Don Shula Expressway and up to Doral. The bus exited into a thriving commercial district dominated by bilingual signs. Serge pulled into the parking lot of a dark concrete building with few windows and even fewer indications of retail commerce.

"Photo fun!" yelled Serge. "Everybody out! This is the head-quarters of the private military contractor behind the assassination of the president of Haiti—a crack operation so professional that they found some of the gunmen hiding in shrubbery . . ."

Two black Crown Victorias with black-wall tires and extra antennae pulled up across the street. The windows lowered just enough to accommodate the telephoto camera lenses and a parabolic microphone.

One of the men lowered his camera. "What's that guy doing now?"

"Talking to so-called tourists about that debacle in Port-au-Prince. It's so weird that he must be running a big op."

Parked a block behind them was another Crown Vic, which had been sitting on the military contractor's office. The occupants swilled coffee and munched egg salad sandwiches from one of the wildcat convenience stores prevalent in the area. "Who the hell are these new guys?"

"The school bus?"

"No, that pair of Crown Vics up ahead. They look like they're on stakeout."

"Oh, those guys are from the regular CIA station. The ones who reopened JM-Wave."

"Do you think they made us?"

"Them? They couldn't find their own dicks if they had three hands . . ."

A block ahead, binoculars peered out the back window of a Crown Vic. "Uh-oh, I think we've got company."

"Who is it?"

"Probably the secret cell."

"The first or the second?"

"Can't tell. They're wearing hats."

"Hats?"

"Hats are always a problem."

"What do we do?"

"Don't get fired," said the Miami station chief, turning his head. "Now another black Crown Vic pulled up. Who *are* all these people?"

"This guy from the bus giving the tours sure is popular. He may just be the key to this whole secret thing."

"What whole secret thing?"

"You know . . ." A wink. "The *secret* thing."

"The first secret thing?"

"Or the second. We don't know what it is yet."

The lens of telephoto camera lowered from a car window. "My vision is getting blurry."

Another grabbed his stomach. "I don't feel so good."

"Those egg salad sandwiches?"

He covered his mouth and his cheeks bulged.

"Not in the Crown Vic!" yelled the boss. "Open the door!" . . .

. . . Ten minutes later, the Colonel stepped outside a cavernous metal building. "What the hell?"

Serge stood next to a white bus and a tourist mob on the sidewalk, taking photos. "And this is the famous Water Bed Barn, home of the budget military contractor that advertises on the Internet . . ."

Chapter 37

MIRAMAR

The snarled, corkscrew confluence of turnpike and interstates let off near the signs for the horse track. A Subaru took the first exit.

It was child's play for Debbie to track down Reevis's address. Then the degree of difficulty increased when she arrived at his apartment. Landscaped with smooth white rocks and sea grapes. Everything else was also white except for the doors, shutters and roofing trim, a sherbet shade of orange.

She leaned over the wheel as her car pulled up behind the yellow crime tape. An officer approached her window and she flashed a badge. "What's going on here?"

"Someone trashed the place," said the officer. "Professionally. Floorboards pried, wall fixtures yanked out."

"What about the resident?" Debbie asked with dread.

"He arrived just after we did," said the officer. "Pretty shaken, which I don't blame."

"Where is he now?"

"At the station for questioning—"

Before the officer was finished, the Subaru skidded backward and gunned it up the road. Debbie got on her satellite phone. "Sir? They have Reevis . . . that reporter for the *Free Paper*. Honduras, the bunny suit . . . What do you mean, I can't call you? I'm on the satellite phone. . . . I know you said I'd be disavowed but—" The line went dead. Debbie dialed again. She got a recorded message. "This number is no longer in service."

She burst into the local police precinct and slapped a badge against a glass security window in the lobby. "You're interviewing a crime victim here named Reevis Tome? I have to see him. Matter of national security."

The officer on duty at the front desk inspected the badge. "Right this way . . ." He led her down a hall and opened the door. A lieutenant was sitting across a stark table from Reevis. "Sir, she has credentials. National security."

"Let me see," said the officer.

Debbie handed it over. "I must take this man into custody."

The lieutenant folded her badge and handed it back. "Okay, since he's only a crime *victim*, we don't need red tape to release to your custody—" A cell phone rang. "Lieutenant Yarmouth here. Yes, we were just interviewing him now. Custody? You're on your way over? Okay, we'll see you then." He hung up and turned to Debbie. "Sorry, but it seems someone else from your agency wants to hold your person of interest."

"Time is of the essence!" said Debbie. "He must come with me immediately or if anything happens—!"

"Can't do it," said the lieutenant. "We'll wait until the next guy arrives, and you sort it out with him. If I hand him over to the wrong people, that could be my career."

"Call my people in Washington," said Debbie.

"Why don't you call your own people," said the lieutenant. "Figure out who has dibs on this guy?"

"Because we're compartmentalized." Debbie shook her head. "If it wasn't this serious, I would tell you about it, but I can't. You've heard of the proverbial ticking-time-bomb situation. If you really care about your career, you'll make that call."

"But I don't have a secure line in here."

"Trust me. You need to find one."

The lieutenant rubbed the top of his head. "You people don't make any sense."

"We're not trying to be difficult."

"I'll be right back."

The door closed, and Debbie spun to Reevis. "Get up!"

"For what?"

"Run!"

She burst out of the interview room, and the reporter followed. Reevis practically dove headfirst into the Subaru as Debbie patched out.

"What just happened back there at the police station?"

"You're not safe."

"Gee, you think?" said Reevis. "Just take me to the newspaper office."

"They'll have guys waiting in the parking lot. Maybe even a sniper."

"Now you're really scaring me."

"I can only say so much," said Debbie, "but it's Honduras."

"What about Honduras?"

"You were at the ambassador's house. You wrote stories. But most of all, people have now linked you with Yandy."

"Is that why they threw me in the trunk?"

"At the time, it was a case of mistaken identity. My guess is a private military contractor got wires crossed. But now you're on their radar."

"As what?"

"Another loose end."

"I'm totally lost," said Reevis. "There are huge gaps in this story."

"Something happened in Honduras," said Debbie. "A clandestine operation didn't go swimmingly. Now some people think you know things you don't. I've already said too much."

"What are we doing now?"

"Finding Yandy before it's too late."

Locating Reevis's apartment was easy-peasy, but Yandy's digs were something else. She chose the obvious starting point. The Subaru headed over the MacArthur Causeway.

"Where are we going?" asked Reevis.

"Back to the nightclub."

"Why?"

"Yandy's employer should have his address."

"I have it," said Reevis.

"Have what?"

"His address. He lives with a cousin."

Her head swung. "How'd you get it?"

"His boss gave me all his contact information," said Reevis. "In case I had any follow-up questions or wanted to do more stories. He was really pushy about publicity for his place."

"Jesus, if *you* got it that easy, then anybody . . . I just hope we're in time. Here's my phone," said Debbie. "Enter his number and give it back."

He did.

Debbie put it to her ear. "Yandy, don't hang up. It's Debbie, from the club as well as the ambassador's party. The cowgirl. I'm on your side. I think you're in danger. Has anyone been following you?"

"No . . . wait, a sedan just pulled up. A Crown Vic . . . Wait, now another Crown Vic."

"What are they doing?"

"Taking pictures of each other."

"Get out! Now! Grab your phone! We'll pick you up!"

Yandy darted out the back door and sprinted down an alley. He panted on the phone as he ran two blocks and took cover in a self-service car wash.

"Stay put," said Debbie. "We'll pick you up."

She made time across the city. "I'm in a white Subaru. Stay concealed until you see me. We're minutes out."

"I see the Crown Vics," said Yandy. "Both are rolling slowly like prowler cars . . . Where'd that third Crown Vic come from?"

"Stop talking. Just listen from here out . . ."

Debbie turned a corner into the neighborhood and saw the bright sign for the car wash at the next intersection. She also saw several slow-moving sedans going both directions. But she figured they wouldn't expect her there or know what she was driving. "Reevis, get down!"

A Crown Vic passed in the other direction, none of the occupants giving her notice. Then a second passed by without detection. The Subaru pulled into the car wash, and Yandy jumped out from behind a commercial vacuum cleaner. They sped away.

A third Crown Vic pulled out of a side street, turned on its headlights and began following at a discreet distance.

Debbie reached a ramp for the Dolphin Expressway and got back on the phone. It was one of her close colleagues from the agency who sat a desk away. "Roger?"

"Debbie? Is that you?" Then hushed tones. "What's going on? There was some mysterious shit today about not talking about you. Not even acknowledging your existence if asked."

"I need a big favor."

"I could have guessed," said Roger. "What is it?"

She pulled into an all-night bodega. "Drive by my apartment and tell me what you see . . ."

A half hour later, her phone rang. "Roger?"

"Not good. Police everywhere. They've blocked off the street."

"Okay, thanks," said Debbie. "You've done enough, so just—"

"Right, this call never happened." He hung up.

"We need to find a safe place for the night," said Debbie. "I mean really safe. I have to think."

"Screw this," said Reevis, pulling out his own cell phone.

"What are you doing?" asked Debbie.

Reevis punched buttons. "Calling a safe place. It will seem counterintuitive because it will definitely appear the opposite of safe, but right now it's the only option I absolutely trust."

"You're just a civilian with no training in espionage tactics," said Debbie. "How can you come up with a safer place than me?"

"Oh, like you people are doing such a bang-up job," said Reevis. "With what I don't know about Honduras, what I don't know about the police station, why my apartment was trashed, or this Yandy, or all these sedans. Thank you very much, but I'll take my chances with my own resources." He put the phone to his ear. "Hello, it's Reevis. I know I'm calling pretty late, but I've got a problem . . ."

Chapter 38

ISLAMORADA

A firm knock on a fourth-floor door.

Serge skipped across the living room in glee and unfastened the locks. "Reevis! Come in! Make yourself at home! Stretch those legs out! Want something to drink?"

"Want a bong hit?" asked Coleman.

"And this must be Debbie." Serge winked at Reevis. "Are you two an item? You could do worse . . . Cinnamon, over there on the couch packing a bowl with Coleman, is my current galactic squeeze. Came to me via a vending machine. Yowza! The code word is 'gibberish.'"

Debbie glared with professional sternness. "I don't know what any of that means. But no, we're just friends. A current alliance of necessity."

Serge stepped forward and extended a hand. "And you must be Yandy! I've heard a lot about you! Actually not, but it's always polite to lie about that. Some shit went down in Honduras? And you're a desperate man? You a fan of Zevon? . . . Alexa, play 'Lawyers, Guns and Money'!"

Guitar riffs and marijuana smoke filled the condo.

Debbie turned to the journalist. "Can this reek any more of bad judgment?"

"He'll grow on you. Give me a moment." He pivoted. "Serge. We have important business to discuss. And I'm sorry, but we may have placed you in danger."

"Then whoever it is," said Serge, "*they're* now in danger. That's how I roll with my friends."

"Excuse me," said Debbie, "but Reevis wasn't too clear. What exactly is it that you do?"

Serge spread his arms and his smile. "What else? Dig Florida!"

"And how is it that Reevis claims you can keep us safer than my contacts?"

"I don't know your contacts," said Serge. "But I've been doing this for decades and you don't see any handcuffs on me yet. At least, none when I'm not with Cinnamon." He reached in the kitchen nook and produced a flat cardboard box. "You can't think on an empty stomach. Pizza, anyone? It's cold, but that makes it better. As a matter of fact, the more you abuse a pizza, the better it is. Want a slice? No? It will still be around in the morning after I retrieve it from where Coleman will leave it under the sofa. If nothing else, he's predictable."

"*. . . Hiding in Honduras . . .*"

"Alexa, stop playing music," said Serge.

"Alexa, make a Sir Farts-a-Lot fart," said Coleman.

"*Pfffft, pfffft, pfffft—*"

"Alexa, stop," said Serge.

"What the fuck?" said Debbie.

"You just need pizza," said Serge. "Your brain's clouded."

She grabbed Reevis's arm. "We're out of here."

Reevis pulled away. "No. I trust him. He's one of the few people I know who's rock solid when it comes to integrity."

"Like Mount Rushmore," said Serge. Cinnamon was rubbing against Serge and whispering in his ear. He smirked impishly. "Excuse me for a moment. This won't take long."

They went into the bathroom . . .

"Reevis!" Debbie tightened her grip on his arm. "We're in more danger here than I thought possible! What do you really know about this man?"

"More than I ever care to want, and I don't want to know any more," said Reevis. "But here are the things I know about Serge: He has a huge heart and moral compass, and he doesn't take any shit. But that's just if it's about himself. When it comes to friends, I've never seen anyone so protective. If he cares about you, and you're threatened, you don't want to see the aftermath."

"And this unstable person is your best idea of safety?" asked Debbie.

"Okay," said Reevis. "Then let's go back to the police station to meet this other person at your agency who wants to take me into custody."

She stood mute.

"Just like I thought," said Reevis. "I still don't know why we had to run out of the station, or why you can't contact your CIA pals. There's something you're not telling me, probably a lot. It's my life, so I'm going with my gut and trusting Serge—"

Voices from the bathroom: *"Oh yes! Oh no! Oh yes!"* shrieked Cinnamon. *"Talk gibberish to me! . . ."*

"What's the deal with eggs? They're all grade-A. Where are the grade-B eggs? What aren't they telling us?"

". . . Yes! Yes! Harder! Screw me harder! . . ."

"Is pimento still the best we can do for green olives? I suspect nobody is working on this."

". . . I'm coming! . . ."

"Waka-waka-waka. Pac-Man. Someone actually had to program that."

"Ahhhh! Ahhhh! . . ."

Debbie set her purse down. "This makes Alexa's farts sound downright Norman Rockwell."

Alexa: "*I don't understand that, but here's a Royal Fart...*" Trumpets sounded. "*... Pfffft!...*"

Coleman exhaled from the Maltese Iguana. "You have to be careful about saying her name."

Down in the parking lot, binoculars angled up at the fourth floor through the windshield of a black Crown Vic. A dossier of eight-by-ten photos sat in the driver's lap. "Looks like the whole cast is here. Debbie from the CIA, Reevis the reporter, Yandy, and even the driver of that fake tour service..."

Suddenly, high beams rounded the far corner of the building.

"Everyone, duck!" yelled the driver. They peeked over the dashboard as another Crown Vic entered the opposite end of the parking lot and turned off its engine.

Back up in the condo, Serge and Cinnamon reemerged from the bathroom. "So, what have you crazy kids been up to?"

"Serge," said Reevis. "Debbie hasn't gotten to know you. I think she's concerned about us staying here."

"Is it sleeping on pull-out couches?" asked Serge. "I can add an extra comforter."

"I don't think that's it," said Reevis.

"How about this?" said Serge. "Stay the night, because you're too exhausted to make important choices. Then in the morning, see how the day proceeds and make your decision then. How weird can it get?"

Chapter 39

THE NEXT MORNING

An olive-green armored tactical transport vehicle sat in a parking lot in Doral. It had been dropped off overnight by an unknown person or persons.

All the employees who arrived for work in the morning noticed it. They didn't ask questions.

Nearby, another typically encrypted Miami satellite phone rang in the supervisor's office of the Water Bed Barn. "Yes, I saw the tactical vehicle. What?—" The person on the phone immediately pressed a button concealed under the lip of his desk.

A red beacon began rotating below the ceiling of the cavernous situation room, and an intermittent buzzing sound painfully echoed off corrugated steel walls.

The paramilitary team members jerked around at their desks.

"What's going on?"

"Is this a fire drill?"

"I don't know. It would be a first."

The Colonel ran into the situation room. "Everyone! Gear up!

We got the green light from the secret cell! Deploy to the transport vehicle they dropped in the parking lot! Go! Go! Go! Repeat, we got the green light!"

Someone pointed up at the ceiling beacon. "It's a red light."

They all ran to the western wall and an array of hooks suspending every conceivable kind of war accessory. The team swiftly strapped on the ridiculous amounts of equipment with the choreography of a metro fire department. Moments later, the gang sprinted into the parking lot and jumped through every door of the tactical truck. It was the kind of vehicle that the military donates to local police departments for use in the event of free speech.

ISLAMORADA

An elevator door opened on the ground floor of the Pelican Bay condominium, and Serge led his overnight guests into the Hemingway Community Room.

The residents had already gathered, carefully sipping hot coffee and munching from variety boxes of doughnuts.

Debbie whispered sideways to Reevis. "We're going on a sight-seeing tour? That's the antithesis of a safe house."

"He has his own methods," said the reporter. "They've worked till now."

"Everybody!" yelled Serge, doing a cartwheel and sticking the landing. "Why am I so fevered this morning? Because I have an extra-special surprise for our next installment of Serge's Florida Keys Underbelly Spy Tours! . . . Over to my left are defrocked CIA agent Debbie—don't ask why—and Honduran espionage operative Yandy, who's playing multiple sides and laying low, plus award-winning journalist Reevis, in danger from his upcoming exposé that will blow the lid off everything!"

The residents clapped politely like someone had sunk a two-foot putt.

Debbie stared daggers into the side of Reevis's head. "*This* is supposed to put me at ease?"

"Everyone thinks he's making it up," said Reevis.

Serge began windmilling his arm. "To the bus! . . ."

The neighbors cheerfully climbed aboard as Serge sprang up and down in the driver's seat . . .

. . . The scene was magnified in binoculars watching every move.

"How's it looking?" asked the driver of a Crown Vic. "Jackpot. I knew Debbie would lead us to them. I've got a solid on her, as well as Yandy from that fiasco in Honduras, and that reporter whose involvement is still murky but worrisome."

"What are our orders?"

"Just observe and report. Headquarters will give the go if we have to make a move."

Behind another set of binoculars in another Crown Vic. "The gang's all here. Debbie, Yandy, and Reevis, plus the mystery man behind the wheel."

"What's the directive?"

"Terminate loose ends. The private contractor is on the way."

"Where's the secret cell?" asked the driver.

"We're the secret cell."

"I mean the other one . . ."

. . . Back on the bus, Serge grabbed a microphone. "First stop, upper Key Largo, where you'd poop yourselves if you knew what happened a half century ago."

The white bus pulled out of the parking lot, followed slowly by a black Crown Vic and another. They spread out on U.S. Highway 1.

Serge headed east a dozen miles until an unmistakable landmark came into view. Here and there along the Keys, the median strips widen to accommodate commerce, and this was one of the most recognizable. Near the entrance of John Pennekamp Coral Reef State Park stood a narrow four-story concrete shop—"Scuba-Fun"—that had been painted on all four sides by the famed marine muralist Robert Wyland, featuring manta rays, marlins, manatees and dolphins. Serge took an acute right-hand turn down Fishermans Trail. The bus drove through a quiet neighborhood of homes with docks located on boating canals. The two Crown Vics hung back at a cautious distance.

Serge grabbed his microphone. "It appears far different today, but back in the early 1960s, this was the site of the sprawling yet classified CIA Cuban Intelligence station in Key Largo. Farther north on the island are the ruins of the radar towers for the missile pads, which you can view from Google Earth." The bus stopped at a security fence. "Strain your eyes down the road, which leads to more finger canals. In the 1960s, it was all blinding-white strips of crushed coral and dust, populated by scores of tiny trailers and speedboats. The CIA was just throwing money at the problem—'Everybody, simply look busy'—and it ended up operating more like a vacation fishing camp."

The bus backed up from the security fence and patiently made a six-point turn.

The Crown Vics were right behind them, forced into the harsh light of obviousness to make the same high-profile turn. Serge waved down at them from his bus window as he passed back to the highway.

Another side street was coming up, and another car was waiting at a stop sign. The Crown Vic sat until Serge went by, then pulled out in front of the other pursuit vehicles.

"Sir, how did you know he'd be here?"

"Logical choice," said Gus. "He's hit all the other agency historical touchstones on his way south and this was the last one. I just can't figure how Debbie knew about this 'Serge' character."

"What do we have on him?"

"The file was a bit thin, but he's been connected to dozens of suspicious deaths and yet never been caught. Which means he's working for someone who's protecting him. That's why we can't make a move. There's no deeper shit than blowing the cover of a long-term field operative."

The passenger nodded. "Pensions."

"But there was an unconfirmed note in his file," said Gus. "He might have thwarted the assassination of a Latin American head of state ten years ago when they held the Summit of the Americas in Miami."

"I never heard of that attempt."

"Precisely," said the station chief. "And I think a lot of people would like to keep it that way. That's why this whole 'Serge' situation is so delicate."

The increasing number of trailing vehicles returned to the Overseas Highway and followed Serge southwest, turning one by one onto the road, pretending it hadn't become an obvious parade. The vehicles proceeded leisurely through Key Largo and Islamorada, eating sandwiches and drinking take-out coffee. Just before Marathon, another vehicle shot onto the highway, cutting off the other trailing cars and almost causing a chain reaction of rear-enders. Hands grabbed dashboards to brace. "Where the hell did that tactical vehicle come from? . . ."

. . . In another Crown Vic: "What took them so long to get here?"

The driver of the armored transport rubbed the scar on his chin and silently bore down on the white prison bus. The passenger rammed an insane magazine into an assault rifle that was also fitted with an RPG, short for rocket-propelled grenade launcher. The passenger glanced in the side mirror at all the Crown Vics stacked up behind him. "I've been waiting for this since I can't remember." He loudly racked a combat round into the chamber. "I hope the agency isn't going to pussy out."

"They won't have the chance," said the Colonel.

"What do you mean?"

"The secret cell already authorized this op to deal with loose ends, which are all conveniently gathered in that bus," said the Colonel. "Our Honduran contact, that reporter, the mystery bus driver and Debbie."

"Debbie?" said the passenger. "But she's one of ours."

"Then what's she doing on that bus?" said the Colonel. "I should have smelled that rat, obviously a plant to spy on us . . . No, there won't be any aborts today. We've got the go. Any countervailing orders from now on will simply be ignored."

"But how will we explain it to our men?" asked the passenger.

"Like this," said the Colonel. He reached up for a microphone, which broadcast back to the men, locked and loaded, sitting in the back of the transport along the walls. "Listen up, everyone! We've been given the final go. No other authorization is required. We're totally kinetic now. Any instructions to abort are sabotage communication from the enemy."

The passenger, in a camouflaged helmet, nodded aggressively. "Fuckin'-A, sir! . . . Do you mind if I do some cocaine?"

"Go for it." The Colonel pulled a small capsule from his shirt pocket and popped two Viagra in his mouth. "This rocks."

On the far end of Vaca Key came the first glimpses of the always-anticipated Seven Mile Bridge. Serge had been checking his rearview ever since they left the condo, counting upward.

Reevis and Debbie approached the driver's seat. "Serge," said the reporter. "I think we're being followed. There are at least—"

"Four," said Serge.

"What are we going to do?"

"Nothing for now."

Debbie stepped up next to Serge's throne-like driver's seat. "You have no idea what you're doing, do you?"

"We won't find out until the credits roll," said Serge. "But right now my plan is proceeding perfectly . . ." He looked up in the rearview. "Right, Cinnamon?"

She gave him a thumbs-up from the back of the bus, licking salt off her hand for tequila shots with Coleman and bong hits from Malty the iguana.

"Coleman!" yelled Serge. "Didn't I tell you that the iguana is cursed? Prepare to hide it, because we're deep in some international CIA shit and don't want to be pinched for pot."

"I'm working on it." *Cough, cough.*

"See?" Serge told Debbie. "Nothing to worry about."

Yandy leaned over to Debbie. "Are you really in the CIA?"

"I can neither confirm or deny that. Why?"

"Is this how you always run an operation?"

"Actually, I don't see any operation at all."

"Have faith," said Reevis. "Serge has methods that aren't obvious at first. Wait and see . . ."

Traffic had been unusually slow for a weekday, because of all the rubbernecking. Far worse than a wreck: the filming of a major movie on the closed-down original Seven Mile Bridge running parallel just to the north. Nobody had seen such a furnace of activity since the last movie.

Cameras, lighting scaffolds and silver umbrellas to defeat shadows. Craft Services buffet tables under one of those soccer parents' tents. Superstars and gaffers and grips and assistants to assistants.

At the east end was the highway approach for all normal traffic accelerating toward the new Seven Mile Bridge. The older side was blocked off to everything but authorized personnel. So Serge took it. He reached into the breast pocket of his tropical shirt and removed an important-looking badge on a lanyard and looped the cord around his neck.

A Monroe County deputy at the sheriff's checkpoint stepped into the derelict road in front of the white prison bus and held up both hands for Serge to stop. He walked up to the driver's window and pointed with authority. "You'll have to turn around."

"Sorry, chief." Serge shook his head. "Can't do it."

The deputy took a stutter-step back. "What?"

"We have a movie to make." Serge pointed ahead. "They're about to film the climactic scene, and they can't do it without us."

"I didn't hear anything about you guys."

"Rewrites from the studio suits," said Serge. "Change in demographic research."

The deputy turned to a cameraman standing near the bridge's southern guardrail. "Did you hear anything about this?"

"I'm just Camera Twelve. They don't tell me shit."

Coleman staggered up the aisle. "What's happening? What am I missing?"

"Just making the acquaintance of Deputy"—he leaned over to read the name tag—"Shaughnessy . . . Didn't I tell you to ditch that bong! We're into global shit now! I'm not about to blow this just because Malty is cursed!"

"Where do I stash it?"

"I don't care," snapped Serge. "You're the master on hiding drug shit when the Man arrives."

"Sure thing." Coleman took off back down the aisle with rare purpose.

The deputy got on his tiptoes. "Let me see some authorization."

Serge removed the lanyard around his neck and handed everything out the window.

In the delay at the checkpoint, all the following vehicles were forced to abandon their otherwise clandestine surveillance technique of creating broad separation between cars, and they all began to bunch up onto the otherwise empty and prohibited approach to the old bridge, forming a parked motorcade. All the CIA vehicles' occupants nervously glanced forward and back at everyone else. The station chief closed his eyes. "This is embarrassing."

The deputy studied the badge in his hands. A government seal and a logo of a vintage Hollywood camera. Then the words: MONROE COUNTY MOTION PICTURE AND TELEVISION DEVELOPMENT OFFICE.

Shaughnessy glanced up from the badge to the driver's window. "I've seen a lot of badges out here on this movie, but none of them look like this. Where'd you get it?"

"Oh, right. Like I just spit it out on my computer," Serge said sarcastically. "Then I went down to the corner print shop and encased it on one of those official lamination machines that is available to the general public."

The deputy then noticed all the vehicles stacked up behind the bus in numbers not seen since the movie production crew first arrived. The deputy, talking to himself: "Who are all these people?"

"They're all with me," said Serge. "My credentials cover them too."

"But who *are* they?"

Serge turned around briefly. "That big olive-green monstrosity is a private military contractor working for the CIA to do deniable missions abroad. Then in all those black Crown Vics you've got two CIA secret cells, plus the official CIA station in Miami, where people can just walk in off the street and spill secrets. Don't ask me which is which because I can't keep them straight."

"But what's the CIA got to do with the film?"

"Government assistance to make the film better," said Serge. "They've learned it's a great recruiting tool, like when the Navy lent an aircraft carrier and a bunch of F-14 Tomcat fighter jets when Tom Cruise was filming *Top Gun*. Next to that, these few vehicles are less than the money that falls off the table during congressional junkets."

"I don't know," said the deputy. "I think I need to call this in for verification."

"Suit yourself," said Serge. "But ask yourself this question: Do you know how much shooting delays cost, especially factoring in several CIA teams? Are you used to your ass pinching buttons off a chair sitting in an office of a federal government agency? Or, even scarier, the Monroe County Film Development Commission?"

"I'm still not sure." The deputy rubbed his chin.

"Then do you know how much fuel per hour one of those clandestine black helicopters burns?"

"You don't have a black helicopter."

Suddenly, a whooshing sound. From below the level of the

bridge, a black helicopter shot up into view and began hovering over all the vehicles waiting at the checkpoint.

Back in one of the secret-cell Crown Vics, an assistant pointed. "There's our helicopter."

"Right on time," said Gus, looking out the side window. "We'll get to the bottom of this yet."

The deputy shielded his eyes as he looked up. "Okay. You can go."

Coleman leaned over his buddy's shoulder. "So where'd you get that badge anyway?"

"I encased it at the corner copy shop in an official laminating machine that the general public has access to. Add that to the list of the bold: orange safety cones, clipboards, reflective vests, hard hats."

"So you were actually honest with him this time?" said Coleman.

"He can't handle the truth," said Serge.

The bus drove on, and the other vehicles began pulling up, preparing to display credentials. But the deputy just waved them all through—"You're good, you're good, you're good . . ."—and they all followed the white bus onto the decrepit bridge, trailed by the black helicopter.

Chapter 40

SCENE 327

As anyone in the movie business will tell you, if there's a major climactic scene that is so expensive and dangerous it can only be shot once, then you can never have enough cameras.

And they were all there, loaded, focused and positioned everywhere on the new bridge and the old, and down in an armada of boats, and up in drones and fixed-wing aircraft. Someone at the middle of the old bridge held up one of those new digital Hollywood clapboards with lighted red numbers. He slapped it closed. "Scene 327, take one."

Someone else: "And . . . action!"

Commandos emptied from limos, firing blanks from machine guns. Explosions and fire.

In the other direction, toward Serge, the vehicles started picking up speed, slowly at the beginning as the various players gained separation on the rickety, decaying old decks, then faster and faster. Serge looked up in the bus's giant rearview mirror and saw the armored military truck quicky accelerating until it was right on his bumper.

"Reevis!" yelled Serge. "Get up here!"

"Why?"

"I need you to drive."

"Me?"

"Like I'm going to ask Coleman?" He waved fast. "Now, get over here!"

Reevis arrived and Serge leaped out of the driver's seat.

"Shit," said the reporter, jumping into the chair and grabbing the wheel. "What do I do?"

"Just keep it straight and constant, no fluctuations in velocity."

Reevis leaned and bore down over the wheel. "What's going on?"

"That military vehicle is about to try to disable our bus, then board us and grab you."

"Me?"

"If it makes you feel better, they're also going to grab Debbie and Yandy and myself."

"But why?"

"Reevis, the other day you were thrown in a trunk in a bunny suit," said Serge. "We're way past logic."

Serge trotted back through the path between the seats. "Debbie, what are you doing?"

"What?" She looked at her hand, holding her service-issue nine-millimeter Glock that she always carried.

"Shooting won't be necessary," said Serge. "I'm a big fan of de-escalation. Ask anyone. Or maybe not."

"But the passenger up front has his gun out," said Debbie. "I think he's going to shoot out our tires."

"Try to," said Serge. "But that armored door is too thick for him to get his arm far enough out for an accurate shot. Unless he wants to play hero and dangle out the window."

"You're right," said Debbie. "He's having trouble, trying to twist around."

Bang.

"There's the first shot," Serge said with a smile. "Missed everything, which is great because I got a deposit down on this bus."

"He's aiming again," said Debbie. "I could pick him off, except that glass is too thick for my pistol."

"Don't worry," said Serge. "I have a plan."

. . . Back in one of the Crown Vics, someone was on the radio. It wasn't even a secure signal, but he didn't care anymore. "Unknown helicopter, acknowledge! Who do you work for?"

A pause. Then a crackle over the airwaves. "It's a secret."

"Listen carefully. This is Miami station chief Virgil Gus. If you're taking orders from a secret cell, it's your ass. You're under my command now. Stop that military transport! It's a private military contractor that's gone off the rails."

Another pause. "Yes, sir."

The helicopter swooped in and hovered between the bus and the truck.

Someone in another Crown Vic was on a secured satellite phone. "Colonel, abort the mission! Repeat, abort the mission."

"I can't make out what you're saying." The Colonel popped another Viagra. "Too much static."

"I'm ordering you to abor—!"

Click.

. . . Serge took up a position in the back of the bus's aisle. Ahead was the large speaker on a tripod, and in front of that, right up against the emergency door, the Coke vending machine. "Debbie, make your way to the last row of seats, and when I give the signal, throw open the back door."

"He's about to ram us!" yelled Debbie. "And shoot again."

Bang.

"His aim's getting closer," said Serge. "Now!"

She grabbed the lever handle on the emergency door and flung it open, banging against the back side of the bus. Serge busily worked the electronic controls and aimed the speaker . . .

. . . Back in the military transport, the Colonel was behind the wheel about to blow blood vessels from both temples. "Who taught you how to shoot?"

"The door's too thick."

"So hang outside it!" barked the Colonel. "Be a hero for once."

The gunman looked up out the windshield. "What the hell is that?"

"The landing rail of a helicopter." The rail lowered until it was in front of the driver. "He's trying to force us to stop."

"I thought he was on our side?" said the passenger. "You said in the plans—"

"Plans have no allegiance. Fuck this noise." The Colonel accelerated and smacked the landing rail, causing the chopper to jerk-rotate thirty degrees.

The copter's co-pilot grabbed his harness. "He's crazy! He'll crash us. Pull up!"

The pilot held steady. "You've never played chicken?"

Another voice on the radio. "Chopper One, what are you doing? The armored vehicle is on *our* side!"

"Who was that?" asked the co-pilot.

"A secret cell—"

"Belay that order!" said Station Chief Gus. "I'm in command."

"Roger." The chopper turned its landing gear toward a windshield again . . .

. . . The passenger in the armored truck dropped his gun. "Ohhhh, ahhhh."

"What's the matter now?"

"Don't feel so hot," said the passenger. "I just want to lie down and watch TV."

"In the middle of a mission!" shouted the Colonel. "You're fired! . . . Wait, what's that? Ohhhh, ahhhhh. My ears are ringing. Do things look blurry to you?"

"I can't understand you," said the passenger. "Your voice is echoing too much."

"Dear God!" The Colonel grabbed his stomach. Then, in rapid

sequence, he threw up, his head fell, unconscious, against the steering wheel, and his right foot pressed the gas pedal all the way to the floor . . .

Up the road, near where the bridge crossed Pigeon Key, the official movie climax scene had just kicked off. Automatic weapons fired blanks, flash pots released fireballs, smoke grenades exploded, a black helicopter swooped down over the tiny island under the bridge.

In the other direction, the raging chase came east up the bridge, toward the scripted climax on the span over Pigeon Key. The director turned. "Who are those people?"

"Shut down?"

"No, keep filming! . . ."

. . . "Serge!" yelled Reevis. "We're coming up fast. A bunch of cameras and movie people and shit. What do I do?"

"Hang in there," said Serge. "Just a little longer . . . Just a little longer . . ."

Several cameramen along the bridge's railings looked over their shoulders at the speeding bus.

"What's going on?"

"I don't know. I thought the climax was that way."

"Maybe it's this way."

"Maybe it's all around us and we missed a rewrite."

"Fuck it. I'm not going to get fired for missing the one-time finale."

"You three cameras film that way, and we'll cover the rest."

Half the cinematographers swung in the opposite direction.

. . . Back on the bus, Serge watched the advancing military vehicle, where the blacked-out Colonel still had his foot mashed on the gas. Serge gripped the rear of a seat. "Everyone! Brace for impact!"

All the bug-eyed condo passengers didn't need to be told twice and grabbed whatever they could.

The military truck slammed into the back of the bus at high speed. The Coke machine catapulted out the bus's emergency door, followed by the giant speaker on the tripod, both landing on the hood and smashing into the windshield. The Colonel abruptly awoke, and reflexively hit the brakes, sending the vending machine forward off the hood.

"Enough of that shit," said the Colonel.

Not quite. The vending machine crashed into the road, and the military truck rode up onto it, where it got stuck in the undercarriage and disabled steering. Which screwed up the helicopter's plans.

"Watch out!" yelled the Colonel. He and the front passenger flattened themselves across the front seat as the back end of a hovering landing strut came through the windshield. It broke off, destabilizing the chopper.

"Mayday, mayday, we're going down!" The helicopter twisted sideways as the pilot fought for control, veering down over the side of the bridge.

The military truck was next, wildly skidding side to side across the bridge, still rudderless with the Coke machine wedged up under its front axle. It made one last desperate swerve before crashing, vending machine and all, through the north guardrails of the old bridge and plummeting into the sea. Followed by the helicopter, going down sideways with propellers making quite the cinematic show slicing the tips of the blades off the waves as they broke off one by one. Reevis hit the brakes, and the bus finally skidded to a stop barely feet away from the ashen movie crew.

Silence.

The chase was over in an abrupt, stunned, breath-evacuating halt. Everyone was quiet as they exited all the vehicles and walked tentatively and haltingly to the bridge's broken railings as yellow and purple smoke from the effects grenades wafted over everything. Everyone except those in a pair of black Crown Vics at the back of the parade, who squealed tires and spun around and couldn't get back to Miami fast enough. The Florida Marine Patrol boats were already on the scene because they were required by regulation for safety reasons whenever movie stunts were being performed near waterways. The divers in the water kept surfacing and making hand signals that it didn't look good for the military contractors in the armored vehicle. But then other divers broke the surface of the water with the surviving crew of the helicopter.

Cheering broke out, louder and louder. Cast, camera people, everyone formed a circle and tightened closer and closer around the action director, Branson Van Zack. Whistles, shouting. "That was your best!" "Legacy!" "You'll kill at Cannes!"

Branson stared down and smiled slightly with fake humility while accepting congratulatory handshakes and pats on the back. There was immediate talk of a pre-wrap party. "Tonight let's all get drunk at the No Name Pub!" Then more talk of Golden Globes and Oscars. In the crowd, the director finally spotted his longtime assistant director and ultimate confidant, Spike Lowe, and seized him by the shirtsleeve and yanked his ear to his face. "What the fuck was all that about?"

"No idea," said Lowe. "I was going to ask you as soon as I could, but didn't want to say anything in front of the others."

Van Zack glared a short distance up the road at the white bus and everything. "Who *are* these guys? And what's with the script? The studio? You know it's just like the suits at Vistamax to make rewrites without telling me. They've had their knives out for years now."

Lowe shrugged. "The good side is that everyone is saying this is your best work ever."

"So what should we do?"

"Keep it to ourselves."

"But what if the CIA or whoever comes clean with the real story that we had nothing to do with most of the climax?"

"Preemptively praise them," said Lowe. "Trust me. I know people in government . . ."

Van Zack looked over the bridge's railing at a grisly sight. "What about the bodies they're recovering from that military thing?"

"Blame the CIA."

"Praise and blame at the same time? That's beyond cynical."

"What don't you understand about this town?"

. . . Coleman stood forlorn. "I lost my cool bong."

"How?" asked Serge.

"I stashed it like you said." Coleman told him where.

"*Now* do you finally believe me that it was cursed?" said Serge. "Little good has happened since it came into our lives."

"But Serge!" said Coleman. "How do I get rid of the curse?"

"Mythology has it that curses are passed along to the next person who acquires the object."

All the residents of Pelican Bay climbed off the bus with a consensus that this was the best underbelly tour ever. They brimmed with glee as they socialized with the cast and had their photos taken with A-list actors.

Someone else arrived. "Cinnamon!" Serge pulled out a money clip and began peeling off currency for the loss of the vending machine. "Anything else?" asked Serge. "How about some gibberish? . . . I saw a TV commercial where the husband asked his wife why Hawaii has an interstate highway."

From the other side, Debbie approached, grinned, and patted Serge playfully on his arm. "That was amazing. You know, I was sure you were out of your tree, and we should never have gotten in the bus back at the condo. But Reevis kept saying wait and see, wait and see, his style is weird."

"He knows me well."

"You kept mentioning your plan." She started chuckling. "I never remotely thought it would save us."

"What are you talking about?" asked Serge. "I had no plan to save you."

"Then what was your plan?"

Serge contentedly gazed up the bridge at where the cast and crew were still celebrating. "What else? To get in a Florida movie."

Epilogue

The Central Intelligence Agency launched a massive inquiry into a maelstrom of mind-bending events stretching from Honduras to the Florida Keys. Then, suddenly, all questions screeched to a stop. That's what happens when a famed film director like Branson Van Zack wins the Palme d'Or at Cannes and profusely thanks the agency, "without whom the film would never have been possible." The film had gone through several working titles until Van Zack, in the same acceptance speech, made the name official. *CIA: Kinetic.*

Spy offices in Washington were abuzz with ecstasy and popping Champagne corks. In one of the largest conference rooms in Langley: "What a public-relations bonanza. This is a better recruiting tool than *Top Gun*!"

"On top of all that, it's a two-for-the-price-of-one. The contractors weren't part of a rogue operation to kill American citizens on that bus, but hired stuntmen in a scene that went tragically wrong."

"But what about the director also pointing the finger at us for the deaths of the military contractors?"

"That's the beauty of our buffer strategy to hire budget contractors. We praise their valiant efforts, and blame their incompetence."

"Is that ethical?"

"What don't you know about this town?"

Soon after that, several agents, including Gus and Debbie, received commendations and pay bonuses for exemplary work promoting the agency. In return they only had to swear to support the new narrative that the stink of everything bungled in South Florida was actually the agency's cooperation with an international blockbuster that showcased America's intelligence apparatus in the best possible light.

Debbie said it would only work if they tied off the loose ends that could blow the cover story, which would subject the agency to one of its worst scandals in history. They asked her how. She said: Easy, give everyone—Yandy, Reevis, Serge and Coleman—clean bills of health and widely circulate urgent hands-off memos for all of them.

Done. Pensions.

Secret Cells One and Two had a harrowing close call at being discovered on the Seven Mile Bridge before spinning around and racing for the mainland to dissolve back into the anonymity of the western Miami asphalt grid. But their troubles weren't over. Because of the cells' exposure during the whole debacle in the Keys, regular agents were able to develop a number of promising leads. They were getting closer and closer on a daily basis until it was just a matter of time.

Secret Cells One and Two began to sweat every hour as they felt the net tightening. So they got together for a meeting and decided to change their names to Secret Cells Three and Four, falling off everyone's radar, never to be heard from again.

The only people to ever face any consequences were several residents of the Pelican Bay condominium complex, who were summoned to appear before a local judge, where they pleaded no contest for events that transpired at their next Monopoly Night. They were sentenced to probation that stipulated community service and not to play any more board games for six months.

The raucous send-off party was one to beat the band. The Hemingway Community Room was packed to the gills, and the numerous tables were covered with pot-luck platters and casserole dishes: meatballs on toothpicks, ten different things wrapped in bacon, three-layer taco salad, tubes of salami with cream cheese, shrimp cooked every which way, and enough booze to stop a battleship from deploying.

A cheer went up as Serge and Coleman arrived. Noisemakers blew and streamers fell.

"We sure are going to miss you . . ."

"If you ever decide to drop anchor for good . . ."

"Are you certain we can't do anything to change your mind? . . ."

Serge shook his head, just before being grabbed from behind and spun around by Cinnamon for a tongue-wrestling kiss.

The crowd, in unison: "Wooooooo!"

"I didn't know you'd be here," said Serge.

"I didn't either," said the redhead. "But something made me have to say goodbye. You are one fucked-up dude."

"I'll make sure to connect you with the guys who do my tombstone."

She just smirked and mischievously poked him in the chest and headed off for her shift to mine tourists' wallets at the club.

The shindig lasted into the wee hours. Food tables a disaster zone. Liquor flowing like a faucet. Skee-Balls flying off the table and ping-pong balls being crushed. Then it was time for the hugs and tears. Serge held each of his neighbors by the shoulders, promising never to forget them and that yes, someday he would return.

Then it was that moment. Serge and Coleman waved back at everyone gathered outside the condo as they climbed into the Galaxie, speeding off through Key Largo, then onto the "Eighteen-Mile" into Florida City and Homestead, and another long run up Krome Avenue through the endless agricultural expanses with those massive sprinkler machines. Their windows were down, whipping their hair with brisk atmosphere. In the crisp pre-dawn blackness of four a.m., they pulled up to a stoplight at the intersection with the Tamiami Trail. No cars. To the right, the Dade Corners truck stop and airboat culture store. Ahead to the left, the still ridiculously out-of-place Miccosukee casino. The traffic light was unusually long, as was usual, and the cool breeze continued blowing through the open windows. They were at one of those few Florida places that could genuinely be described by any bone-deep native as the Crossroads.

"What now?"

Serge smiled. It was a rare moment so quiet and uncomplicated that you could actually hear the ticking of the traffic light's unseen machinery attached to a pole. "This is one of my absolutely favorite things in life. No pressures or agenda from a boss or anyone else. Just a few seconds where you have no direction or any direction. Freedom."

Coleman pointed. "The light just turned green. Why aren't you going?"

"Freedom," said Serge, swiveling his head. "There are no other cars around. How often do we realize that we have the liberty to just *sit* at a green light?"

"Okay, so what do you want to do at this green light?"

"Put the coda on our Art of Slowing Down life phase."

The tranquility of the green light passed, and it turned yellow.

"Uh-oh," said Coleman, fastening his seat belt.

The traffic light hit red. Tires squealed in place, generating a thick cloud of smoke. Serge finally let his foot off the brake and cut the steering wheel left, slinging the Galaxie west, its taillights fading down the road under the dim, vague silhouettes of herons and vultures, into the darkest reaches of the Everglades.

It was an awe-inspiring engineering feat to observe as a massive mobile crane sat on the old Seven Mile Bridge, hoisting out of the sea an olive-green armored military vehicle. Saltwater drained from all the doors as it was slowly lifted over the railing and set down on the bridge's deck for disposal. Environmental crews positioned inflatable berms to corral any damage that might occur from leaking engine oil and transmission and brake fluids, et cetera. Then another crane on a barge snagged the helicopter. Yes, impressive. But the whole double-crash sequence had been so violent and chaotic, with varying witness accounts, that not everything could be accounted for.

Six months later, in the middle of the crazed lobster season, a trio of scuba divers swam efficiently beneath the old Seven Mile Bridge. Bubbles crawled toward the surface in intermittent bursts as they continued skimming along the bottom with mesh collecting sacks, plastic carapace rulers to measure for legal length, and tickle sticks to coax their quarry from tight hiding holes in and under the rocks.

The lead diver was the first to see it, suddenly turning around and waving urgently. Even at a distance he knew what it meant. The others caught up and swam toward a rusty Coca-Cola vending machine with its door ripped off. To mix metaphors, it was shooting fish in a barrel. The divers quickly began filling their sacks with huge Florida spiny lobsters, known affectionately as bugs, just lying in layers all over themselves, all fat and happy inside the machine.

When their sacks were full and the soda dispenser empty, they prepared to swim back to their dive boat. Just then, the last diver noticed something stuck in the bottom near the change box. He wedged it loose and studied it a moment before giving a big thumbs-up to his dive pals. He triumphantly raised his right fist, gripping the Maltese Iguana.

ABOUT THE AUTHOR

Tim Dorsey was a reporter and editor for the *Tampa Tribune* from 1987 to 1999, and is the author of twenty-five other novels: *Florida Roadkill, Hammerhead Ranch Motel, Orange Crush, Triggerfish Twist, The Stingray Shuffle, Cadillac Beach, Torpedo Juice, The Big Bamboo, Hurricane Punch, Atomic Lobster, Nuclear Jellyfish, Gator A-Go-Go, Electric Barracuda, When Elves Attack, Pineapple Grenade, The Riptide Ultra-Glide, Tiger Shrimp Tango, Shark Skin Suite, Coconut Cowboy, Clownfish Blues, The Pope of Palm Beach, No Sunscreen for the Dead, Naked Came the Florida Man, Tropic of Stupid,* and *Mermaid Confidential.* He lives in Tampa, Florida.

BOOKS BY

TIM DORSEY

THE MALTESE IGUANA

MERMAID CONFIDENTIAL

TROPIC OF STUPID

NAKED CAME THE
FLORIDA MAN

NO SUNSCREEN FOR
THE DEAD

THE POPE OF PALM
BEACH

CLOWNFISH BLUES

COCONUT COWBOY

SHARK SKIN SUITE

TIGER SHRIMP TANGO

THE RIPTIDE ULTRA-GLIDE

PINEAPPLE GRENADE

WHEN ELVES ATTACK

ELECTRIC BARRACUDA

GATOR A-GO-GO

NUCLEAR JELLYFISH

ATOMIC LOBSTER

HURRICANE PUNCH

THE BIG BAMBOO

TORPEDO JUICE

CADILLAC BEACH

THE STINGRAY SHUFFLE

TRIGGERFISH TWIST

ORANGE CRUSH

HAMMERHEAD RANCH
MOTEL

FLORIDA ROADKILL

MORROW